*"Bastard," she flared.*

William chuckled deeply, his eyes flashing angry amusement as an arm went around her waist and drew her sharply against him. "*Milord* Bastard, Isabel. Remember, you did promise."

He tightened his hold around her waist as his other hand unwound her hair from its plait, his fingers lacing in her hair as he brought her mouth to his.

Braced for his anger, her senses shocked at the startling gentleness of his kiss. She desperately tried to block her mind from the feel of his mouth on hers and the length of his hard body pressed against her own. But her nerve endings sharpened with anticipation as a deep ache of desire kindled—and Isabel deClare knew she was lost, lost, lost . . .

*   *   *

*"Five stars. A must for your summer reading pleasure."*
—AFFAIRE DE COEUR

# DAWN OF THE WHITE ROSE

## MARY PERSHALL

BERKLEY BOOKS, NEW YORK

To Meg Blackstone

Who taught me to stand tall
so that I might see the horizon.
. . . and in memory
of my father,
Manly Wayne Nelson


DAWN OF THE WHITE ROSE

A Berkley Book / published by arrangement with
the author

PRINTING HISTORY
Berkley edition / June 1985

ISBN: 0-425-07961-9

A BERKLEY BOOK® TM 757,375
Berkley Books are published by The Berkley Publishing Group,
200 Madison Avenue, New York, New York 10016.
The name "BERKLEY" and the stylized "B" with design are
trademarks belonging to Berkley Publishing Corporation.

PRINTED IN THE UNITED STATES OF AMERICA

## AUTHOR'S NOTE

In writing a romance it is normal to depict the hero as larger than life. That devilishly handsome rogue who sets fair hearts atwittering with a mere glance from his devastating eyes. The love of his life is beauteous, graceful, with a fire that can only be matched in her hero. We escape into the fantasy of two wonderful human beings.

In researching *Dawn of the White Rose*, I found that two such human beings had actually lived, and loved. Two people considered exceptional by their own peers, and those of us privileged to share their history. In writing their story, I found myself with the unusual dilemma of expressing the truth of their lives in a believable way, fearing that the results would appear as a fantasy, characters too good to be believed. Simply, Isabel deClare and William Marshal were extraordinary individuals.

Isabel was, in fact, beautiful. "Beautiful, fair, a courteous lady of high degree." She was wealthy, holding the estates depicted in this book. She was capable, ruling her domains, and held in such esteem by her husband that her hand was set to many legal documents, next to that of William's.

William Marshal was, in fact, tall, exceptionally handsome, and talented in every endeavor he chose to pursue. The anecdotes presented here barely touch upon his varied and vast adventures, and each is accurately told. I have not even mentioned his talents of song and story. Nor have I mentioned his ability in sports of the day. However, respect for this man was such that even in his sixtieth year no one would accept his challenge to combat, nor was his word ever discounted. Such was the mettle of the man, that upon his death, the sovereigns of three nations wept at the loss.

It is from such as this that dreams are made.

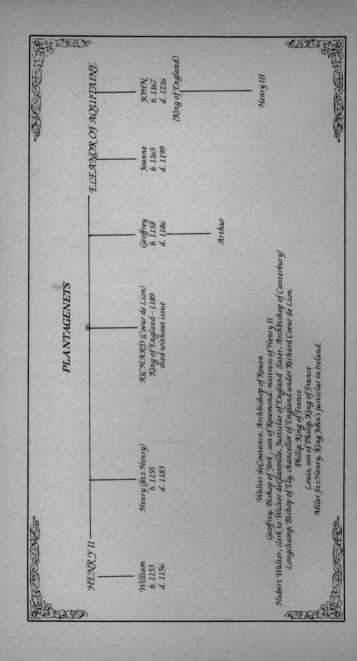

# PLANTAGENETS

HENRY II — ELEANOR OF AQUITAINE

William
b. 1153
d. 1156

Henry (fitz Henry)
b. 1155
d. 1183

RICHARD (Coeur de Lion)
King of England—1189
died without issue

Geoffrey
b. 1158
d. 1186

Joanne
b. 1165
d. 1199

JOHN,
b. 1167
d. 1216
(King of England)

Arthur

Henry III

Walter de Coutance, Archbishop of Rouen
Geoffrey, Bishop of York, son of Rosemond: mistress of Henry II
Hubert Walter, clerk to Walter de Glanville, Justiciar of England (later, Archbishop of Canterbury)
Longchamp, Bishop of Ely, chancellor of England under Richard Coeur de Lion.
Philip, King of France
Louis, son of Philip, King of France
Miles fitz Henry, King John's justiciar in Ireland.

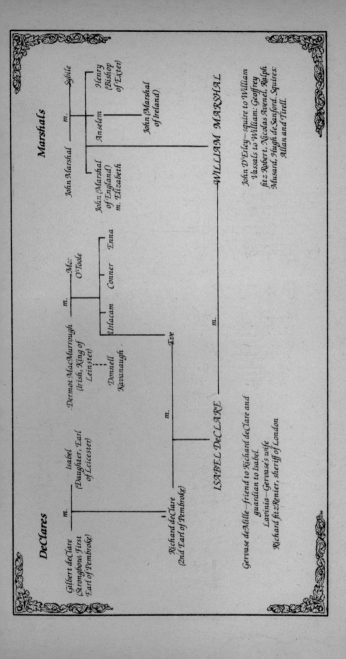

**DeClares**

Gilbert deClare **m.** Isabel
(Strongbow, First          (Daughter, First
Earl of Pembroke)          Earl of Leicester)

Richard deClare
(2nd Earl of Pembroke) **m.**

ISABEL DeCLARE **m.**

Gervase deMille—friend to Richard deClare and
guardian to Isabel.
Lavinia—Gervase's wife
Richard fitzRenier, sheriff of London

**Marshals**

John Marshal **m.** Sybile

John (Marshal    Anselm    Henry
of England)                (Bishop
m. Elizabeth              of Exeter)

John (Marshal
of Ireland)

WILLIAM MARSHAL

John D'Erley—squire to William
Vassals to William: Geoffrey
fitz Robert, Nicolas Avenel, Ralph
Musard, Hugh de Sanford. Squires:
Allan and Tirell.

Dermot MacMurrough **m.** Mor
(Irish, King of              O'Toole
Leinster)

Donnell
Kavanaugh

Urlacam    Conner    Enna

Eve

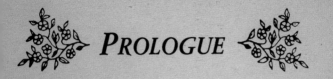

# PROLOGUE

## Ireland,
## February 1189

My Dearest Friend,

How I pray that things are not with you as they are in England. The land is torn, the people tremble as they await the decisions borne from those in power. When the great, the mightiest fall, how can the meek, the helpless, be expected to persevere? Do you recall when Richard was among us, how we depended upon his strength and wisdom, the calming influence he would impart where we would never fear the outcome? Forgive me that I should seek to remind you of that man's gift, to you who knew him best and held him the most dear. You must know that while he was yours he belonged to all of us. If only that miscreated arrow had not taken him in Normandy! How I covet his presence now, when it is so sorely needed!

Henry, our king, lies dying in Normandy, his eldest playing traitor upon his deathbed. Oh, how the vultures await to devour his flesh! How Richard would have grieved! That one who would call Henry friend, loyalties given, even when such loyalty harvested betrayal!

Oh, but I do transgress. Forgive me, dearest friend. I will hie to the reason I take pen in hand . . .

Eve lowered the letter to her lap, unable to go on. The reference to Richard tugged at her heart. The wound left from his loss, though so many years past, was still fresh and gaping. So Henry lay dying. The great king lowered to that of other men, deceived, betrayed, and dying alone. What would Richard have felt? Sadness? Aye, for his loyalty was that. Her eyes narrowed, biting back unbidden tears as she glanced from the window to the inclement landscape he had so loved. His adopted home, Ferns, nestled deep within Ireland. He had risked everything to be here, even to challenge his king in a dangerous game he had won—while he had lived. If only he had lived.

She pushed back her unruly hair, the tendrils now streaked with grey from the deep golden auburn he had loved. The lovely face was now touched with lines, the rosy complexion softened to a pale hue. The eyes still held a vibrant emerald sparkle, now glistened with tears, and the determination of survival that had carried him forward was still there. She sighed raggedly and forced her eyes back to the letter.

. . . Such a responsibility you have given us when you sent her to be fostered at Chepstow! We have loved her like our own and now, alas, her future has been taken from us, and there is precious little that we can do!

Eve drew her eyes away from the letter, knowing what would be written. So, it had come at last. Isabel, their child. Eve closed her eyes and called up the image of her face, so like his own. There had been moments, while watching her grow, when it was hard to find something of herself in the child. The same startling grey eyes, and the spark of humor . . . comforting in their familiarity and painful with the reminder of the loss.

Richard had treated her like a son—nay, not a son,

not as a daughter, but somewhere mysteriously in between. He had ignored the modes that were firmly established for one's offspring, treating her instead as a special being, devoid of normal rules. *Does she remember?* He seemed to take delight in what she was, asking the best from her while reveling in what she had to give to those around her . . .

She was their only child, after the small boy who had lived only a few months. The pain plucked at her, and she had to push it forcefully aside as she recalled the grief that had almost caused her separation from Richard. She had so needed his comfort to carry her through the pain and had never understood his need to be alone. The crisis had come the day she had embarked amid an overcast morning with the cold winter winds snapping over the forbidding landscape, clad only in a coarse woolen kirtle, her feet bare against the frosty earth, to walk the six-mile vigil to the church in tribute to her lost child. Richard had caught up with her only a mile into her journey, reining in his mighty black warhorse, Taran, as he gaped down at her in furious disbelief. She had expected him to bear her with him back to Ferns much as he had done upon their first meeting. Instead, his face became etched with love and longing as he dismounted, and removing his boots, he joined her in silent companionship for their lost son.

Ah, but how he had loved his daughter! The two of them, so alike. *If only he were here now, none of this would be necessary. . . .* The years lost etched her heart with loneliness. But for her there were the memories, rich, full. Aye, they had been blessed with a love so vast. . . . She took a deep breath and forced her eyes to focus on the letter once more. *I must be getting old,* she thought. *I seem to live more and more in the past—and there is this present to deal with now . . .*

I do not mean to deride you, dear Eve, now at this moment, but you must have considered her fate when you sent her to us, placing her so assuredly in Henry's hands. Whatever will her fate be now that he is dying?

I fear to tell you, but there is no easy way. She was taken, by order of Henry, to the Tower of London. We should have written to you sooner, as soon as it happened, but we hoped that there would be no need—that he would see reason and release her! Alas, his own troubles in Normandy, and from his own blood, took his attention elsewhere, and now it is too late. The matter now rests with the new king—we know who that shall be and I cannot help but to wonder as to that source! That Plantagenet's mind and soul have never rested with England! I fear that his decision of whom Isabel shall marry will be considered only to the extent that it will bring coin to his coffers—to finance a new crusade!

She is so young and has been so sheltered! She must be terrified! Tell us what you would have us do, a word we might carry to her.

Eve sat back in her chair and smiled. Richard deClare, lord marcher of England, Ireland, Normandy, and Wales; his daughter terrified? Hardly. But her mother's heart reached out, wishing that she could confide in them. It could not be helped. Decisions had been made, plans set, and she did not regret them, knowing it to be the only way. Still, something had to be said. Eve turned to her writing desk and picked up a quill, dipping it into the inkwell. Pausing for a moment in thought, she began to write. . . .

My Dear Lavinia . . .

# PART ONE

## ISABEL

# 1

*London*

THE moon cast its spreading light through thin, drifting fog to the murky water; the shadows from half-submerged refuse floated out in ever-widening circles to the dank stone walls that lined the Thames. Large rats, fierce combatants for the cats that roamed the city by night, scurried along the walls, pausing to chatter to dark companions before disappearing into piles of rotting garbage. The only other sound heard in the quiescent night was the gentle lapping of the river against the sheer walls and its steep steps reaching down into the blackened current.

A single boat approached silently from the river's mid-current, coming abreast of the steps as a boatman leapt from its side and lashed a stout rope to a ring set into the wall for the purpose. A tall man heavily cloaked against the fog stepped from the boat. Ordering the boatman to wait, he crossed through the shadows of the ancient Roman wall and approached the towering fortress. The moon drifted from behind the clouds, illuminating the sheer walls of the mammoth tower and its four turreted corners. The visitor viewed the structure grimly, well believing that it had been constructed by

The Conqueror for the intimidation of London's citizens, to be a constant reminder of the power of the Norman conqueror.

He paused at the massive doors to the keep, drawing his knife from his belt to pound its hilt against iron-studded oak. He had to wait only a moment before the portal swung open and he blinked against the sudden light from within.

"Has she been told of my arrival?" The visitor turned sharply to the jailer as the door closed behind them. He glanced about the small, dim room with distaste as he threw back the hood of his cloak and shook out its heavy, damp folds.

"Nay, milord. 'Er room is ta the top, ta the left," the jailer answered, jerking his head in the direction of the stairs. He eyed the knight with curiosity, wondering at the power that could admit a visitor to the Tower of London at such an hour. The message from Ranulf deGlanville, the justiciar, had been succinct. He was to allow the girl this visitor upon his arrival, no questions were to be asked, and no witnesses would be present. It was highly unusual, and in spite of his orders his curiosity overcame him. "Thought it were a pity that the girl 'ad no other visitors, milord. Such a pretty young thing, she is. Can't imagine wa' she done to warrant such, milord."

"She has done nothing," the knight snapped. "Her only sins are with God."

"Aye, milord," the turnkey muttered. He stared at the departing back as the knight began ascending the staircase. Disgruntled, he knew he would continue to wonder about the questions he had harbored since that night, nine months before, when the lass had been brought to the Tower under heavy guard.

Finding the door, the knight paused for a brief moment, bracing himself for what he might find within. It had been almost a year since King Henry's men had come for her. What could that year have done to the lass? He swore softly, cursing himself anew, feeling for the thousandth time the helplessness he had felt the day they had taken her, the anguish over vows broken, hav-

ing been made to another so long ago. He removed his
helm, tucking it beneath his arm as he pushed back
the coif of his hauberk, revealing sandy-brown hair
streaked with grey. His strong jaw tightened as he
rapped softly on the heavy door, the lines about his blue
eyes deepening with apprehension. No answer given, he
turned the large key set in the door and pushed it open
as his eyes narrowed in the darkness that met him. The
soft lights of flickering candles and the low fire on the
hearth cast dim shadows about the few pieces of furniture that dotted the room. His eyes moved about the
room until he found her where she sat on the edge of the
raised hearth, bent to the meager light of the low fire as
tapered fingers worked a needle through a small tapestry. So absorbed was she in her task that his knock had
gone unheard, affording him a moment to observe her
unawares.

Her slender figure was clothed in a coarse woolen
gown of dark blue, her striking hair of tawny smoke left
only to his memory beneath a stiff coif and wimple of
white linen, accentuating the paleness of her lovely
young face. When he had last seen her, her skin had
been flushed with a golden tan from hours in the sun
and now held a pallor that struck him to the heart with a
jolt of fear. Had she been ill? Her eyes were lowered to
the work, hidden beneath brushes of thick black lashes.
He prayed that when they raised to his they would still
hold the sparkle of determination he remembered.
Those startling grey eyes, their look of mischief declaring uneasy moments for those who would attempt to
control her.

"Isabel?"

She looked up with a start, her eyes growing wide at
the sight of him. Her lips opened as if to speak, and he
heard her breath draw in a sharp gasp as his identity
registered.

"Gervase!"

She leapt from the hearth, spilling her needlework to
the floor. He barely had time to shut the heavy door
behind him before she was in his arms. He enveloped
her in a fierce bear hug, relief coursing through him as

he felt the strength in her body.

"Oh, Gervase, is it really you?" She laughed delightedly, pulling back to see him better.

"Aye, little one, as you can see." He added with a throaty chuckle, " 'Tis no specter."

Her laughter ceased and her eyes grew wider and fear passed over then as she stiffened in his arms. "But why —why have they allowed you to come? Has something happened? Is it Mother—or Lavinia?"

"Nay, Isabel. Lavinia is well and we have had a letter from your mother but three days past. She sends you her love. But what of you? DeGlanville insists that you have been well cared for. I would not believe him until I could see for myself." His mouth twisted with barely controlled anger as he recalled the verbal battles that had raged between them.

"I am well, Gervase," she assured him with a new lilt to her voice. "Oh, it is good to see you! Boredom has been the worst of it! But come, remove that damp cloak before you catch a chill. Lavinia would never forgive me if I sent you home with a fever."

She bustled about, her pleasure at company after long months of solitude showing in the flush to her cheeks and the shine in her lovely pale eyes. She hung his cloak on a hook by the hearth, then hastened to pour him a goblet of wine. Touched by her attempt to act the cheerful hostess, his eyes passed over the room. While it appeared spotlessly clean and somewhat comfortable, he bridled at the meager condition in which she had been made to live. He forced a smile as she crossed back to the hearth. Kneeling before it, she warmed the brew with a hot poker laid in the coals of the fire.

He sank into a chair in front of the hearth, his shoulders slumping wearily as he watched the steam rise off the goblet with a sharp sizzle. He took the offering with a smile as she settled on the edge of the hearth before him, wrapping her arms about her knees. He took a long, welcome draught of the wine, and she drank in the sight of him, the misty grey of her eyes filling with tears as she fought to keep her emotions hidden. She knew him well, this man who had been so like a father to her these past years; knew that the sight of tears would be his undoing. She did not need to cry, she told herself, though a hard lump formed at the back of her throat; she wasn't dreaming, he was here, she could touch him.

"Isabel," he said softly, his eyes searching her face for some sign of what the past months had done to her. "My thoughts have been haunted by the memory of those last moments you were with us. The confusion, the terror you must have felt. I had not even the chance to comfort you, to bid you farewell . . ."

"Aye. . . ." She swallowed, her eyes now brightening with tears in spite of her resolve. "That was the worst of it. I could hear you shouting from the great hall as they took me away. I was afraid that they might harm you—that you would . . ."

"Do something foolish?" he finished for her. "Aye, I would have, given the chance. It took three of the bastards to hold me." He gritted his teeth. "And the king's written order that you would not be harmed if I did not interfere. It was the only thing that kept me from taking to horse with all of Striguil's vassals to bring you back."

"They did not harm me," she assured him, reading the pain in his expression. "Actually, they were quite courteous. The most frightening thing was that they would not tell me anything. They brought me here," she glanced about the room and her eyes touched briefly on the door. "And shut me in—and I saw no others for weeks, except for the serving woman who comes each day with my meals and to tend to my personal needs. But she hardly speaks to me."

"You've seen no one else, all of these months?" Gervase gasped, the color in his face beginning to rise.

"Only Hubert Walter, deGlanville's clerk." She shrugged. "He comes once a week and spends a little time. He continually apologizes for the state of my keep. He insists that with Queen Eleanor locked away in Winchester and the court in Normandy there is no one to authorize more comfort—or company—for me." Her voice trailed on the last words, but she looked up at him again and her eyes brightened. "But he has tried to make it easier. Once he recovered from the shock that I could read he brought me books—and he tells me of court gossip—who is doing what with whom. It is odd how interested you can become in people you do not know when you hunger for any manner of news.'' Her eyes twinkled. ''I have heard some interesting tidbits of gossip about people we do know, Gervase. Someday I must tell you of the gracious ladies who attend the court. I understand now why you kept me cloistered at Chepstow.''

''Aye, I did do that,'' he said slowly, regret heavy in his voice. His brows furrowed as he paused, and he peered intently at Isabel. ''My protectiveness of you, I fear, is at least partly responsible for your being here. Henry commanded that I bring you to court time and again. I ignored the order, trying to buy time, thinking that I could reason with him. But now—I suspect that he was correct. It was safer to bring you here.''

''Safer?'' Her eyes widened at the word as she stared at him incredulously. Then they narrowed, and she felt herself suddenly gripped with a rising surge of anger, which threatened to shatter her control. All of the months, the terror, the terrible gripping loneliness, the endless unanswered questions consuming each hour, themselves marked only by the lightening and eventual darkening of a small window overlooking the Thames, bubbled to the surface. ''Safer?'' she repeated, nearly choking on the word. ''Safer from what? For nine months I have been kept here, no word of why I had been brought here or a suggestion of when I would be released!'' Her voice broke as she leapt from the hearth and spun away to begin pacing, her happiness over seeing him dissolving in a rage that began to take control of her reason. ''Men!'' she spat, as if the word were distasteful to her. ''Henry signs an order, I am taken from my home in the middle of the night. I am locked in here for months on end with only an occasional visit from a spineless clerk who is too afraid, or insensible, to answer my questions! I spend my hours reading the same books, or with needlework, or writing letters I suspect will never be delivered, or staring at walls I've memorized to the last line in the mortar, while asking why! Why? Now, after all of these months, you come here overwhelmed with concern for my welfare, when it is obvious that you suspected something might happen long ago! Why did you not tell me? You could have prepared me . . . "

The sound of his laughter filled the room, bringing her to a halt in mid-sentence as she spun back to him, her mouth still open on her last words. "Isabel! I feared they had broken your spirit!" he chortled with relief. "I should have known that somehow you would manage to survive, even in this place!"

A fine brow arched as she planted her hands on her hips and she regarded him with an angry gleam. "You still have not answered my question," she said quietly, too quietly, and he could hear the bitterness in her voice.

He frowned unhappily as he suddenly focused his attention on the goblet he slowly turned between his palms. He was no coward; the scars on his muscled body attested to the battles in which he had fought in the service of Isabel's father, and since in protecting the lands left in his care, and all lay claim to his bravery. Gladly, at this moment, he would have found himself amid any one of those battles, save one, than to face the battle that was now raging within him.

"Aye," he sighed raggedly. "It must be met. Bear with me, little one, and allow me the recounting in my own way." He rose heavily from the chair to pour himself another measure of the heady liquid as he sought to collect his thoughts. "Isabel," he began slowly, "to answer your first question, why it is safer to be here, you must understand about the greed that drives men to do what they do." He turned from the table and crossed again to the hearth where she had again settled, to stand beside her. "Do not count such as honor and duty, as they are too often luxuries enjoyed only after greed is met.

"When your father was killed in Normandy, fighting for Henry, and your mother fled here to England with you, it was because she knew that you both could become pawns in Ireland. She knew that there was bound to be an uprising, a struggle for power following his death, as indeed there was.

"For a few years there was peace, and she was content to raise you in England, among your father's people. Queen Eleanor was your mother's greatest ally, and she managed to keep Henry at bay—you know that your mother had no wish to remarry . . . " He turned to look at her, and his eyes were touched with an old, remembered pain. "The marriage she had with your father was for a lifetime. However, the time came when the queen's tongue plagued Henry once too often, and Eleanor was locked away, as was her influence for you both. It was then that Eve took you back to Ireland, when you were twelve.

"I knew, from the innocent things you would say when you first returned to us, that she had not discussed these matters with you, and I deferred to her judgment. However, I do lament that decision if you have been hurt by your innocence." He leaned a shoulder against the hearthstone and drew again from his goblet. "For years Henry demanded that she return to England with you, but your mother is a powerful woman, Isabel, and she has learned throughout the years how to use that power. With the Irish chieftains behind her, foremost of whom is your uncle, Donnell Kavanaugh, he dared not confront her—not without sending arms, badly needed arms, into Ireland. I must admit," he added with a deep sigh, "as much as I love having you with us, I do not understand why she chose to send you to be fostered with us at Chepstow instead of keeping you in Ireland." His mind turned in torment, questioning for the endless time Eve's decision to place Isabel so firmly in Henry's hands.

"She said that it was time for me to take my place among my father's people and learn of the responsibilities to my inheritance," she said quietly, her eyes shrewdly watching him for the truth. "She felt that I should begin to learn about my father's lands, as she could never return to claim them. She wished for you to teach me what I needed to know about the deClare holdings, as you have, Gervase. Would you have had it otherwise?''

He grunted, crossing once again to the wine, where he poured himself another healthy measure, deliberately avoiding the question while knowing that her large grey eyes followed him as surlily as the regrets that tormented his soul. Oh, Richard, my dear old friend, he thought miserably, I vowed to protect your daughter and I have failed you. Perhaps, had I been quicker to act, to outthink Henry. But then, Henry knew I would ship her back to Ireland—that is why he locked her up in this damnable place! And now any freedom of choice she might have had in her life had been taken away from her. He returned to his chair, sitting heavily as he cleared his throat.

''Isabel, you must know that King Henry has died . . . ''

''Aye, of course,'' she replied. ''I am not so completely isolated, Gervase. Hubert Walter told me of the king's illness—the bells of London told me of his death.''

''Isabel . . . '' He drew a breath and plunged on with grim deliberation. ''Henry brought you to this place to protect your estate, not to mention your virtue—until he could determine which of his vassals would be given your hand in marriage—to his own best advantage, of course.''

Isabel's face paled at his words, but she continued to regard him evenly, though he winced at the slight tremor in her voice when she finally spoke. ''I would truly be mindless had I not suspected, Gervase, though . . . '' She smiled weakly. ''Until now it was only reasonable speculation. I have had endless hours to imagine a host of reasons, but they have always led back to this. However,'' she took a deep breath, letting it out slowly, ''I thought—hoped, that with Henry's death, and that I had heard nothing—I would be released.''

''Richard is now our king,'' he said grimly. ''But Henry did choose for you, Isabel, shortly before he died, and our new sovereign has affirmed the choice. I fear that you will not leave this tower except as a bride.''

"But—the prince hated his father, Gervase!" Isabel stammered, a feeling of dread deepening. "What choice would be suitable for them both?" It had seemed so simple before, to speculate on the possibility that a husband would be chosen for her. But now. . . . The fact that it had come to pass left her feeling light-headed, and something deep within her pulled into a tight, clenching knot. "Who is he to be, Gervase?" she asked tightly.

"You are pledged to Sir William Marshal."

"Marshal?" She allowed the name to trip over her tongue.

"He has been seen little in England in the past few years." Gervase shrugged, drawing from his wine. Then he set to studying the remains of his goblet.

"But you know him." When he did not answer she felt her ire rise with her deepening dread. "Gervase, I am of a mind that my marriage is of far more importance to me than the wine in that goblet is to your palate, particularly considering the poor fare these accommodations have to offer. 'Twould be best for us both if you were to tell me of what is on your mind and have done with it."

Gervase looked up as a feeling of unreality crept over him. The lass was not a little unlike her mother. The child was becoming a woman. "I know Marshal well," he began, then laughed bitterly. "Indeed, all of England knows him! And Normandy, and France, and . . . " Shocked, he suddenly realized that he was becoming slightly drunk. He shook his head to clear it and continued. "The confidant of kings, he is called," he said expansively with a wave of his hand. "Henry's closest friend. More than that, the man virtually raised Prince Henry before he died, as only he had the king's faith to do so. Moreover, you are correct. Richard Plantagenet hated his father, as he had hated his older brother and all those who were loyal to him. But damn me if he does not trust Marshal! For the life of me I'll never understand it! Why, Marshal slew Richard's horse out from under him during a battle the prince fought against his father. Yet what were Richard's words to the scoundrel, over his father's barely cold body, when pressed to honor Henry's promise of marriage to you? 'By the Legs of God, my father did not give her to him, he merely promised to. But I will give him freely both the lady and her lands!' '' Aye, he thought to himself, I am becoming drunk, and the better for it, as it will make the telling easier. Perhaps you are a coward, Gervase, he reasoned. At least in the matters of women. With that thought he took another long draught of the wine.

"Gervase—you said he raised young Prince Henry." She swallowed, fearing to hear the answer to her next question. "How old is he?"

"Heh?" He looked up at her with a puzzled frown. "How old? About thirty-and-five, I believe. Aye, about that. Why?"

"No reason." She let out her breath, not realizing until then that she had been holding it. That was reasonable, she mused. Aye, a husband should be somewhat older to her ten-and-nine years. But not too old. Then what? There was something. "What does he look like?"

His brow wrinkled at the question, but after a moment's reflection he understood the lass's need for assurance that she would not be wed to an ogre. "He is manly enough, I suppose." His mouth suddenly twitched with a smile. "No warts or malformations that I can recall."

She flushed at his teasing while feeling relief that he had nothing untoward to report on the man's appearance. "Then why are you at odds with the match?" she pressed.

The blunt question sobered him, and his brows now lowered in anger. "Because the match is ill-suited!" he snapped, with more anger than he had intended to show to her. "The man is landless! Well, practically landless if you discount a few paupered holdings mismanaged by his forebearers—for all of his father's title as marshal! There is no doubt about it—the man must have coerced Henry, playing upon the emotions and fears of a friendless, dying man! I had hoped that when Henry died the match would be set aside. I cannot understand Richard's reasonings! By the Legs of God, the man is merely a knight! I cannot believe they pledged you to him!"

Isabel's love for Gervase kept her from saying anything to hurt him, and she knew that his concern for her was genuine. How could she explain that her own concerns for her marriage did not parallel his? Lud, she thought, so he was landless, without title. There was a time, so her mother had told her in gentle reminiscing, when her father had been without means, all having been taken from him by old King Stephen, before Henry took the throne. Yet he had regained all, and more, by his abilities. Too often Isabel had seen sons of great families lose all by their ineptness. Nay, it was the manner of the man that was important, not what he was born with. She needed, wanted, a man who could hold what was hers. Besides, at the moment her concerns led quite a different path.

"And when shall I expect to receive this one who is to become my husband?" she asked, feeling her stomach roil as she asked the question.

"At his leisure," he grumbled, staring into the fire. Realizing what he had said, his look darted to Isabel. He had not meant to be so blunt, and he regretted his words when he saw her face drain of color. "That is why I have come now, lass," he added softly. "He is—even now within the city."

Wordlessly, she rose from her place on the hearth and crossed to the small window that was the only one in the room. For a long moment she stared out into the night as if she could detect Marshal's arrival through the thick fog that had settled over the Thames. "I would have hoped for a little more time," she said quietly, her words barely reaching him.

"Even to remain in this place?" he grimaced, glancing about the dismal room. "Do you not wish your freedom?"

"How much freedom will I have in marriage?" she returned, turning to smile at him with a look of irony.

He coughed, chagrined at the truth of her words, and sought to change the subject. "I have ordered the items you will need to be brought to you; trunks your mother had sent some time ago . . . " His voice trailed off awkwardly.

"None are to attend me on the day of my marriage?" she gasped.

"Of course," he answered gruffly, suddenly feeling out of his realm. "By Marshal's order we will be traveling to Striguil. The marriage is to take place there, at Chepstow castle."

"Oh, Gervase!" she exclaimed, afraid to believe what he was saying. "Is this true? Am I to return to Chepstow to be married?"

"Aye," he answered, relieved that she was smiling again.

Her eyes began to twinkle and she grinned at him. "By Marshal's order, you said. Could a mere knight give such orders?"

"He has some influence." Gervase shrugged, not wanting to give anything to Marshal, especially his gratitude. He could have added that while William's elder brother, John, now held the title of marshal of England, it was William the people referred to as the marshal. "He will be joining us for the journey," he said.

Isabel closed her eyes, awash with a feeling of relief as she mentally thanked her husband-to-be for this unexpected offer of generosity. She would be married among her own people, her vassals, on her own land. The knowledge gave her strength and a warm, rushing feeling of peace. It occurred to her that a journey would also give them the opportunity to come to know one another, a promise of a better beginning. A beginning. The thought subdued her, drawing from her joy in a rush of nervous anticipation. Jesú, she thought, a few days, weeks, perhaps a fortnight. How well could she come to know him in that time? What if, upon making his acquaintance, he proved to be more than she could bear?

She crossed to the table with the wine and poured herself a generous measure, from which she took a heady draught, grimacing as she swallowed. "Well," she said tightly, " 'twas my reasoning, in the past, to prefer a man of the land, one content to see to his estates and family. I despised of marrying a marcher lord whose interests would forever take him from me—but now I know better. A knight is little at home, and the better my life will be for it!''

"Isabel . . . " Gervase squirmed under the bitterness of her words. "You know that had it been within my power, you would have married for love . . ."

"Aye, Gervase." She smiled wistfully. " 'Tis not your failing but the result of my birth." Her face grew suddenly angry as her eyes burned with feeling. "Had I been a son I would now hold incredible power in this hand." She held her hand up before her, clenching her slender fingers into a fist. Then she slowly lowered it to her side as she added intensely, "As it is, my worth is only in what I bring to the marriage bed and what my body can yield in the way of sons. It does give me pause, Gervase, why my mother was so intent upon my education; why you strove so to teach me of matters which will now be taken from my grasp."

She turned to regard him levelly with eyes now darkened to a deep grey, shocking him in remembrance of another as they waited in unspoken challenge. They were Richard's eyes. He shook his head to clear it of its thoughts but they prevailed. Why had he never noticed the uncanny similarity? Was it because he had thought of her only as a child? Aye, she was her father's daughter, in more ways than one, and there would be no avoiding the questions when she sought the answers. He felt deeply guilty that he had none to give her. Moreover, he worried that she would not rest until she found them. He had given her desires, the knowledge to be more than she was, and he feared that it would now lead her to grief. If only he had kept his council and had listened to Lavinia. But then, perhaps he had not erred. Had he given her something of what Richard would have given to her, had he lived? He could only pray that he had done well by her.

Greying light gave shape to the small window as objects of the room began to take form, and still Isabel had not slept. Gervase had returned to his lodgings many hours past, yet she lay restlessly on the narrow bed, tossing and turning with thoughts of her future and what the new day would hold for her. Giving up, she threw herself from the bed and pulled a shawl about her shoulders. She crossed to the dying fire, her bare feet dancing across the cold planking of the Tower room. She stirred the coals gently with the poker, seeking a spark among them, and added kindling, blowing softly on the red glow until it caught life. Carefully nursing the small blaze, she added more kindling until it was firmly caught, knowing that if the fire extinguished itself, she would be forced to wait until someone came with her breakfast before she could have it relit. Her task done, the fire began to crackle, and she curled up in the chair, tucking her long legs beneath her. She chewed her lower lip pensively, her mind turned to all that Gervase had told her in the hours past, and she struggled to digest it all, to face what was going to happen to her.

William Marshal. Gervase had been so typically a man about it, so vague to details she thought important, in spite of her prodding. What was Marshal like? Tall? Short? Ugly? A ghost of a smile appeared for a moment as she recalled Gervase's assurance that the man bore no wart upon his countenance. Did he have a temper? Would he be kind to her? What manner of man was he? And—what would he think of her?

She rose, taking a candle to the table she used for dressing and peered at her reflection in the tray of polished silver that served as a mirror. She smoothed her fingers over her face, noticing for the first time how pale she had become in the months in the Tower. " 'Tis the fashion,'' she murmured. But somehow, in her judgment, she felt that it did not suit her. She unpinned her hair, letting it tumble about her shoulders and down her back. It had been, as near as she could recall, a riot of colors ranging from gold to almost white, and now it had turned to a dull bronze mass. She had never been one to concern herself with appearance, accepting herself for what she was. But now, as she tried to see herself as another would see her, she was less than pleased. "He will probably think I am an invalid, wan and sickly,'' she said to herself. Picking up a hairbrush, she took it back to her chair.

Married. Her husband was now within the city. The thought made her tremble in a sudden wash of nerves, yet it held an undeniable excitement. Isabel was not one to delude herself, to lose herself as so many other giggling girls in fantasies of romance—in fact she had always held them slightly in contempt. As she had become acquainted with her wealth, she had reasoned, quite on her own, that someday her husband would be chosen for her, and the odds against falling in love with a complete stranger were infinitesimal. Yet her mother had loved her father, with a love that had allowed no other in her life. Gervase had always loved Lavinia, and they had been allowed to marry—due to her father's influence, as she recalled now. But he was not here to make a match for her.

On the other hand, she reasoned, there was her Uncle Donnell. He had loved Katy when he married her, or thought he did, until she turned into a shrew. Or had she always been a shrew? Perhaps love had not allowed him to see it. Nay, Aunt Katy had always been a shrew, she thought with a smile, and Uncle Donnell had been too blind to see it.

Nay, only one thing was certain. There would be no more delays, which were always with the possibility that she would leave the Tower to return unwed to Striguil, the great seat of the deClares, or even to Erin. Was she prepared? At moments in her life she had certainly thought so. Was a girl's life not prepared to this end? Painstakingly prepared by all aspects of those formative years. Carefully nurtured to the fine points of overseeing a large household for her future husband's comfort; versed in the fine art of needlework to enrich the finest fabrics for his home and person; and accomplished in voice and lyre for his enjoyment—and she never questioned the importance of what she had learned—well, almost never.

There were moments when her exuberant nature had wanted to rebel, to experience the deep feeling of life within her. She had quickly acquiesced, unaware of an alternative. She had observed the young men of her age, knowing their lives to be as structured as her own. Indeed, she would not have traded places with any one of them. At the beck and call to the needs of their knights in service to yet another, with not as much freedom as she had experienced—until now.

There was something, a feeling sealed deep within her, never quite examined, but there, that somehow she was different. Did everyone feel this way, she wondered, as if they were on the outside looking in at the world, unable to quite touch it? Thoughts of Lavinia, her mother's closest friend and wife to Gervase, came unbidden. She remembered the kindly woman's displeasure when Gervase afforded her privileges Lavinia considered unwomanly. Isabel's most treasured memories of Chepstow were the hours spent talking with him of past battles. Even, after much prodding, of the one in which her father had fallen and Gervase had been gravely wounded. The politics, the reasonings of men, he had shared with her. Isabel embraced such dialogue readily, for her mother had talked freely of such, as did Uncle Donnell. But then, women in Ireland involved themselves in the affairs of their men. It had only been a matter of time before Isabel had come to realize the differences in England. Awareness came not only from the deep frowns brought to Lavinia's fair brow as she ushered Isabel off to another task, but from the scandalized attitudes of young women her own age—though they treated her with deference to her position and sought to cultivate her friendship in spite of their disapproval. She had resolved to ignore these differences as problems, happy with herself and content to approach life in her own way, totally disregarding what she considered to be the unreasonable expectations of others. Then Henry's men had come for her, and she began to view the prospect of what the future would bring, a future contrived and resolved by others. A husband chosen by others.

Thus, she had been somewhat content in her tower, desperately wanting her freedom but knowing that what she might face when she left could be far worse. How she cherished her freedom! Even the past months, in this place, were preferable than to be at someone's beck and call, "by his order."

Perhaps, even tomorrow, she would look upon his face. Before, he was vague, merely someone who might come in the future. Now he was real. Tomorrow he might look upon her, speak to her, perhaps—even touch her. What color are his eyes, she thought, his hair? Does he have a sense of humor? Oh God, she prayed, please let him have a sense of humor!

What will he expect from me? Surely he will know that I am inexperienced—Henry has seen to that! He is older, by fifteen years, Gervase said. Will he be patient with me? She was fully aware of what would be expected of her in the marriage bed. The giggles, the whispers, the hours spent discussing the matter with her friends had sparked her interest. Living in a large household had served her curiosity to the act itself; the heated groping in darkened alcoves by servants and nobles alike, the only place lovers could meet in a crowded manor when men were relegated to knight's quarters or pallets in the great hall, and the ladies to the women's quarters. The warmth and longing that would come into her mother's eyes when she spoke of her father had eased her mind to the pleasure to be found. All had been tantalizing supposition, wrapped about a dreamlike figure who was part of the future, leaving her young body eager in anticipation. But to think on it now—to imagine a stranger's hands upon her body . . .

She stared into the orange-and-yellow flickering of the flames, losing her thoughts in their unmeasured dance. Finally, as a solitary spark leapt from the flames to sputter to lifelessness on the hearth, she sighed, a deep, ragged sound that she felt in the deepest part of her being. "What does it matter?" she said aloud. "None of it makes the least twit of a difference! Tomorrow I shall be introduced to the man with whom I shall spend the rest of my life. Oh, lud."

# 2

AT dusk the inhabitants of the city drew into their homes, securing themselves against indecision, knowing their lives to be set by the whims, the uncertainty of man. The heavy fog swirled about the solitary horse and rider, the sharp hooves of the large war-horse striking an echoing clatter against the cobblestone as it picked its way along the narrow London street. The rider knew it unwise to be riding without escort at such an hour, but his decision to make the journey alone, though protested heatedly by his men, had been essential. His eyes moved beneath his helm to the doors locked tightly against him, felt the silence about him, and reconfirmed the importance of his errand. The messages he carried to deGlanville from Queen Eleanor were meant for no others. Even suspicion that he carried messages involving matters of state could lead to serious complications, giving his enemies substance for accusations of treachery, affecting not only his own life but that of England itself. Nay, those aware of his presence in London must think he was there only because of the girl.

The girl. He shrugged his shoulders uncomfortably,

feeling the bitter cold, made the more miserable by the chain-link hauberk, which seemed to bite through the heavy padded gambeson beneath. How could the days be so miserably hot and the nights so bitterly cold, he swore to himself; the weather had gone as mad as the times. He drew his fur-lined cloak more tightly about him. Feeling more comfortable, he allowed his thoughts to drift once more. Thoughts of the girl had been placed aside, events of state more pressing, but now in his loneliness he allowed himself the luxury of thinking of her.

Eleanor had said the girl was exquisite. Charming, poised, a real beauty; but then the queen had a way of bringing matters to her way of thinking. When Henry had first proposed the match, he had been horrified. Of marriage, first of all, and to a girl of nineteen? Sweet Jesú. It was hardly uncommon for a man of his age, or one much older for that matter, to take a wife of even more tender years, he reasoned. But then, he wasn't other men.

Marshal sighed deeply, shifting in the saddle with uncomfortable thoughts. He probably should have married years ago, but there had never been time. Or had there been? Was it merely his own reluctance to commitment that had deterred him?

Isabel deClare. He eased the name about his mind. Beautiful, wealthy, titled. Damnation, William, he mused, you've come a long way. But even as he thought the words, he developed a hard knot in his stomach. He wanted nothing given to him like this! He had not asked Henry for the match—or Prince Richard either! It was Geoffrey, Henry's chancellor, who had reminded the prince of his father's wishes. The matter had come to a head when Richard had informed him that he was to leave for England to release his mother, the queen, from Winchester Castle, where she had been imprisoned the past many years. It was a mission William had relished. There had been many harsh words over the years between Henry and himself as to Eleanor's confinement, to no avail. It was upon his departure that the chancellor had brought the matter to Richard's attention, pointing out to the prince that William's return to England would be time for the match and a perfect cover for more political matters.

William was no longer landless, a fact not commonly known as yet. One of Richard's first acts as king was to award him with lands in Oxford and Crendon in Buckinghamshire, manors with the service of forty-three knights. But he knew, without an actual accounting of Isabel's property, that his would pale by comparison. A fine beginning for a man who had lived by his honor.

William reined in his mount, having arrived at his destination, the home of his host, Richard fitz Renier, the sheriff of London and an old friend. He dismounted and quickly seized the bridle of the now riderless animal. He murmured soothingly to the nervous, high-strung destrier as two of fitz Renier's groomsmen approached. The destrier's eyes rolled and he pulled back, his massive body shifting nervously as the men took the bridle on either side. Fighting a smile at the oaths given by the two as they struggled with the horse, William climbed the steps to the large manor.

Renier awaited him in the main room of the house and joined with William's own men, who rose from their chairs upon his entrance, their faces spelling their relief at his safe return. John d'Erley, William's squire, a ruddy-complected young man with large, honest brown eyes, leapt from his chair, his ale forgotten, as he rushed to take William's cloak and helm.

"God's breath, Sir William, we were worried about you! You were expected hours ago!"

"My business took longer than I expected," William answered as he accepted the ale that was thrust into his hand. He took a long swallow, welcoming the warmth that filled his throat and stomach, then glanced about the room at the expectant faces. "The news was well received," he answered to their unasked questions. He glanced briefly at fitz Renier before he took another draw of the ale, and his men knew that old friend or not, nothing more would be said in front of the sheriff of London.

"We will take leave of you, then, Sir William," one of the older knights said as he set his tankard on a table. "Now that we know you are safe, my mind is of bed."

"Aye, Beaumont." William smiled, rolling his shoulders against his fatigue. "Another measure to relax and warm me, and that is where I am bound. A matter awaits me on the morrow for which I will need my wits about me."

Broad smiles and not a little amount of elbow punching were passed about at his words by his departing men. Beaumont frowned blackly at the open jests, knowing how touchy William was about his approaching marriage.

Once alone, Renier turned to William with a speculative look, and his mouth became set with determination. "I have the information you wanted, William," he said quietly. "Do you wish to see it now?"

William turned on Renier's words, a dark brow arching with question as Renier removed a sheaf of rolled papers from his desk. He spread them out on a large table in the middle of the room, placing candlesticks on the corners of the documents to make them lie flat, then removed himself to a nearby chair and his ale, allowing William time to absorb what was written.

After a while, William, who had read the parchments silently, his jaw tightening with increased tension on each line, let out a long, slow sigh. "Jesú. I suspected but I did not fully realize. According to these she owns three score knight fees scattered through nine shires plus Weston in Hertfordshire, Badgworth in Gloucestershire, Chesterford in Essex, her father's seat of Striguil of over one hundred miles between the Wye and the Usk, including the great castle of Chepstow. In Wales she holds the county of Pembroke from Saint Brides Bay to Carmarthen and north toward the Teife. Not to mention, in passing, one full fifth of Ireland. It is listed here as the counties of Wexford, Queens, Carlow, Kilkenny, and Kildare."

"And control of these lands is absolute," Renier said. "She enjoys the privileges of a baron, owing only her fealty to the crown."

They exchanged a long look, then slowly Renier's mouth slipped into a wry smile. "It would seem, my old friend, that you are about to become one of the most powerful barons in England."

William swore under his breath, almost sloshing ale on an expensive inlay table as he poured himself another measure. Understanding his anger, Renier rose and went to William's side, laying a hand on the taller man's arm. "William," he cautioned. "Be careful, my friend. I know you; while most men would bay to the moon with such news you take it as some sort of insult."

William glared at him, then took another draught, the thought passing over his mind that it would be a good night to become exceedingly drunk.

"William, listen to me," Renier pressed. "The Lady deClare is to be married to someone, the match is long overdue. Do you realize how many of us thank God that Henry had the foresight, the wisdom, to match her with you? Had Richard deClare lived, the matter would not be at issue, but he left a young heiress, one ripe for the taking. The lands, wealth, and power he amassed are open for one less responsible, less able. The result could have been disaster! Why do you think Henry had her locked away in the Tower this past year? To protect her power, not her chastity! William, do not look at me that way. You were Henry's closest friend, the only one he trusted. Even the prince—ah, the king—knew he could depend upon you, in spite of your differences. One thing you can be counted upon, in spite of your personal feelings, is loyalty to the crown and to England. Consider, if you turn your back on this marriage, who might take that power."

William said nothing, merely gifting Renier with an angry glare before he tossed off another large draw of ale. "Have it your way, Marshal!" Renier threw up his hands and turned away to pour himself another tankard. "I will get drunk with you. Perhaps then we can have a meeting of minds." He paused and turned back to William. "Tell me, what did the queen say?"

"She supported the match." William shrugged.

"Supported it?" Renier laughed. "I suspect that she planned it!"

William jerked his head about with surprise.

"Oh, come now." Renier smiled. "Would Richard do anything without consulting his mother?"

"Tell me something, Renier," William asked with a smirk. "Why are you merely a sheriff?"

Renier chuckled deeply. "From you I take that as a compliment, William." Then he answered with a shrug, "It suits me, I never desired more. Unlike you, I have no further ambitions apart from wealth, as too many demands come with responsibility. Now, you tell me," he added slyly. "How much of England's administration is to be part of your duties until Richard arrives?"

William's eyes barely flickered at the question. "Now I know that you have lost reason, Renier. Do you imagine that I would have any control over England?"

"Of course not," Renier answered with wide-eyed innocence. "I only wondered about the sixteen knights and over thirty men-at-arms that were sent into South Wales against Rees ap Griffith upon your arrival. But then, what do I know?"

William's mouth twitched as he fought a smile, but he left the comment unanswered and returned his attention to his drink. The two men retired to chairs before the fire and relaxed into a comfortable companionship, easing the tension of the past day as they sipped from their tankards in easy silence. Finally, it was William who broke the silence in a lazy drawl. "I have decided to take the lady back to Chepstow. The marriage should take place there, among her own people."

An awkward silence followed, and William could feel a sudden tension from Renier. Finally, Renier came out with it, his voice unaccustomingly strained. "I fear that I cannot allow that to be, William. You must take the lady to wife here, in London, and as quickly as possible. I cannot permit you to take her from the city unwed."

"You cannot be serious!" William protested.

"Those are my orders, William. They came from Henry before his death, and Richard has confirmed them."

"You must allow it," William said grimly.

"I cannot, William. I have my orders. You, more than any, understand duty."

William glanced at his friend, then his gaze returned to the fire. "You must understand," he said quietly. "I have not the funds to marry the lady here. I must see her to her own estates to marry her fittingly."

Renier winced inwardly at William's confession. He knew what it must have cost him to admit his circumstances, and he swore silently at his king. Typical for a knight-errant, Renier grimaced. The king would think nothing of "borrowing" a few coins from his vassal when he found himself temporarily short of funds, but never would he think of William's needs. Another reason he did not seek to associate himself with the court. Damn, Richard should have thought of it; for that matter, Eleanor should have provided the means. Renier felt intense anger, an emotion foreign to his nature, being normally one who accepted life's little blows as something to ignore less they interfere with one's pleasure. In this case he allowed himself the luxury. William was one of the few men he admired, as he saw in him a man of extreme honor and loyalty, a man with true principles guided by intelligence and ability, a combination he respected for its rarity. His shrewd mind worked quickly, searching for a way to salvage Marshal's pride while solving the problem.

"Worry not about the means, William. The queen has pledged funds to see you to your purpose," he lied. "The only condition is that you are to wed the lady quickly and see her from London." Jesú, he would see to the matter himself. It was only part of a lie, he reasoned; he was certain that the queen would have advanced the funds had she thought of it. His position had found him well set, he being a shrewd investor, and he knew that he could do worse than to use his own coin for the purpose. Instinct suggested that the return could be far greater than the amount he might advance.

"So be it." William nodded begrudgingly. He knew that he had no choice. He did not doubt that Renier had his orders, and they were reasonable. Until Lady deClare was wed, she was fair game for anyone feeling strong enough to take her—and a party traveling half the breadth of England was tempting. But he did not delude himself for a moment over Renier's offer. Had Eleanor provided the funds, she would have told him when he was with her. But he was grateful for the lie and the opportunity to save face before his friend. And he would make certain that the loan was repaid as soon as he was wed. His friendship with Renier was based on a thorough understanding—and he had no doubt that Renier would ask the favor returned someday. He had no intention of placing himself in that position. Clearly he recognized the offer as the only reasonable solution. But God, it rankled!

"So be it," he repeated. "I shall inform the Lady Isabel of the change of plans, and two days hence shall wed her and remove her from your jurisdiction and responsibility immediately thereafter."

The two men exchanged a look of understanding, then drank deeply, settling back into silence, each turned to his own thoughts.

# 3

"PERHAPS this one, milady?"

The maid lifted yet another gown for Isabel's approval. Isabel's attention, however, was on the bustle of activity in the room. Quite a difference, she mused silently. For months I have longed for company, and now this. Amazing the difference one night can make—or one knight. Her mouth twisted into a smirk at the thought as she turned back to the waiting maid who had arrived with the first of the trunks.

"Nay . . ." She shook her head. "Not that one. Here, the blue one." She reached past the bemused woman and pulled a sky-blue silk from the pile on the bed. Crossing to the mirror she held it before her and affirmed her decision with a quick nod. "Aye, this is the one I shall wear. Work out the wrinkles as quickly as you can."

The maid dipped a curtsy and scurried from the room as Isabel turned back to the confusion and was gripped with a moment of petulant anger. Hubert Walter had arrived with the dawn, filled with self-importance as he ordered the placing of sumptuous furniture about the room, soft rugs to be laid on the floor, and the large postered bed in place of the narrow pallet she had used over the past long months. Among these were the trunks Gervase had promised. Isabel suspected, from their dusty condition, that they had been stored elsewhere in the Tower for some time. A large copper tub had been placed before the fire, which now burned warmly with the fragrant smell of oak, and buckets of hot, steaming water were being carried in to fill the large vessel. Isabel looked at it longingly, her usual fare a singular container of tepid water brought each morning from which she completed her ablutions.

When the last of her things had been set, Isabel closed the door upon the departing servants and leaned against its frame. She bit her lower lip in a confusion of mixed feelings: gladness that her imprisonment was almost at an end, anger that the imminent appearance of a man was needed to effect a change in her circumstances, and a trembling fear as she considered the prospect of her soon-to-be visitor. "Well," she murmured, taking a deep slow breath to calm her tumbled emotions. "There is no time but to take each step as it comes."

She looked to the tub and to the water steaming in soft misty trails that beckoned her to its warmth. Stripping off the wool gown she had come to detest, and the chemise beneath, she slipped into the soothing water and let her body relax in its warmth. She allowed her mind to drift, enjoying the moment for itself as the water soaked into her body, easing the tightness of her muscles as well as her thoughts. She was now relaxed, thoughts of the hours past invaded, and her eyes began to fill with tears. Among the trunks she had discovered a small casket containing her mother's jewels. There were jeweled torcs, or necklaces, of fine Irish gold. Rings, bracelets, and armlets. Girdles of intricate lace handiwork of exquisite Irish gold and studded with costly gems; combs and droplets for the ears. Her mother's small jeweled dagger was there, and finding it Isabel had been overwhelmed with emotion. It had first belonged to Isabel's grandmother, and Eve had cherished it as a symbol of her own independence, for Isabel had rarely seen her without it.

Confused, Isabel had opened the letter tucked into the lid of the casket. Her eyes misted as she read the words of love from her mother, the concern for Isabel's happiness, and her wish that she could be with her daughter on this most important day of her life.

At the bottom of the casket she discovered a small, linen-wrapped bundle, and its contents caused her to sit heavily on the edge of the bed. Within lay a magnificent emerald suspended from a delicate gold chain. Isabel wondered at its source, as she had never seen her mother wear it. Her fingers had trembled as she opened the yellowed parchment lying beneath the stone, and her heart seemed to stop as she realized that it was a letter from her father. Tears began to trip from the corners of her eyes, tracing an unheeded path down her cheeks as she read the words he had written to her so many years before. He told her that the emerald had first been a gift to her mother on the day of his knighting. The night before he had left for Normandy they had laid it away for the day of her marriage. He spoke of his love for her, his wish for her future, that it would hold all the brightness and joy that she had given to him. It was almost as if, somehow, he had known that he would not be with her on the day she was to wed.

Forgotten memories came rushing back in feeling more than form, and the aging parchment crackled in her trembling fingers. She realized then that her entire body shook with the tears she was trying to hold back. Carefully, tenderly, she rewrapped the letter and the precious stone in the linen wrappings, and gently she returned it to its resting place. Too overwhelmed to think on it, she forced her attention to her wardrobe, unwilling to face the realization that neither of her beloved parents would attend her on the day of her wedding.

Now, with tensions easing in the comfort of the warm water, she faced her thoughts and found that she had never felt so desperately alone. Feelings of loss suddenly defeated her, and she gave in to her grief, allowing the tears to come in heartfelt self-pity. At last, totally drained, when no more tears would come, her emotions swung to anger, directed at her lack of self-control. As she washed her face, splashing it in the cooling water, she vowed never, never again would she give into grief over something beyond her control, hating the exhausted, helpless feeling it had left her with.

She lathered and rinsed her hair and was drying herself when the maid returned. The tiringwoman set to brushing her hair, stroking it until the original shine began to return. "Your hair is lovely, milady," the maid offered, admiring the smoky golden mass that now hung in soft waves and ringlets about Isabel's shoulders and down her back.

"Hummm," Isabel murmured, her attention elsewhere. She leaned forward toward the mirror and pinched her cheeks, once again dissatisfied with her paleness. Never mind, she thought, it will have to do, as she refused to wear the sheep fat and tinted rouges so common of the day. Well, at least I will not require a skin whitener, she mused drolly.

Rising from the table she slipped from her robe and allowed the maid to assist her into a thin linen chemise and silk stockings, gartering them at the knee. Next came soft leather slippers and finally the sky-blue silk gown. It clung to her waist with a finely linked girdle of amethysts and pearls, which lay about her slender hips. The sleeves were long and fitted, flaring below the elbows, the inseam reaching to her hem, where the outer sleeve covered just the tips of her fingers. The gown smoothed up over her full breasts with a high collar that encircled her throat and was studded with pearls, as was the lining of the revealed sleeves. Her hair was left loose, and she wore only a thin circlet, or fillet, of lace gold and seed pearls about her forehead.

She studied her reflection in the mirror, turning to see the effect. Not bad, Mother, considering, she mused. But then, you did have nine months to prepare. She glanced back at the maid, whose eyes were wide with admiration, and she flushed. "Try to set the room to right," she ordered gently, touched by the woman's response. "I suspect that we will soon have company."

The tub was removed, and they were just completing their efforts when a light tap was heard at the door. Isabel froze, her eyes swinging to the source. She drew herself up, trying to ignore the heavy beating of her heart as the maid answered the knock. Her knees felt weak when it was Gervase who entered. He halted abruptly when he saw her, his face breaking into a broad grin. "My Lord, Isabel, you are breathtaking!"

"Under the circumstances, it will have to do," she said modestly but with a grateful smile as she offered her cheek to him for a kiss. His gaze darted about the room and his brows arched with surprise before returning to her. "The powers that be have suddenly seen fit to attend to my comfort." She shrugged, but a wry smile tugged at the corners of her mouth.

"Humph," he grunted, but his eyes fixed on her again, and they warmed at the sight. He dismissed the transformation of the room and was transported, marveling in her exquisite beauty. What had happened to the braids and the freckles that used to dance across her nose? Her smoky blond hair tumbled about her shoulders, smoothing over full breasts and a small, trim waist. Her nose, slightly tipped at the end, was so like her beautiful mother's, as were her full, enticing lips and oval-shaped face, delicately arching brows, and high, graceful cheekbones. But her eyes, for whatever she had taken from Eve, those were Richard's. Soft, luminous grey, changing with her moods to a darkness that could penetrate with their intensity. Damnation, he thought, his anger swelling with emotion, if she comes to any harm at the hands of that scoundrel . . .

"I see that you have everything," he said quickly, noticing the trunks, then shrugged. "I wish there was more that I could do for you. If we had more time there is so much I would say to you . . . "

Further conversation was lost as there came a sharp

knock at the door, and they both tensed. Recovering, Gervase glanced at her with a comforting smile and noted how pale she had become. He patted the hand that lay on his arm, then crossed to the door, but his jaw, now turned away from her, was set grimly.

As the door opened, two men seemed to suddenly fill the room. The first was Ranulf deGlanville, the justiciar of the Tower, his dark eyes flashing a warning to Gervase as he nodded in greeting. But Isabel never heard what he said, as her attention was fixed upon the tall knight who had entered with him. As the door had opened, she had drawn in her breath in an attempt to stop the wild beating of her heart, which now seemed to stop completely for an instant at the sight of him. Sweet Mother Mary, her mind raced. She attempted to lower her gaze, realizing the impropriety of staring, but she could not help herself. He was tall, his shoulders broadly filling a costly, well-fitted tunic of dark blue velvet, the collar of the white linen chanise beneath in startling contrast to his deeply tanned face. His hair was dark, almost black, in soft waves where a few, unruly curls wrapped about his ears, and a wide brow over strong, strikingly handsome features. While her eyes, seemingly with a mind of their own, would have continued on their course, they were drawn inexplicably to his own. She gasped softly, her body stiffening as her heart lurched in her chest, her eyes now locked with the depths of startling cerulean blue, which seemed to hold hers in their intensity. But it was their coldness that made her tremble to the very core of her being. Beyond that they were unreadable, and she felt her cheeks grow warm under his frank appraisal. She was all too aware that moments before she had been guilty of the same as his eyes moved slowly over her, then he suddenly turned to Gervase.

"You represent her family? Gervase de Mille, is it not? I have heard well of you, your name is revered, sir. Your place in Ireland, as well as Normandy, is to be remembered. I am honored." He extended his hand, clasping Gervase's wrist in greeting. Gervase took the knight's arm in offering, gauging him carefully as they openly judged one another. They turned to Isabel, but she barely heard Gervase's introduction, her eyes now lowered modestly, though her mind still burned with the remembrance of those startling cold blue eyes. She heard her name in greeting and was shaken by the intensity of his voice while impressed by the richness of its timbre. But she held her composure; this moment was too important to falter, and all of her instincts forced a show of womanly poise and manner.

"My lord, welcome," she said softly as she curtsied deeply, her eyes still lowered while she would have preferred to look him squarely in the eye, though her body trembled at the thought of doing so. Why was he so angry?

"Leave us."

She tensed, her gaze darting to Gervase as she rose. He looked momentarily confused, then tensed visibly as the order registered. He seemed about to protest, but deGlanville laid a warning hand on his arm. He shrugged unhappily, following the justiciar from the room with a quick, guarded backward glance at Isabel. When the door had closed behind them, Marshal turned to Isabel and sighed, a sound that almost held a quality of relief.

"Would you be so kind as to pour me some wine, milady? I am most weary."

The sudden softness to his voice unsettled her as much as the simply given request, and she opened her mouth to speak. Thinking better of it, she turned away to comply. Anything, she thought, but to stand there and stare at each other. As she handed him a goblet, he settled into a chair by the hearth and motioned for her to take the chair next to his. They sat in silence as he drew from the goblet, and she struggled not to look at him, unconsciously biting her lower lip as she pondered the situation and considered whether or not she should speak first—and what she could possibly say.

"Do you always chew your lip when you are nervous?" he asked.

"What?" She blinked, raising her eyes to find him watching her.

He repeated the question, this time with a hint of a smile.

"I—I don't do that!" she flushed.

"Aye, it appears that you do. 'Tis most natural to be nervous under the circumstances, milady." She saw that his eyes were now filled with amusement. "I understand how difficult this situation is for you, Isabel. It is for us both."

Suddenly rankled by his attitude, she felt her nervousness dissolve. Why should he be angry with her? And now he was laughing at her! "You appear to be at ease, milord!" she snapped.

"Oh?" He rubbed his lips with his fingers in thoughtful contemplation as he studied her. "And why would you reason that this is not equally difficult for me? We are strangers, yet we are to spend the rest of our lives together, by orders of the king, our liege lord. . . ."

"Was it only by order of the king?" she queried, arching a brow with doubt. "Are you saying that you had nothing to do with the decision?"

His eyes glittered dangerously as his mouth slipped into an easy smile. "So you imagine that I arranged this, and the possibility displeases you. Milady, you give me more credit than I deserve. But tell me, why would it bother you if I had?"

"Since we have never met I can only presume that your interest in marriage is for reasons other than desire of the lady," she answered evenly, forcing herself to meet his gaze.

He returned her look, and she shuddered inwardly at the coldness in his eyes. "Ah," he said softly. "So we come to it quickly. You are a very blunt young woman, Isabel, but perhaps it is as well. At the very least we shall know where we stand." He rose from his chair and took the goblet to the fire, where he leaned an elbow against the mantelpiece and stared into the flames for a long moment. Waiting for him to continue, Isabel took the moment to further her assessment of this stranger who had walked into her life and was to become so important a part of it. Her gaze moved brazenly down over the dark curls at the nape of his neck to the broadness of his shoulders and to his waist, pausing on muscular thighs and calves beneath form-fitting black chausses, to his cross-garters and the soft black leather of his boots. She suddenly felt the small hairs on the back of her neck tingle, and she looked up to find him watching her, his eyes dancing as his mouth played with a smile. She flushed deeply, dropping her gaze to her lap where her fingers began to worry a fold in her gown.

"Do not be embarrassed, Isabel," he said, almost gently. "I am just as curious about you. But to your question," his voice and eyes hardened once again as he ignored her blush. "The marriage came as much of a surprise to me as it did to you. Frankly, I had not considered marriage. I had not the time or the leanings toward it."

"If that is true, milord, you did not have to accept," she parried. "But you obviously did—why?"

He shrugged, turning to her as he leaned his back against the mantel. "When Henry first told me of the match my inclination was to refuse. In thinking on it I decided that perhaps it was well overdue, and I found the prospect not as displeasing as I once would have. And," he added with a flash of an honest grin, "Henry pointed out, in his own inimitable way, that I was not getting any younger. As for the lady herself, she was said to be 'the good, the fair, the wise, a courteous lady of high degree.' So you see, I did know quite a bit about you."

The fading color returned to Isabel's cheeks. "Is such truly said about me?" she murmured. "I did not know the court was aware of me."

"Would you otherwise be in this place?" he laughed —she noticed how his eyes crinkled at the corners when he laughed. "A less fair maid would not find it necessary. Speculation about you has been rampant at court for some time, Isabel. Had you not returned to Ireland, you would have been espoused by the time you were twelve. You are an extremely beautiful young woman, milady, not to mention wealthy. You would be quite a catch for any man."

"Especially for one who is landless?" she blurted out, then winced, regretting her words as soon as she had spoken them. "I—I am sorry. It is not my place . . . "

"You need not apologize," he answered calmly, though she noted with regret that his eyes had turned cold once more. "You are accurate, Isabel. The lands in my family have been held by my brothers. What I have has been earned in tournaments and in service to my king. Indeed, it is a good match for me—do not doubt it. You will have to decide the manner of man who is to take you to wife. From there our relations will develop —whatever they may be."

"I did not mean to offend you, milord," she answered. "I merely wanted to know—how you felt."

"I know," he sighed. "And you have every right to wonder. In my abruptness please believe that I did not mean to hurt you," he added gently, his voice touching her in a caress that brought a new flush to her cheeks. Perhaps, she thought wistfully, he was capable of gentleness. . . . Her attention was brought back from her musings as he took a step toward her. "As we are discussing this matter, Isabel, do not call me 'milord.' I have no title, I am merely a knight."

"Merely a knight?" she repeated, gifting him with a generous smile, eager to make up for her rudeness. "Hubert Walter, deGlanville's clerk, told me that you are the foremost knight of our age. Gervase said that you are a confidant of kings."

His head came up abruptly. Was the lass making fun of him? He caught the sparkle of humor in her large grey eyes, but with it there was admiration and more, an intelligence, a depth that did not delude him. A dull hope began to stir. She was everything Eleanor had said and more, much more. Absolutely exquisite. Could she know what that smile had just done to him? Nay, she was innocent, that was also obvious by the easy blush to her fair cheeks. But—could it be that the lass was actually intelligent, as well as beautiful? He could have told her that the main reason he had never married was that he had grown quickly bored with the women he had known. Even the intelligent women he had known had, to his frustration, refused to use it, preferring to act in simpering roles. Nay, William, he reasoned, you could not be that fortunate. "You should not listen to everything you hear," he grumbled.

"About the man I am to marry?" she countered. "Of course I shall. But if you wish for me to truly know about you then you should tell me yourself."

"You might find yourself quite bored," he answered, wanting to change the subject.

"Well," she said softly as she focused her attention once again on her hands. "We shall have time to come to know one another as we journey to Chepstow. Perhaps we might even become—friends."

His head jerked about and his dark brows met in a heavy scowl. Damn, he had forgotten. "I have had to change our plans, Lady Isabel. We are to be married in London."

At first she did not think she had heard him correctly, then her heart sank at his words, and her lower lip began to tremble. She bit it to hold back the tears of disappointment that were threatening to gather in her eyes. "London?" she asked softly. "But Gervase said . . . "

"The plans have been changed," he answered shortly, his own discomfort of the situation giving his voice more anger than he had intended. God's breath, was she going to cry? He wanted to reach out, to comfort her, already longing for the brightness in those incredible eyes when she smiled. But he held back; his emotions were still too confused about what was happening to be able to offer her comfort. He knew it was unreasonable to feel anger toward her for something beyond her control, but since he had read the documents Renier had so painstakingly compiled, anger had loomed just beneath the surface. He watched as she brushed a tear from those pale cheeks, and he knew he had to say something. . . . "Isabel . . . "

"I understand," she stopped him, raising herself up to stand before him. "You have determined that our wedding shall take place in London. May I ask when it is to be?"

His brows lowered into a frown as she stood stiffly before him, her hands clasped in front of her, a new tightness about her mouth and determination in her eyes that he recognized as acceptance—with not a little anger of her own. It was just as well, he thought. Perhaps, after all, it would help to carry her through the next few days far better than wishful thinking and girlish dreams.

"On the morrow, Isabel," he answered with a quiet grimness. "At midday, in Christ's Church. DeMille will escort you there."

"Tomorrow?" She blinked, her resolve beginning to falter.

"Aye," he answered firmly, ignoring the fear that had leapt into her eyes. " 'Tis important that the wedding take place as soon as possible, and there is no need for further delays."

She winced at the coldness of his words and swallowed as she fought back the tears of anger that were forming at the back of her throat. Fighting for control, she regarded him evenly, wanting him gone before her hard-met resolve crumbled. "Then, perhaps, milord—ah, Sir William, we should see an end to this meeting as there is a little time to prepare and I have much to do."

He glanced about, his brows rising in question, but he gave her the moment, realizing her need to be alone. He nodded then bent over her hand, his lips touching their icy tips, noticing that they trembled slightly at his touch. "Good day, Isabel," he said softly, deeply regretting this poor beginning. "Until tomorrow."

# 4

ISABEL stared at the gown on the bed, her mouth tight with anger and frustration. The gown was breathtakingly beautiful; a heavy silk brocade of deep gold lavished on the bodice and skirt with intricate patterns of pearls and priceless jewels. A golden diadem similarly encrusted lay next to the gown, the morning sun streaming in from the small window to catch the many facets, releasing sparkles of rainbow hues. It was the gown and diadem her mother had worn when she had married her father; they had been carefully packed away, cherished, and held for the day her own daughter would wear it.

"Take it away," Isabel snapped to the waiting maid. "I will choose another."

"But—milady!" the woman gasped. "It—'tis so beautiful!"

" 'Twas a gown worn by an Irish princess when marrying a lord marcher," Isabel answered tartly. "Totally inappropriate for this occasion. Remove it!"

The maid stared at her, puzzled as she glanced at the breathtaking gown and back to Isabel. It seemed totally appropriate to her way of thinking. But then, she shrugged, who was she to question?

When the maid had left, Isabel sank onto the edge of the bed, depressed and irritated with herself for her behavior to the woman. She would have to find a way to make it up to her; it was hardly the poor woman's fault that she was in such a foul mood!

How could he? To raise her hopes, promise her something so very important to her, then rescind it in such an uncaring, hurtful manner! She was to marry alone, attended only by Gervase, and he did not even seem to care! But why should he? What was she, after all, but a means to an end?

She derided herself for caring, for hoping that there might be more for her than a cold, loveless marriage. What a fool, what a silly romantic! Those moments with him for just a moment, when she had thought—and why, because he was handsome? Oh, he was that—male, virile—her thoughts froze, and she felt heat begin up her neck to her cheeks with her thoughts. Passing off uncomfortable thoughts, she allowed her anger to return. Oh, lud, false hopes changed nothing. In a few hours she would be wed . . .

Well, Isabel, she thought, what else could you expect? Perhaps it was just as well. She had begun to think of the journey to Chepstow as a courtship and now, she suspected, that it would merely have given her more time to regret her wedding day as she grew to know him. She threw herself back on the bed and stared at the ceiling above her. She felt so alone—but then, she had been, for a long, long time. She knew that her only resources would have to come from within herself. She could crumble and feel sorry for herself, that would be easy enough, part of her even felt she had the right. But what good would it do? Who would it hurt but herself? He would not even notice.

Slowly, an idea began to pluck at the back of her mind. Aye, she should not be the one to pay. Careful, Isabel, she thought, think calmly. Revenge is a dish that should be served unheated. Slowly, her mouth drew into a smile, and she laughed aloud, the sound filling the room.

"She is late."

Renier glanced once again at the doorway of the small room where they waited. He pulled at the heavy gold chains about his neck, showing his agitation, then strode to the window overlooking the sanctuary. Every pew was filled, the immense room filled with those who had come to bear witness to the marriage of William Marshal to the heiress of Striguil. Unfortunate that there had not been more time, Renier mused. Perhaps, had there been, the king himself would be here. Still, he wasn't displeased. While he had helped as a matter of friendship, it never hurt to help oneself.

"Give her time," William said calmly, apparently unruffled by the bride's tardiness. He was slumped in a chair by the window, his legs stretched out before him and his head resting on the heel of his hand.

Renier glanced at him and silently approved. The black and velvet surcoat trimmed in silver braid was rich and costly and complemented the well-fitted chausses of matching color. Appropriate, Renier thought with relief. Since their talk the night of his arrival William had seemed far too casual about the marriage, almost acting with indifference. He would not have been surprised if Marshal had shown up for his wedding in a fur tunic and leather leggings, an outfit of which he was particularly fond. "She has had ample time," Renier grumbled, glancing again at the door. He suddenly paled. "You don't think that deMille whisked her back to Ireland?"

"Hardly." William grinned. "DeGlanville would have known of it before they reached the city gates. Relax, Renier, it is her prerogative to be late; this is an important day for her. You are acting like the mother of the bride."

"Since you mention it, she too should be here," Renier snapped, regretting his words as he watched a dark shadow cross William's eyes.

"You make a good point, Renier," William said evenly. "If you step again to that window you will notice that the lady's people are spare. No groomsmen to accompany her, save deMille, no maids to carry her dowry by my side. No minstrels to mark our way to the church door; indeed, that portal is to be passed by entirely, Mass dispensed with, and the vows themselves said at the altar. A remarkable wedding, would you not say? Remarkable in that time will be spared for the vows. Can you blame her for dallying to the event?"

"William, you know that . . ."

He was stopped by the sound of the door opening and John d'Erley entered. His face was flushed, and he was wearing a pleased smile. "She is here, Sir William, and Lord, she is beautiful."

William waited at the altar, aware of the eyes that had turned to him expectantly and with great curiosity as he had entered the sanctuary to take his place. But now, his own eyes were fixed upon the vision proceeding down the long aisle toward him. John had been entitled to his enthusiasm. She was radiant in a rich brocade gown of deep gold studded with jewels, which fitted her slender figure to graceful folds that swirled about her feet as they peeked beneath the hem. The sleeves of the garment were fitted, the inseam reaching to the hem and lined in a plush matching velvet. Her fair, smoky hair was long, hanging in graceful turning waves and crowned by a diadem of emerald-and-ruby studded gold, from which hung a golden coif of transparent gauze. About her narrow waist was a girdle of golden links, from which was suspended a small jewel-encrusted dagger, and about her neck, suspended into the deep cut of the gown, hung a magnificent emerald, its facets catching the light that broke in narrow spears through the high windows of the sanctuary. The first murmurs heard about the room were hushed as she began her walk down the aisle. The speculation about this daughter of Richard deClare and his Irish princess, the rumors of the beautiful young heiress, were finally satisfied. When word had spread that the girl was to be married to Marshal reactions had been intense, though mixed. Marshal's enemies had grumbled, some loudly, and those loyal to the renowned knight had been enthusiastic, feeling it his just due and that Marshal was the only one who could control such power. Those feelings could be felt now throughout the sanctuary and eyes, awed and impressed by Isabel, turned to William to note his response.

But William's reaction was well hidden as one used to presenting an impassioned face to the world, a talent gained by a man who dealt daily with the demands of diplomacy. Inwardly, however, it was a different matter. He noted her poise, the proud tilt to her head, the graceful sway to her slender body as she approached on deMille's arm. He missed nothing, including, unseen by others, the defiant gleam to her eye as Gervase laid her arm on his. He fought a smile, his face remaining impassive as he took her hand in his and knelt with her before the altar.

He could feel her tension as they recited their vows, though her voice was strong and even. He saw her bite her lower lip as he repeated his vows, and his heart went out to her in sympathy, understanding her nervousness and doubt. But, as they rose to accept the blessing from the priest, she glanced up at him, and once again he saw the defiance return to her eyes. A dark brow raised slightly, and she blinked at the answered challenge.

Renier watched the young bride where she sat on the narrow window seat of the small antechamber, her back stiff with pride and hurt as she stared out to the street below. Damn, William, he thought, to leave her now, even for a short time! William had been called away to another part of the city, an urgent message d'Erley had said with an embarrassed look at the bride, only moments after they had signed their names to the marriage contracts. He recalled the hostility he had read between the couple upon the news, and suddenly he made a decision, much to his disgruntlement. Even as he crossed the room his thoughts bid him keep his own counsel, but compassion, though he would not have recognized it as such, moved him forward until he found himself sitting next to her.

"Lady Marshal?"

It took a moment before the address registered and she turned to him, her face softening as she recognized him and she forced a smile. "I have not thanked you for what you have done for us. Gervase told me that it was you who made the arrangements for the wedding."

He laughed. "Are you quite certain that it is your thanks you wish to offer?" But then he sobered, remembering his intent. "I must apologize for William. There were matters to which he was compelled to attend, most urgent matters . . . "

"You need not apologize for my—husband," she said with a touch of bitterness in her voice. "I reason that he does exactly what suits him." Then, more gently, "It has nothing to do with you. Your kindness will not be forgotten."

"You misjudge him, milady," Renier answered, determined to continue now that he had committed himself.

"I think not," she murmured, turning once again to the window.

"Can you know him so well?" he asked gently. "But, you see, I do. He is a man given continuously to great responsibility, often to his own disadvantage."

She turned back to him, her expression filled with doubt. "Oh, would this be so? He has told me himself that he is merely a knight—surely a knight's vows would not keep him from those made so recently to a bride."

"Ah, but there you have it. William is truly an enigma of our time. He will claim that he is merely a knight, and in fact it is so. Yet, his responsibilities carry him into a realm which neither you nor I can follow. It will be for you, not I, to understand and live with him."

"What are you trying to tell me, Renier?" she asked, now giving him her undivided attention.

"Only that you have married a man that few of us will ever truly understand, though I pray that you will be one of the few, for your sake and his." He leaned back against the window casing and regarded her carefully. "Tell me, what is it that bothers you about him?"

She started visibly at the astuteness of the question, and from a mere stranger, and she bristled in self-defense. "You do overstep your bounds, sir, with such a question!"

"Perhaps," he answered calmly. "But the answer is important, or I would not have asked the question. William is friend to me and I care deeply, though I would not admit it to many. I would help, even at the risk of your displeasure. Lady Isabel—as to the demands of which I spoke—if you are to have a chance of happiness—you must accept that there will be times you will have to live with disappointment. William is bound for greatness, this I truly believe. The needs of the king will always come first for him, his duty, even as love may lie elsewhere, his own desires placed aside."

A commotion was heard from without, and the pair looked up upon William's entrance with d'Erley. William's brow furrowed speculatively as he regarded the two on the window seat, obviously deep in conversation. The moment passed as he crossed to them and extended his hand to his bride. "Forgive the interruption, my lady," he offered. "There were unavoidable matters which needed my attention but they have now been reconciled."

Isabel rose, giving a soft smile to Renier, who had risen with her to draw to one side as she laid her hand on William's offered arm.

"The hour grows late, and we must be away if we are to make Surrey before nightfall," William said, picking up her cloak to lay it about her shoulders.

Isabel stopped short. She stared at William, then her eyes darted to Renier for answer, but the latter merely offered a gentle smile. "But—would we travel such a distance for the wedding supper?" she gasped. It couldn't be—all of her plans! What could he mean?

"There shall be no wedding supper," William answered.

Renier cleared his throat to the hostile glares passing between the couple, and he gestured to d'Erley to take his leave. "I shall see to your mounts, William."

Once alone, she spun on William. "What is your meaning, sir? To spirit me away without even the comfort of a wedding supper?"

"And what comfort would you gain from that source, Isabel?" he asked, regarding her steadily. "To sit before the company you observed in the sanctuary? Nay, we were bade to wed in this city, without attendance of family or retainers, but I will not place us in the ordeal of a wedding supper. I have chosen for us a pleasant, restful place suitable for a honeymoon, generously offered by an old friend of my father, Engerrand d'Abernon, at Stokes d'Abernon on Surrey. There, perhaps, we may find some time for us."

She was speechless. Intent on her own plans, now thwarted, she did not hear all of what he had said, only realizing that everything had been changed. Her cheeks flushed with anger as her eyes flared at him. "Evidently you have seen to everything!" she snapped, her fury allowing her to speak boldly. "And who shall witness our bedding, husband?"

"Do not concern yourself, wife," he answered with a grin. "It shall be seen to."

Before she could collect her thoughts he took her arm and led her from the room and to the waiting horses. Once mounted she could say nothing as they left the city, d'Erley and William's knights falling behind. As they rode south, Isabel divided her time between trying to reason with her anger and adjusting to the feel of a horse beneath her, her legs weakened from the long months in the Tower. What manner of man had she married? she thought as she rubbed against the soreness in her thighs. Was he as selfish and inconsiderate as she had reasoned or the man Renier was convinced that he be?

William was surprisingly kind and solicitous, seeing to her needs before she could ask, pacing their journey to her comfort. He engaged her in light conversation, his mien relaxed and comfortable, while her own was in turmoil. She attempted to sort out the things Renier had said to her, to apply them to this man who rode next to her, to whom she had been wed but a few hours past. She was certain that Renier was correct about one thing: the man was an enigma. His face, now lightened with laughter as he exchanged quips with his men, appeared youthful and at peace. Yet, there remained a hardness about him that confirmed the things Hubert Walter and Gervase had told her and to which Renier had alluded. Power. She could feel it when he entered a room, detect the deference by his vassals and peers, even though his manner was comfortable and easy with them. It both excited and frightened her and caused a great deal of curiosity. She was still furiously angry with him and not inclined to forgive—at least not yet, as her anger remained a comforting barrier of protection against the confusion of her thoughts. But she knew that eventually her temper would have to be placed aside, if only to make her life more bearable. The relationship could only suffer by continuing anger, and she was certain to emerge the loser. The realization fed her rage, intensified by frustration and a feeling of helplessness. Nay—she grimaced—never helplessness. A way would be found; it could always be found.

They arrived at Stokes d'Abernon in Surrey as the sun set amid blankets of gathering clouds, promising that the new day would arrive in stormy greeting. Isabel's cloak whipped about her in the increasing wind as Marshal helped her from her horse, ushering her up the steps into the manor of their host, a large two-storied structure formed of dark heavy timbers and bleached fieldstone gathered from the surrounding countryside. As Isabel entered through the tall oak doors, she experienced a feeling of peace, and she glanced at William, suddenly awash with an unexpected feeling of gratitude. If he noticed, he gave no evidence of it as he turned to d'Abernon's steward, who had appeared upon their entrance, and gave swift orders for their settling in. They were advised that their host was not in residence and had left the manor for their use in his absence. William's lips twitched with a hint of smile in acknowledgment of d'Abernon's tactful consideration. His vassals were bedded down about the spacious manor, and the newly wedded couple were led to a large comfortable chamber on the second floor, where a warming fire had been laid against the encroaching dampness. Time was taken in settling in; servants scurried about unpacking their chests into wardrobes and the laying out of fresh garments until William, his temper having begun to gather into a storm, snapped orders for the confusion to cease.

"But, milord, the room has not been set to right," the scandalized steward protested.

"Morning will see to the matter," William growled, waving the man away as he settled heavily into a chair. "Bring us some supper, something more substantial, and see that my men are fed as well."

"Aye, milord," the steward conceded. "I will see that someone is sent to assist you while the meal is prepared. A bath, perhaps, and fresh garments. In my Lady d'Abernon's absence I shall send . . . "

"Nay."

The men turned with surprise to Isabel, who had been standing by the hearth, warming her hands against the crackling blaze and had, until this moment, remained silent. "See to the supper, and when we have eaten you may bring the baths. I will see to the needs of my lord—alone."

"Milady?" the steward said, blinking.

"You may leave now," Isabel said firmly then turned back to the fire.

The obviously confused steward departed swiftly, leaving the room in a heavy silence. William leaned back in his chair and studied the form of his wife, who was half-turned away from him, where she seemed to be studying the actions of the flames on the hearth. She could feel his eyes upon her and she could sense the questions lurking there. Taking a shallow breath, she determined that it was time to begin answering them.

"William." She swallowed as she drew herself up. "Many traditions have been broken this day. No groomsmen were allowed for my escort to the church, save Gervase, who insisted upon his place in lieu of my father. No maidens accompanied you with my dowry as token of what I bring to this marriage, nor did you give coin to the poor as blessing upon us. We were taken from the church door and our vows said at the altar though the weather would have permitted it. No wedding supper was allowed me, and I find myself ensconced without witness on my wedding night. I have made no protest, indeed have gone willingly, as they are more your traditions than mine. However," she took a deep breath, grateful that he had remained silent. "While nothing of me, save myself, has been part of this wedding, there are traditions, again yours, which I shall protest. To begin with, I know that it is customary for the lady of the manor to bathe and dress male guests; you take this as a matter of course, I do not. I will not degrade myself to washing a strange male's . . ." Her mouth worked as she searched for a suitable word. "Backside!" A strangled sound was heard to come from William, but when her eyes snapped to his, his demeanor was as before. She looked back to the fire quickly, the view being safer for what she had to say, and continued. "Moreover, I will see to your needs, William, as your—wife." She swallowed again. "But I will be allowed privacy to do so. I am not accustomed to bathing as a social event. Furthermore, I expect that you will *not* allow another lady to attend you. Now, I have given this matter much thought and . . ."

"I respect your wishes, madam," William interrupted suddenly, bringing Isabel's attention to him. His face was impassive, and he continued to regard her with the utmost seriousness, but she noticed that his eyes had strangely begun to water. "However, there is one point I must address. It would appear that should I remain away from your presence for any great period of time I should become rather—gamy." His lips began to twitch, but he pursed them quickly in an introspective manner and covered them with his hand.

"Naturally I do not expect you to adhere to this agreement when we are apart," she snapped, her embarrassment over discussing the subject playing on her nerves. "If you cannot manage to bathe yourself, milord, and your squires are not about, of course you must avail yourself of whatever help is offered. Just refrain from telling me about it!"

With that, William was no longer able to contain himself. It began as a choke and erupted into uproarious laughter as Isabel drew herself up indignantly and glared at him. Finally, with great effort, he brought himself under control as he noticed the fury in his bride and that her lips had begun to tremble in quite a different emotion. "Isabel," he coughed. "Isabel, I apologize. Please, do sit down," he ordered, gesturing to the chair across from him. "It has been a long day for us both." She sat, though she was unconvinced of his sincerity, as she could still detect a glint of humor in his eyes. "I will try to respect your wishes, as it seems to be so important to you. Although, I will admit that I do not understand your feelings; it is such a minor thing."

"Minor?" she repeated, her eyes flaring once again. "Perhaps, William, to you. Half of me is English, both by blood and heritage, having spent some years on my father's lands—and in your tower. 'Tis a conflict I may never settle, for I feel the pull of both parts of me. But simple things are clear, in those I can only relate to what I know best. In that I am my mother's daughter, and Irish."

Isabel's words and her intensity sobered him. He began to suspect, at that moment, what a complex woman he had married. "I will try to respect your wishes in such matters, Isabel. However, in matters I deem important I will expect you to comply."

"Aye, William, that is fair," she answered softly, then brought her gaze up to his with a new flair of determination. "I do ask one more thing."

"And that would be?"

"If I should find it difficult to comply to a request, you will allow me the courtesy to express my feelings. I hope that you will attempt to understand them."

He stared at her for a long moment as he rubbed his hands against his chin in thought. A voice within him pressed for outrage. Was she trying to dictate to him? Was she suggesting that he should give into every whim? Perhaps he had been wrong to give in so easily on the matter of the bath; had he set a dangerous precedent? But it was a voice seeming to belong to another, an imposed voice of reason, not of feeling. Emotionally he could not take issue with her request. Would he not want the same from her? How much easier their life would be if she would do the same for him. "Would you do the same for me, Isabel?"

"Of course."

A long, heavy moment passed. "Then I shall try. However, my final decisions are to stand firm, and you will obey."

She nodded, the tension of the past moments sweeping over her. Oh lud, she thought, I am so tired.

The steward returned with their supper, a moderate but sufficient repast of roast pigeons stuffed with nuts and spices, tails of crayfish boiled lightly with butter, and paindemain, pastries cooked in yolks of eggs and fried in clarified butter and sprinkled lightly in sugar. They devoured the meal in almost total silence, neither realizing how hungry they had been. While traveling, Isabel reasoned that she could not have partaken of a mouthful, her mind and emotions being too full to even think of food. Until the repast was set before her and the actual sight and aroma of the delicacies took over. When the last crumb had been devoured, she sat back in her chair with satisfaction, her mind blissfully content. Then reality struck her on the heels of the ever-present steward, who knocked softly then opened the door to admit servants carrying the tubs and buckets of steaming water.

Once again alone, she stared at the tubs, bracing herself to carry through what she had wrought. She had meant what she had said. She had been scandalized when first returning to England as a young maid to realize that she would be expected to attend visitors. Lavinia had tried, at first, to explain to her that one did not really *look* at a man, one's eyes were carefully averted . . . but she quickly acquiesced to Isabel's sensibilities, knowing the manner in which she had been raised. Had she had a father or brothers in Erin, she at least would have attended their needs. But she had not and had therefore been most sheltered.

William watched her dilemma, aware of the conflict that was raging in his young bride, and he sensed the depth of the matter. Part of him was angered that she had been so unprepared, even to the sight of a man. Sweet Jesú, what were they placing on him? Not only did he have the responsibility to bed her, but to overcome her shyness about men, a matter that should have been resolved years ago! But a gentleness in him overcame his disgust, and his concern focused on her, dismissing all else.

"I am in need of some air, Isabel," he tossed, rising from his chair to grab his cloak off the hook by the door. "Perhaps you would like to refresh yourself while I am gone," he offered to her puzzled stare. "Take your time, I shall be gone a while."

The room had darkened, and the fire played its tentative highlights about the room before William returned, shutting the door quietly behind him. He turned to hang his cloak before his eyes sought her out where she sat by the fire. She had bathed and was dressed in a sheer, long-sleeved chemise covered by a soft, sleeveless robe of embroidered linen tied beneath her breasts, accentuating their lovely fullness, which pressed against the sheer fabric. She clenched her hands, which were folded tightly in her lap, not noticing the frown that came to William before he looked quickly away, nor realizing that his thoughts were fixed on the delectable way she looked in the robe or the way her hair curled in soft damp tendrils about her ears and the nape of her neck.

"They took the tubs away, William," she said, her eyes wide with question. "The steward said that you had bathed in the knight's quarters and would not require them."

"Aye," he answered, settling into the chair next to her. He stifled a smile as he recalled d'Erley's surprise when he suddenly appeared and ordered a bath. "Would you be so kind as to pour me some wine, milady?" he asked, changing the subject. He watched as she jumped to comply, noting her nervousness as she did so. He accepted it with thanks and stretched out his long legs to the fire as she settled herself once again into her chair. They sat before the fire in silence as William's mind turned for what he might say to her. He was acutely aware of how she looked and the knowledge that she was his bride was ever present. A part of him was tempted to act as he knew he was entitled to and force her to the bed and to the act that was undoubtedly on both of their minds. But something held him back. He could force her, it would be all too easy. But then, what of the morning, all the mornings thereafter? What would she feel for him then; how much of their future would depend on this night?

He had hardly been celibate; he had known many women in his life. Some he had loved, or thought he had at the time, though the feeling had never lasted for long. There were women used at his convenience, many provided to him by generous hosts, not least of which his king. That is, his former king—oh, how he missed Henry, that one with voracious appetites of his own. Indeed, women were offered as a course to a meal, the last course as a prelude to sleep. But never before had one been his bride. His wife. He would return to her following each journey; he would live with her, day by day. She would bear his children, be mother to them. He would grow old with her, companion with her when matters of sexual comfort held less importance. Was he merely facing a prospect others had faced countless times before him? He dismissed the thought as unimportant. The answer to his questions would be important only to his life—and hers. He stole a glance at her and he knew. Aye, it was important, she was important. He must not make a mistake. She had been given so little, and this, at least, was within his power to give.

"Are you cold?" he asked softly, noticing that she trembled.

"Nay, William," she answered. But when she looked up at him he saw fear but also a determination and resolve to accept whatever was to come.

"You are cold," he said, rising from his chair as she trembled again. He pushed his chair aside and crossed to the bed, pulling deep furs and pillows from it. Then he returned to the hearth, where he spread them on the floor before the fire. He offered her his hand, saying nothing as she regarded him with open wonder. She took his hand at last and allowed him to draw her from her chair and down to the warmth of the furs, where he wrapped her in his arms. He could feel the tension in her body but ignored it as they fixed their attention upon the flames leaping before them in measured dance.

"I would have you understand why I brought you here from the church, Isabel," he said at last. When she did not respond he continued, while not missing the fact that she stiffened in his arms. "Our marriage was decided upon by others, and I felt our lives being taken from us. Renier, though he meant well, would have displayed us for London, and I would not have it. I decided that this was the only way to give us some control over what has happened. I simply could not allow them to use us further. As for your concern over the lack of witnesses—I promise you that no scandal shall touch you. The court's absence allows us more privacy than we normally would have." Could she be aware of what he had saved her? The stripping, her body exposed to the company of witnesses for evidence of flaw—giving him the right to repudiate her? His own distaste for the practice, to have what was his exposed to the lusty leers of others, had encouraged him to make his decision—coupled with his anger of wedding her without witness of her family and friends. What ladies would have stood by her, to cover her quickly and give comfort? And he had not even known then of her shyness . . .

Isabel had listened and the gentleness of his words and voice began to touch something within her. Distrust remained; a few well-spoken words could not change the feelings of hurt and betrayal, but acceptance began to grow and the realization gave her strength and comfort.

William became aware that she was no longer listening, as her fair brow furrowed in her own deep thoughts. He allowed her silence, watching her beneath lowered lashes as conflicts passed over her face in an inner struggle. "Will you tell me now why you have been so angry?" he asked finally. His voice was gentle and spoke of an attempt to understand.

"I—it is nothing, William," she answered, glancing at him briefly, only to find that she could not hold that questioning gaze. Nay, the matter must now be put aside, forgotten.

He considered her answer for a moment but would not be put off. "I will ask you again, Isabel, why you have been so angry." His own thoughts had been giving answer to his question, and he had to know. If he was right, this marriage could prove difficult to them both. "Is it that you feel that you have married beneath you?"

She twisted in his arms to stare at him. "Nay! I do not feel that way!" When she saw his look of doubt she rushed forward, unguarded. "Please, believe me! Why, I argued with Gervase about it! He . . . " She froze, realizing what she had said, and flushed, turning her face from his. Inwardly she cringed, knowing that she must have hurt him, and she cursed her tongue for its looseness. Then she started, turning back to him as she heard him chuckle.

"So, you defended me, did you?" he grinned. "Do not dismay, Isabel, for it was reasonable for your guardian to feel so, but I have marked well your defense of me. So, if not my landless state, what then?"

She did not want to answer him but knew that she must if he were not to doubt her. "I—was hurt, nay, disappointed that we were not to marry at Chepstow as you had promised. I wanted to hurt you for that."

So that was it! Damn you, Marshal, for a fool, he thought. "Isabel, the blame for your unhappiness does lie with me but for reasons other than you have fixed upon. My silence is what has caused you pain, not my intent. It was not my decision to marry in London but the king's." He smiled as she turned in his arms to look at him, knowing now that she was listening. "Chances are excellent that we never would have made it to Striguil, for there are many who would have risked much to take you from me. Henry was right, but then he usually was."

"Oh, William, I am sorry," she breathed. "I did not understand."

"The fault is mine, for I should have thought to explain it to you."

They sat quietly in a reflective silence, and he knew, by the way that her body had relaxed against his, that a wall, however small, had been breached. Her face, now turned away from him toward the fire, saved him cause to wonder what else troubled her as she began to chew on her lower lip.

Armed with the knowledge that she had misjudged him, she was overwhelmed with guilt. Though she had protested, she knew that she had been less than truthful. She had harbored that to which she had so vehemently protested; to dishonor him at their wedding supper, to remind him at every opportunity that he was a usurper to nobility. The plan, now faced from a more rational mind, was viewed with horror. Venomous thought wrought of anger had nearly led to disaster, for that was what it would have been. No few words of explanation would have brought understanding or forgiveness had she publicly humiliated him as she had planned, no matter whose fault it would have been.

Married beneath her? Gervase's words, not hers, to that she had been honest. Only spite had caused her to consider it as a means to revenge. Aye, she was well versed in the dowry she brought to her marriage. She had taken to Gervase's instruction eagerly with attention to detail and understanding that would have made Richard deClare beam with pride and approval of his daughter. But it came not from a desire to please her late father but an instinctive will of her own. She was fully aware that her estate was surpassed among Englishwomen only by the queen dowager herself, Eleanor. And she knew that it would take a man to hold it—or lose it. Her thought suddenly focused into a startling clarity that fate had quite possibly brought her that man. Not because of the deference paid to him, or the words of Gervase, Walter, or even Renier, but the power, the assurance, she read in him. She wanted to be part of it, to share in her inheritance, which she could only retain by his sufferance. And she had almost destroyed it before it had a chance to begin. The realization caused a terrible shudder to run the length of her body.

William started at the movement, misreading the manner of her disquiet. His own thoughts had taken a vastly different track in their companionable silence as his eyes moved over the length of her long, slender body. He had become entranced by the way the fire's light would move suggestively over the silk of her robe where it clung to her form, leaving little to his increasingly heated imagination. The realization that he held his bride in his arms only added to his discomfort, which proved a sore trial as he felt his loins tighten uncomfortably, and he wondered how long he would be able to remain in this position before the matter became obvious. He had about decided to bring the issue to hand, and his arm began slipping about her shoulder to turn her to him when she had shuddered. Assuming the response to be directed toward him, he groaned inwardly and pulled his hand back to her shoulder while racking his brain for the best way to proceed. Jesú, he thought, he felt like a smooth-faced boy frantically attempting to mount his first conquest, and it angered him, fed by frustration and the aching in the lower part of his body. Damn, if he fumbled now he might as well be that fur-cheeked boy, and that he was not.

Isabel, unaware of William's struggle, had reached a decision of her own. While love might never be a part of what they woul d have, she could learn to live without it and be content. She would make something of her marriage, she thought with grim determination, only vaguely aware of William's fingers, which stroked her shoulder softly. She would not be a weak, self-serving woman, spending her life wallowing in self-pity and living fantasies of what might have been. The choice was hers at this moment, to accept what fate and King Henry had given her. Her mind fixed upon what this man could bring to her and to her children. Perhaps he was even a man strong enough to accept what she needed to give. With her thoughts, the child in Isabel clung for a brief moment, clinging in a desperate final hold, then released with only a moment's subconscious regret.

On the other hand, William reasoned, he could give her time. Time to come to know him better, perhaps time to care for him. The thought almost made him groan audibly, but he forced himself to consider it. Nay, there was another matter, apart from his own needs, though it did not escape him that it suited his own purpose. She would have to be bedded this night. While he had shown consideration to absent himself for their wedding night, William knew that d'Abernon and his lady would most certainly present themselves on the morrow—to observe the bridal sheet and its evidence that the marriage had been consummated. A report that would carry swiftly to his supporters—and his enemies. Without such proof to bind the vows, Isabel would be vulnerable to any that felt they could take her from him. William's mouth twisted into a sardonic grin at the thought. He would like to see anyone try.

Nay, this last tradition he could not save her; even were he to find the inner resources to do so, the danger would be too great. With relief that the matter was resolved, he placed conscious thought aside and pulled her to him.

Isabel tensed as he drew her to him and looked up at him with wide eyes. She had been mesmerized by the flames as she lay comfortably in his arms, lost in her own thoughts in a growing security only to be startled out of it by his sudden action. Reality came rushing back to stun her, giving her no time to prepare. He felt her tense and looked down at her with concern. His hand reached out to cup her chin, forcing her to look at him. "Isabel," he said quietly, with a strange thickness to his voice. "I would not hurt you. I want you to come to me willingly." He found himself bluntly voicing his earlier thoughts. "If it were up to me, if it were your wish, I would give us time to know one another before I forced you to this. Do you realize why I cannot? It must be met or our vows mean naught and you cannot be safe."

She looked up at him with confusion. Why was he telling her this? Of course the marriage had to be consummated, else he could not promise to hold her to him. The flashing thought that another could take her from him crossed her mind, and she felt a rush of fear, denying the possibility. At that moment she fully realized the importance of not losing him, something deep within her confirming the decisions she had made about him.

But William again misread her expression as she lay looking up at him, and he struggled to make his meaning clear to her. The remembrance of the difficulties involving the bath returned only to make the matter more awkward. His finger trailed down her cheek as he looked at her gently. "Do you know what is going to happen?"

She flushed at the directness of his question and dropped her gaze to his chest where she focused on his open shirt front. She could feel the muscles in his chest where they lay against her side, and something deep within her began to tremble. "Aye, William," she answered softly. "I understand."

He lifted her chin, and his mouth came down on hers gently, lingering in a sweet embrace meant not to frighten her. He was surprised at her response as she leaned against him, meeting the kiss as her lips moved beneath his willingly. Encouraged, his hands began to move over her gently, stroking her body through the thin robe, moving to the ties at her throat, pulling them apart to push the garment from her shoulders. He swallowed at the sight of her full pale breasts pushing against the low cut of her chemise, but he held himself back, determined to bring her slowly to awakening. His hand moved to a breast as his lips covered hers once more before moving to the lobe of an ear and then to the nape of her neck, trailing down her shoulders as his hand caressed with gentle encouragement. He pulled the chemise aside, and his lips followed his fingers to the crest of a breast. He heard her gasp as his tongue trailed a gentle path about its tender sweetness. His lips pulled gently, suckling until she began to moan and move beneath his attentions, until finally a sob escaped her as she arched against him.

Her mind was spinning with what he was doing to her as she focused on the rush of warmth that spread over her body and the odd tightening in her belly. She had received his kisses with eager curiosity, marveling at the response of her body as his lips had moved to discover the tenderness of her neck and shoulders, points of sensation she could not have imagined. When she realized that he had parted her gown and his hand was on her breast, she had started—but only for an instant. Her embarrassment was dispelled quickly as she felt the shock of pleasure his fingers and mouth were bringing to her. Her thoughts tumbled. As his lips drew at the tip of her breast, she gasped, conscious thought fleeing as she gave into new, exquisite sensations.

Slowly, a hand traced a gentle teasing path down her waist to her hips, where it eased up her chemise until it met the smooth silk of her thighs, pulling them gently apart to search further. She gasped, arching her hips to his attentions as his fingers found what they were seeking. His mouth moved to her other breast, which was aching for attention, proof given as she arched her back to meet his probing tongue. Her response both surprised and excited him, though for a flashing moment he wondered if Henry had been too late in sending her to the Tower. What a joke that would be on both of us, old friend, he thought, and he would soon know.

Stroking her, he whispered soft words of love, encouraging her to give herself to him, and was rewarded as her hips began to move beneath his attentions. Her thoughts were spinning wildly, her emotions trapped by the spreading tension that consumed her body. Pressing her head into his shoulder she moaned, fearing she could not stand more, yet fearing that he would stop. Expert fingers played, coaxing patiently until finally he felt her draw up to him in a deep shudder as she cried out softly. He pulled her arms gently from where they were tightly bound about him and pulled the chemise from her, then kissed her deeply. He smiled, realizing that even in the sweet aftermath of her satisfaction she was feeling amazement, and he bent to kiss her again as she sighed against his lips. Suddenly she found that she was swept up into his arms, and he carried her to the bed as his lips nuzzled the nape of her neck.

"Now it must be here," he whispered as he pulled the covers of the bedding from beneath her. In the relaxed glow of what she had experienced, she was unaware of the moments he was not with her except for a disquieting feeling of loss. But he was soon there, and she was shocked at the feel of him, realizing then that he had left her to discard his clothing, and she felt for the first time the length of his body against hers. Instinctively she reached out and pulled him to her, wanting the difference against her. He kissed her tenderly, and she relished the feel of his lips against her own and his tongue, which sought out the inner depths of her mouth, meeting it in quick response as she yielded to him. Her mind, still languid with the satisfaction he had given to her, became aware that he had pulled her beneath him. She felt the swelling of his member against her thigh, exciting her with a strange curiosity. She marveled over the warmth that began to grow once again deep within her, the strange ache that began between her thighs. She opened her legs to him, wanting the feel of him, wanting him to complete what he was going to do. She felt him enter gently, and she raised up to him, pushing as she sought to have more of him. Suddenly she felt the pain that the recesses of her thoughts had expected yet forgotten in the depths of her pleasure. She tensed, drawing away from him in surprise, but she quickly willed herself to lie quietly, realizing that it had been done. A small, secret smile began at the corners of her mouth as she realized that she was now his, irrevocably his, and she was rewarded with a peace that settled over her. He began to move within her and astonishingly she felt no more pain, only a sweet bliss, a bittersweet intimacy. She felt him pause, then felt a shudder that seemed to involve all of him, and she sighed softly, knowing that he had found pleasure with her. She felt wonder at the feeling of power it gave her, the deep feeling of contentment.

She lay in his arms, sharing peace and belonging in the aftermath of their lovemaking. Her back was nestled against him, her legs curled up against his longer ones with his arms wrapped protectively about her. As he nuzzled her neck affectionately, her mind drifted. We are wed, she thought sleepily. A truly wonderful end to the day, she smiled softly, in spite of a rather poor beginning. Together, what shall our life be? It will not be easy, but all things are possible. Oh lud, I shall but try . . .

# 5

THE storm battered against stone and timber of the isolated manor; shutters pulled in strain against their hinges as trees bent in protest of the driving rain that came in sheets to whip and pelt against the lowlands. Dawn passed as the blackened storm clouds caused those within the manor to turn in their sleep and recapture their dreams. Only those the most unalterably bound to their duties rose from their pallets with deep yawns and resentment for those still sleeping, to bank the fires and light oil-soaked torches scattered about the walls of the great hall.

In the large chamber above, Isabel stirred, drifting reluctantly from sleep. A feeling of unreality gripped her, a disorientation to her surroundings that caused a momentary feeling of panic. Then she remembered. She lay still in the greying quiet, unwilling to surrender those first thoughts, needing them to gain touch with reality.

It would all be different now, her life was changed. She drew her legs up involuntarily, remembering, and she felt wonder pass through her. All of those years spent speculating about what it would be like, discussing it with her friends, laughing over nervous jokes, the hours spent alone, imagining. Times that her young body had ached for something intangible; it had now happened. She was a woman, he had made love to her. A smile pulled at the corners of her mouth. Now she could well understand the frantic groping she had viewed in the shadows of the keep, the misty longing in her mother's eyes when she spoke of her father, the endless courting and flirting she had observed between men and women; observations she had viewed with curiosity and now with a measure of understanding. Bliss. Her skin trembled as she recalled the intimacy—the feel of his hands on her body. Would it have been like this with any man? She considered men she had known, but it only brought confusion, repulsion, then incomprehension. Was it merely acceptance that made the difference? Nay, she felt an excitement with him, a frightening yet pleasurable nervousness. What was there about him that had conquered her so easily? His countenance? Aye, he was handsome. His virility? The thought brought a warm flush. Nay, not only those, she reasoned. Others she had known were handsome, strong. Well, perhaps not quite so handsome nor quite so virile, but she knew there was more. His confidence, touched with such gentleness. . . . Oh, it was so confusing! In these thoughts of him, she turned impulsively to find him but the bed was empty next to her, the covers thrown back. She sought him out, her eyes darting about the room until they came to rest upon a shadow by the window. "William?" Oh, why had she said his name? She would have had more time . . . but he turned at the sound of her voice.

He came to her as the sound of the storm beat against the shutters from without, and he settled on the edge of the bed, reaching out his hand to touch her face in the dim light of the remaining candles that flickered about the room. "I thought you were asleep."

"It must be morning."

"Aye. Though you need not rise, the storm has kept everyone abed."

"Can you not sleep?" She reached out and covered his hand with hers, pressing her cheek into its warmth. A bold thing, it surprised her, and she quickly withdrew her hand. Her thoughts, the warmth she had felt, fled as she pulled from him, leaving her with an acute feeling of embarrassment. As the silence lengthened she began to feel an unreasonable grip of fear. What did he expect her to do now? Why had she called to him, she could have pretended sleep, been alone to reason out her feelings . . .

He shed the fur robe he had wrapped about himself and lay beside her, pulling her against him to draw warmth from her warmth. She shivered, then waited, expecting him to do more. He merely held her against him, and then as he felt her relax against him, he kissed her gently behind the ear, a lingering tentative kiss beneath her earlobe, a tender spot that sent shivers of feeling through her body to her toes. Sharpened remembrance of pleasures invaded her mind, and she moved slightly with anticipation. His hand moved to a breast, cupping it as his fingers began to tease the nipple as she could feel his breath in easy rhythm on her back. She lay still, wondering what she should do, what he expected, as a rush went through her body with a dizziness that made her want to turn to him. Would he think her bold?

As she turned, he gathered her into his arms, and his lips came down upon hers, smothering her in an embrace that left her breathless and excited. Her sensations rose to a tension that could only be relieved by a deep moan, the sound coming from someone apart from her.

She gave herself to him, feeling his hands on her, each part, his touch making her want to cry out as she held the cry back, fearing that it would break the experience, the feel of what he was doing to her. Oh, God, is this what she had been waiting for, it had to be a sin, how it felt . . . She gave in to everything then, giving herself to him.

He plied her with experienced hands, and she met him eagerly, taking what he was offering with a passion building to match his own. The tension within her peaked, and she cried out as it broke over her, her fingers digging into his back as she sought to hold it for as long as possible; a feeling of wonder was touched with disappointment as it receded. Pulling her under him, he entered her, bringing her up to him with a hand beneath her hips. She gasped, feeling the tension build again as he moved within her. Excitement was building within her as she realized that there was more than he had given to her before, a promise of new, greater discovery. But with her thoughts the feeling ebbed, and though she tried desperately to recapture it it remained illusive, somewhere out of reach as she rose with him, taking him within her, again experiencing the warmth, the intimacy she had felt before, until he finally shuddered and lay against her. He nuzzled her, his hands stroking her body softly, and she felt a rush of emotion, of deep affection for this man who held her so tenderly. There was something else. She had felt the beginning of it and the knowledge excited her. Give it time, she thought, it will come. For now this was enough, nay, more than she could have hoped for, the satisfaction he gave her, the gentleness, the caring she could feel in him, and the sweet promise of more . . .

She felt him move as he rose up and leaned on his elbows, and she opened her eyes to find him looking down at her, a hint of a gentle smile before he leaned down and brushed her lips with his, then gently caressed the corners of her mouth and her eyes.

"You must not try so hard, love," he murmured. "There is much more to give you if you but relax and let me love you."

She startled, wondering for a moment if he had read her mind. He chuckled softly at her look of surprise and bent down to plant a light kiss on the tip of her nose. "Give it time, and all things will come."

She flushed, suddenly wanting to change the subject. "What were you thinking?" she whispered.

"When, now?" he grinned, looking down at her. "Do you need my thoughts, as well?"

"Of course," she said, blushing, but laughed in spite of herself.

"Greedy wench," he snorted, rolling off of her. He propped the pillows up behind them and pulled her into his arms, suppressing a smile as she carefully arranged the blankets about her.

"Before," she pressed. "When you left me, when you were sitting by the window. Were you thinking of us?"

"Aye, and other things," he answered. "I was thinking on what we have said to each other, how quickly everything has changed, and of many pressing matters I must attend to." Seeing her brow furrow into a frown, he smiled. "Nay, there is nothing I must see to immediately, now is for us."

His words brought a tantalizing tingle with them, and Isabel turned in his arms and nestled against him, laying her cheek on his chest. "William?" she said after a while.

"Humm?" he answered lazily, his finger pausing where it had been rhythmically wrapping itself about strands of her smoky blond hair, his thoughts focused on its silkiness and the feel of her soft body pressed against his.

"Is it not . . . odd . . . that we appear to be so . . . comfortable with each other?"

"Aye, truly a marriage brought from heaven," he said, smiling.

"Is that wherein Henry resides?" she quipped. "Can you be so certain?"

" 'Tis not for me to say," he chuckled, appreciating her barb. "Though I would not be surprised if he divided his time. He was a man of contrasts." He looked down at her questioning face, and his eyes grew warm with understanding. "Aye, we are fortunate," he said softly. "It has not gone badly for us." How fortunate they had been he could not begin to explain to her; how totally at odds they could have been, virtually abhorrent to each other. William had seen it all too often, apathy between couples, even hatred, from the moment of first meeting, and it had continued for a lifetime. He felt something in this girl, an unspoken communication that was unique. Aye, in her words, comfort, but more, and he found himself looking forward to discovery. "Perhaps, if we endeavor to care enough it will be a good marriage. We have much to learn about each other."

"Aye," she agreed softly, a pensive frown wrinkling her brow as she gave thought to his words.

He smiled at her seriousness, knowing that her thoughts were on other matters than to what he was again fixed. Her passion had surprised and pleased him, as he knew now for certain that she had come to her marriage bed innocent. He recognized instinctive passion, part of her nature that he sensed would be carried to everything important to her. It was that physical passion that interested him now. A wickedness entered his voice that escaped her for a moment. "We have much to learn about each other." He reached up and pulled the blanket gently from her, exposing young, tender flesh of her high, firm breasts. Aware now of what he was doing, she looked up at him in question. A flush crept up her neck to touch her cheeks, which he ignored as a hand rose to those tempting orbs. His fingers closed on a nipple as his eyes fixed upon what he was doing with an objective appreciation for her beautiful body.

Her first impulse was to cover herself, but she remained transfixed, feeling a strange excitement that he would look at her so, with such blatant possessiveness and interest. Suddenly, she was aware that she wanted him to look at her, and the realization made her belly and loins tighten with desire. A new aspect of love, it pleasured her, making her feel expanded. She remained still, enjoying the moment and wanting to prolong it, unaware that she finally moved, arching her back to him in an unmistakable message that he read clearly. He lowered his head, closing his lips about the tightening nipple and sucked gently, pulling, teasing with his tongue until she began to moan and move beneath him. She tried to slide down in the bed, wanting the feel of him against her, but he stopped her. With hands placed firmly at her waist he pulled her on top of him, his lips nuzzled in her breasts. "A new lesson, my lady," he murmured, taking a breast in his mouth. He pulled her legs to either side of him then, and releasing her breast with a flick of his tongue, he raised her up and brought her down on his erect shaft, causing her to gasp as he plunged upward, gently at first as she opened to him, then more deeply until she moaned with pleasure, arching her back, and the muscles of her belly tightening in response. A hand reached up to cup a breast as the other went between her thighs, his fingers seeking that swelling bud of desire, stroking, coaxing, as he moved within her. She tightened with the unbearable pleasure that was mounting within her, the heat that began growing with waves of tension from her body when she suddenly burst within. A cry tore from her as she soared apart in shattering fulfillment, a part of her realizing that he had joined with her in his own release. She collapsed against him, her heart pounding as she gasped for her breath, her arms going about his neck as she clasped him to her.

Sweet Mother, she thought. It was as if she had been only half a person before and now she was whole, complete; now, with him. But with the thought there came an unexpected emotion of rushing fear, without form but so strong a feeling that it startled her. Illusive, it was gone before she could deal with it, but with it the memory of her passion. She clung to him, afraid to move, willing the feeling of joy back to her, but it remained apart. She felt drained, empty, and suddenly very aware of his body, and the difference. She pulled herself from him, lying by his side, where he cradled her in his arms, unaware of the change in her. She felt him kiss her softly on the top of her head, and she closed her eyes, trying to recapture the bliss she had felt with him. Oh Lord, what had happened? What had she been afraid of? She felt no fear now, only a deep unexplainable loss, but the realization frightened her even more.

He stretched with a deep, sated sigh, then tensed suddenly, his head turned toward the shuttered window.

"What is it?" she asked, watching him.

"Listen."

She listened for a moment but then looked back at him, even more puzzled. "I do not hear anything."

"Exactly," he answered, then tossed back the covers and left the bed to cross to the window. He threw open the shutters. "Just as I thought, the storm has passed. You had better drag yourself from the warmth of that bed, my lady," he said, crossing to the wardrobe, gathering his scattered things on the way. "As pleasant as this has been, I expect we will soon have company.''

"Company?"

"D'Abernon and his lady.''

"Oh," she said in a small voice, finally understanding. She began to leap from the bed, then remembered her bare condition, which seemed to glare at her in the bright morning light left in the wake of the departed storm. She looked up in time to catch the robe he tossed to her with a chuckle, and she offered him a slight smile in contrast to the pink that flared from her cheeks. Sliding more contritely from the bed, she turned her back to him to slip into the robe. Turning as she pulled it about her she froze, her eyes fixed on the bright red splotches that glared at her from the white linen sheet. She felt her face grow hotter, and she reached to snatch the sheet from the bed, but he was suddenly there to stay her from her obvious intent.

"Nay, it must remain," he said deeply, and reached over to throw the covers over the bed. "Now hurry and dress," he offered in a lighter tone, ignoring her embarrassment. "I've of a mind to take a ride, would you enjoy that?"

"Aye!" she brightened, eager at the prospect, but then became sober again. "But . . . should we? If d'Abernon and his lady are expected . . . ''

"They will be here when we return," he offered with a grin. "It is not my mind to share you, not just yet." He was gratified by the look of pleasure that shone from her and knew he had said the right thing. There was no need to enlighten her about his true intention, hoping to save her the added embarrassment of d'Abernon's inspection of their bedchamber, wanting to postpone their greeting until it was done. Besides, to his surprise, he found that his excuse was true enough.

They rode out across the lowlands and the air was rich with the smell of rain-soaked grasses, filling their nostrils with the heavy scent as the sharp, crisp air bit into their faces and the world seemed new. They stopped beneath a spreading oak and set to eagerly devouring a breakfast of bread and cheeses, quickly prepared by a steward, washing it down with watered ale, then set to linger more leisurely over warm apple tarts they found at the bottom of the knapsack.

Isabel's fear had left her, leaving her to wonder what could have caused it as she dismissed it completely in the warm pleasure of William's company. With prodding, he began to tell her something of his life, at first reluctantly, as a man unaccustomed to talking about himself. But he soon had her in giggles, proving that he was fully capable of telling a joke on himself. She collapsed on the blanket in laughter as he rolled his eyes, telling of the time, following a most important tournament, when others had departed to enjoy the pleasures earned and he had been left behind beneath a blacksmith's efforts as the man sweated to remove the helm that had been twisted backward on William's head, a task lasting well into the night.

She delighted in his humor, feeling a genuine warmth of affection grow for this man who had so suddenly become her husband. But she grew more serious as he recounted times of his childhood. "Was your father truly a hard man?" she asked finally, noticing that while there seemed to be no bitterness in the recounting of his family, there appeared to be no affection for his father.

"Aye, that he was," William said, nodding. "Possessed with ambition, greedy and cold."

"Did you hate him?"

"Hate him?" He looked at her with surprise. "Nay. It is just the way he was. I remember. . . . " He smirked at the recollection, then shook his head as if to pass it by. "He fought bravely for the Empress Mathilda when the majority of nobles in England saw fit to sit on their laurels while hoping that King Stephen would become a better ruler. But then, you would not remember those days, my young bird, for you are far too young," he added, lifting her chin with his fingers and gifting her with a gentle smile.

"I recall my mother speaking of it," she said pensively. "King Stephen was the reason my father went to Normandy and lost his lands—to aid Henry in taking the throne since his mother had failed so miserably."

"Aye, and his name on the treaty at Wallingford attests to his success," he agreed, then returned to his musings. "My father fought bravely for her. I could never understand his obsession about Mathilda when the only other thing in his life that could stir him was greed. It was, perhaps, the only time he reached for something higher. He was blinded in one eye while defending a castle from Stephen's forces, defending the empress's retreat with only one other knight to aid him. And he succeeded. I think it was the most noble moment of his life." His voice trailed off as if his thoughts were far away, there at the battle where he might understand his father's motivations.

"Such a man could not be so hard," she offered.

"Nay?" he grinned, returning to the present. "When I was seven he was defending his castle at Newbury against Stephen's forces. The keep was poorly garrisoned and stocked, so he gave me as hostage to Stephen, assurance that he would release the castle, when in fact it was to give him time to send for aid. When he continued to defend the keep, Stephen sent him a message, a reminder that my life held in the balance. Can you guess what my father's rejoinder was, when reminded that I would be hanged?" He grinned. " 'I have the anvil with which to forge even better sons.' "

"Nay!" she gasped, her eyes wide with horror.

"Aye, and he was firm."

"What happened?"

"I was hanged."

"Oh, William!" she cried. "Be serious! What happened?"

"Obviously, Stephen relented," he laughed. "Oh, there was some discussion as to my disposition. Some suggested that I be catapulted over the castle walls into my father's lap. But Stephen decided on the promised hanging. However, as we proceeded to the tree where the deed was to be done, I noticed one of the knights swinging a particularly attractive new lance. I remember that lance, it was a beauty. Being seven, and totally unaware of what was about to happen, I asked to play with the lance. Evidently, Stephen was so moved by my innocence he picked me up in his arms and carried me back to the camp. We spent the remainder of the siege playing 'knights' with the plantains which grew about—if I recall he allowed me to beat him.''

"Oh, William, you could have died!''

"And you would not be here with me now, kitten. I wonder who would be sitting beneath this tree with you?''

"Stop it!'' she admonished.

"Do you care so much?'' he asked with a smile, leaning over to brush his lips against hers.

She pulled from him, shocked by the feelings that rushed through her body at his touch. She found that she did care, but she did not want to face that now, she wanted to know more about him. "William, your father was a terrible man; how could he do such a thing?''

"Nay, Isabel, he was not terrible, at least in the way you mean. Perhaps he was a good judge of men, perhaps not. He knew where his loyalties, his principles lay, whatever they were, and nothing would interfere.''

"Humph!'' she snorted. "Some principles, to sacrifice a child! I'm sorry, William, but I do not think I would have liked your father very much.''

"Neither did I,'' he shrugged. "But I respected him.''

They rode back into the courtyard as the sun rose to its highest, its warmth escaping in streaks of brilliance from scattered high clouds leaving a patchwork sky of blue and grey. Horses were tethered before the manor, and William exchanged a reassuring glance with Isabel, who looked at him for confirmation that their hosts had arrived. He helped her from her mount, and they ascended the stairs, his hand at her back with a reassuring presence as they entered through the wide double doors of the hall. William grinned upon their entrance as d'Abernon rose from his seat near the warming fire and came to greet them. He was an aging man with hair of snowy white and kind brown eyes that moved over Isabel with interest. Nervously, she sought out Lady d'Abernon, whom William had warned her was a stiff-necked lady reserved in a coldness that left her slightly unreachable; but the lady was absent. The hall was crowded with William's and Lord d'Abernon's retainers, many of whom sat before the fire while others gathered about gaming tables with chess and backgammon. William smiled broadly at d'Abernon's approach. He reached out an arm in greeting as from the corner of his eye he noticed d'Erley approaching swiftly; his manner seemed agitated. Before he could acknowledge his squire, his host grasped his arm firmly in greeting, and at the same moment he felt Isabel stiffen at his side and heard her breath draw in a sharp gasp. He turned to his wife, noting that the blood had drained from her face and her eyes had become widely fixed at something above them. His eyes followed her shocked gaze to the balcony at the head of the stairs on the far side of the room. There, hanging from the railing, was the bedsheet with Isabel's blood glaring at them brightly.

It took a moment for the truth to register, but as it did William turned on d'Erley, who had reached his side. "Take it down!" he said through gritted teeth in surging rage. John looked at William helplessly, then drew himself up with a look of contempt at d'Abernon as he spun away and rushed to do William's bidding. William pushed Isabel behind his broad back, where she could no longer view the offending object, and he turned to d'Abernon.

"I apologize, William." The man shrugged with embarrassment. "My lady insisted that your wife's family were of old traditions and it would be fitting."

"How would it be that your lady knows of my wife's family?" William rejoined.

On cue, Lady d'Abernon swept into the hall from a side door, her dark skirts swishing with impatience. Seeing the small group standing near the center of the hall, she paused briefly, apparently forgetting some dissatisfaction left behind her as her mouth drew into a smile. "William!" she exclaimed with pleasure. She crossed the room to them, her hands outstretched to take his. She held one hand slightly aloft for his lips but William, in no mood for such amenities, smoothly stepped aside as he released it. A frown touched her smooth brow, and her dark eyes flickered with a moment of surprise, but then her gaze came to rest on Isabel.

"May I present my wife, Isabel, Lady Marshal," William said in an expressionless tone.

Isabel tensed at the sound of William's voice as he presented her and completed the introductions. His apparent indifference struck her cruelly. Was he ashamed to present her to his friends? She swallowed and shifted her gaze from her husband to the others as she murmured a greeting. In the moment her eyes rested on her husband she missed the angry gleam that came into the eyes of Lady d'Abernon as they had passed over her. When their eyes met, Lady d'Abernon smiled sweetly. "She is simply lovely, William! Though she appears somewhat peaked. My dear, you are not one to take sickly, are you? That would never do! To be married to one such as William Marshal, you will need great strength and fortitude! Well, well, come now," she rushed on before anyone could react to her words. "Come and sit with me, we have much to talk about. You were in the Tower many many months, were you not? You must tell me all about it!" As she led a bemused Isabel toward the great hearth, her dark eyes darted up to the railing where John was overseeing the removal of the bedding sheet. A small smile touched her lips for an instant before she continued on with her stream of questions. "Sit here," she indicated a chair near the one she was taking.

Isabel had listened with amazement, bereft of speech in face of Lady d'Abernon's manner. The woman, some years younger than Lord d'Abernon, perhaps near the age of her own mother, was still somewhat slender, though thick at the waist. Her face was deceptively smooth but for a few lines about the eyes and mouth. Perhaps it was the whitener she wore, Isabel mused. It effectively hid some evidence of age but left the wearer with a rather skull-like appearance but for the addition of the rouge which accentuated her high cheekbones. Her lips were thin with tight lines of disapproval, evidently the lady's normal manner, about their corners. The stiff wimple and coif she wore hid the color of her

hair but added to the severity of her face, broken only
by her large heavily lashed dark eyes, which were far
and away her best feature.

William, who had been drawn away to a chair at the
far end of the hearth by Lord d'Abernon, watched the
women covertly from over his host's shoulder. Knowing
the couple, he was not surprised that Engerrand would
seek any opportunity to draw away from his wife, but
under the circumstances he would have preferred to remain near to his. Unlike Isabel, he had not missed the
anger in Lady d'Abernon's eyes when they had come to
rest on the younger woman. And then there was the
matter of the bedsheet. Something was seriously amiss,
and it forebode ill for his young wife. As he half listened
to Engerrand, who typically was discussing nothing of
particular importance, his mind searched his memory
for some clue to what grievance Lady d'Abernon could
be holding against Isabel. It was obvious that it could
not be for Isabel herself; if they had ever met, she
would have said something upon greeting. Nay, it had
to be something, someone else.

William had known Richard deClare. They had spent
some time rousting together in Normandy and, of
course, he had known him when at court. While the differences in their ages—William had been but a squire
then—had not allowed familiarity, he had greatly admired him. The Earl of Pembroke had occasionally
been the good-natured butt of jokes regarding his addic-
tion to his wife. Only rarely would Richard show interest in whoring and then only when well within his
cups and following long absences from the countess.
Knowing deClare, William could not believe that he
would become involved with the likes of d'Abernon's
wife—before or after her marriage to Engerrand. But
there was something, he was certain of it. He had seen
that look too often not to recognize it. Lady d'Abernon
hated his wife.

William's thoughtful expression encouraged Lord
d'Abernon to launch more deeply into his subject, his
surge of enthusiasm bringing about William's attention.
Feeling slightly guilty for his inattention to his host,

William struggled to listen to what was being said and was soon drawn into the conversation, Isabel's problem momentarily forgotten.

A soft cry was heard, and the two men turned to find that Isabel had jumped from her chair, her face struck with horror and rage as she stepped back from Lady d'Abernon, who was wearing a most innocent and surprised expression. They could not hear what was said, but the anger was clear in Isabel's voice before she spun about and rushed from the hall to their chamber above. The men rose and William would have started after his wife, but he saw John standing near the women's chairs with a dumbfounded expression on his face. He suspected that his squire, who had apparently just reentered the hall, had arrived in time to overhear the women's conversation. As Lord d'Abernon, his face fairly exploding with rage, closed on his wife, William crossed to John and motioned for him to join him on the far side of the room. He glanced at Lady d'Abernon as he crossed near her and was shocked to see the self-satisfied expression she now wore even as her husband bore down on her. "Gwen!" the older man roared, "by the Blood of God! What have you done to that young woman?"

William found Isabel in their chamber, the only evidence of her anger the way she snatched at the garments she was removing from their wardrobe chest. He paused at the door as she glanced up at him and offered an unconvincing smile. Her show of good humor touched him, and he felt a wash of relief. He knew so little about her, this young woman who was suddenly his wife, and he had no way to judge what her reaction would be to what had happened below stairs. He had spoken to John, who had indeed overheard what was said—the content shocking William as much as it had his squire. He had wondered, as he had climbed the stairs, what he would find. A screaming shrew, deriding him for bringing her here, or a weeping bundle of simpering mass, flinging herself on him for comfort. But she merely continued at her task, her spine straight, only the tightness of her mouth giving away the tension she felt.

"Isabel?"

"A moment, William," she answered, carefully folding a chemise, which she bent to lay in the trunk.

He went to her side, laying a hand on her arm and turning her toward him as he sought to study her expression, seeking what was there. "Isabel, I am sorry."

She laid a hand on his chest and shrugged. "Do not concern yourself, William. It is nothing."

"Nothing?" His brow arched with doubt. "Do you make it a habit to cry out angry protests to your hostess and flee the room over nothing?"

"She is a witch." Isabel shrugged again, turning from him. She removed her sewing basket from the chest along with the torn chemise she had sought and crossed to a chair near the window's light. He watched her, giving in to a smirk at her comment. "You know, Isabel," he said lightly as he shrugged out of his surcoat. "You are my wife now—all things we may share. There is no reason for you to hide your anger from me."

Seeing what he was doing, she lay down her needlework and went to him, her fingers quickly undoing the lacings. "There is no need to involve you in such—such pettiness, husband," she answered, her mouth still tightened with anger. "I do not wish to speak of it." She crossed to the door, jerking it open, and shouted for a tiringwoman to order a bath for her lord. William stifled a smile at her manner, turning away toward the fire to hide his amusement. He stretched wearily, then sighed deeply, and as he stared into the fire he could hear her angry movements behind him as she prepared the items for his bath. There was much more involved than the matter at hand that concerned him. He appreciated the fact that she was not one to complain to him, expecting, needing him to settle every disquiet in her life. He suspected that she would prove to be self-sufficient and capable, and the thought pleased him. But this was no small matter. He knew that she had been deeply hurt, and it bothered him that she would not share it with him. He watched her from the corner of his eye, his lips pursed in thought as he sought the best way to bring the matter to hand. Recalling her forthrightness upon their arrival, his mouth drew into a crooked smile, the solution found. He waited until the bath was brought and the servants had departed, settling himself comfortably into a chair near the fire. When the door closed upon them he rose and waited for her to come to him. He controlled his mirth, which threatened to burst, as she fixed upon her purpose to undress him, her face rigid with her intent, the strain of what was required of her adding to her already foul mood.

She unlaced his chemise and helped him pull it off his head, then bent to unlace his cross-garters. He offered little help as she removed his boots nor, to her obvious discomfort, when she faced her next task—the unlacing and removal of his chausses. He observed her blush and waited—bracing his hands on his hips as his fingers itched to wrap themselves in the soft tendrils that curled about her temples as she bent her head, her own nervous fingers pulling at the laces at his waist. He shook his head slightly as he again realized how truly naive she was. Had she been accustomed to such efforts she would know, as did any high-born gentlewoman, how to minister to a man without ever seeing, a blocking of the mind and eyes to the sight of a man. But he did nothing to help her. He could feel her growing tenser and he fully planned to use it.

She pulled the chausses from him and twisted away to toss them onto the pile of the clothing nearby. She waited by the tub, her hands clasped in front of her, her eyes staring ahead of her. He stepped into the tub and lay back, allowing her to scrub him thoroughly, not even allowing her to hand him the cloth and soap when more intimate areas were reached. When he finally stepped dripping from the tub, he knew her nerves were set to a raw edge, even as she picked up the towel that had been hung to warm by the hearth to dry him. As he turned for her to dry his back he heard her sob softly.

"Engerrand is a fortunate man," he said lightly. "This is a most restful place," he added, stretching as she moved in front of him. "I think we shall remain a while. Ah, aye . . . most definitely. I had thought to leave soon, but Engerrand has generously offered a hunt. He has a lodge not far from here, and he has offered a few days in his woods. I understand that the game is most plentiful and the roe are . . . ''

"A hunt?" she looked up at him with shock. "A hunt? You would go on a hunt?"

"Aye." He sighed with pleasure. "It has been a long time since I have had the pleasure of a hunt. Not since—nay, even before that. Good Lord, not since last fall!"

"You would go on a hunt?" she repeated dumbly, staring at him, the damp towel limp in her hands.

"Is there any reason I should not?" he asked innocently. "Isabel, please. I am freezing, another towel . . . ''

The wet towel suddenly became a missile, wrapping about his head as he heard her shriek. "There is your damn towel! You miscreated, loathsome, damnable whoreson! Go on your hunt! Stay a week, a month! Why should you care what happens to me!"

He managed to pull the towel away, sputtering into it as he fought to control his laughter. His expression was surprised innocence when he managed to face her again. "Isabel? Is something wrong?"

"Wrong?" she shrieked. "What possibly could be wrong? We are but a day wed and you speak of a hunt! You would leave me—with that—that bitch!"

"Bitch?" he blinked. "Such language, Isabel," he chided as he drew on a robe. "You mean Lady d'Abernon?" His expression dawned with sudden understanding. "Ah, you mean that little disagreement below stairs. But you said yourself that it was nothing . . . ''

"Nothing!" she cried. "Nothing? She said that my father loved *her!* That he had been *forced* to marry my mother, that he never loved her! That they had always loved each other—that they had been miserable apart! That—that only my birth had finally forced him to stay with mother . . . '' Her voice broke in a sob as her eyes filled with tears.

He wrapped her in his arms, murmuring to her softly until her crying had stopped. "Isabel," he said softly. "Can you believe what she said? Look inside of yourself. I knew your father, I heard and saw him when he spoke of your mother. He loved her deeply, of that I have no doubt. As for their accuser, consider. Lady Gwen is spiteful, she has always been so. Had I had the misfortune to marry her I probably would have strangled her years ago." He smiled when he heard her giggle. "Are you going to take the word of such a one?" he asked. "If you were to have the truth from her, which is unlikely, most likely it would be that she held an affection for your father which was not returned. Imagine her delight to find you within her grasp after all these years—the opportunity to repay your father for rejecting her and your mother for being the one he loved."

She sniffed and leaned her head back to look up at him, her eyes brimming with gratitude. "How is it that you are so wise, William Marshal?" she asked softly.

"Wise?" He looked down at her with mock surprise, then he strove to look most thoughtful. "Nay, I believe it comes from a vast experience with jealous women. There was a time . . . "

"Do not dare!" she gasped, struggling to pull from him as he broke into laughter. Suddenly she ceased in her struggles and stiffened in his arms as her brow furrowed with a worrying thought. "Oh, William. Did you mean it when you said you would leave me for a hunt?"

"Do you think me mad?" he chortled. "Nay, I would not leave you with her—even if we were not so recently wed." His eyes flared with his meaning, making her blush. Then his voice softened. "Which reminds me. You must try to forget about the bedding sheet. It was obvious that she did such to embarrass you. Believe that my men are now loyal to you as they are to me—they are most angered for you . . . "

She reached up and placed a finger on his lips to silence him. "Nay, do not speak of it. While it did discomfort me greatly, it was not life-shattering. In fact," she smiled wickedly, "the message that will be carried because of it will only add to the confirmation of our bedding. She actually did us a great favor, as no man will now be able to dispute your claim to me."

A dark brow arched appreciatively at her reasoning.

"Is that so important to you?" He grinned.

"I believe that it might be." Her eyes glowed with some hidden meaning as she returned the smile.

"Then, for the moment we are content." His eyes narrowed slightly as he wondered what thoughts could be giving her such obvious pleasure. "We have no choice but to remain for a few more days—I would not offend Engerrand by leaving now. He has enough to bear with such a wife without adding offense to his guests to the burden. But soon, a few days at most, we will depart, I promise you."

"Where do we go?" she asked, puzzled.

"Where?" he smiled down at her. "Where else but where I wished to take you from the beginning? Chepstow, of course. I would see what you have brought to me."

"Oh, William!" she cried, throwing her arms about his neck. As she clung to him she realized that he was still quite damp from his bath. "Oh, William!" she repeated, this time with horror. "You must be freezing!"

"Hardly," he murmured, drawing her back into his arms as his fingers began to work down the back of her gown. "But if you are truly concerned with my needs we will have to divest you of this."

"But—it is the middle of the day!" she gasped even as she could feel her body begin to respond.

"Love, that has nothing to do with it." He chuckled softly as he pulled the gown from her shoulders.

# 6

THE morning dawned in a riot of color. The rains had covered England in a cleansing wash, bringing forth new life in fresh, tender grasses for grazing cattle and sheep; budding grains burst through the soil, reaching for warmth to spread, heads cracking. Animals ventured out, tentatively at first, then with more courage to seek food, braving a moment to roll in the warm sunlight and experience the joy of another day.

A party of travelers paused at the ridge of the hill, twenty-three knights and twoscore of men-at-arms, headed by a singular knight, his chest emblazoned with a red lion rampant, its jaws open in challenge against its field of gold and green. Deep blue eyes moved beneath the helm as they moved over the scene before him, the rising dawn illuminating massive battlements laid to his critical gaze. The woman at his side moved her horse forward, disturbing the still morning air with the sound of creaking leather as she waited for his response.

Finally, he turned to her, and he reached up to push back the visor on his helm. His eyes locked with the surge of pride he read in her own. "Aye," he said softly, "it is everything you said, and more."

His eyes shifted back, and convoluted feelings surged through him as his eyes fixed once again on what lay before him in the valley below. A massive castle crowned the hill, beyond which the river Wye swam lazily, trailing through the valley rich with farms and hamlets. But it was the battlements that drew his experienced eye as he mentally tested the parapets telescoping to rows within, then to the towers that stood massively at each corner, and the cliffs that reached up to its base, defying siege. Little wonder, he mused, that deClare settled on this place for the seat of his power. He made a promise to himself, at that moment, that never, while it lay in his care, would it fall.

Isabel rode silently at his side as they made their way down into the valley, leaving him to his thoughts as her mind filled with her own. She sighed with pleasure, remembering the days passed, and closed her eyes. They had spent the nights of their travels at inns, with the exception of one when none suitable could be found. That night was spent by a campfire in a tent hastily constructed for William and his lady. But wherever they lay, upon a cot or the soft feathers of a fresh-smelling mattress brought out for the arrival of a fine lord and his lady, the result was the same. Their days passed with exchanged looks, anticipation, an eagerness to be alone. Touches, glances built to that moment, with doors closed or in the isolation of a secluded tent, when William had drawn his bride to their bed and their tension was released in a whirl of loving touches, caresses to set their blood to racing; his lips and fingers stroking her to a peak of surrender that left her breathless, yet wanting more.

She felt as if she were living an incredible dream; drawn up into a heaven where she was set apart from mere mortals; a part of her sorrowing for other women who could not experience what she had. There was only him. The vibrant, striking blue of his eyes, the tremble of anticipation that would overtake her when they came to rest upon her. His voice, rich and full, the timbre felt down to her depths when he spoke to others, gently melting something deep within when it was gently turned upon her.

As they traveled, she had mused over which was best —to have him riding with her, to talk quietly with him, to laugh at his teasing while responding with her own wit, giving as good as she got. Or when he rode ahead with John, where she could watch him, drink in the sight of his broad shoulders, his narrow waist, the way he sat his destrier, his easy laughter as it would carry back to her, the look in his eyes as he would draw back to join her once again. Isabel had completely, amazingly, and totally fallen in love.

They clattered through the outer bailey, making their way by Chepstow's villeins, who paused in their labors to stare at the arriving company, their gladdened eyes fixing upon Isabel, who greeted them with a warm smile. Their lady was home! Word passed faster than the progression of the arrivals. Laundry was left in steaming tubs filled with lye soap. Weavers rushed from their wall huts, axes were plunged into stumps, and chickens were left half dressed as small boys rushed to see what had caused the commotion, joining their elders, who left buckets of water by the well and rude hoes dropped in garden rows. Their lady was home, and many memories reached back to her lady mother and their great lord, plentiful days filled with bounty. They reached the inner courtyard and held back, collective eyes fixing on the entourage that surrounded her and the large knight on a great brown war-horse at its head. Unfamiliar coat of arms reached out to them, the familiar red chevrons they knew so well now absent, a ferocious red lion agape with angry jaws in its stead. All eyes moved to their lady, and to the tall knight at her side, and they waited, wondering what this would mean to their lives. Silence fell over the bailey and they waited.

"I have brought a husband with me, your new lord!" she called out to those who had gathered. "William, knight of England, by the grace of His Majesty, Richard. By his signature he is lord of Striguil and all that is mine. You will do him homage as you have done to me and to my father before me. What he wills is my will, and you will honor me by giving honor to him.''

There were guarded smiles, but silence pervaded as eyes now turned to the knight. She had married! He was now their lord, and who knew the manner of man who would now control their lives?

The massive doors to the keep opened, and a small man with silver-grey hair hurried out to pause at the top of the stairs: Waverly, steward to Isabel and to her father, and to his father before him. In his eighties but still administrator to Chepstow; too capable, too cantankerous, to relinquish the title to a lesser applicant. With a snap of his fingers, servants began to rush about to see to the baggage, and Isabel knew that within the keep there was a scurry of activity, though it would be unapparent when they entered.

William brought the activity to a halt with a wave of his hand, and he looked down at the steward who awaited his orders. ''It would seem, steward, that there is cause for celebration. I will leave this in your able hands—a day of feasting and rest in honor of your lady's return.''

''Aye, milord,'' Waverly answered with an unaccustomed hint of a smile. ''And for the arrival of the new lord of Striguil.''

''Ah, but you appear to be most prepared for our arrival,'' William observed, his eyes narrowing in speculation. ''You have inner knowledge, perhaps?''

''Nay, milord, I do not claim to be a seer. Suffice it to say that I was given reason to suspect.''

William exchanged a bemused look with Isabel, who stared at Waverly in wonder. He must be losing his faculties, she mused, slipping from her mount as William came to her side. However, as they entered the great hall they assumed the mystery to be solved, as Gervase and Lavinia came forward in joyous greeting, having reached the hall upon their entrance. Lavinia swept Isabel into her arms with a cry of joy while Gervase stood by, beaming at them with approval. His eyes then moved to William, where they clouded with doubt.

Isabel ignored his guarded look, flinging herself at un-prepared Gervase and rained kisses on his face until he finally gave into hearty chuckle.

"Isabel, you look positively radiant!" Lavinia ex-claimed, her blue eyes sparkling as she glanced at the handsome bridegroom. William bent over her hand, and to Isabel's amusement, Lavinia flushed at the atten-tion as she stammered a greeting to the tall knight. Her hands went to her coif and wimple, the stiff white linen headwear Lady deMille was never seen without, for some nonexistent adjustment. Her still lovely face beamed with approval as she turned to Waverly with orders for refreshments.

"I reason we must take our repast in the solar, my dear. I believe that Isabel will find it a most pleasant place to spend the morning hours," Gervase suggested with a hint of a smile.

"You finished it?" Isabel cried, as the room had only been begun when she had left Chepstow rather hur-riedly.

"Aye," he answered, taking her arm in his, leaving William and Lavinia to follow as he started toward the stairs. "The glass we ordered from Venice is as lovely as you thought it would be. Come, and I will show it to you."

But it was not the precious beveled glass that stood in tall narrow windows, allowing shafts of bright morning light to fill the room in soft shadows that took Isabel's breath away—but the sight of the slender figure stand-ing before a far window who turned as they entered. Her coif, hiding the greying streaks of her auburn hair, her body still willowy and graceful as she took a step toward them, her regal bearing defying age as bright green eyes came to rest on Isabel, then moved to William as he entered behind her.

"Mother!" Isabel gasped, then flew across the room and into her mother's embrace, leaving a startled William and a grinning Gervase. Lavinia, whose eyes had begun to fill with emotion, motioned to her hus-band and closed the door quietly behind them.

"But how . . . when . . . ?" Isabel blubbered, wiping tears of disbelief and joy from her eyes. "No one told me!"

"No one knows," Eve said calmly. She turned to William, who waited nearby, his gaze fixed with fascination on this still breathtakingly beautiful woman about whom he had heard so much. An Irish princess, one of fire and passion, who had led a great lord marcher a merry chase until, he suspected, she had caught him. He had conquered a kingdom for her and now, seeing her, he could well understand why.

"My lady," he said quietly, bending over her hand.

They regarded each other silently. Eve took careful measure of the man who had taken her daughter to wife, then nodded tentatively with a slight smile. "Sir William, welcome to Striguil."

"Mother, you still have not told me how you came to be here!" Isabel cried impatiently, ignoring the exchange between her mother and her husband.

"In good time, Isabel," Eve replied, retiring to a chair by the windows as she gestured for them to sit by her. She poured them each a goblet of wine from a table next to her, then settled back with a look of love for her daughter, her eyes drinking in the sight of her young, eager face. "Eleanor, of course, is responsible. She secreted me into the country and here. My word, I have not used those stairs hidden in the wall by the river since . . . " Her voice trailed off as her mind was taken to another time, and her eyes began to hold a misty memory.

"What stairs?" Isabel blurted out. "Are there secret stairs?"

"I shall show them to you later," she said, smiling. "Or, perhaps I should show them to William." She laughed, apparently in the realm of her own private joke. "Never mind," she answered to their puzzlement. "Isabel, I regret that I could not have been here sooner. I would have given a ransom to be there when you married but I could not. Only in this way could I see you at all and only for a short time. I must return to Erin before the king arrives in England.''

"My lady," William interrupted, "you are now under my protection, and if it be your wish to stay . . . ''

"I thank you for the offer, William, but it is impossible. Firstly, I would not place you in that position with your king. Secondly, it is my power in Erin that Richard would seek to control, and you would not stay him. It is for that I have come, and to see my daughter, however brief my stay must be.''

They took their supper in the solar, as only a few among the most trusted servants knew of Eve's presence. The evening was spent in reminiscing, enjoying the short time they were to have together. Isabel had watched her mother earlier, as she had stared from the tall, arched windows, her gaze lingering with longing at the reaching countryside, and she knew how she ached to ride out over those beckoning hills, to experience remembrances of the past in their company. Memories of her father, undoubtedly, and the years spent with him here. She wanted to say something, but somehow she realized that her mother preferred to deal with her memories in her own way.

The Countess deClare had also watched, her shrewd eyes noting the ease between Isabel and William. It was obvious, by word and gesture, that her daughter was deeply in love. She noted with approval William's gentle and caring manner with which he returned Isabel's affections—but her eyes narrowed as she searched more deeply for signs that would indicate whether or not he was, indeed, the man she was seeking.

The remains of the supper were cleared away, and with a glance from Eve, Gervase and Lavinia begged fatigue, taking the servants with them. Once alone, Eve leaned over to refill William's goblet. Their eyes caught and Eve blinked at the sudden twinkle of amusement she read in his. "There is another matter which has brought you here, milady, is there not? Aside from your wish to visit with your daughter and to view your son-in-law. One that would bring you such a distance, through much danger.''

"Aye," Eve sighed. He was quick, she thought. "I would not come now, intruding upon your time together, so important to both of you, were it not of the utmost importance." She glanced at Isabel who was looking most puzzled at the exchange, and then she returned her gaze to William as her eyes set with determination. "William, you are now lord of one full fifth of Ireland. Your responsibilities there, I pray, will be faced with equal importance as your holdings in England, Wales, and Normandy."

"They shall be."

"And if they were threatened?"

"They would be secured."

"Mother, what has happened?" Isabel blurted out.

"Nothing that has not been happening for quite some time, and it must be stopped."

"Tell me," William said flatly, waiting.

"Prince John," Eve spat, her voice filling with contempt for King Richard's younger brother. "Henry's gravest mistake was making him lord of Ireland. How I rue that whelp's birth and that Henry had no other land to give to him! The man has no manners!"

"Manners?" Isabel laughed at her mother's choice of words.

"He has a responsibility to care for the land entrusted to him!" Eve snapped. "Yet he has no understanding of what that means! Greed, avarice! He leaves his men to run free, unguarded! They raise unlicensed castles, despoil the country, subjugate the people, and they do this in Leinster, William, in your holdings!" She directed this to him, and held her breath, waiting for his response. She had relished the past hours spent with him, gauging the man, and she felt encouraged, but. . . . She was all too aware of his loyalty to the Plantagenet family, the depth of his feeling for Henry. Did it extend to John? Would he be blind to that one's actions, perhaps even condone them? If so, she had gravely erred, and this was the moment of truth.

William had been silent, listening as he turned his goblet in his large hands. The moments lengthened heavily, then finally he answered, his response carefully worded and firm. "I shall send men to Ireland to establish my authority, madam, and they will break any resistance to what is mine. Furthermore, I shall speak to Richard on this matter when he arrives in England. But do not mistake me, I will not take arms against John until I have much more on which to act—he is my lord in Ireland."

Eve gifted him with a smile, which startled him in its similarity to her daughter's. "I could not ask for more than that."

William grunted in response, turning his attention to his goblet as his brow furrowed into a deep frown. Why did he have the feeling that he had been manipulated? He had made his own decision, according to his own dictates. Hadn't he?

Lavinia wiped the tears from the corners of her eyes and gasped as she broke into laughter again. "Oh, Eve, how I have missed you!" She giggled. "Oh, Lord, and do you remember when Richard was chasing that yellow cur you insisted on giving a home . . . "

"It had snatched a new glove of Richard's, as I recall." Eve chuckled.

"Snatched?" Lavinia's eyes teared with her mirth. "It ran with it—and Richard slipped into the mud as he would have caught it and . . . " she could continue no longer as she burst into laughter.

"I don't know who was the more surprised," Eve joined her, nearly collapsing with the memory, "the bull—or Richard as he rolled into the pen. I didn't know he could move that fast!"

"Neither did the bull!" Lavinia chuckled.

The two friends sat reminiscing in the solar as they enjoyed the warmth of the early morning sun and shared memories. Their morning had been deliciously private, as Isabel had not emerged from her chamber as yet and William and Gervase had ridden out early to ride Striguil's boundaries.

"I am pleased that Gervase has finally seemed to accept William," Lavinia observed with a sigh, wiping her eyes as she changed the subject. "I feared for a time that it would not be so."

"Gervase is as a father to Isabel," Eve answered affectionately. "It is reasonable that he would feel that no man would be good enough for her. I am certain that if Richard were here it would be much the same. No man can fully accept the fact of his daughter being wedded and bedded."

"Aye, he hears of Robert's and Richard's exploits with almost pride," she offered, referring to their sons who were fostered with the earls of Leicester and Norfolk, respectively. "But I am certain had we had a daughter he would have been as unreasonable with her as he is with Isabel. But is it not wonderful?" she sighed, almost dreamily. "She appears to be so happy."

Eve merely grunted as she bent to her needlework, suddenly engrossed in the task.

"Eve?" Lavinia frowned. "What is it? Are you not pleased over Isabel's happiness?"

"Of course I am." Eve shrugged, laying down the work. "But I am not as convinced that all is well with her as you seem to be."

"What are you talking about?" Lavinia frowned. "It is obvious that she is head over heels in love with him! And why not? He is handsome, virile, and wonderously gentle with her. He . . . "

"Lavinia!" Eve laughed. "I think you are a little in love with him yourself!" Lavinia, sputtered indignantly and Eve chuckled. "Do not fret. I, more than any, know that there never has been, nor will there ever be anyone for you but Gervase. But you do seem a little cow-eyed."

"Even an old woman can appreciate a fine figure of a man when she sees one," Lavinia parried indignantly. "And do not try to tell me that you did not notice."

"Of course I noticed." Eve laughed. "And I am more than delighted for Isabel. He is all that you say, and more, much more. He is everything I wanted for her."

"Aye, she was very lucky."

"Aye," Eve murmured. "Most fortunate."

"Eve." Lavinia's eyes narrowed. "What are you afraid of?"

"No man is perfect." Eve shrugged. "But the problem, I fear, is that Isabel reasons he is. Nay, that is not the correct choice of words—she is not reasoning at all."

"Is that it?" Lavinia smiled. "But it is perfectly natural. She is in love!"

"She is not just in love, Lavinia. She is living in a dream world, one of her making."

"Just because she dotes on him and . . ."

"And hangs on each word," Eve interrupted sardonically. "And marks each breath he takes for fear his exhale will not be followed by an inhale. Lud, I fear the lass would suffer apoplexy should he display normal male behavior; she would probably expire on the spot if he farted. Nay, such behavior would be normal in many maids, Lavinia, but not in Isabel. Have you ever known her to be so compliant, so . . . insipid?" She sighed raggedly. "Nay, I fear that she must awaken from that fantasy in which she has been existing, or she is heading for sore trouble."

"Oh," Lavinia said in a small voice. "Oh, Eve, perhaps you are right, now that I see it. Perhaps we should stay . . ."

"Stay?" Eve's brow furrowed as she sought Lavinia's meaning, but then she shook her head, suddenly understanding. "Nay, Lavinia, you must not. I know you mean well, and I love you for the thought, but you have already done more than you should. Gervase has longed to return to his own lands, to be well rid of the responsibilities placed on him here. Do not mention this conversation to him," she warned. "You know that if you do he will never leave regardless of his own needs. Nay, Isabel must learn to face her own life and all that will come with it, the bad as well as the good."

Isabel sank into the warmth of the tub in the privacy of her chamber, having dismissed her tiringwoman in

her need to be alone. Why was a bath always such an aid
to thought, she mused. Was it the warmth, the comfort
of the water, or the solitude it brought? She had awoken
early to find her bed empty, the first such occurrence
since she had been wed. Her maidservant had entered as
soon as she had stirred and had answered her anxious
questions as to William's absence. Disgruntled, and
somewhat embarrassed in front of the woman to discover that he had gone out with Gervase at dawn without a word to her, she had rolled over and had gone
back to sleep. Rising late, she had eaten a light meal in
her room, missing Mass, as she did not want to see anyone in her petulant mood—particularly her mother,
who had a habit of seeing quickly to the heart of a problem. Admittedly, she knew that she was being unreasonable, which alone kept her from facing Eve, but the
realization did nothing to improve her humor. Finally,
out of boredom more than anything else, she had
ordered a bath. As she soaked in the tub, her thoughts
eased. Unwanted thoughts invaded her mind in spite of
her resolve not to think of him. Thoughts of the desire
that rose from a look, a glance, the sight of dark curls
wrapping about the back of his neck, the broadness of
his shoulders in a well-fitted tunic, a frown that would
crease his brow, drawn from heavy black brows as he
pondered a problem to which she knew he would find a
solution; his voice, the rich timbre of his laughter . . .
and hating herself for it, she felt a surge of desire, a
wanting . . .

But her anger fled as the door opened, and her
thoughts scattered as William entered. He paused for a
moment as his eyes came to rest upon her in the tub.
They lit with interest, moving over her slowly, where
they came to rest where the water swirled about her
breasts, and lingered. She smiled wickedly, recognizing
the look, her mood changing quickly, all thoughts fleeing from her mind but awareness of the way he was
looking at her, and she felt a rush of excitement, of anticipation.

He grinned and rolled his eyes, obviously appreciating the picture she made. "Good morning, love," he tossed out. With that he crossed to the chest at the end of the bed, throwing back the lid to rummage through the contents. He brought forth a small enameled set of chess, inlaid with silver and ivory, one of his most precious possessions, gifted from Henry in a moment of affection. Even as she waited, a soft seductive smile on her lips, she found herself staring at the door that had closed behind him. He left, without another word! She sat there for a long moment, dumbfounded. Gradually she became aware that her nipples were taut and that her body had been left with a dull ache of disappointment and unfulfillment. Suddenly she let out a great shriek and rose from the tub, splashing water on the floor as she grabbed up a towel and began drying herself with angry strokes. The anguished bellow brought the tiringwoman, her brown eyes wide with fear that something dire had befallen her lady. She had cause to regret her appearance, as Isabel bent her fury on the unsuspecting woman, snapping orders and throwing garments about as she sought something to wear.

Eventually somewhat mollified, Isabel left the chamber. She had no intention of spending what was left of the day in her chamber alone, and she was just as determined not to spend it with William! Let him spend it with Gervase, she thought, grimacing, she'd be damned if she'd care! Discovering that her mother was alone in the solar, she made her way down the long hallway to the west wing as she strove to improve her humor. She knew that her mother was not easily fooled, and she had no desire to discuss William with her—not when her own emotions were in such a state of confusion.

However, as she entered the room, she found that she did not have to force herself to affect a lighter mood. She found Eve sitting by a window, her fair brow wrinkled into a frown as she bent over the embroidery on which she was working. "You must be bored," Isabel laughed as she approached. "Since when did you voluntarily take up needlework?"

Eve looked up and smiled with relief at her daughter's

interruption. "Since I've become old and discovered a limitation to my energies."

"You? Old?" Isabel chuckled with disbelief. "Mother, you'll never be old."

"Humph," Eve snorted, "visions of the young. You only see what you want to see. I've found that needlework passes the time, but you are correct, I'll never enjoy it. It seems such a monumental waste of time, at least for me, though I admire the art of those who do it well."

"Here, let me see it." She took the work from her mother and gasped, then broke into laughter. "Mother, this is truly terrible!"

"You need not seem so pleased."

"I am sorry," Isabel rushed to add, biting her lips to hold back her laughter. "I fear that we will have to rip out half of this, the rest might be manageable."

"I fear that you are right," Eve sighed. "Where you gained your talent for the art I will never know. Perhaps from your father's mother, your namesake. 'Tis her tapestries which adorn the great hall; she even allowed me to help with a small part of them."

"Really?" Isabel looked interested.

"A small part, the corner near the buttery, the one that hangs in the shadows." Eve grinned.

"Well," Isabel chuckled, "let us see if we can set this to right."

As Isabel bent to her task, her concentration taken to her efforts, Eve used the luxurious moment to study her daughter, her unfailing eyes astutely drinking in the sight of her, memorizing. Then her eyes fixed on her daughter's hair, the smoky mass shining in a riot of color in the light shafts from the window. Suddenly, another thought struck her, realization of something unformed, which had been bothering her since her daughter had entered the room.

"You are not wearing a coif or a wimple," she said dully.

Isabel looked up with surprise. "What?"

"Your hair is loose!"

"Aye." Isabel looked at her mother strangely. "Mother, what is the matter? You look stricken."

"Your hair, it is loose!"

"Aye." Isabel's fingers went to her hair as she looked at her mother with puzzlement. "Why do you find that strange?" She looked at her mother's coif, the stiff white linen covering her hair, and the wimple of linen wrapped about her chin and neck, and understanding began to dawn. She fought a smile, recalling, at last, how her mother detested the English headwear. "Mother, you need no longer wear the wimple or coif. They are out of style, Queen Eleanor saw to that. She now wears a small cap that ties beneath her chin called a barbette, and then only when she must."

"Damnation."

Isabel laughed, realizing at that moment how much she had missed her mother, and the strong easy words she had grown up with. Eve reached up and unpinned the headpiece, followed by the constricting wimple, which landed in a pile at her feet. "The only reason I wore that bloody thing was that I thought you would be scandalized if I did not, or that William would be. I know that Lavinia would have been."

"Since when did you care about what others thought?" Isabel chortled.

"Since I wanted to impress your husband," Eve answered bluntly.

"Impress William?" Isabel blinked at her. "But why? You need not," she added tightly as she averted her gaze from her mother.

Oh, dear, Eve mused, there was trouble in paradise. She leaned back in her chair and looked intently at Isabel. This woman-child, their daughter. So much Richard had taught her as his wife. Had she passed that on? Had those years been filled with only the mundane, however precious, or had she taught her well? "Isabel, I've missed you terribly. However, it was not the main reason I have come, as you know. Since the first day you have not asked me about Erin, not a word, even as you heard my plea to your husband. Even as he and I have spent many hours over the past weeks in discussion. Do you care so little?''

It shocked her to learn that William had spent so much time with her mother. "Are things truly bad?" She felt chagrined; her mother was right. She had not thought of it once.

"They are that, and more."

"Tell me," Isabel said softly.

"Isabel, if there is a fault to be found among the Irish people, it is their insufferable, their damnable pride!" Eve shook her head as if to rid it of uncomfortable memories, then she fixed her daughter with a determined stare. "You put ten Irishmen in a room together to solve a problem, and they will emerge with ten solutions and a donnybrook to prove their own point of view, and enjoy every moment of it! They simply will not see past their own noses! And their faith! Blood of Mary, they will not see the evil of others! While they lay claim to it, it never becomes a reality until it has destroyed them! Then they are surprised, outraged!

"Your father had ambitions, Isabel, never forget it. I loved the man, I love him still, but I recognized that ambition years ago and learned to live with it. Why should I not? I had ambitions of my own, and though I loved him I used what he could offer, to me and to Ireland. He took Erin for his own purposes, but he came to love her, nay, cherish her. He knew that she would not survive the modern world as she was; her very nature would not allow it. He strove to give her the best that was Norman, and Anglo-Saxon, knowing that it would be the only means to her survival. The very devil was coming, and he wanted to make her strong. God alone knows why he decides upon his plan." Eve shook her head as if to dispel unwanted memories, then forced herself to continue. "If your father had lived . . . but he did not," she said, drawing up her chin with a resolve to accept what was. "No man, after him, was strong enough to preserve Erin against the plague that overtook her, and now, what he . . . we were frightened for, has happened.

It is merely land, to be used or misused for the greed of others. With no love, no longing to make it what it can be . . . ''

As Isabel listened, an awareness began to stir, a feeling that she was discovering something within her that had for too long remained dormant. She was caught up in her mother's passion, and a link that had been missing suddenly emerged, forming into a strength of purpose that she knew would never, never leave her.

"It has come," Eve continued, drawing in her breath as she gave herself to the inner depths of her feelings. "Eleanor, as much as I love her, is much responsible. It was she who gave Erin to John, her youngest, prodding Henry to provide for him. Oh, Richard warned me years ago, more years than I care to remember, that it would be so. John Lackland, they called him, the poor prince without land of his own. Can I blame a mother for providing for her children? Aye, in this case I most surely can, for in doing so she despaired of a people. Few are truly worthy of power, and John most assuredly is not. He cares not for Ireland, but only for what it can bring to him. His men take, never giving, never caring, for they are not made of that mettle. It takes a special man to give.'' She looked up at Isabel, drawing her thoughts from her own personal torture to find reason with her daughter, her eyes a bright emerald green as they sought understanding. "I think—perhaps—that you have found such a one. I pray that he is.''

"William?" Isabel asked, her mind spinning.

" 'Aye, William,'' Eve said flatly. "Oh, I do not delude myself. Once freedom is lost, no simple solution, no easy time, will regain it. When your father died Erin became chaos, each faction fighting among themselves to gain control, to return to the old ways, dismissing the unity he had gained. So tragic, for it was the only way she could have gained her sovereignty. Now, I fear, it is much too late. No one man will be able to throw off the yoke she has placed about her neck—but a man, a strong man, can aid her, give her the will to retain her identity. I must believe that William is that man, perhaps the only one."

Silence fell over the large room as Isabel stared at her mother, a silence so deep that one could almost hear the dust motes as they traveled through the light shafts that settled about them. Reasoning began to form, focusing into a reality that gripped her in a pain almost physical in intensity.

"Sweet Mother of God," she breathed. "It was you. Not Henry. Not Richard. You! You planned it, arranged it, you chose him!"

They exchanged a long look of understanding, the silence more telling than words, as Eve did not flinch from her daughter's demanding stare.

"Why? Oh, Mother, why? Could you not have told me?"

"I am a product of all that has gone before me, Isabel," Eve answered with no apology in her voice. "A product of my mother, who died a terrible death in protecting her clan. My brothers died, save one, because of revenge. My father, and grandfather before him, died in dishonor because they fought the only way that they could, to preserve the life that they knew. Your father taught me something that, of us all, only my mother knew—that before personal desire there comes loyalty to a greater purpose. The individual is important, Isabel, but only if he contributes to a society that can grant and protect those rights. When all is lost to the wants of one selfish motive, there is no chance for anything better. Why did your father choose to meld himself with Erin? He could have simply taken it, he had the power. Instead he manipulated Henry, held Erin while he strove to integrate himself and his followers to the land, to the people, to give to them the best of what he was. Why? Because he knew that there is no way to stop change, it is the nature of things, but a man's choice can make it good—or destructive. It rests on personal goals.

"Aye, I chose William for you. Eleanor and I have

been in correspondence for many years; even in her cap-
tivity she knew what was happening. William Marshal is
the only man with the strength to give what is needed. I
pray that you will find within yourself to give what is
needed to aid him, to bring him to what he can fulfill for
Erin.''

Isabel was dumbstruck. No words would possibly express what she was feeling. How could they; her
thoughts were a tumble of confusion. She rose from her
chair and reached over to wrap her arms about her
mother in a tight embrace, then she left the room. There
was so much to think about, so much to consider. It was
far too much. It would take time. She would take each
point, carefully considering all that her mother had
said, now mixed with her own problems, and try to deal
with it.

They gathered about the fire in the great hall. The
solitude granted each a moment of reflection, a time of
sharing the companionship of others, that most human
need required in a world tormented with doubt and
question. Only Lavinia was truly peaceful, occupying
herself with her ever-present needlework, satisfied with
its existence in her knowledge of Gervase's presence, a
fact she never had cause to doubt in his stability and
comforting support.

Gervase was focused on his own thoughts, the responsibilities to Chepstow and his own lands, the matters of
daily living, the care of those entrusted to him. The
spring planting reaching into harvest, while overlaid
with subconscious relief that the matters of his king
would no longer take him to loftier planes.

Those were held by William as he slowly turned his
goblet in his hands. He stared into the fire as he sought
solutions to the endless problems pressed upon him,
matters taken to a depth that only years would tell him
if they were beyond his experience. He stretched his legs
out comfortably as his brow deepened in thought, his
mind miles away from where they sat, turning on

messages that had arrived for him from Eleanor . . .

Isabel tried not to focus on anything except the work in her hands, the needle as it pulled through the fine fabric. Proper tension, pull, knot. Her mind was too full, her thoughts would take time—to sort, to reason. How could she deal with it all now? Her mother was leaving in the morning; only that fact had caused Eve to leave the upper floors, knowing that she would be gone before Richard entered England to learn of her presence. Supper had been joyous, laughter, sharing. A premonition pressed on her that it would be the last time her mother would see England. Did her mother care, truly? Her heart was in Erin, her breath. But it was here that she had spent the first years with her father. How did one leave those behind, knowing? Her thoughts turned to William. What memories would they have, years from now? Would they be as rich, as full?

Eve watched her daughter, and her heart reached out, aching with the inadequacy of a mother faced with the need to share with her child her wisdom and experience, yet she was frozen to silence. It seemed that with the young nothing could be accepted but that which was learned, taken by a passion of their own feelings, never by design of others. It was there, a subtle strain developing between Isabel and William, tenuous, but obvious to the caring eye. She was gladdened that Isabel was awakening from the fantasy she had spun about her husband—but knew that Isabel now faced the hardest challenge of all, to learn to live with the difference.

She fixed her eyes upon her daughter now so firmly engrossed in menial pursuits as if in escape. Oh, Isabel, she thought, listen to me. He is a good man, as good as I had, and such a man is rare. How blessed we are both to have found him. I could tell you these things as I know, from the depths of my feelings, wherein your problem lay. I have been there. In seeking the answers you will find yourself. I would not take this from you. The best that I can do for you, my darling, is to leave in silence. Allowing you to find your own way.

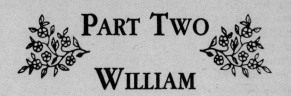

# PART TWO

# WILLIAM

# 7

ISABEL closed her eyes and drew in the heady fragrance of the roses that climbed the walls of the keep. A light breeze wafted through the open window to carry their sweetness with cooling relief on the warm July morning. With a soft sigh she struggled against a growing restlessness, unable to concentrate upon the light chatter from the ladies who had gathered in the solar to pass the morning. Reality stirred her guilt. She knew she should not feel this way, she spent little enough time with the wives and daughters of her vassals. But then they had not her responsibilities, she told herself with stirring anger. Another sigh and she pushed aside her petulance, realizing that they were not to fault for her restlessness. She did not even know why she should feel so. Her life was full, busy, everything she had expected it to be. No more, no less.

Soft laughter drew her from her reverie, and she shifted her gaze to find Elizabeth Marshal, wife of William's older brother, John, watching her. Elizabeth was a small, almost fragile-looking woman—which Isabel had quickly come to realize was most deceiving. Her large blue eyes, while kind, held a shrewd intelligence missed only by the least observant. That she loved her husband was obvious, and their easy and loving rapport was something Isabel envied. Isabel had felt drawn to the kindly but blunt older woman from the first moment they had met—not knowing that Elizabeth had sensed from the first the need in Isabel for a friend, and her kind heart had reached out.

"Your mind is not on your work, Isabel," she observed with a smile, glancing down at the cloth lying idly in Isabel's lap. "You will have to redo that last color."

Isabel glanced down at the work with dismay, realizing that her sister-in-law was right. The threads were uneven and the stitches were hopelessly loose. "Lud," she said softly. She glanced up at Elizabeth with a timorous smile. "I hadn't noticed."

"Obviously," Elizabeth laughed, then her expression softened. "You miss him." Her eyes narrowed as she saw the younger woman's mouth tighten at the question.

"On the contrary, Elizabeth," Isabel responded as she began to pick at the threads. "My life is full; I have more than I expected."

"Of course," Elizabeth agreed, her eyes watching Isabel speculatively.

"Milady, you promised to tell us of the coronation!" The question came from Jocelyn, the young raven-haired wife of Elizabeth's oldest son. Her large brown eyes fixed expectantly on Isabel. "There have been so many rumors, please tell us all of it!"

"Feel fortunate that you were not there, Jocelyn," Isabel said, grimacing. "It was a dire affair. I wish that I had been spared."

"It is said that a bat flew into the hall during the ceremony," another lady offered, affecting great knowledge.

"Aye, 'tis true." Isabel smirked. "It circled about the coronation chair, and no one could dissuade it, not even the priests who attempted to shoo it away, for it seemed intent upon landing at the king's shoulders. Moreover, at the precise moment the crown was placed upon Richard's head there was a mysterious tolling of the bells of Westminster."

" 'Tis said that such are great omens, decrying the reign of the Coeur de Lion!" blurted out another with wide eyes.

"The goings on were mysterious," Lady Elizabeth agreed. "The priests who cared for the bell tower were questioned, and they swore that no one was near the bell when it happened."

"The king became deranged when it was over," Isabel added, remembering. "He was certain that the demons were intent upon his soul. He ranted and raved, and it took William over an hour to calm him."

"It must have been horrible!" Jocelyn breathed. "The poor king!"

"What do you expect from a man who believes that his grandmother flew out of a chapel window on a broomstick," Isabel murmured, fixing her attention on her needlework.

"What did you say?" Elizabeth asked.

"Nothing."

"The mayhem lasted quite a while," Elizabeth continued, picking up the story. "The coronation banquet was delayed for hours while everyone was questioned, but not a clue was discovered."

"No one questioned the bat," Isabel murmured with a smirk as she pulled out a row of thread.

As they chatted on, the ladies happily absorbing Elizabeth's recounting of who had attended, what was worn by whom, and the vast fare that bent the groaning tables for the banquet celebrating the coronation of Richard, Coeur de Lion, Isabel's thoughts took another, more sober, path. Her thoughts turned reluctantly to the real mark of Richard's coronation, and to his reign. Damn him, she thought, a lump forming in her throat as remembrances she had willed aside returned with their discussion. It had begun for her when John d'Erley had appeared at William's shoulder during the banquet. She had heard William swear softly before he turned to excuse himself from her, then left quickly. The next twelve hours proved to be one of horror, the more so as so few seemed to feel as she did.

Upon Richard's orders, Jews and witches had been

forbidden from attending the coronation. The latter
obeyed the edict, while, unfortunately, two members of
the former had misunderstood. The Jews of York,
thinking that the edict had been lifted, had sent two representatives, Jossen and Baruch, to present a gift to
their king. As they milled with the crowd outside of
Winchester, a rumor began to circulate that an attempt
had been made on the life of the king. The crowd
rapidly became a mob and turned on the two most likely
suspects, suspicion against the Jews having heightened
by the church in light of the coming crusade and the
funds that would be needed to finance the venture.
None of this Isabel knew until later. She spent the evening lost in a maze of strange faces, her anger growing
toward her husband, who had left his bride to the mercy
of blunt propositions by nobles who seemed to gravitate
to the beautiful, unescorted lady they found in their
midst. As unsettled as the awkward situation made her,
it did not take her long to realize that no one dared force
himself upon her. Their regard for William's power and
sword arm became obvious when she would but mention his name, but it rankled nonetheless.

She was in high humor by the time she arrived back at
their lodgings. Her anger had been sharpened when she
was forced to beg assistance from Elizabeth, whom she
had just met that day, to secure an escort to return to
Renier's manor. But she did not see William until the
following morning when she came down for breakfast,
finding him with Renier. Her anger was tempered by his
appearance, as his eyes were bleary with dark circles as
evidence of his lack of sleep. Moreover, the tension in
the small room between William and Renier caused her
to slip quietly into a chair as she stared at them across
the table. It was then that she learned what had happened. John d'Erley, who had been returning from an
errand for William, had observed the porters eject
Jossen and Baruch from the hall into the waiting mob.
William had acted quickly, but before he could reach
them the two were badly beaten. Baruch eventually died
from the abuse he suffered, but William was able to
return Jossen with an armed guard to York. Renier, as

sheriff of London, was outraged that William had taken matters into his own hands; thus the tension between two old friends.

How odd, she mused, that moments full of the richest promise often rise from our darkest thoughts. Perhaps it is only then that our mind is truly open to hope. She had had such a moment with William, so fleeting, but full of that promise. Renier had been called from the room, the door barely closing behind him before she had burst into a fair tirade over what had happened to Baruch and Jossen, only to be brought to a halt by her suddenly bemused husband. Her outburst brought his attention upon her, and his eyes narrowed speculatively. "Since when have you felt sympathy for the Jews, Isabel?"

She had blinked at the question. "I—I've never thought about it." She shrugged. "I've never known a Jew. It just seems to me that they cannot be so very different from us."

"The church would be dismayed to hear you speak so," he observed as a hint of a smile touched his lips.

"Pah." She shrugged, and then a glint flared in her eyes. "You forget that I am half-Irish. We believe in the Mother Church, William, but only to a point."

"And that point is?"

"As long as we agree with what she says."

William laughed, his eyes crinkling with delight. "That attitude could well find you in serious trouble, Isabel."

"Are you warning me to keep my opinions to myself?"

"Not at all. I would not ask of my wife other than what I would expect from myself. I caution you only to use discretion. Do not voice such thoughts carelessly, especially now." He became serious but his voice was gentle. "I expect you to stand by your beliefs, and I will support you. However, bear in mind that our heads might be involved, so I ask only that what you voice be very dear to you."

A warm thrill had run through her at his words and by the way he had said them. He meant it, she had thought, he truly meant it! She readily accepted his terms, vowing to never abuse the precious gift he had given to her, a freedom shared by no other woman she knew. And with it, realization that he cared, about her thoughts as well as her body, a gift greater than any other he could have given to her.

And then he left her. Without warning, he announced that he was going to Normandy with Richard as the king's emissary to Philip of France. From there he would accompany Richard on the Third Crusade, to be gone for years. And he was gone, leaving her to return to Chepstow alone. He had knighted John d'Erley before he left, leaving her in his care along with her own knights and retainers. But he had left. Lud, what had she expected? She had married a lord marcher. It was her own undoing if she had expected more. Was that not what she had wished for, to be left to her own devices, to live her life as she wished? Her deep musings were ended by a sudden outburst of laughter from the other women, and she forced her attention to them, needing relief from her dark thoughts.

"They should have known better," Lady Isamond huffed. "Imagine, thinking that they would be accepted."

"Aye, they only received their just dues." This from another of the ladies.

Isabel stirred uncomfortably, sensing what had become the object of conversation. "I was daydreaming, I fear," she interrupted. "What are you discussing?"

"Lady Elizabeth was telling us what happened during the banquet," Lady Isamond explained, her brow arched haughtily. "I do not understand why she seems disturbed. It is incomprehensible to me that the Jews do not know their place by now."

Isabel felt an explosion go off inside of her, a burst of red light that seemed to flash behind her eyes. " 'Just dues'?" she repeated. "Can you be so shallow-pated?" she asked quietly, too quietly. "Let me enlighten you, Margot, as to the results of that night. It began with those unfortunate two. But it spread, in and beyond London. Unknown to William's men, they were followed to York when they returned Jossen. When they left, taking their protection with them, the mob was waiting. They robbed, looted, killed. Did the baronage of York attempt to stop the despoiling? Would they, when they were to a man in debt to the Jews of York? Over a thousand people retreated into the palace of York, followed by a mob screaming 'death to the disbelievers.' They tried to hold out until help arrived. When it was apparent that they could not they—killed themselves, Margot. Men, women, children.''

Lady Isamond drew herself up in the face of Isabel's anger. ''Are you actually grieving for Jews, Lady Isabel?'' she spat, her lip curling in contempt. ''Disbelievers who . . .''

Isabel stood up and regarded the other woman coldly. ''Lady Isamond. It is understandable that you would forget your husband's position to me, and thus your own, in the face of my mother's recent visit. That I will forgive you. However, you would be most wise to remember that you are here by my grace. I would not dismiss your husband from my service because of the ill-found words of his wife, but I can remove your presence. I expect my ladies to be above the lower values, to act with charity and kindness toward their fellow man. I will not tolerate less.''

''But the church . . .'' the woman sputtered.

''The church does not rule here,'' Isabel answered, cutting her short. ''Now leave me and do not return until you have thought well upon it. All of you, please, I wish to be alone.''

The ladies left quietly while exchanging wide looks of shock. Tongues were certain to wag as soon as the doors were closed upon them, but for the moment each thought it wise to respond quickly and quietly to Isabel's order. Isabel turned her back on them, waiting for the sound of the closing door as she fought to control her trembling anger. Unaware that she was still clasping her needlework to her, she crossed the length of the long solar to a far window, where she sat down on the deep window embrasure, welcoming the warmth of the morning sun on her face and shoulders as she leaned back against the stone arch and attempted to bring her strained emotions under control.

"Well, well. There is no doubt that you have become the mistress of your domain." Isabel jerked her head about to find Elizabeth standing near, her eyes dancing with humor. "Be assured, I'm delighted. Margot needed her comeuppance and I agree with your point, though I would not have phrased it quite that way. You need not look at me like that, I have no intention of leaving, not yet. And do not attempt high-handedness with me, my dear, I shall simply ignore it. That done, there are a few matters I wish to discuss with you."

Isabel stared at her for a moment then erupted into laughter. "Oh, Elizabeth, what would I do without you?"

"It would be hard to imagine. But you survived before we met and you will again, should we be parted. Now, I have been sneaking glances at that banner on which you are working, though you keep it carefully folded. Let me see it."

Isabel regarded her with puzzlement as she extended the needlework. "Of course you may see it, I have not been trying to hide it."

Elizabeth merely grunted as she took the large cloth, unfolding it. She blinked, a frown creasing her brow, and her eyes darted up to Isabel. "Is this to be your banner?"

"Aye," Isabel answered, mystified by Elizabeth's response.

Elizabeth stared at the coat of arms, and her brows drew together in dismay. William's device was there; at first glance, it appeared as it should be. The lozenge-shaped cloth was divided in half, with William's device, as her husband, to the dexter, or right; the half-green, half-gold background dominated by the bright red lion standing ferociously on its hind feet, mouth agape in a feral snarl. The sinister, or left half of the banner, bore her own coat of arms, given by her father. Gold background boldly overlaid by the three red chevrons of the deClares. But there was something. What was it? "The colors!" Elizabeth blurted out.

"The colors?" Isabel stared at the banner. "What of them?"

"The chevrons . . . they appear to . . . dominate."

"Nonsense." Isabel frowned, suddenly irritated by the criticism. "They are all of the same hue. You are imagining it."

Elizabeth studied the banner. Nay, she was not imagining it. Could Isabel not see that she had used a thread of a different hue for the chevrons than she had for the lion? The sinister side of the banner was definitely dominant. But she sensed that Isabel would not see it or accept it. Sighing, she handed the cloth back to her. But she could not help wonder if William would notice.

She sat down on the sill next to Isabel and studied the younger woman for a moment. "You feel abandoned, don't you?" Isabel blinked, stunned by Elizabeth's bluntness. "You need not answer, my dear, your thoughts and feelings are your own. Just listen. I could tell you that it becomes easier over the years, but it does not. You will learn, as I have, to keep that part of your heart tightly locked, opening it when he walks through that door."

"You mean, pretend that he does not exist?"

"More or less. Focus on other matters. Do not allow yourself to dwell on the fact that he chooses a life without you. Wait patiently, keep his home ever ready. You are mistress of a large domain, and for some reason William has allowed you to keep it under your control—a shocking development, I must say." She shrugged. "Why you would not prefer his castellan in his stead I cannot imagine. But that is between the two of you."

Isabel suppressed her irritation. Nothing would be served by pointing out to Elizabeth that her domain had been hers long before William Marshal entered her life.

"Have you told him?"

"Told him what?"

"That you are expecting a child."

"How did you know?" Isabel gasped. "I have not told anyone."

"My dear, I have borne eight children." Elizabeth smiled. "Your body tells the story. Your waist and your breasts are fuller, and I have noted a certain paleness when you attempt to sit to midmeal. Now answer me. Have you told him?''

"Nay."

"Why not?"

"I don't know how."

"You mean you don't know if he cares."

Isabel began to protest, but in the face of Elizabeth's penetrating stare she merely shrugged. "I cannot believe that he does."

"Oh, child of course he cares! It is his child that you carry! Sometimes, my dear, we must remind men of what is important to them. Now, you shall write to him immediately. Keep it loving, but light-handed. Fill him with news, draw his interest to income and profits, then drop it lightly as a matter of passing, a matter of vital importance to you while understandably an issue he need not concern himself with. A small matter you will see to while he deals with the important cares of the world."

Later, as dusk deepened her chambers to a softening subdued grey, Isabel lit a candle and sat at her writing desk, determined to follow Elizabeth's advice. She smiled as she recalled the older woman's counsel, recognizing the wisdom of experience. Still, she felt sobered, facing terror as she began to pen the letter. Where would he be, what would he be doing, what matters would be pressing on his mind when he read it? And how would he react?

He was shaking with anger when he opened the letter. The morning had been spent with Philip, king of France, and the monarch had been in a particularly irascible mood. Difficult at best, always set to matters of his own making and mood, Philip had enjoyed baiting William, knowing his favored envoy would speak his mind when few others dared. The subject was the coming crusade, and each vied for financing, position, and glory, the matters dear to the heart of a king. Angry, William opened the letter with mixed emotions, his mind still for England's position in matters of state.

He began to read through the letter and gradually relaxed, the beginnings of a smile appearing as he warmed to the news of home. Then suddenly he froze, his eyes focusing on a singular line.

He took another long swallow of his ale as his eyes moved over the darken atmosphere of the tavern, his gaze falling on the other occupants without really seeing. Unwillingly, his mind was fixed upon that which he would not face. Duty lay here. There was nothing else for him. That which was first . . . Certainly a man could not split himself in two, two loyalties, two parts of his heart divided . . .

Seeking an escape, his gaze fixed upon two men who had entered the tavern, the cut of their dress apart from the other occupants about him. They moved through the crowded room, and to his amazement they moved in his direction, coming to a stop before his table. Had he not been so well into his cups, William would have realized that his was the only table available. As it was, his brows gathered at the interruption to his solitude, his manner intent upon mayhem.

"May we sit, friend?" one of the men spoke.

"Only those I know well may call me friend," William growled.

"Our mistake," the other replied in a friendly tone. "Unfortunately, yours seems to be the only table vacant."

William glanced about, assessing the truth of the stranger's statement. Then he frowned blackly, grunting at them in hard-won concession. As they took the chairs across from him he glowered deeper, promising himself to ignore their presence. Moodily, he stared into his tankard, his mind once again returned to the contents of Isabel's letter. A child. He should have been filled with elation; part of him was. A son to teach. He visualized time spent with his son, sharing with him, watching him grow to manhood. Or a daughter, a miniature of Isabel, and his expression softened at the vision. A delicate creature climbing up into her father's lap, large grey eyes, or would they be blue? Nay, they would be as Isabel's. Eyes plying him with instinctive feminine wiles.

He was certain he would find himself helpless to her demands. Aye, the thought of their coming child filled him with feelings of immortality and joy. It had seemed so easy in the past to look forward to this day, the time when children became a reality in his life. But it had always been dreamed of as the future, not as part of today. Only now could he begin to face what it was to mean to his life.

In a month's time he was to accompany Richard on the Third Crusade. Glory, honor, riches would be for those in the king's company. William's memory returned to past conquests: Normandy, France, the Second Crusade; exotic lands and people, the heady adrenaline that would race through his blood in the midst of a battle. Mental agony, followed by cold calculations in forming battle plans; the abiding satisfaction reaching into his depths as a painstakingly orchestrated attack was set into motion, his seasoned armies moving as pieces on a chessboard to their objective. But more than all, to lead them, to be first to the wall, to experience that surge of power behind him when the enemy was met. And he would know it again. Plans were set, in spite of Philip's obstinacy, and in a few short weeks it would begin.

Aye, he thought, feeling better, his life with his family would begin upon his return. In fact, he would see to it in short order upon his return that Isabel began another child. Aye, he wanted a large family. . . . It bothered him somewhat that he would miss many years of his children's lives. It was something he would have liked to experience. However, there was nothing to be done for it. He was a soldier, had always been, would always be.

His mind lightened, he motioned to the passing barmaid for another tankard. He watched her walk away, her full hips swaying beneath the thin wool of her skirt. It would be an easy conquest, he mused, recalling the way her expressive blue eyes had moved over him, the invitation clearly there as she looked into his, a seductive smile as she took his order, suggesting that she would be all too happy to take another. He was amazed that he viewed the promise mentally without evidence of physical response. Delectable creature, he thought, knowing that normally the evening would lead to a most certain conclusion. Isabel, he mused; thoughts of her had simply left him uninterested in another. It did not bother him overmuch, knowing the decision to be his. He reasoned that in the coming long months his physical needs would prevail, but for the moment he rather enjoyed the special feeling that Isabel had left him with. His thoughts drifted to moments they had spent together, the remembrance of silky golden hair spread on a pillow, large grey eyes darkened with passion as they stared up into his, soft arms wrapped about his neck as she pulled him down to her. . . . He felt a tightening in his loins, his musings bringing the result that the buxom barmaid had not. Throwing down a large measure of his ale, he thrust his mind to a different path, unwittingly turning to the other occupants of his table. Sipping from the tankard, he was amazed to realize that they were heatedly involved in a discussion of some vague theological point. He peered at them through half-closed lids, unwilling to eavesdrop on their conversation even as his curiosity was sparked. The smaller of the two, with thick brown hair that seemed to drop onto his forehead though it was pushed back repeatedly in an almost subconscious gesture, had fixed on the other with penetrating brown eyes, which gleamed with an excitement not matched to the placid expression he wore. William fought a smile, recognizing the look. Whatever their discussion was about, the smaller man was warming for the kill, a point caught, a win at hand. He shifted his gaze to the stranger's companion and felt himself tense. Black eyes burned with a discerning ferocity William had rarely seen before. Involuntarily, his memory focused on another, long forgotten, and he shifted uncomfortably in his seat. Suddenly, he became aware that their conversation had ceased and they were looking at him.

"I am sorry," the smaller man offered with a warm smile that met his honest brown eyes. "Did we disturb you? 'Tis a habit, I fear. We become so involved in our own verbal sparring that we forget that we might be disturbing others.''

"Nay," William shook his head, offering a smile as way of apology for his own earlier rude behavior. "But I could not help but to overhear your conversation." His gaze lit lightly on their apparel, his puzzlement deepening. They were dressed as merchants, though the taller man's garments were obviously rich and costly. Then he remembered the tavern's proximity to the University of Paris. "You are teachers at the university?"

"Aye," the stranger answered with a grin, pushing back the unruly forelock once again. "Though priests, we often assume this guise, to allow needed time to ourselves. I am Stephen Langton, and this is my good friend, Lothario de Conti de Segni."

William blinked. "Of the noble family of Scotti?" He stared at de Segni numbly.

"You know of my family?" the dark-haired man asked, his eyes glinting with humor.

"Aye, milord, there are few who do not know of one of Italy's most noble families. I am honored to meet you." William fought a smile of his own, almost laughing out loud as he recalled how he had been prepared to toss this man out into the street on his ass for daring to speak to him. Noting the grin, it was obvious that the other man's thoughts ran in close parallel with his own.

"You need not address me as 'milord,' sir," he offered, "I am a priest and my heritage is no longer at issue. Stephen and Lothario, I believe, should do for this evening. And you, sir. Your accent is—ah, Norman French, heavily touched with Anglo-Saxon, therefore I assume you are English. Will you be in Paris long?"

William realized that he had been rude, and unwise, to ask such blunt and personal questions of his table companions. But they appeared unaware of such rudeness, and their manner was friendly, and he saw no reason not to answer their question in turn. "Only for a few weeks more. My business has been with Philip."

"Ah," de Segni smiled, "an envoy from King Richard, are you not?"

William started at de Segni's perceptiveness. He had an unsettled feeling that this one, as with the other of his memory so like the dark-haired priest, could look into a man's soul and extract the truth no matter how hard he tried to hide it. "Aye, I am William Marshal, envoy of my lord Richard, Coeur de Lion."

"William Marshal. Of course." De Segni smiled, but William did not miss the slight narrowing of his eyes. "I have heard of you. Your exploits with Henry Plantagenet caused those here on the continent many sleepless nights and not a little discomfort."

"You are too kind, Father de Segni," William answered evenly.

De Segni chuckled at the answer, and Langton grinned with delight as he ordered another round. "Really, Marshal," de Segni protested, "you must call me Lotario, if only for this evening! I insist that we must be on a first-name basis, for there are many questions I would ask of which only friends may discuss."

"If we might exchange answers," he said quietly.

"Ah, William. But of course. Answers, information, but nothing, I assure you, to compromise. Agreed?"

"Agreed."

"There is much we wish to know about what is happening in England, William," Langton said, his enthusiasm evident. "Information we receive here is, ah, somewhat biased."

"What could I possibly tell you?" William asked casually. "Surely the church informs you of what you need to know."

"Only on matters of religion or politics," de Segni shrugged. "Of the people, their feelings, we know very little."

Their conversation ceased momentarily as the barmaid returned with sloshing tankards of ale, which she set on the table, pausing as she set William's in front of him. She leaned over unnecessarily to afford him a generous view of her breasts, which strained against the thin material of her low-cut chemise, the only other garment worn with the full wool skirt. She paused, locking her eyes with William's for an instant, her tongue passing suggestively over a full mouth before she turned on her heels and sauntered away.

Langton's gaze followed the woman for a moment before he turned back to William and grinned. "An eager wench, she appears to be somewhat attracted to you."

"Not interested," William said lazily, turning to his tankard.

Langton glanced at the barmaid and back to William, his brows drawn in puzzlement.

"Tell me, William," de Segni interjected, looking at William with amusement, "what is it about me that bothers you?"

William started. His first impulse was to pass off the question politely, but his accustomed manner of bluntness saw him to the question. "You remind me of another I knew long ago."

"Oh?" De Segni looked truly surprised. "And who might that be?"

"Thomas Becket." William ignored the slight gasp from Langton as he regarded de Segni with an even stare.

"Really," de Segni answered. "You knew Becket well?"

"Very well," William answered, turning the tankard slowly between his fingers.

"I would ask what you thought of the man, but it would be obviously compromising," de Segni observed with a smirk.

"The man was an enigma." William looked up at de Segni. "His personality was of incredible power. Often, when we spoke, I sensed a deep, disturbing unhappiness. A drive he little sought to understand himself but one that took him to his end. It was as though he had forseen his future and could do little, nay, *would* do little, to stay it."

"You see me driven to a dire end?" De Segni's brow arched, though he regarded William keenly.

"Nay, Father, that is not the similarity I see. But the desire, the obsession, to see you to your purpose, your fate. I trust that the result will be far different than our archbishop of Canterbury's."

"It shall be, William," de Segni answered, exchanging a long look of understanding with him. "I assure you that it shall be."

"The matter remains unclear—about what happened," Langton interjected. "You were close to Henry. Tell me, did he truly plot Becket's death?"

"Not in the way that was said," William answered, pulling his attention to the question. "Henry often said things in his cups which he barely remembered the next day. Oh, he was angry with Becket, I would not deny it, but he loved the man, he never would have harmed him. But he was king, and as such his word . . . I warned him often to caution himself about Becket or there would be some who took him at his word. . . . We were in Normandy, as you probably know. Henry was drunk, ranting and raving about what he felt was Becket's unfaithfulness. I attempted to see him to his bed, but he would have none of it. In a moment it was done, the words spoken that the man who would rid him of Becket's presence would find great favor. He saw to his bed after that, but it was too late. Three left the hall, making their way to England where they saw to it— expecting to find favor with the crown. Stupid fools!" he added softly, lost in a memory. "Henry did not even recall saying it . . . "

"A king cannot afford such leisure," de Segni murmured.

The three fell to silence, intent upon their thoughts as they drew from their tankards. At last, it was Langton who broke the silence. "It is said that Henry's favor was often found by those who served him well. As with you, my friend. You are favored with Philip, and he had made no secret of his pleasure that you have been so honored."

William glanced up sharply, his eyes narrowing with a flare of guarded anger. Damn. Whenever he sought to forget, there was always someone to remind him. "To what honors do you refer, Langton?" he asked quietly.

"Do not bristle, Marshal." Langton smiled. "I refer to your marriage and the lands it brings to you. Oh, aye, news does travel of such an event. When one has become the most powerful peer of the English realm we are likely to know of it. Before you anger," he added, noting the storm that was beginning to gather in William's eyes, "know that Henry's decision is deemed with approval by the church. You are seen as one who can appease factions which would otherwise bend for war. It can only be viewed that God guided Henry in his choice."

There was little that William could say in answer to that statement. He could merely shrug as he moodily returned to his cup. Gradually, their conversation turned to other matters. By the end of the evening he found himself warmed in easy sodality, sharing an ease with them he had not experienced for many years and with few friends. Odd, with these two he had only just met. Perhaps that is the easiest way, he thought in a moment of clarity. It is easier with those who do not know you too well. No pretenses, no reason for guarded device, as they will never be seen again. As the hour drew late and they sensed the end of the evening, Langton called for the last round.

"You have not told us of your plans," he asked. "I presume that you will be leaving with King Richard soon for Acre."

"Aye," William nodded. "We leave before the end of the month." Even as he answered Langton, he wondered why the prospect gave him no thrill, the accustomed surge of pleasure he normally would have experienced strangely absent. Shrugging, he passed off his ferment, forcing his emotions to accept what amazingly seemed suddenly so hard-won.

De Segni watched William as he answered, and his shrewd dark eyes narrowed speculatively. "Indeed," he smiled. "For those whose hearts strive toward Jerusalem, there is no more noble quest. Our blessings go with you, William—wherever your soul shall lead you."

# 8

ELIZABETH had been unerring. Isabel's days were filled with the needs of her lands and people, giving her little time to dwell upon the fact of her loneliness. She could not have imagined how she could have dealt with it but for the endless responsibilities and decisions that placed their demands upon her, finally releasing her into a welcomed, exhausted sleep each night.

Her morning began just before dawn when her maid, Corliss, awoke her. Isabel had chosen the young woman for her sunny disposition and easy manner; Corliss's large brown eyes constantly glinted with mischief and humor. Isabel would not have embarrassed the young girl with unnecessary familiarity, but in spite of their positions an easy relationship developed, giving Isabel considerable ease.

Isabel pulled herself from the warm bed as a part of her longed to fall back and steal another hour's sleep. As she gave in to a yawn, she noticed through sleep-filled eyes that while Corliss moved about, tending to the needs of her mistress, her young mouth was drawn in a tight, disapproving line.

"Corliss, what is it?" she asked against another

yawn. "Is there something that troubles you?"

The girl looked up from the washbowl she had filled with warmed water from the kettle over the fire. She straightened at the question and tugged at the long apron that reached to the floor over the dark brown wool skirt she wore. "Nay, milady," she said a bit tightly.

"Tell me," Isabel insisted, pulling herself from the bed. She crossed to the washbowl where she splashed the sleep from her eyes and accepted the warmed towel the girl handed to her.

"Well, milady, 'tis just that . . . well . . . 'tis you, milady. We're all most worried about you, with the babe, and all. You've been working too hard."

Isabel was deeply touched by her concern, and it was obvious that the subject had been discussed among the household. "And Waverly." Isabel smiled. "Does he agree?"

"Nay, milady," the girl sniffed disapprovingly. "He said 'twas good for you, and that he'd be the one to decide when it be too much for you."

"I suspect that he is right." Isabel laughed. "Truly, Corliss, I am fine. I am touched by your concern, but Waverly is right, the work is good for me. Now fetch my gown, as there is much to do today."

Mass was followed by a quick breakfast of bread and wine, and Isabel began her day with the irascible steward, reviewing the accounts and the inventory of the manor's provisions. Instructions for letters to be written were given to father Delano, the chaplain, before Isabel could make her way to the kitchens to discuss the results of her inventory with Julia, Chepstow's able head cook. The formidable woman was the only one of the enormous staff who did not quake in fear of Waverly. In fact, fur usually flew, and anything else within reach, when the two strong-minded individuals battled wills. Isabel had given up trying to convince Julia that, as steward, Waverly was most certainly in charge of Julia's precious stores. It never would have occurred to her to retire one of them; they had been with the family since her father's time. But she now understood her mother's reluctance when she had been forced to interfere between the two.

As Isabel entered the kitchens, the heavy smell of the roasting venison that was turning on large spits over enormous fires assailed her. She grasped the edge of the table nearby, feeling her stomach heave as her head began to spin, and for a frightening moment she thought she was going to be sick. Suddenly, large hands grasped her shoulders, and she found herself propelled through the kitchens and out the door to the kitchen yard, where she was plopped unceremoniously onto the steps.

"Put yer head 'tween yer legs, milady."

It was Julia's gruff voice, and Isabel found herself complying without argument.

"Jus' a bit of the queasy, lass. Had it meself when I was bearin'. Few more weeks, 'haps a fortnights, and it'll stop grabb'n ye. 'Twas the smell of the roast that done it. Aye, it'll do it every time."

The dizziness did pass and Isabel's stomach began to settle into place. She raised her head slowly and looked up into Julia's round face where she stood before her, her hands akimbo on her broad hips. "Yer color's comin' ba. Ye'll be all right now. Know it gets bad but I promise it'll pass, luv."

In the face of Julia's easy affection Isabel felt suddenly overwhelmed. Her loneliness, the heavy weight of responsibility and fear of the future suddenly came upon her. She sniffed, biting her lower lip to fight back the tears that pressed at the back of her eyelids. Seeing her grief, Julia sat down beside her and drew her into her beefy arms, cradling her against her large breasts. "Now, now, luv. I know how ye be feel'n. Yer too young ta be goin' through all this without kinfolk ta help ye or the comfort of a husband. But ye'll do it, yer made of sturdy stuff. It'll be right. And the babe'll come and ye'll have a new life to fill yours."

Isabel swallowed back the tears and sat up. "Thank you, Julia," she smiled, sniffing. "I do feel better. We can go back to the kitchens and . . ."

"Nay, milady." Julia stood up with her and again drew behind a thin veil of formality. "I advise that ye wait each day 'til after midmeal when ye 'ave somethin' in yer stomach. It'll see ye better ta the task."

"Perhaps you're right." The memory of the cooking meat caused her stomach to flop unpleasantly. "I'll see to the spring shed instead. The pantler's accounts of butter seems drastically low, and I should check it. It is cool there and I should be fine."

Isabel entered the spring shed, where the butter and cream were stored, a low thatched-roof structure cooled by a small spring that ran through its center. She began to check the figures the pantler had given to Waverly but soon gave it up. Suddenly, she simply did not seem to care. It all seemed so unimportant. She sat on a low barrel, resting her chin in her hands as she watched the water of the spring trickle by, her thoughts fixed on the water as it tripped over and around the cobbled rock-bed. How long, she thought. How many years would he be gone? Their child would most certainly be walking before he returned. He—or she—would be a stranger to him. So little time they had been given, how much they both will have forgotten. It would be like beginning again. How strange—they would have a child, but it would be so new. Would he change? War must certainly change him. He had been through the same before . . . but never with a family at home. Would he even wish to return, after so much time?

She had not told him about her mother's part in their marriage, uncertain of how he would react. Their relations were still so tenuous, with enough problems besetting them, she had no intention of introducing a potential wedge that might further widen the chasm. Of one thing she was certain: her mother had used Eleanor as well. She had been presented to the queen at Winchester during the celebration of Richard's coronation.

The queen had been warm and solicitous, inquiring about her mother and then about her marriage. But Isabel had been quick to read between the lines. Eleanor's interest was concerned with the wealth and position given to a favorite, one she considered loyal to her son, and it was obvious that she looked upon the match as beneficial to the crown. Isabel wondered, her lovely mouth drawing into a grim smile, what the queen would say if she knew Eve's true reasons for giving her consent. Consent? The thought made her chuckle. She could see her mother's fine hand molding and shaping their lives, even that of the queen's, Henry's, and Richard's. A common mistake of the powerful, she mused, to assume complete control of those beneath them, to be so confident in their power that they overlook subtlety in others. A lesson she would consider most carefully.

She leaned back against the wall of the shed and closed her eyes. After all was said, what did any of it truly matter? I have the lands, the power, and I am lonely, so very lonely. His child grows within me, and he is not here. And when he returns, what will he want—what do I want? Intimate thoughts washed through her mind, the feel of his hands as they stroked her body, the sweet bliss he could bring and tears of regret bit at her eyes.

She could not put him from her thoughts, in spite of Elizabeth's advice. She could not. To do so would be denying his existence. To think of him, the memories, were bittersweet but as necessary now as breathing. Nay, good or bad, he would be part of her life until she no longer drew breath.

A sound from the far corner of the shed startled her out of her musings, and her head jerked about to the source. She saw nothing, and for a moment she thought she had imagined it. A rat, she thought with a shudder. I must have someone come and check for vermin. She leaned back once again, closing her eyes to reescape into her dreamings when she felt something brush against her legs. She gasped and drew back, a shot of repulsion shuddering through her body. Pulling them up against her, she leaned over and stared with amazement into the large yellow eyes of a half-grown grey-striped cat. It sat there looking at her with detached aloofness as its long tail wrapped about its legs, the tip barely twitching.

She lowered her legs and leaned forward. "Hello," she said softly. "Am I intruding?" The cat got up and rubbed against her legs, allowing her to stroke its back. After a few moments it walked a few feet away and sat down again, fixing her once again with the same detached stare. "Are you content here among the cream and butter?" she said, then laughed at herself. What was she waiting for, a response? She really had to do something about herself—now she was talking to a cat! She stood up and finished her inventory quickly, then left the shed, shutting the door tightly behind her. As she began walking across the inner bailey to the keep, she sensed something nearby, and she turned to find that the cat was following her. "Where did you come from?" she laughed. "Obviously you have your own way out of that shed." She continued on, glancing over her shoulder occasionally to find that the determined feline appeared to be staying with her. The fact gave her an odd sort of comfort, and to her surprise she found herself hoping that it would continue, even as she knew she was being quite ridiculous.

She crossed to the steps of the keep, through the doors and around the screen to the great hall. Waverly was entering the hall at precisely the same moment, and he came to an abrupt halt, his wizened eyes growing wide as he fixed on a spot immediately behind Isabel.

"Milady, there appears to be a cat following you," he observed as one grey brow arched.

"Apparently so," she returned, continuing across the hall. "When the men return from their hunt see that the dogs are securely tied." She fought a smile as she crossed to the stairs, knowing what his expression must be.

As she opened the door to her chamber and stepped

inside, she turned to see if indeed her companion had chosen to accompany her this far. The scrawny animal whipped through the door, and Isabel shut it with an odd feeling of satisfaction and happiness.

The cat raced across the room and landed in the center of the bed, whereupon it immediately set to bathing itself as if its presence in the chamber were the most customary course of events. Corliss, who had been tending to her mistress's gowns, peered about the door of the wardrobe, her eyes coming to light on the newcomer, and they understandably widened. "What is that?" she squeaked, forgetting to add the proper term of address for her mistress.

"By all accounts it appears to be a cat," Isabel replied, repressing a smile.

"I know it's a cat! . . . ah, milady." Corliss flushed in spite of her surprise. "But what is it doin' here?"

" 'Twould seem that it has come to live with us." Isabel smiled. "Go to the kitchens and bring a met of cream." When the startled maid did not respond Isabel repeated the request. "Oh, aye, and a small amount of raw meat."

Too astonished to reply, Corliss left the room quickly, and Isabel had to repress her laughter, knowing what the conversation in the kitchens was sure to be. She sat on the edge of the bed and tentatively held out her hand, fearing that she would frighten the animal. To her surprise and delight the cat paused in its methodical bathing and turned its head to lick her hand with the same steady intent of purpose.

"Well," Isabel said softly, "I believe that you have truly decided to stay." She watched the cat for a moment as it returned to its own grooming. "You must have a name," she said aloud. "I will not call you 'Cat,' nor shall anyone else." She thought for a moment then smiled. "Of course. Shadwell! It means 'from the shed spring.' The perfect name! What do you think, Shad?" The cat paused for a moment, its pink tongue extended slightly from its mouth as it seemed to consider her words. Isabel giggled at the ridiculous picture it made, but the animal quickly regained its poise and returned to its cleaning.

Corliss, who had barely recovered by the time that she had reached the kitchens, was then horrified to realize that she was expected to ask Julia for a met of cream and a "bit of raw meat"—for a cat. Trembling, she approached the grandiose head cook. Julia, as fate would have it, was in a high temper over a matter of a haunch of pork left too long on the spit. Noting the cook's mood, Corliss fervently prayed for the ground to suddenly open and swallow her up. To her shock, the request from Chepstow's mistress elicited a mere raise of surprised brows and a quizzical look, followed by a shrug and the requested items. Mystified, but fervently thanking her patron saint for deliverance, Corliss scurried away with her burdens, leaving the kitchens abuzz.

By midmeal d'Erley had returned with Chepstow's knights. He was met by Waverly, who calmly informed him that the dogs were to be chained. "Are there guests expected?" John asked as he motioned to his men to comply with the order.

"It appears that one has arrived," Waverly answered, leaving the bemused knight to return to his own duties.

The men were well into their meal when Isabel came into the hall. Wide eyes, elbow punching, and torn meat half protruding from mouths met her entrance and that of her companion who trotted confidently behind him. The dogs came up against their chains, and the hall was quickly filled with the sound of the baying hounds. A stunned d'Erley finally recovered enough to bellow at the animals, lowering the din to anxious and dissatisfied whining. Isabel calmly took her place as Shad jumped to a spot at the end of the vacant table, whereupon he promptly set to another bath, particularly tending to the claws on his front feet.

"Milady," John cleared his throat, now understanding the steward's quip, "may I ask where *that* came from?"

"*That*, John, is a cat. It came from the spring shed," she replied, her mouth twitching. She took a measure of meat from the mazer which Thomas, John's squire, was holding for her. The youth's eyes were widely fixed on the animal. "His name is Shad."

Though it took some members of the household longer to accept the situation than others, Shadwell apparently accepted it as his just due. It soon became a common sight to see the young mistress of Striguil with her ever-present companion. Soon even the most hardened knights could be spotted slipping Shad a morsel from their trenchers or giving the cat an absent-minded scratch behind the ear when he rubbed against their legs for attention. But only Isabel was favored with true affection from the animal, as he curled up in his mistress's lap when they sat before the fire in the great hall of an evening. Perhaps it was the independent yet possessive nature of the animal that changed their opinion. Or perhaps it was due to the change in Isabel after his arrival. She took more time to care for herself, napping in the afternoons with Shad curled up next to her. She took time from her duties to play with the animal, and in general she appeared more relaxed, more content than she had since William's departure. Whatever the reason, Shad assumed a prominent position, even with Waverly, who could be caught occasionally giving in to a hint of a smile over the cat's antics.

The summer weeks lengthened into August; the hedgerows were cut to allow the cattle into harvested pastures, barley, wheat and rye having given a generous yield; and daily chores were met by those of Striguil to assure a winter without want. Isabel moved about her duties, seeing to the needs of her people and her lands, fulfilling each with enthusiasm while appearing more content, seeming less driven. But there remained a sadness, an element missing that was all too obvious to those about her who cared.

Julia sent for her one morning after a particularly heated row with Waverly over the matter of rose sugars. "How am I expected ta make flathon without sugar, might I ask?" Julia snapped. "They're yer favorites, milady, I only wished ta please!"

"Aye, Julia," Isabel sighed. "They were quite delicious. Perhaps you might serve fruit for now. The sugar must be conserved, as you know. We have no idea when the next shipment may arrive from Cyprus. While I am here we should check the supply of candles," she added, wanting to change the subject.

"More are needed," Julia grumbled, knowing that Waverly had won this round.

"An appropriate chore for this afternoon. Have the boys bring the tallow, and we shall see that they are begun." Isabel left no room for argument as she spun about and left for the room below the kitchens where the candles were made.

By midmorning the small room was filled with the heat of the boiling kettles of melting tallow, the fires kept high as the sour smoke filled the room, burning the eyes of those who worked. The light blue linen of Isabel's gown clung to her with sweat as she supervised the dipping of the wicks into the molten liquid, dipped again and yet again until the candles reached the appropriate width, then were tied to poles strung about the ceiling to dry. Her hair had long since escaped from its pins. Damp tendrils clung about her face as rivulets of moisture beaded on her flushed cheeks. But she gave no thought to her appearance as she directed boys in the making of the precious candles, noting each in a tally in her ledger as the winter's supply was met.

As the day lengthened, she felt a dart of pain through her back and she stretched, rubbing the small of her back as the other hand rested on her growing stomach. She glanced at the row of small windows along the far side of the room, promising herself that she would have them widened to allow more of the heat and the smoke to escape and wondering why it had not been done before. Just then a sound attracted her, and she turned in time to see one of the boys drop a line of finished candles into a vat of bubbling tallow. Heat, fatigue, smoke, and the pain in her back overcame her and she snapped at the youngster, immediately regretting the sharpness of her words as his small face paled under her reprimand. Her expression softened and she opened her mouth to retract her words when another voice was heard.

"They are not lost, only misplaced for the moment. I fear that you will have to do the work again." The boy's face lightened, then paled as he gaped at the source, his large brown eyes staring past Isabel to a point behind her, as did all in the small room. Isabel spun about at the sound of a familiar voice, her mouth dropping open as she identified its source.

"William!" she gasped.

He was leaning against the doorway, still in full armor of mail, his surcoat dust-caked and grimy from his ride. She wondered in a flash how long he had been standing there watching. Immediately she became painfully aware of how she must look, hot, sweaty, and disheveled. "Are you not going to greet me, wife?"

"Where did you come from?" she asked, not believing.

"France." His eyes moved over her slowly, and she felt herself cringe under his appraisal.

"But . . . did you not go with Richard . . . on the crusade?"

"Apparently not." He grinned.

"But . . ."

He held out a hand to her and smiled. "Perhaps we could find a better place to speak of this. You can send another to help." His eyes fixed again on her belly, and his manner became more serious. "I do not reason that this is the best place for you, considering other responsibilities you carry."

They sat in the great hall, their chairs close but separated by an awkwardness, a shyness unspoken but lying between them with its own presence. Isabel had felt it as they had crossed through the kitchen, aware of the speculative glances thrown in their direction. Her pride had kept her manner light before others, but now that they were alone it descended like a heavy blanket. This man was her husband, she told herself, it was his child she carried within her. He was no stranger. But he was.

The man she remembered, had fantasized about in his absence, seemed different than the one who sat so close to her now in reality. This one was of flesh and blood, had expectations that suddenly seemed apart from the dreams she had molded so exquisitely night after lonely night.

"Why, William?" she asked softly. "How is it that you are here?"

"That sounds slightly like an accusation," he commented, watching her.

"Of course not!" she protested. "I simply meant that I did not expect you! You were to be gone for . . . for years! How is it that you are not on the crusade? Has it been delayed?"

"Nay, Richard has left for Lyons." He shifted, stretching his long legs out before him.

"I—do not understand. Why did you not go with him?"

William did not answer, and she could not be certain that he had heard her. His thoughts were apparently distracted as his eyes moved over her slowly. Her mouth opened to repeat the question when the words froze on her tongue. She recognized the look he was giving her as one every wife knows, and she flushed, suddenly feeling terribly self-conscious.

He was slumped in his chair, his head resting on the heel of his hand as he studied her. "How have you been feeling?" he asked quietly.

"I am fine, William," she answered awkwardly. Why was she so nervous?

"No sickness nor vapors?"

"A little," she said, shrugging. "But less and less now." She hurried on with a timorous smile. "William, I have been thoughtless. You must want a bath and a hearty meal. I know I could use a scrubbing. I must look a fright." She cringed inwardly, hoping that he had not noticed the nervousness in her voice.

"You are beautiful," he offered with a smile. "However, the bath is in order and as for the meal, I have not eaten since . . . "

Their attention was drawn to a commotion heard behind the hall screen, and d'Erley entered with a contingent of Chepstow's knights, his face bright with pleasure. "William! God's breath, I knew it must be you! Who else would head that rag tag mob of men-at-arms without!"

William rose to greet his old friend and former squire, and the two clasped arms in affectionate greeting, William's pleasure as great as d'Erley's. "Rag tag, is it, John? You used to be part of that mob, if I recall."

"William!" Isabel exclaimed. "Have you truly left your men without? Has no one seen to them?"

"I was anxious to see you." William grinned. "But never fear, Waverly is even now finding quarters for them. The knights have been given the lower wing by the river."

"Sweet Mother Mary," d'Erley rolled his eyes. "You should see to yourself, William. You look as if half the soil of England is upon you, and the odor I detect hanging about confirms it. Have you been unable to obtain a squire of my caliber? 'Tis understandable, of course."

As if on cue a gangling young man in William's colors appeared from behind the buttery screen. His sandy blond hair was in need of a trim, and his large green eyes darted fearfully about as his hands clenched at the sides, betraying his nervousness.

"Have you seen to it, Allan?" William asked.

"Aye, Sir William," the boy answered, his voice cracking slightly.

"What do we have here?" John laughed. "William, have you taken to using children for your squires?"

"Actually, John, I decided that a younger lad was called for so that I might train him earlier, hoping that he would not develop the bad habits of his predecessor," William quipped with a smirk.

"Point taken," d'Erley chortled.

"Would you be wanting a bath now, Sir William?" the boy asked.

"Nay, lad, you may see to yourself." Then he added, his deep blue eyes crinkling, "My lady will see to my needs. In fact, she insists upon it." He ignored the sharp draw of breath that came from Isabel's direction, and he turned to d'Erley as Allan left the room. "His name is Allan fitz Ulred. He came to my attention from a priest I met in Paris. His family was killed in a siege upon their castle in Anjou, and the boy has been on his own since he was twelve. The bishop had taken him in, but he felt that Allan was unsuited for the clergy. He shows promise; I think you'll be impressed." He turned to Isabel. "Now, milady, about that bath . . ."

As they walked down the long hallway to their chamber, the servants bustling ahead of them with steaming buckets of water and warmed towels, William leaned over to Isabel and spoke low in her ear. "You see, milady, I have not forgotten your wishes. In fact, I have remembered everything about you."

# 9

THE servants departed and they were alone. Isabel wondered fleetingly where Shad had departed to. His mornings were normally spent curled up in the window embrasure for as long as the sun warmed the stone. But thoughts of Shad were quickly dismissed as she became fixed on the two steaming tubs that centered the room.

Nervously, she helped William remove his hauberk and gambeson, folding them with great care as she set them on the war chest at the foot of the huge bed. Then she stood frozen, wondering what she should do. There were two tubs. Was she expected to assist her husband, or should she see to her own bath? The long months spent without a man in her life had left her as nervous as a bride. Indeed, she was barely that, though she felt she should be more, and she felt totally inadequate.

"See to your bath, Isabel."

She glanced up at William and flinched at the amusement clear in the startling blue of his eyes. Those eyes of which she had dreamed. In her dreams it had seemed so simple, their relations so natural. Why did she feel now that she was roomed with a stranger? She turned away, willing her fingers to work as she slowly unlaced the ties to her gown. Once done, she had no choice but to shrug her shoulders from the blue linen and let it drop to her feet. She felt her body tremble at the sound of splashing water behind her as he entered his bath. Painfully, she reached for the shoulder strap of her chemise, willing herself to numbness as she determined to see the matter through.

"Isabel, would you hand me the soap?"

She let out her breath, thankful for the respite, and turned to comply. She handed him the soap with a timid smile, forcing her eyes not to travel from his face to the tub. She began to turn away, but he grabbed her wrist, pulling her gently to him. "I am reminded that you were firm on the matter of my bath, Isabel? Would you prefer that I call another to help?"

She swallowed, feeling the heat rise in her cheeks even as the thought of another tending him straightened her back, and she took the soap from him. Awkwardly, she began to scrub him. Beginning with his back, she did not see his mouth twitch in his struggle not to laugh. She lathered his arms and hair, then she picked up the pitcher of water nearby and poured it over his head to rinse. She smiled in spite of herself as he sputtered and struggled to wipe the soap from his eyes. "You could have warned me, woman!" he coughed.

She picked up the soap again and began to lather his chest, her hand lingering over the hard muscles of his arms and body, and her cheeks pinked again as her imagination began to wander. He leaned back in the tub and watched her expression, reading her mind as his eyes began to gleam with speculation. "There are other parts of me calling for attention, milady," he said with calm deliberation while his eyes danced.

She missed the amusement in his eyes, hearing only the sternness of his voice, and she took a deep breath, determined to see the matter through. As her hand disappeared beneath the water, he gasped.

It happened without warning and with a squeak she found herself in the tub with him. His laughter filled the room as she struggled against him, screaming profanity that would have done a hardened soldier proud. He held her to him, in spite of her struggles, until he brought her mouth up to his, ceasing her tirade with a kiss that took the breath from her. Her lips softened beneath his as her memory responded to his touch, recognition sharpened to the feel of him as nothing else could have done.

When she lay relaxed in his arms, the water swirling gently about them, he pulled his mouth from hers and looked down into languid grey eyes. "Where did you learn to swear like that?" he asked, truly interested.

"From my mother," she whispered, wishing he would kiss her again.

"From your lady mother?" he chortled with disbelief.

"My lady mother was raised among men," she parried, noting the way the dark curls of his hair wrapped about his ears when wet.

He planted a kiss on the end of her nose. "Are you comfortable?"

"We are wasting water," she observed, remembering the other tub.

"I would hardly consider it a waste. Though I do not think you need this." He pulled her chemise from her and let it drop, dripping, to the side of the tub. "There, is that not better?" he asked huskily. His mouth came down upon hers once again, his hands moving over her body with a sudden eagerness that made her gasp beneath his lips. She opened her mouth to him, drawing in his tongue, which searched eagerly as his hand moved to a breast to fondle until his fingers found a hardening nibble. He rubbed it slowly, savoring the feel of her after so many months, determined to experience fully each step of an experience he had fantasized over and over again in his journey back to her. He raised his head from her once again, his eyes matching hers with desire as his mouth pulled into a smile at the puzzlement he read in her expression. "Finish my bath," he murmured.

She complied, passion dispelling her embarrassment

as she studied her task, her skin tingling with promise as she touched each part of him. He returned the favor, lingering over each part of her beautiful body, their tensions heightened to a taut pitch before it was done. He rose, lifting her from the tub to set her on the rug; then, taking a towel, they set to drying each other. Isabel became light-headed with desire and pleasure as William's eyes moved over her, lingering on each part he dried with a blatant possessiveness that made her think she would go mad. He swept her into his arms and carried her to the bed even as he wondered if he would be able to contain himself much longer. As he lay down beside her, she reached down and took him into her hand, bringing a sharp gasp from him. "Oh God, Isabel, no," he moaned. He reached down and slipped his fingers between her thighs, almost moaning with relief to find her moist and ready for him. He had wanted to bring her slowly, but he knew he could not wait. The months of waiting, the softness of her body against his, her hands upon him, had done their damage and he knew he could wait no longer. He pulled her beneath him, spreading her legs with his knees and entered as gently as his driving body would allow. He held himself back as long as he could, plunging with measured deliberation as he tried to bring her with him. To his relief her hips began to move beneath his in measured rhythm, but he came quickly, exploding within her as his large body shuddered in release.

She had trembled as he entered her, taking him within her in a wash of love, wanting the feel of him, the deep comfort it would bring, the intimacy she had longed for the past long months. She sensed that he could not wait for her; she could almost feel the pain of his need. Smiling, she thrust her hips up to him, knowing that her movements would make the decision for him. He was home and she knew that there would be a new beginning.

As his breathing returned to normal she stroked his back tenderly, the hardened muscles comforting beneath her palms. She closed her eyes and experienced the feel of him on her body and still within her, deliciously aware of the pleasure, the release that she had given to him. She wished that he would give her the full pressure of his body, pressing her into the soft down of the bed, but she knew he would not. He rested on his elbows, and she was aware that it was because of the child that grew between them. He lifted his head where it was nestled at her ear and traced a line of gentle kisses across her cheek to the corner of her mouth. "I have missed you," he murmured.

"As I have, you," she whispered. "Are you truly home, William?"

"Has a specter done this to you?" he grinned.

"If it could I would have conjured it up before this," she parried.

"Oh? Have your needs been such?" he asked as he nuzzled her ear.

"You left me wanting more, milord," she breathed. "Aye, I will admit it. I have longed for your hands upon me, the delightful things you do to me. Is it a wonder why women look elsewhere when their men go to the crusades?"

He tensed, raising up to look down at her. "Are you excusing infidelity, Isabel?" he asked.

"Nay, of course not, but can a woman be expected to again become innocent once she has known love? The months have been overlong, milord. Can you say that you have been faithful all this long time that we have been parted?"

"Are you expecting me to account for my time?"

"I am expecting you to answer the question you yourself have posed."

He rolled away from her onto his back. "I have held no other woman in my arms since the day that we were wed, as it has been my choice to do so. Is that what you would hear?" His voice was quiet and even. She could hear an edge of anger, but she was warmed by the knowledge that he had been faithful to her and was amazed that it should anger him so to admit it. "Truly?" she asked softly.

"I have said so," he snapped, turning his head to look at her.

She started, her own anger rising in the face of his unreasonable attitude. "Why are you upset? What have I done?"

"I do not like explaining myself," he grumbled, staring moodily at the ceiling.

"I did not ask you to."

"You asked me if I had been faithful."

"Oh, William, the question was rhetorical. I truly did not expect the answer you gave me."

He turned his head to look at her with a puzzled frown. "Do you find it so amazing that I could be faithful?"

"I do not know you that well, William," she answered quietly as she looked away.

She could feel him watching her, but she would not look at him. She was deeply hurt by his attitude, and angry that he could treat her so. They lay there in a tense silence. Slowly she sensed a changing current between them and realized, with horror, that he wanted her again! How could he, after treating her like this? The distant sound of the bell for midmeal was heard, and she literally leapt at the excuse, flinging herself from the bed as she saw, from the corner of her eye, that he had reached for her. "They will be waiting for us," she tossed over her shoulder as she pulled a robe about her shoulders. "You must appear, William, or they will be sorely disappointed."

They entered the hall to a rousing hail by the knights and their ladies in tribute to William's homecoming. As they settled into their chairs at the empty table, Allan appeared to pour wine for them both, which was raised in a toast as d'Erley rose from his chair to launch into a short speech. The room turned to happy banter as servants rushed in, and soon the tables bent beneath the weight of Julia's tribute to his homecoming, and the wine and ale flowed freely, adding to the merriment. By the third course, William was already becoming quite full, but the next event whetted his appetite anew. Julia herself emerged from the kitchens bearing a met with a large salmon encased in a layer of pastry sculptured to resemble sea coral, wafts of steam escaping in light trails from slits marked along the sides. The succulent aroma of the salmon filled the room, and William's mouth watered, his eyes rolling with comic pleasure over Julia's efforts to prepare his favorite dish. The met was placed before him, similar dishes carried out on other arms to those at the trestle tables, and Allan quickly carved the fish and served an ample helping on William's trencher.

It happened so quickly that even though it became the subject of conversation for many days, all well out of William's hearing, each version of the story differed. As William bent to the mouth-watering task of dipping his fingers to the flaky fish, a grey flash appeared from nowhere, a large ball of fur was suddenly in his trencher, and then it was gone and with it, the fish.

"What the hell!" William roared.

"Oh Sweet Lady Mother," Isabel groaned.

"Damnation, that cat!" Julia shrieked. "I'll skin his hide when I catch him!"

"Cat?" William asked dumbly, staring at Isabel while vaguely aware that the room had erupted into uproarious laughter.

"Shadwell," Isabel answered meekly, wishing that everyone would stop laughing.

"Shadwell?" William repeated, his face coloring with anger.

"Well, I call him Shad," she answered, her voice trailing off.

"There's a *cat* in here?" He glanced about, noticing for the first time that the dogs were chained. It struck him passing strange that they seemed not to have noticed the cat's presence. "A *cat* took my salmon?"

"It appears so. Now, William, there is more. Allan, please serve William more . . . "

"The devil you say!" William blurted, glaring at the company, who had begun to attempt to control their mirth. "A goddamn *cat* took my fish? How did it get in here?"

"Now, William, please," Isabel pleaded. "I told you, his name is Shad, and I am certain that he did not realize . . ."

"I *hate* cats!" William bellowed.

"Please, William, he did not mean to take your salmon."

"Did not mean to?" he shouted. "He took it! It's gone!" Allan served up more fish, and to Isabel's dismay his face was contorting painfully. She hoped that William would not notice, but he was too busy looking under the table.

The meal continued without further untoward event, but something had gone out of the evening for William, though everyone else seemed to be enjoying it. He ate with one hand guarding his trencher, and before long Isabel, watching him, found her own humor in the situation, though she too watched from a corner of her eye for Shad's ill-timed reappearance. Occasionally she emitted a sound suspiciously like a chortle, though when William would glance up accusingly she affected a bland response. Good lord, she thought, did he truly hate cats? They were in for trouble. Particularly in that she had no intention of giving up either of them.

The company polarized to various pursuits following the meal; gaming tables of backgammon and draughts for those intent upon contest, and a comfortable group gathered in the lesser chamber with their lord and lady for those who preferred conversation. William's disposition improved considerably as he had finally managed to satisfy his appetite with a new dish of salmon. As the culprit did not reappear, the incident receded into the background, much to Isabel's relief.

With little prodding from John, William launched into a rather detailed accounting of his experiences during his absence. "The king has appointed William Longchamp as chancellor?" John asked, stunned.

"Aye, and as bishop of Ely, as well. I know it is difficult to believe," William answered, shaking his head.

"I remember him," d'Erley said slowly. "In fact I recall you ranting and raving about him."

"Aye, even then he left a bad taste in my mouth. Henry banished him to Rouen, not trusting him. But while Henry saw through him, but I fear that Richard believes him to be a friend. Fortunately, Hugh de Puiset will share the reigns of government with him for the north. As a palatine bishop he is a fine soldier and a most capable administrator. He has a level head on his shoulders, and I trust him."

"The bishop of Durham?" Isabel blurted. "I met him years ago. Though cousin to the king he seems to lack the aggressiveness of the Plantagenets. Do you really feel that he will be able to control Longchamp?"

"We shall see," William answered, affecting patience as he returned his attention to the others.

She blinked at his abrupt dismissal, and she felt her cheeks grow hot, both from embarrassment and anger to be treated so. So much for his promises, to stand behind her, to. . . . Nay, he had promised to stand behind her beliefs, to support her against those who would disagree. He never promised to agree himself, or even take interest in her opinions. "The king has appointed associate justiciars to act in his absence. Perhaps we may exert some control over the little weasel."

"We?" John blurted, nonplussed.

"Aye," William shrugged. "Geoffrey fitz Peter, Hugh Bardoff, William Brewer, and myself."

Isabel barely heard the exclamations of the others. For a moment she felt as if she had ceased breathing, as pain dulled her other senses. She stared at him, vaguely aware of the laughter in his eyes and the whiteness of his teeth against the deep tan of his face as he grinned at a pleasant retort from John. An associate justiciar, and he had not bothered to mention it to her. ". . . not too pleased with it," she heard him say. "It will keep me from Striguil more than I would have wished." Good, she thought, her hurt deepening. That is fine with me. You see to your life, William. I shall see to mine.

It was late when William came to their chamber. He found her bent over a large bound volume, leaning to the meager light of a thick, flickering candle. "You retired early," he commented, shrugging out of his surcoat of deep blue linen.

"I was tired," she answered without glancing up.

"But not too tired to see to your accounts?" he observed, glancing at the journal. Then his eyes became fixed on her lap. "Good God, is that it?" he sputtered.

"Aye, this is Shad," she answered as her eyes lowered softly to the grey-striped cat curled up contentedly in her lap. "I believe that you have met."

"It is not going to sleep in here?" his voice rose.

"You need not shout, William," she answered calmly. "He has slept in here since he was a kitten. I certainly cannot now throw him out into the cold."

"Cold? Good God, Isabel, it's August!"

"Nevertheless. He has been a great source of comfort to me, William. I have grown very fond of him. I assure you that he will be no trouble. You won't even know he is here." She looked at him evenly, her eyes growing stony.

"I will know he is here," he grumbled, settling into a chair near her. He stared at the cat with displeasure. A cat, for God's sake! And she had obviously made a pet of it! Why not a dog, or a horse? Or a falcon? Aye, that was it, he would train her to a falcon, and then they would have done with this nonsense! Why was the damn thing staring at him? Begrudgingly, he noted the tender way she was stroking the animal. Unbelievable, but she actually seemed fond of the creature. Harmless enough, he supposed. As long as it left his food alone. And you will, cat, he thought, returning the animal's even stare, you will.

She had left them soon after his startling disclosure, unable to deal with her emotions in the presence of the others. But she had dealt with them, in the hours past. They were wed, for good or ill. Once again she was faced with the choice of wallowing in self-pity and being miserable—or learning to live with her disappointments and hurt. She had tried to consider him objectively, and her marriage to him, thus awakening from a fantasy woven about dreams of sharing and love. She would give to him what she could and take whatever he would offer when it suited him. And she would survive.

"Did you like your gifts?" he asked suddenly.

"Aye," she answered, suddenly brought back to reality. "The silks were lovely. And Julia is overjoyed with the sugars and spices you brought to her. You cannot realize how many problems you solved by your choices."

"Good," he said, looking boyishly pleased. "There is another gift I bring you, Isabel, one which solves another problem, at least for the present. Richard has confirmed my presence in Ireland."

"John will withdraw his men from Ireland?" she asked, her interest suddenly sharpened.

"He will comply, if not willingly. At first he agreed to concede to my claim only if his men were allowed to retain their holdings as given by him."

"But he virtually divided all of Leinster between them!" she cried.

"Calm yourself." He smiled. "I said that the matter had been settled. You could not expect him to give up a full fifth of Ireland without dispute. Only his butler, Theobald Walter, will be allowed to keep his fief, and, only then as my vassal. While John is still my lord in Ireland, I will do only homage to him as such. The charters and title are mine." He laughed at the gleam that came into her eyes.

"I shall write to mother tomorrow." She smiled distractedly. "She will be most pleased."

"I imagine so." He grinned. "Do you realize that this is the first I have seen you smile since I returned? I shall make note of it—to make you happy I merely have to give you a country."

Her smile disappeared. "It takes much less than that, William," she answered quietly.

He did not hear her as Shad chose the moment to vacate her lap, and William's attention became focused on the opportunity. He reached over and she found herself ensconced in his lap with an arm about her as a hand came to rest on her growing stomach. His look softened as he regarded the swelling, and his voice was gentle as he spoke. "My life, while not always easy, has been good, Isabel. I have fought, all of my life, but I have succeeded, and loved every minute of it. I will be honest with you. Perhaps, had you not been given to me, my life never would have changed. Most certainly I would be with Richard in Lyons now, pulling at the bit to see Jerusalem. But I found myself sitting in a tavern in Paris, drinking myself into delirium after receiving your letter. I realized that night, much to my amazement, that I wanted to come home. To you, to our child, and to the lands."

Stunned, she tried to reconcile what he was saying with his earlier actions. "To me?" she asked.

"Of course to you, twit," he laughed. He moved his hand up from her stomach, sliding it into her robe to a breast. "It appears that I have not had my fill of you. I needed more . . . of this . . . " He pushed the robe aside, lowering his head as he took the tip of a breast into his mouth.

She gasped, sparks of feeling shooting through her body at his touch, even as her mind raced to make sense of it. How could he be so cruel, and yet so . . . her mind spun as he plied her nipple with his tongue. Oh, God, she thought desperately, is this why he returned, is this what he wanted, what she meant to him? Only this? She tried to draw her emotions from what he was doing, to think clearly, but her starved body, suddenly anticipating what was going to happen, needing what he could give her, vanquished all other thought. Her arms went about his neck, and her fingers wrapped in his hair as she pressed him down to her. Her back arched against him as she surrendered to the moment and her great need for him.

# 10

THE dust rose in heavy blankets about the group of riders, seeping beneath hauberks and gambesons to mingle with sweat, adding to their discomfort beneath the sun as they made their way along the long road to their destination. As he rode, William's mind was fixed upon that behind him. A morning spent in one of Striguil's many hamlets, meting justice in local disputes and in old antagonisms between villeins, each laid with heavy importance before their lord. William had found his mind wandering while he faced intent pleas for justice only he could impart. He caught himself in moments where his mind would drift to battles where life was imperiled; to glory found in tournaments, for the victor ransom and acclaim in hard-won celebration; to moments in dispute with peers of the realm in presence of the king, the outcome to determine a nation's sovereignty. His thoughts wandered thus, only to be brought to focus once again on a face heavily lined by sun and toil; to hopeful eyes waiting and watching with anticipation for a decision he would give down as law. It was hard to define the way he felt, certainly to himself. He did not minimize the needs of those with whom he dealt. Their needs were many, their lives difficult, and only the most callous could ignore them. But he found himself restless and irritated as he endeavored to listen and guilt overwhelmed him, sharpening his ire.

At Chepstow a hot bath and supper awaited him. Jesú, but he was hungry! They passed a cluster of huts, little more than a space in a clearing beside the road crowded with mud-and-wattle structures with thatched roofs, smoke from cook fires rising to give credence to life within. It was the mount tied before one of them that gave him pause, pulling his thoughts from their self-serving pursuit to focus a fraction of a second before they had passed. With a shout he brought the party to a halt. Puzzled glances passed about as he studied the mount with a heavy frown, his eyes fixed upon the hut as he made a decision. "Return to Chepstow," he grumbled, pulling his destrier about. "There is something here which calls for my attention."

His men departed quickly, eager to see to their own needs before William could change his mind, but his own thoughts were captured by what he knew he would find within; his supper was forgotten. He dismounted, tying the restless stallion apart from the docile mare. Crossing the clearing, he stroked the gentle animal's nose, his mind fixed upon the rough door of the villein's hut. Should he just barge in, or should he wait? Indecision pulled at him with a feeling of unaccustomed awkwardness. God's breath, he had entered a king's chamber with less trepidation! He gathered himself to storm the door, to demand entry for what he knew he would find, when the door opened and she appeared, her face lightening with surprise.

"William!" She closed the door behind her, her arms laden with bundles.

"Why are you here?" he growled, leaning against the mare as he gripped the pommel of the saddle.

"There is sickness within, William," she answered, baffled by his gruff attitude. She crossed to the saddlebags and began to stuff her burdens into them. "I was called to help early this morning, soon after you left. Why else would I be here but to see to their needs, much as your day was spent." She paused to stare at the saddle with empty eyes. "I can only pray that I have. The child will live, but I am not so certain of the mother. She has borne six children before this one, and she is not strong . . . " Catching herself, she glanced up at her husband. "But how came you to be here?"

"I was returning . . . and saw your horse." He suddenly felt uncomfortable, at odds with his own attitude. "I realized that my wife was within. Would I not wish to be with her?"

His eyes seemed to reach into her, seeking something to which she wanted to respond, drawing her to him even as a presence fell between them, a vague, wispy cloud holding them from completion. A deep feeling of sadness engulfed her, and she fought to release it, to reach out to him. "Are you hungry?" she heard herself asking.

"Famished."

"I . . . I have food in my saddlebags." She noticed that the blue of his eyes deepened with interest as he listened, and he seemed to lean imperceptibly forward on her words. "It is early yet. A picnic, perhaps?" Had she said that? She wanted to return to Chepstow, there was so much to do. "I always bring something with me, they have so little . . . " Her voice trailed off as she waited for him to answer.

He reached out and grabbed her about the waist, and she found herself in the saddle. He fixed her foot in the stirrup and her knee about the pommel, draping her skirt about her. Then he crossed silently to his own mount and swung into the saddle.

They found a quiet grove, drawn from the world, secluded beneath reaching oaks heavy upon their years, whose limbs reached to afford gentle shadows to the bed of soft grasses beneath their sheltering cover. William spread his cloak, and they laid out the repast of meat, bread and cheese, and a skin of wine.

"Do you always eat so much?" William asked with a knowing grin as he stretched out across from her.

"I sometimes share a little," she answered with a shrug.

"Sometimes?"

"Usually," she answered defensively.

"Isabel, I do not disapprove." He laughed, reaching for the bread from which he tore a huge hunk, wrapping it about a generous piece of cheese. "Besides, but for your generosity you would not have the means to share with me."

They passed a restful afternoon, filling themselves contentedly from the contents of the saddlebag. Then they stretched out in the warm afternoon sun, whereupon they both took advantage of the peace and quiet, the absence of demands, and napped. As the shadows lengthened William stirred, a cramp in his shoulder awakening him. He found Isabel sitting up, her arms wrapped about her bent knees, as she stared vacantly at some distant spot. He lay still, wondering as to the sadness of her expression. How could he reach her? There had to be a way to breach this wall that was forming between them. God's breath, he did not even know why it was there! What had happened to them? It had begun so well.

In his time of life he acknowledged his fortune in finding her. He rejoiced in that he had been given a wife who was intelligent, knowledgeable. Aye, she was that, and generous, caring, gracious. Everything he had dreamed of, however subconsciously, in his longings over the years. And she was lovely. Her face, her body, the way she moved. Her hands. He found himself fascinated watching those hands as she moved about her daily tasks, caring, emphasizing. The smile she would gift him with while unaware that she was doing so. Natural, giving, could she know what joy it gave to him, what solace? . . . And she carried his child. That alone made him want to care for her, protect her. Why was she so unhappy? And he knew, clearly, that she was.

"Isabel," he said softly, "what is it that you want?"

His question startled her, and she was shaken by his bluntness and the kindness in his voice. How could she answer? Could he truly not know? She wanted to be back at Chepstow, among people, to be busy. Alone with him now she felt an inevitability that she would have to face the answers to his questions, to bare her soul, and to what end? He was as he was, nothing would change. Desperately she looked about the glade for an escape, however improbable, and miraculously, she found it. Growing at the base of the oak she spied a rare herb she had been seeking, a form used to kill pain when used with great care and knowledge.

"Oh, William, look!" She leapt up and rushed to the base of the tree, falling to her knees, and she began to dig up the plant with her bare fingers, oblivious to the dangers of touching the dangerous herb in her eagerness to collect it—and to avoid William's pointed question.

Her scream came out in a muffled, shocked cry as he wrenched her about, knocking the plant from her hands. His sharp expletive of profanity was heard in the still afternoon air as he shook her wrists to free them from the offending dirt. Dragging her back to his cloak, he pulled her to her knees as he grabbed up the skin of wine and poured the contents over her hands. Wiping them off with the edge of his cloak, he looked up at her, his face fused with fury. "Damnation, Isabel! What were you thinking of?"

"I . . . " Her voice broke off and she began to tremble, realizing what she had just done.

He turned her hands over, inspecting them for cuts where the poison from the deadly plant could have entered. Relief spread over his face when he found none, but the anger, the fear was still there as he regarded her. "Jesú, Isabel, what were you trying to do?"

She drew in a gasping breath, turning her face away from the anger in his eyes, and shook her head, unable to answer.

"Why should I ask?" he said, his voice barely controlled. "It is all too obvious, is it not? Anything to avoid facing what is between us, even to rushing headlong, without thinking, into danger. Am I so abhorrent to you? Do not worry," he grimaced at the look of horror she gave him. "I won't touch you." He dropped her hands and stood, stepping away from her.

"Nay, William!" Her eyes filled with pain at the look she read in his face.

Stung, he stood unmovable, watching her with a detached feeling of anger as he threw off her protest. "What then?" When she did not answer, his anger sharpened. "God's breath, Isabel, I am not going to harm you! Will you not answer me?"

"I . . . I only wish to share in your life," she whispered, sniffed loudly.

"Christ." He bent down, drawing a kerchief from his tunic. "Here, blow your nose." When she had done so, and wiped her eyes, he merely shook his head. "Who, more than you, has ever shared my life?" It must be the babe, he reasoned. Emotional, quick to cry. What else could it be?

"You . . . you do not care about my thoughts, my feelings . . ." she said, and hiccuped.

"Of course I do," he answered, drawing her into his arms. Aye, the babe, he reasoned. He should have been more aware, more prepared. But it was a relief to know at last what had been bothering her. "Let me take you back," he murmured, realizing that fog had begun to settle in. "I don't want you to chill." He pulled her up, drawing his cloak about her shoulders. "Do not weep," he said softly. "All will be well, I promise you."

As they rode the distance to the keep Isabel noticed that William's mood had improved considerably. He told her of his day and solicited her opinion on a number of the decisions he had made. She was surprised for a moment but soon suspected that she was being patronized. Fine, she thought slyly, let him think what he will, for now. At first he affected a patient demeanor, listening politely to her suggestions. Then, as her eyes slid covertly to him, she saw that his brows had gathered, the thoughtfulness deepening with amazement over her ability to quickly discern the problems, offering in hand perceptive and sagacious solutions.

Upon their arrival a messenger awaited them from Winchester, the letter he carried requiring immediate attention. William tore it open, retiring to a chair near the fire, where his eyes scanned the first page, a smile at the corners of his mouth as he settled more comfortably in his chair and returned to the first line.

Isabel attended to the messenger, seeing to it that he

was well fed and given suitable quarters for the night. Supper had been served before their return, and slowly the vassals and their ladies departed the hall for their own quarters; the servants retired to their pallets along the far walls, leaving the large room in silence. The sound of the fire, with its occasional hiss and crackle, was the only sound to be heard. She was alone with William, for she knew that no one would approach the area reserved for the family without permission. She occupied herself with needlework and her own thoughts as she left William to his, sensing his need for silence as he stared into the flames, the letter lying forgotten in his lap. A manservant came into the hall to retire, and Isabel gestured toward the fire, suspecting that it was to be a long evening. The man added wood, building it to a roaring blaze before he sought his bed, leaving them to their own company.

The hiss of the fire mesmerized her thoughts, and she drifted into a comfortable feeling of peace. That their lives could truly be thus, she mused; quiet, shared comfort. She had not meant to cry earlier. In the face of his anger and her fear she suddenly had been unable to control it. He then had been so gentle, treating her with such tender concern. But did he truly understand, even now? She suspected that his solicitousness on the ride home had been for all the wrong reasons. She could only hope that she had gained a point, however small.

"What are you working on?" he asked suddenly, startling her in the heavy silence.

She looked up at him and smiled. "I thought it was time I finished my coat of arms." She held up an edge of the cloth for his view, the red head of the rampant lion beginning to emerge, its mouth open in a challenging snarl.

He nodded, then stretched as he reached over to his goblet, which sat on a small table at his side, and frowned to find it empty. Before he could rise she was up, grasping up the pitcher to refill the empty vessel. He took a draught as she settled on the edge of the raised hearth before him, wrapping her arms about her knees as she glanced speculatively at the letter in his lap.

Lowering the goblet he caught her look.

"So, now I know what you are about." A dark brow raised as he pursed his lips in mock seriousness. " 'Tis not my needs that keep you from your bed, but your curiosity. The letter keeps you here."

"That is not true!" she protested. "I knew that the message was important, that it disturbed you. I merely wished to . . . " As he began to laugh she could not help herself, and she joined with him, caught in her own ploy. " 'Tis true," she admitted, smiling sheepishly. "Of course I wanted to know what you found so important. It is from the queen?"

"Aye, it is."

She waited, but when he said nothing more she began to squirm from frustration. "Well? Will you not tell me what she said!"

He grinned, but opened the parchment, scanning over its beginning once more. "It is typically Eleanor," he said, "she is wallowing in her new-found freedom. God knows she should not have been kept imprisoned all of those years, she did not deserve it, however difficult she was to live with. A husband should be able to control his wife, as toilsome as it may be . . . " he added, glancing at Isabel. He grinned at the flare to her eyes, then continued before she could remark on the statement. "She has been using her time well, traveling from town to town, releasing all those imprisoned under the game laws set by Henry, asking them only to pray for his soul as condition for their freedom."

"It is only just," she blurted out. "Men should not be imprisoned because they seek to feed their families by the only means they can!"

"They were his forests," he reminded her. "And the law was clear."

"But he took the best!" she protested, feeling outrage. "He took more than he could ever use for himself, leaving people nothing, not even game needed for their very survival!"

"It was the law, Isabel . . . "

"An unjust law!"

"Unjust laws should be changed, not broken."

"And who will change them? The barons who benefit by them? I wonder, William, what lengths you would go to to feed your family if we were starving?"

He could have informed her that many years of his life had been spent in near-poverty, and he had made his way, without breaking the law. But he had never had to explain himself to anyone before, and he was not about to begin now. "Do you wish to dispute the matter now or hear the rest of the letter?"

"The letter," she answered, her mouth drawing into a pout. His eyes narrowed as she answered through gritted teeth and he knew that in spite of her words she would much rather argue. He sighed, and continued to read but was unsurprised when she interrupted again. "Will you be able to effect changes, unjust laws, as a justiciar?"

"Nay," he answered, laying down the letter again. "Our purpose is only to assist Longchamp and de Puiset."

"You have reservations about Longchamp, don't you? What if he proves to be incompetent, unjust? Is it true that he is a dwarf?"

"Isabel," he answered with a sigh. "You have the most disconcerting habit of asking two or three questions at a time. Aye, he is a dwarf, but more importantly he is a weasel. As for your other questions, my responsibility is to Richard and to England. As long as Longchamp protects both interests I will support him. I would act, but only if he were to break the laws you seem to hold in such little esteem."

"I believe in laws, William." She frowned. "But not one which hurts people. Laws made to protect the interests of only a few!"

He leaned back and regarded her speculatively. "Even laws that protect your own lands?" he asked quietly. Slowly his mouth drew into a smile. "Anger becomes you, my love. Your eyes brighten and your skin takes on a most becoming flush."

She blinked, her color heightening with his words. "Is that all that I have said means to you!" she sputtered.

"Do you fault me for finding you attractive?" he parried; his eyes were filled with amusement.

She jumped up, glaring at him as she drew herself up indignantly. "Far be it from me, William, to find fault with you about anything!" She spun away and strode from the hall, leaving him in a thick silence. He stretched lazily, then stood up to cross the hall to the stairs. An interesting turn of events, he mused. She was angry, her senses sharpened. With a little coaxing it should prove a most interesting and pleasurable night.

"By all that is holy, William, he must be stopped!"

Isabel refilled William's goblet and then that of the large blond knight who sat with him. She saw to their needs herself, having dismissed the servants who had risen from their beds upon the arrival of the visitor. In her present mood, Isabel viewed the interruption with relief. William had joined her in their chamber only moments after she had stormed from the hall. The look in his eyes, the smirk of speculation he had given her, had added to her rage. She was all too aware of what he was about, and she had no intention of giving in to what she momentarily considered as his baser instincts. She was prepared for a battle royal.

As he approached, fairly stalking her across the room until he had backed her against the bed, the cry of exchange was heard from the guard on the tower wall, the sound carrying easily on the still night air through their unshuttered window. Cursing, William had stormed from the room, ignoring her soft laughter, which followed him into the hall.

They met with the visitor in the lesser chamber off of the great hall, drawing a heavy screen across the archway in their need for privacy. The man was as large as William, his hair as fair as William's was dark, his eyes of a lighter hue. In his dust-ridden hauberk it was difficult to believe that the man was a bishop, but when one met his eyes once, one sensed that while he was fully capable of wielding a sword, his desires were more inwardly directed to the mind and soul.

"Longchamp was Richard's choice, Hugh, as were you."

"Aye, William," Hugh de Puiset grumbled, "but the man is unscrupulous! England will not fare well under his hand."

"Why have you come?" William asked, his eyes narrowing with speculation. "What can I do to help you?"

"You might ask more what you can do for yourself, Marshal," de Puiset answered as he arched a sandy brow. "But I will not pretend that I have traveled here just to protect your interests. You must know what has happened while you have been settling into your new estates." He glanced at Isabel, who had taken the chair next to William. "He is devious, and shrewd—I'll give him that. We both were attending Richard in Rouen and, fool that I am, I actually felt flattered when the king requested that I remain." He gave a short, bitter laugh. "The little ferret had planned it! He left immediately with writs impressed with the Great Seal giving him full authority, while convincing Richard that I remain to attend him!"

"I know that he has replaced men of position with those of his own," William muttered. "My brother, John, was replaced as sheriff of Yorkshire by Longchamps's brother, Osbert. Obviously I already have a grudge for the man."

"He replaced John?" Isabel blurted out, stunned. "William, you did not tell me that!"

"Word came only a few days ago, Isabel."

"Did you not think that I would be interested?"

"Of course, but our days have been filled with matters of our own."

"Our properties are well set, William. But anything that concerns their welfare such as this is certainly of interest!"

"The man, as disputable as he is, is the arm of the crown. He has the power to place in office who he deems fit."

"And what will he 'deem' next? Will Chepstow or Caerphilly suit his needs?"

"Do not fear on that point, Isabel," William said, smiling grimly. "There is a line over which the man shall not pass."

De Puiset watched the exchange with fascination. They seemed to lose themselves in their own verbal sparring, and he felt the emotion that crossed between them, their eyes lit with the exchange, the subject matter almost secondary to a battle of wills. He had observed such a relationship once before, between a strong-willed queen and her king, now dead. Eleanor must miss Henry, he mused. He recalled that stormy relationship, knowing that they had indeed loved each other, though neither had ever found a way to show it to the other. He had been nurtured among them, cousin to Richard and to Philip of France. Observing these two, he remembered and sighed softly. He would say a prayer for them, he thought, that their love might make a better end.

"Ahem," he coughed, reminding them of his presence. They glanced at him, as if surprised to find him in their company. "It is clear, William, and your lady is most correct, that the matter strikes closer to home than you would wish. Longchamp seeks to weaken the Marshal influence and power. John is only the first step."

"What else has he done?" William gritted his teeth, now giving Hugh his full attention.

"What has he not done?" de Puiset snorted. "Where do I begin? He has traveled about England, selling positions to the highest bidder. He auctions posts, settles lawsuits by bribe, selling lands and forests to those with the purse."

"Does Richard know of this?"

"Know of it? He supports it! I wrote to him immediately, informing him of what was being done, and do you know what his answer was? 'By God's feet! Find me a purchaser and I will sell very London itself!' "

"The devil knows its prey," William muttered. "Longchamp knows that the way to power with Richard is by providing the means to his crusade."

"What are you going to do?" Isabel interrupted.

"Do? My love, in spite of your outrage, Longchamp has done nothing illegal. As Hugh has admitted, the chancellor's actions are by the king's writ. Would you have me begin a revolution?"

"So you will do nothing?" she glared accusingly.

"Not until he breaks the law," William answered sternly. "Isabel, if each of us interprets the law unto himself there can be no order. With it I may protect England; without it, who may serve her, who can be trusted?"

"You have not answered the question of Longchamp."

"He will make a mistake, madam, be assured of it. When he flaunts the law, then, and only then, I will act."

"You have it," de Puiset said, bringing their attention back to him. His eyes gleamed as he set to the purpose of his visit, the ground laid. "It seems, William, that he has chosen to lay siege to your castle at Gloucester."

William stared at him for a hard moment, his eyes growing dangerously cold. "On what grounds has he dared to attack me?" he asked quietly. Isabel remained wisely silent, knowing the moment was won.

"Apparently none are needed. Geoffrey de Lucy came to me upon his return from Normandy. He had met with Longchamp, who happened to be laying siege to your holdings, my friend. Longchamp dared to ask Geoffrey if he should continue. Geoffrey replied that if he desired peace he would lay down his arms."

"Why has Ralph not sent word?" William said, gritting his teeth, referring to Ralph Musard, his constable at Gloucester.

"He tried but the couriers were set upon."

The eyes William turned to Isabel were chilled to a pale blue. "Well, my lady, you have your issue. The man has broken the law. He has made his mistake." He rose and left the chamber without another word.

Isabel and de Puiset sat in silence for a long moment after William's departure. Finally, she rose and turned to the bishop. "Well," she sighed. "You have what you came for, my lord earl of Northumberland. Will you be riding with him?"

"Nay, milady. Nor shall I apologize for my methods. Marshal is needed or I would not have come."

"No one is asking for your apology, milord. Word was to reach him before long in any case. The matter must be seen to."

Chepstow was in a flurry of activity when she found him in their chambers with Allan, readying his armor. She waited quietly as he gave instructions to the squire for the items he wanted readied, making her presence known only when Allan had left. She closed the door behind him, unaware that Shad had taken the moment to slip in. "Hugh informed me that Longchamp seeks favor with the king by supplying him with an never-ending supply of funds, taxing barons and villeins alike until they can bend no more."

He merely grunted, concentrating on the sheaf of papers he was holding. He crossed to a writing table, sealing the document with hot wax and the imprint of the seal of his ring.

"Why did you not tell me about John?" she asked.

"There," he said, testing the seal. "Isabel, I want you to see that this is sent first thing in the morning." He looked up and his expression lightened, as if he saw her standing there for the first time. "I am taking d'Erley with me, and I shall leave Beaumont in charge here." She did not miss the enthusiasm in his voice. So, she thought, he is champing at the bit to go. His eyes moved over her slowly, trailing down her body in a deliberate perusal, and he smiled. "Everything is seen to, now perhaps there will be a few hours for us before I have to leave."

She tensed as he took her into his arms and turned her head slightly as he bent to kiss her. He seemed not to notice as his lips traveled to the base of her neck, nuzzling her as his hands roamed her back and hips. Time for us, she thought petulantly. Time for this, only this. He took her chin in his fingers, turning her face to look up at him. "I shall miss you," he murmured. She tried to pull her gaze from his, her mind denying his words, but she was transfixed by his eyes, which seemed to burn into hers, stating a need more clearly than words. She felt her body respond, and she hated her body for want-

ing him. But she could not, try as she might, deny her
own needs. Her skin began to tingle, an ache of desire
beginning deep within her sweeping her up to meet him.
Aye, she wanted those hands touching her. As his
mouth came down on hers, her lips parted beneath his,
and her mind began to spin with anticipation of the bliss
the next hour would bring.

"Sweet Mother Mary and Joseph!"

Isabel came out of a sound, drugged sleep to find
William thrashing about, the bed bouncing as he threw
the covers aside. She could barely make him out in the
blackness of the room, and she instinctively pulled the
covers about her as her mind panicked as to what could
be possibly happening. Were they being invaded?!

"William, what is it?" she cried.

"It's that goddamn cat!" he roared as he struggled to
strike the wick. "It walked across my face!"

"Oh, William, really!" she blurted out, horrified,
while a part of her began to bubble with laughter. "He
is locked in the kitchens, it could not have been Shad."

"It was him, I'd know his feet anywhere!"

"Please, William, come back to bed."

Her plea fell on deaf ears as he finally lit the candle
and held it above him as he began to search the room.
She had to bite her lips not to laugh at the ridiculous picture he made, peering about the room stark naked in the
flickering shadows of the candle, his face grim with
anger.

"William, come back to bed. If he is here, you won't
find him tonight."

He hesitated, then grunted, returning reluctantly to
the bed. Setting the candle on the bedside table, he
glanced about the room once again, peering into the dull
cast from the candle's light, then with a frown, begrudgingly blew it out. She felt the bed dip under his weight as
he slipped in beside her. They lay, side by side, the room
heavy with unspoken words as she knew that his mind
was still on his pursuit.

"That cat dies in the morning," he said at last.

"Oh, William, really." She fought not to laugh, a bit

unsuccessfully. "Perhaps you were dreaming."

"I wasn't dreaming."

"He did not hurt you."

"No cat walks across my face and lives."

A long silence followed, each to their own thoughts.

"William?"

"What?"

"You . . . you wouldn't really . . . hurt him?"

"Go to sleep, Isabel."

Fortunately Isabel awoke before William, and Shad was found and whisked from the room to the kitchens before William roused. It proved easy to locate him, as he had chosen to creep up at a later hour and settle himself for the remainder of the night between William's legs. When the lord of the manor rose, the subject was studiously avoided and soon forgotten as last-minute preparations were made.

The days passed quickly even as Isabel found herself pausing in her duties as her eyes turned to a window facing the north. When visiting the various hamlets and villages of Striguil, she watched the horizon for a rise of dust indicating a large group of riders. But she was surprisingly content. Her soul was immersed in the land and the people, the essence of her being filling with them as she saw to their needs, plotted their futures, planned and agonized in bittersweet contemplation of her responsibilities. She demanded and received news of their lands about England, Normandy, and Wales, keeping her fingers firmly placed upon the pulse of all that fell within her domain. She overlooked nothing that concerned her or the future of the babe that continued to grow within her. Erin was secure for the moment; letters from her mother confirmed that William had made good on his promise. Moments came when she thought about her father. Aye, she would be equal to what he had given to her, it would be secured for his heirs. William would see to it by might and diplomacy, and she by planning and detail.

She found herself missing William dearly, as she had when he had left her before. However, unlike before, distance allowed her to think clearly. She recalled his laughter and wit, the way his eyes would crinkle at the corners when he teased her. His touch, the way he would lay an arm about her waist, or cover her hand with his, unhesitating in showing his affection for her in front of others. The way he made love to her. . . . Her heart tightened as her thoughts drifted to that path. He was a wonderful lover . . . and part of her wished it wasn't so. She did not want to enjoy it so much, to need him so much . . . when it was the only way he seemed to need her. She knew it was wrong to feel this way, but the resentment was there, each time he took her, and it was growing, deepening. She had not the vaguest idea of what to do about it.

He returned in mid-September. Longchamp had quickly fled upon the appearance of Marshal's forces with William at its head. "Did you not even see him?" Isabel queried, wanting the full, gory details as they sat to midmeal.

"What would there be to see?" he answered. "To confront those expressionless eyes of his? If eyes truly be the mirror to a man's soul, then it is confirmed that he has none. He escaped with his tail between his legs when we were within two days' march of Gloucester."

"Then why were you gone so long?" she asked with wifely interest.

"I had not seen Ralph in quite a long time. There was much to do, Isabel."

She did not miss the gleam of pleasure that passed over his expression. Men! So he had enjoyed the past weeks in the company of his cohorts! Fine, it had given her time to see to her lands and their needs as she would have them. See to the matters of men, William, she thought, and I will see to mine.

As he finished his meal he leaned back in his chair, relaxed and comfortable in the knowledge that Shad was securely locked in the kitchens. His eyes moved about the room idly, enjoying the relaxed moment. They moved over their company and then to the banners placed high among the rafters where the coat of arms of the knights in residence were displayed. His eyes froze, becoming fixed upon one. It was at that moment that Isabel had turned to him with a question, the words freezing at his expression.

"That is your finished coat of arms?" he asked quietly.

"Of course," she answered, following his stare. "Is there something wrong?" Elizabeth's words passed through her mind, but she denied them even as she began to feel slightly uncomfortable.

"What is your meaning, Isabel? Are you trying to tell me something?" he asked. His voice was calm but she could detect an underlay of anger in his question.

"What are you talking about?" she asked. She studied the banner but failed to see what was disturbing him.

"Your father must have been very dear to you."

It was all that he said but she wondered at the element of hurt in his voice, though he changed the subject quickly, turning to d'Erley, who sat on his right. Her gaze returned to the banner, and she frowned as she stared at it, wondering what others saw that she could not see.

The situation with Longchamp grew worse. The relative peace of the Marshal's was short-lived when word reached them that Longchamp's flag had been hoisted over Windsor castle. Moreover, his confidence in his own authority dared him to use his own seal in lieu of the Great Seal of England in signing the king's name. The noble but unaggressive Hugh de Puiset was unable to contain the chancellor. When de Puiset dared to confront Longchamp, the chancellor calmly produced a commission, signed by Richard, giving him full authority in England. The rafters of Chepstow trembled when word of Longchamp's bold move reached them. William's rage exploded as he learned that de Puiset's titles and lands had been confiscated and the kind bishop of Durham had been banished to the monastery at Howden.

"I actually thought the little ferret was smarter than that," William said as he readjusted the tethers of Isabel's falcon. "Longchamp weaves his web tighter and tighter, and he will soon strangle himself with it. He acts within the law but not within its intent. He will rue the day when I catch him at it.''

'' 'Tis unfortunate that you did not catch him at Gloucester,'' she parried, wondering if the heavy glove she wore would prove sufficient to the sharp talons of the bird resting on her arm. ''You received a letter from the queen yesterday, did you not?'' she asked, glancing up at him. ''Are you going to tell me about it, or is it a secret?''

''I have no secrets from you,'' he said, frowning as he raised her arm up. ''It was from Eleanor, in answer to my letter—the one you sent when I left for Gloucester. She has made Richard see reason, she's the only one who could. This morning I received a letter from Walter de Coutance, the archbishop of Rouen. He is coming to England with a writ authorizing him to assist in the government in the king's absence. Isabel, do not be so tense, the bird feels it.''

''The bird is smart. So another is being sent to assist Longchamp. Wonderful,'' she drawled.

''You do not understand. He will act with the associate justiciars as council. In matters of dispute our esteemed chancellor and bishop of Ely is to defer to our judgment.''

''That *is* wonderful!'' she enthused. ''That means it is over!''

''Isabel, careful!'' he snapped. The bird, shaken by the sudden movement, began to pull against his joices. ''You'll injure him! Do you know how much that bird cost? It is not over,'' he frowned as he stroked the bird gently. ''Longchamp is still chancellor. He will not give up without a struggle. We can only hope he continues to act as rashly as he has done in the past.'' His horse shifted beneath him as he turned in his saddle and nodded to the falconer to release the birds they had brought for training. ''But there is better news. Eleanor has effected the impossible. Richard has allowed his half-brother to be consecrated as archbishop of York. At long last Geoffrey's exile has been lifted, and he will soon be returning to England.''

She gaped at him with shock as the birds were released. "Isabel, remove the hood! You're going to lose them!" He reached over and pulled the hood from the peregrine falcon. The bird looked about with its large yellow eyes, and spying the fleeing sparrows, seemed to disappear from her arm. "God's breath, Isabel! You were almost too late!"

"I am not particularly entranced with killing, William," she replied. "I thought Richard would rather see Geoffrey dead than returned to England. Lud, that news ought to send Longchamp into a veritable uproar even if the archbishop of Rouen's arrival does not."

"We will handle Longchamp. The man, such as he is a thorn in England's paw, has never concerned me overmuch. Nay, there is another who's reaction to Geoffrey concerns me more," he replied, watching the falcon as it circled, then spotted its prey and fell like an arrow to its mark. "Look at that!" he enthused.

"Who, William?" she asked, wincing as the falcon struck.

"Our prince, Isabel," he answered. "John."

# 11

WILLIAM'S frown was concealed beneath the shadow of his visor, which had been pushed back from his helm, the muggy heat of the warm storm-threatened October morning causing him to seek what comfort he could as they rode through the dense forest. As he watched Isabel, his brow furrowed deeply with the doubt that plucked at him. He twisted about, glancing behind him at the large company of over one hundred knights, five hundred men-at-arms and forty Welsh archers that constituted their company as they journeyed to London to meet with the archbishop of Rouen. Turning back to Isabel, he noted her paleness, and his jaw set tightly. He should have not consented to her plea to accompany him on this journey. He would choose a group of knights to return her to Chepstow. "Isabel, you are going back."

"William, I am fine!" she protested. "The babe is fine. It is just the heat. You appear wilted yourself, milord," she quipped.

"Aye, that I am," he agreed. Fortunately, at that moment his attention was drawn by d'Erley, who had chosen the moment to join them. She peered at William from the corner of her eye, relieved that he had accepted the reason for her moodiness. Bless John, she thought, he always seemed to appear when she needed him, although he might not always know it. She certainly had no intention of telling William of what was truly bothering her. A casually laid comment on his part. In truth, it had been brought by her own making. They had been arguing about Count John—her opinion of that Plantagenet was of an even lesser degree than that of his brother who was king. Her concern was for Geoffrey, the best of the lot to her way of thinking, and she feared what might happen to him when he returned to England.

"Geoffrey has no ambitions to the throne, Isabel," he had said, "though Richard will not believe it. I've always wondered if Richard's hatred for his half-brother was due to his concern that Geoffrey might look to the throne, or the fact that his mother was Rosemond, Eleanor's only rival for Henry's affection."

"Did he really love her, as they say?"

"Rosemond was gentle, where Eleanor was not," he answered. "She—answered certain needs in Henry. But to your arguments against John, I do not fear that he will seek to do harm to Geoffrey. He recognizes what Richard will not, that the man is dedicated to God. However, Geoffrey is popular with the people. My fear is that John may try to form an alliance with him against Richard . . ."

But she had stopped listening. Something he had said struck a chord in her that had simply never occurred to her before. Henry had loved Eleanor passionately but had placed her aside in his affections when he had met the lovely, submissive Rosemond. Could William also find one to meet similar needs? She knew that she tried him, their marriage was less than perfect. She could accept that there would be others in his life, those used for need. A wife of her time, she accepted those he might take to his bed in the long months of his absences. They fulfilled a physical need, and she simply did not allow herself to consider them. But another to replace her in his affections, that she could not bear. The realization that the strains in their marriage could actually drive him from her made her acutely depressed—then angry. Lud. Was she expected to give up all that was dear to her in order to keep him to her? To give of herself, body and soul, without qualification, so that he might not stray? She glared at him as he was deep in conversation with John. Not without a fight, William, she thought, her thoughts settling into an irascible mood as she prepared for battle.

They stayed the night in a small inn at Aldbourne. William warned his men to watch their cups, as they would make an early start, soon after dawn, and he would have none falling back due to a pounding head or squeamish stomach. He retired with Isabel to their chamber after a light supper, both too fatigued to eat more than a few bites, and began to ready for bed. He extinguished the candle and reached for her, wanting the softness of her against him as he slept.

Isabel's mood had not lifted. Her earlier angry thoughts, her deep aching exhaustion, combined with the ever-widening chasm that drew between them, erupted. As his arm came about her waist she tensed. Lud, she thought testily, could he think of nothing else? Had he no consideration for her, how tired she was? "William, please!" she hissed, "not tonight!" She felt him stiffen, and he pulled his arm from her, drawing away.

He felt confused by her response but her rejection quickly turned his mood to one of anger. She attempted to dictate to him in other aspects of his life, was it now to be this? Were even his rights in bed now to be rationed, bestowed magnanimously by her whim? Fool! He should have been warned. This is what comes from being generous, allowing her to have her way! Ugly suspicions that had lain dormant came to surface. He'd be damned if a woman of his would feel that she could dictate to him. By the saints, they'd have this out;

they'd settle the matter once and for all. He turned to strike the wick and was fumbling to find the flint when he heard a rapping at the door.

"What is it!" he bellowed, now totally out of sorts.

"William, what is it?" Isabel stirred.

"Be quiet, Isabel!" he snapped, still fumbling as he finally managed to light the candle.

He heard the sharp intake of her breath, and he felt a grim pleasure at having unsettled her as he heard d'Erley's voice at the door.

" 'Tis John. Open up, William, I have important news!"

William struggled into a long wool robe and strode to the door. He paused before he opened it and glanced back at Isabel, who was sitting up in the middle of the bed, her hair disheveled and her eyes wide with puzzlement as she stared after him. "Get up, Isabel, and put a robe on," he growled. When she hesitated, his brows came together in a heavy scowl. "Good god, woman, would you prefer to greet John in bed? Get up!"

She scurried out of the bed to obey, and he thought he saw her chin quiver as she slipped into her robe. He felt a pang of guilt but dismissed it quickly, once again preferring his own foul mood. Seeing that she was now appropriately clothed he turned and opened the door, admitting an overwrought John d'Erley.

John glanced at Isabel with a quick apologetic smile. "William, a messenger has caught up with us from Count John, and apparently it is urgent."

"From John?" William looked surprised.

"Aye, and he will see no one but you," he added.

"Bring him in here."

"In here?" John glanced at Isabel.

"Aye, of course in here. Where else can I see him, in the common room? Obviously the news is confidential."

John shrugged and left the room. William took the moment to glance at Isabel, and the strange way she was looking at him only fed the dull anger that he was still feeling. "Go sit by the window and for heaven's sakes be still, no matter what you hear!'' He ignored the angry look she threw him, and he crossed to a table near the hearth to pour himself a generous goblet of wine. It had been badly watered, and he grimaced as he swallowed. The innkeeper would most certainly hear of this in the morning, he determined. He turned as the door opened, and John reentered with a knight in the prince's colors, his surcoat covered with grime-ridden evidence of a hard forced ride.

"Sir William," the knight acknowledged, glancing at Isabel who now sat with reluctant obedience by the window.

"You may speak freely," William said curtly, drawing again from the goblet. Isabel's brow raised, as did John's, as William made no effort to introduce her to the messenger as his wife. "Well?" he growled, irritated at the speculative way the man was looking at Isabel.

"Sir William, my lord has sent me to you on a matter of the most urgency, or I assure you that I would not have disturbed you at this hour." When he saw the storm of impatience that passed over William's expression, he hurried on. "The archbishop of York is now in England, having landed at Dover four days past."

"Geoffrey is here?" William asked, pausing with his wine halfway to his mouth.

"Aye, Sir William." The man coughed, his throat suddenly gone dry.

"John, pour him some wine, as sorry as it is. Sit down, man, the tale need not be told standing."

The knight took a chair and accepted the goblet eagerly, drawing deeply from it before he continued. "His ship was met at Dover by Madam de Cleres, the chancellor's sister, apparently in the stead of her husband, the constable of that city. Her intent was to take the archbishop prisoner, but he managed to elude her men, escaping on horse to Saint Martin's priory."

"She attacked Geoffrey?" William bellowed, slamming the pewter goblet down on a table with a resounding clatter.

"Aye. Moreover, she would have violated sanctuary,

but the soldiers set to the task refused to enter the chapel to take him."

"Blood of God!" William roared. He gained immediate control, but his eyes glittered dangerously. "Becket is undoubtedly too fresh in their minds to drag an archbishop from the altar." He gritted his teeth, glancing briefly at John. "Where is Geoffrey now?"

"He managed to keep sanctuary for four days, Sir William, standing before the altar in his vestments and holding a cross. On the fourth day she sent men into the sanctuary, hired with enough coin to see to the deed. He was dragged from the priory—and is now held in the dungeon of Dover castle."

Isabel watched William and braced for the explosion certain to come. To her amazement he seemed to grow calm, his eyes turning cold as he regarded the knight. He refilled the knight's goblet, then his own. "What does your lord expect from me?" he asked, his voice betraying nothing of his feelings.

"He rides to London, Sir William. Longchamp has fled to Windsor, and my lord means to lay siege to the keep. He asks for your support."

William regarded the knight for a long moment, then a hint of a smile lifted the corners of his mouth. "John," he said evenly, turning to d'Erley. "Rouse Father Delano and have him strike a message. It goes to the constable of Dover, expressing my displeasure and suggesting that he release the archbishop immediately. Note that if Geoffrey carries so much as a bruise on his person all that is the constable's shall be lost to him. Be certain that the good father expresses how unhappy this turn of events has caused me to be. When he has finished bring it to me for my signature and seal."

John left the room quickly with a grim eagerness to his expression, and William turned once again to the knight. "Return to your lord and inform him that we will soon be at Windsor. I have one hundred knights in my company, five hundred men-at-arms, and forty Welsh bowmen to see to the task. Assure him that Longchamp's banner will be rapidly removed." The knight grinned as he rose from his chair. He began to leave but William stopped him before he reached the door. "One thing more. Also carry this message to your lord: I presume that he will do nothing until I arrive. Not to Longchamp—or to Geoffrey."

Isabel fixed her eyes on William's broad back where he rode a few lengths ahead, her mood still soured from the argument that had passed between them. They had waited in heavy silence until John had returned with the letter, whereupon he instructed d'Erley to rouse the men an hour before dawn. Once John had left, Isabel had turned on him, demanding answers for his earlier foul temper. But he would have none of it, ordering her to bed and sleep, snapping at her that there remained but a few hours before they must depart. She watched him now as she fantasized their next encounter—and various means of revenge.

John rode by her side, watching her expression. He was painfully aware of the tension between William and his lady prior to their departure from the inn, and their expressions when William had ordered him to ride with her. What had happened?

"Are you well, milady?" he asked solicitously.

"I am fine, John," she said as she gritted her teeth.

"Are you certain?" he pressed.

In a sudden need to talk with someone, she voiced her thoughts. "He certainly does act the pompous lord, doesn't he?"

"Who?" John asked, shocked at her meaning. "Sir William?"

"Of course, who else would I mean?" she snapped.

John glanced at the figure in question and shifted in his saddle uncomfortably. His eyes lifted to the banners carried at the head of the company, and he frowned as they fixed on Isabel's. That banner had bothered him since it had been raised to Chepstow's rafters and now, with her words, it disturbed him more. Could she feel that William was . . . well, beneath her? The thought made him angry, and he glanced at Isabel from the corner of his eyes, but the expression on her face silenced his thoughts. Her eyes were unnaturally bright and he recognized this as a sign of unshed tears. Nay, there was something else, but whatever it was between them, he could not interfere in their personal affairs. "William is not pompous, milady, whatever else he may be."

"Oh?" she snapped. "That is not what I see."

"Forgive me, Lady Isabel, but I have known Sir William for many years, and a squire knows his master well."

"So tell me, John, of this marvelous man you served."

At that moment it occurred to John that Isabel did not know very much about the man to whom she was married. But why should she? Living a large part of her life in Ireland, then sheltered in the Tower, and then quickly married. And William was not apt to talk about himself. . . . But how could he tell her?

"Many years ago, milady, when I was but a lad barely into Sir William's service, we found ourselves ensconced in a Flemish inn while he served King Henry . . . the younger, that is."

"Henry fitz Henry?" she asked, recalling the young king who died without reigning, never having grasped the reins from his father or from Eleanor, his mother.

"Aye," John assured her. "He was a sad case, the young king. Given a crown that was not really a crown, but only offered for assurance that he would not seek to gain power during his father's lifetime. William understood that, and accepted the care of the young king, giving him the training he would need. I often think that William was the only one who loved him. His loyalty remained until the day young Henry died, only then did William give it to the father."

"What happened in the Flemish inn?" she asked, her anger dissipating as her curiosity was sparked.

"We had been moving about the continent, spending a goodly sum as usual," he enthused, warming to the story. "And, as usual, we soon ran out of funds. We woke up of a morning to find that the burgess of the town had invoked a petition upon our entire party, shut us in, so to speak, until we could pay our bill.''

"He would not allow you to leave?"

"Just so. Keep in mind, Lady, that he refused the word of a king. Henry was heir to England and had access to half the funds of Normandy. But the burgess would not allow us to leave until funds arrived." He glanced at Isabel. "Sir William presented himself before the burgess and gave, on his word, the promise that the bill would be met. We were allowed to leave within the hour.''

"On his word?"

"Aye, milady. For such was his word, throughout the continent."

When Isabel fell silent, John smiled, knowing that he was making headway. "From this you may well understand what happened later. It must have been an almost unbearable burden for Henry. He was a king, at least in name, traveling about Europe and England from tournament to tournament with a great entourage. William had tried to do well by him, but wherever we would go it was William who was looked to, he who was champion, his word which was taken. It finally came to a head when those jealous of William's favor with fitz Henry circulated the rumor that William had been spending too much time with Margaret. Fitz Henry adored his wife and it gave him grievance, however untrue the accusation was—and I assure you that it was that!'' He added quickly, seeing Isabel's brows arch, "In any event," he continued, "they came to heated words over the matter, and William rode away from him, angrier than I have ever seen him. Word came soon after from fitz Henry that he was to participate in an important tournament at Gournai. He reminded William that his duty was to attend his king. I will never forget it. Upon receiving the message, we rode into Gournai, where he found fitz Henry besieged by a group of knights who were soundly besting the king. He laid them down, each of them, securing the position of the king, then rode out, without a word to anyone. They did not speak to each other for years. Finally, William had had enough. We went to court, whereupon he confronted fitz Henry, challenging his honor by combat with the knight of fitz Henry's choice. The young king, to the amusement of his father, answered that it would be an unfair contest, that no one could best him, therefore it would prove nothing. William then suggested that he engage in combat with three knights over three consecutive days. Still, the answer was the same. Finally, William suggested that a finger be severed from his hand, and he would, with the bleeding finger unbound, combat the knight of Henry's choice. But still no one would come forward to challenge him.''

"Why?" she asked, much moved and intrigued.

"Because, milady," he answered with a patient smile, "there is not a knight of the realm, or of the continent, who will meet William Marshal in combat. Do you not understand? Never in tournament or in battle has he been beaten, nor, I suspect, shall he ever be. There is something about him. His strength, his talent, aye—but something more. There is an honor of purpose, a quality that brings men to respect him."

"Why are you telling me this, John?"

"Because I do not think that you understand him, milady, and I think that you, above all, should. He is not pompous, nor has he ever been, and it is a quality that has always amazed me. I think, in his position, I certainly would have become so, but he remains as he was. Perhaps that, after all, is the secret."

Her brow furrowed as she considered all that he had said. "How did fitz Henry die?" she asked then, somewhat chagrined that she knew so little of the man who was her husband. It had never seemed important to her before, to understand this other part of her heritage, but it came to be now.

"A sudden fever took him. Some say it was food poisoning," he answered. "William held him in his arms as he died—then returned to England, whereupon he pledged himself to the father."

Her mind spun with John's story. It was so much to absorb at once, yet this new portrait of William answered certain questions she had been harboring since the previous night. How William so easily effected the authority he presented in his letter to the constable of Dover, and to Count John. Simple, calm statements of fact, though they had amazed her even through her anger. Aye, she had recognized it on the day of her marriage but had repressed the knowledge in the months that had passed. Power. As before, she thrilled to the fact of it. Pride and the comfort of security warmed her as she thought of the man who was her husband. Pompous? Nay. She sighed deeply. Her husband was a contradiction—a lovely, wonderful contradiction. If only he would try to better understand her.

A great yawn escaped and William gave into it. He sought to stretch his limbs in the saddle, but the high-spirited war-horse sidestepped in displeasure against the change in weight. He drew the destrier firmly back, a part of him longing for the comfort of his palfrey while another enthused, as always, for the feel of the powerful animal beneath him. They would be in London within a few hours, and he had ordered his men to armor and their destriers, knowing that Longchamp might decide to emerge from his hiding place and meet them upon the field. Then there was John. He had lived with the Plantagenet brood too long not to expect the unexpected. He considered the various strategies John must now be tossing about in that dark head of his. The fact that John had apparently cast his support for Geoffrey meant little. If Longchamp provided the means to the throne for the younger son, anything might happen. There was only one thing of which William was certain. Richard was his sovereign, and when he returned, he would be sovereign still.

The sound of laughter carried across the still, muggy afternoon air, and he turned in the saddle. Isabel rode a length behind him with d'Erley and was obviously caught up in some delightful exchange with his former squire. His eyes darkened beneath the helm as he found himself pulling the destrier from the column. He watched them as they approached, apparently so engrossed in conversation that they did not notice him until they had almost passed.

"William!" It was John who noticed him first.

"You may take my place in the column, John," William grumbled, pulling in beside his wife.

Hearing the tone of William's voice, John broached no argument and his mount leapt ahead, leaving Isabel to stare at her husband with wonder. She was piqued by his attitude, seeing no reason for this new show of anger, and she determined that he should be the one to speak first. They rode in silence for almost a mile.

"Damn, it's hot," he growled at last, pulling off his helm and then setting it on the pommel of his saddle. He ran his fingers through his damp hair.

"Well, my lord, as I see it, since you chose to interrupt the story, you will have to finish it," Isabel said, now glancing up at him with the hint of a smile.

"What story?" he grumbled.

"The one John was telling me before you sent him on ahead."

"What was it about?"

"You."

"Me?"

"Aye. You were on a hunting trip in Normandy with your uncle, Count Patrick. You were virtually unarmed when you were ambushed by a group of men . . . "

"John has a loose tongue," he snapped. "I do not wish to speak of it."

She started at the venom in his voice, and she knew it had nothing to do with the anger between them. She fell silent, her eyes fixed on the road ahead as she chewed on her lower lip. Seeing the nervous habit, he softened, regretting his anger. "Isabel, it is a story I wish to forget. John should not have mentioned it."

She looked up at the sudden gentleness in his voice, knowing that he meant it as apology. "John has been telling me about your life together, and it has helped me to realize how much I do not know about you. It is your life before I knew you, and it made you what you are."

A long silence followed and Isabel could see, as he stared at the road ahead, that he was making a decision. "What else did he tell you?" he asked suddenly.

"Only that you were unarmored, yet you managed to hold off six men with only your sword, until another caught you from behind, lancing your thigh."

"Then he did not tell you that my uncle, Count Patrick, died that day?"

"Nay," her voice softened in horror.

"I was taken prisoner, kept in a cell for months, left to die," his voice was low. "They did not even give me the means to clean or bind my wound. I would have bled to death but that a kitchen maid took pity on me and gave me a rag from the kitchen to tend myself."

"Who were they, William? Why did they attack you?"

"The Lusignans, a family with whom we had long had grievances. They murdered him, he never had a chance."

"How did you escape?"

"Eleanor. She paid them a goodly ransom for my release."

"But . . . John said that this happened before you entered the Plantagenet service," she said, confused.

"It did. Eleanor had followed my progress through various tournaments, and when my plight came to her attention she took pity on me."

"Followed your progress? You mean that she was enamored." Isabel grinned.

"I hardly think so, Isabel," William snorted.

Feeling cramped, as much from the conversation as from the hours spent in the saddle, William sighed and stretched out his legs. The destrier chose the opportune moment to turn his head and nipped the tip of William's chain-clad foot. "Damn it, horse!" William swore, pulling his foot from the animal's mouth.

Isabel smiled, seeing no damage done except to

William's temper. It occurred to her at that moment that she had never heard him refer to the animal by anything but "horse."

"William, what do you call him?"

"Who?"

"Your destrier. What is his name?"

William regarded her oddly. "Horse."

"Horse?" she blinked at him. "His name is Horse?"

"What else should I call him? That's what he is."

"But no one calls his horse . . . just . . . Horse!" she protested.

"I do."

"But . . . it seems so . . . cold!" she sputtered. "Do you not have any . . . affection for him?"

"Should I feel affection for something that bites my foot?"

She peered at him, wondering if he was teasing her. She had seen him too often with the animal, talking to him, stroking him. . . . "If you had a dog, what would you call him?"

"I don't have a dog." But with her question an idea flashed through his mind. He glanced at her, then looked quickly away.

"But if you did. What would you call him?"

"I never thought about it. 'Dog,' I suppose."

"You're impossible!" she exclaimed, her brows arching at his grin. But then she smiled, her own mood lightened by the easy rapport that had grown between them. Deep inside she knew that nothing had been settled and eventually it must be faced. But for the moment she was content; the rich feeling of closeness far outweighed the darker moments of solitude.

# 12

THE streets of London thronged with life; merchants hawking their wares, vendors negotiating purchases, individuals making their way to their various destinations as hurriedly as possible with eyes ever watchful for the cutpurse, and ears turned to the warning cry of slop descending from stories above. Girls were pinched overtly, regardless of class, if unwise enough to travel unaccompanied. Urchins waited in sympathetic groups, their large hungry eyes anticipating the opportunity for mischief. All was silently governed by the representatives of the London guilds comfortably established behind neat, deceptively simple storefronts: clothmakers, jewelers, smiths, masons, craftsmen, the silent power of London, the maker of kings.

Industry ceased as the large party of armed knights entered the streets. Expressions became clouded with doubt as they fixed on the green-and-gold banners interspersed among the various colored pennons of the knights. Then they came to rest on the red lion emblazoned on William's chest and his shield, which lay on the arm of his shield-bearer. As recognition dawned, cheers began to rumble through the crowd, catching and building like a wave as they at last recognized the coat of arms. The marshal had come.

William kept a watchful eye on Isabel as he acknowledged the favor of the crowd, knowing that the press could casue havoc with the mounts. He and his men watched closely for the children who would run frequently in their path in their excitement, a quick grasp at shirt-necks often meaning the difference between safety and disaster beneath the razor-sharp hoofs of the high-strung destriers.

"Aye, Marshal!" a voice cried out. " 'Tis 'at yer lady? She's a beauty, she is!"

William grinned in acknowledgment of the caller and chuckled approvingly as the crowd took up in agreement. He laughed as he saw the blush creep up Isabel's cheeks, but she too smiled and waved in the direction of her flatterer.

Word of their arrival passed quickly ahead of them, and their way to Winchester was made the more difficult for it. Isabel noted the pleased expression on William's face, however, and more, a look of affection for the people who had turned out in mass to welcome his return. Eventually they arrived at their destination and what greeted them caused Isabel to draw in her breath sharply before she glanced at her husband to note his response. Before the gates of Winchester there stood a full troop of mounted knights. At their head sat a richly garbed dark-haired man of medium height, and at his side, Hugh de Puiset.

Their party came to a halt within feet of the welcoming committee. William moved his mount forward and clasped wrists in greeting with the dark-haired man. "William, I knew you were within the city only moments after you arrived. Your popularity precedes you." Isabel detected a note of displeasure in the bright, dark eyes though he wore a warm smile.

"Milord," William replied. "I came as soon as I received your message."

John, count of Gloucester, palatine authority of Nottingham, Derby, Cornwall, Somerset, Devon, Dorset, lord of Ireland, prince of England, smiled in response. "As I knew you would. Our friend, Hugh, also lost no time in responding to my request. But then, he has good reason to fly to the opportunity, no?" He laughed loudly and then his eyes came to a rest on Isabel. "Well then, William. Would this be your lady wife?"

"Aye, milord. May I present Isabel, Lady Marshal."

John's eyes passed over Isabel, pausing briefly on her growing stomach, barely concealed beneath the light cloak she wore, and a black brow arched as he gave a ghost of a smile. "You have grown up, Lady Isabel. When I last saw you, you were in braids and had freckles across your nose. William, you are a fortunate man. Had I known she would grow into such a beauty I might have married her myself. In fact, I believe that it was considered at one time."

Absorbed with staring at Isabel, John did not see the dark shadow that passed over William's eyes, but it did not go unnoticed by Hugh. "Milord," the bishop of Durham said quickly. "Perhaps we might repair to a place of more comfort. I am certain that William and his lady would wish to refresh themselves after their long ride."

"He makes my skin crawl!"

"Isabel, I think that you are unduly upset by him."

William and Isabel were alone in their chamber at Winchester, having been escorted there by two stiff-necked pages in the livery of Count John of Gloucester.

"Nay, I am not!" she shook her head vehemently, loosening her hair from some of its pins.

"Are you certain that you do not wish for me to send for Corliss?" William asked as he laboriously unfastened the long column of fastenings reaching down her back.

"I have never heard you complain about undoing my gown before, milord," she quipped, turning her head to look at him.

"In the heat of passion my fingers work with much more agility, milady," he returned. "In that we must attend John within the hour, it does seem a chore.''

"I allowed Corliss time to settle in to her own quarters. By the time she were to be fetched the task would be done. There, see!''

"Aye, and now I must hurry to see to myself,'' he threw back to her, turning to the shaving stand, where he began to lather up soap for his shave.

She could feel his eyes upon her in the silvered mirror as he lathered his face, and she turned her back to him as she slipped from the gown, allowing it to drop at her feet. "If you feel that Longchamp is a ferret, milord, in John I see a fox, beautiful and sleek in appearance while ever calculating his next prey.''

"So, you think John is beautiful?'' he countered, his eyes lit with amusement as he paused in a stroke to a cheek.

"In form, aye, who could dispute it—though he seems to be tending to fat. A black fox. . . . '' She shrugged, bending her head at the washstand to splash her face. She came up sputtering, reaching for a towel, which her husband paused to hand her. "Personally, while I admire foxes, William, for they are most beautiful, I do not trust them.''

"John mentioned that he had known you,'' William tossed out casually, almost too casually, as he worked on his chin. "You never mentioned it.''

"As I recall I was seven. He was a toad. A nasty toad.''

Grinning, William finished his shaving while she dressed her hair. "While you were supervising the unloading of the baggage, John could not help but to wallow in the fact that Longchamp is hiding in the Tower.''

"The Tower?''

"Aye, it seems that he sought to gain support from the people of London by speaking to them in his behalf at the gates of Windsor,'' he said as he pulled on a long tunic of deep gold linen trimmed in the soft green braid of his colors. "Unfortunately the man has never learned to speak English, and his Norman French only served to inflame them. He barely escaped with his skin.''

"So now you have the weasel in his lair,'' she observed, struggling into a deep-sleeved gown of forest-green velvet. She tried to reach the back fastenings and finally gave up, crossing to her husband as he fixed a heavy gold belt about his waist. "Odd, thinking of him in the Tower. I wonder if he has my room.''

"Nay, love,'' he chuckled. It turned to a sigh as he saw her dilemma. He helped her pull the heavy gown about her shoulders and turned her around so he could fasten it. "As pleasant as your room was, his are residence quarters. One I expect to dislodge him from,'' he observed with a crooked grin.

"A pleasant room?'' she parroted, trying to turn to look at him. His fingers gripped on the fabric, and he turned her firmly away as he sought to complete the fastening. A tawny brow arched. "Someday I shall tell you about that.''

He completed his task and handed her the golden link girdle laying on the bed as he turned away to grab up his cloak. She linked the girdle about her waist, adjusting the ends to reach within inches of the hem, below her breast. Going to the mirror she checked the low-cut neckline, adjusting the bodice to reveal the right amount of cleavage. "What of Longchamp's lands?''

"His lands will be distributed, do not fear." Her attentions in the mirror were not lost on William.

"Aye, by John,'' she snorted, fixing a gold fillet of emeralds about her forehead before crossing back to her husband. "He will take them for himself. Tell me,'' she glanced up at William with a sly look, "was it not at Tickhill that Longchamp informed Hugh that he was to repair to a monastery?" She pushed his hand aside and fastened the cloak to a shoulder pin, the tip of her tongue caught between her teeth as she sought to push the pin through the heavy fabric.

"Aye, it was Tickhill. And John does covet it," he answered, a smile at the corners of his mouth as he observed her concentration.

"What if Hugh were to secure the lands?" she asked,

moving to the other shoulder.

His brow creased as he understood her words. Aye, it would work, he thought. Smiling he bent and planted a light kiss on her nose. She returned the smile and they turned to leave the room with a last look in the mirror.

"One thing is certain," she said as he pulled the door closed behind them.

"What is that?" he asked.

"We certainly do look wonderful."

His laughter was heard throughout the corridor as they walked down the long hallway.

An odd war, she thought. To be sitting in a comfortable chamber in Windsor, mending a soft linen chanise he had torn the day before, knowing he would walk through those doors at any moment. A daytime war, called off because of dark, she mused. But she did not delude herself. A stray arrow or lance . . . she shuddered and pushed the thought from her mind.

She thought of other battles he had told her about. More truthfully, they were battles she had come to comprehend through bits and pieces she had put together, knowing what they must have been like from earlier ones Gervase had recounted. The dust, heat, the overpowering fatigue when one pushed on, knowing one's life depended upon it. The noise, ears assaulted by the screams of men and horses, the sounds of metal striking. Always in the back of the mind lurked the realization that the next moment could be the last. But this knowledge was deeply hidden, as to focus upon it would mean death . . .

Hugh was in the north, engaged in a battle much like her musings, and she felt a pang of guilt as she knew that she had been the one to plant the seed. But she smiled in spite of herself as she recalled the excitement clear in Hugh's eyes when it was decided that it would be he who would strike out for Longchamp's lands. He had barely contained that excitement as the evening progressed until he could leave to ready his men. . . . She chuckled out loud as she recalled the stunned look on

Count John's face when he realized that he had been outmaneuvered and that the lands would go to Hugh. William was indeed talented; she smiled in memory. John had not realized what had happened until he had agreed to it.

So now William's forces and John's were ringed about the Tower, and Longchamp's influence was soon at an end. Why, she reasoned, does it take so long for men to come to an obvious conclusion?

"Would you care for something to eat or drink, milady?" Corliss asked, rising from the chair where she had been working on her own mending.

"Nay, I am content." Isabel smiled, realizing how bored the girl must be. "See you to the kitchens, however. We have been at this for hours." She fought a smile, knowing that the gossip below stairs was a far greater draw than food.

"Aye, milady." The girl brightened, eager to be gone before Isabel could change her mind.

Then a feeling of loneliness overtook Isabel, and her thoughts turned to more personal matters. She laid down the mended chanise and picked up a piece of fabric she was embroidering for a surcoat for William. But it too lost her interest as she stared from the window and her teeth began to chew relentlessly on her lower lip. She loved him. More than she thought it possible to love a man, to love anyone. Why then was their life together so filled with pain? He seemed not aware of her existence—until he wanted her. Then he would draw her to his bed, expecting her to respond, after hours, even days, with hardly a word to her. And he knew she would respond, the needs of her body ever betraying her. Each time she pushed down the hurt she lived with, recalling it only later when he had again returned to the world he would not allow her to share. Moments, those few precious times when he allowed her into his life, were rich, filled with such joy, such closeness. Could he not feel it in those moments? Why could he not want it as much as she? He seemed to be so separate from her.

And it had begun to affect even that which they had

shared with such deep pleasure, their physical relationship. Since the night at the inn in Albourne, Isabel found it easier to avoid him—even to pretend sleep when he returned. Involved with his own problems, he had not pressed her. How long, she wondered, would it be before they could no longer pretend? Before they would be forced to face what was happening to them?

She was so deeply lost in her thoughts that she did not hear the door open nor sense that the object of her musings had entered. William paused at the door, closing it quietly behind him. He drew in his breath softly and stood there for a long moment, transfixed by the way she looked. The light from the window encased her in an aura of gold, her hair tumbled about her shoulders, softening the creamy rose of her complexion. He crossed the room, the chain links of his mail clicking softly beneath the heavy linen of his tabbard, but it was not until he bent to lay a light kiss on the top of her head that she realized that she was no longer alone in the room.

"William!" she gasped, jumping slightly as she twisted about.

"I hope that your thoughts were of me," he smiled gently, coming about to sit on a bench beneath the window.

"They were," she answered lightly, hoping to cover how disturbing those thoughts had been. "What has happened, have you routed Longchamp?"

"Nay, not yet," he smirked. "But he cannot hold out much longer. Walter de Coutance has called a council to determine the matter of the chancellor legally. Hugh has ridden in and a troop has been sent for Geoffrey. I came for you, as I thought you might wish to attend."

"Me?" her face flushed with pleasure.

"I thought that might please you," he smiled. "You have just enough time to prepare; the council will be held at Saint Paul's within the hour."

She jumped up, hardly noticing that William reached out to catch her needlework before it fell to the floor as she rushed to the wardrobe, her thoughts excitedly fixed on choosing the right gown. He fingered the fabric, his thumb passing over the careful stitches worked into exquisite patterns of delicate flowers, momentarily fascinated with her ability to transform threads into work that seemed to breathe with life. He glanced up at her with a look of appreciation as she struggled out of her gown. His eyes passed lovingly down her body, now clad only in a thin chemise of soft linen, and his brows drew together in a sudden frown. It struck him that the babe was riding lower than it should, almost as if . . . an uneasy feeling washed through him.

"Isabel," he said softly. "When did you calculate that the babe is due?"

"What?" she turned to him with puzzlement, her thoughts still on the selection of her gown. "Oh, not for well over a month, why?" Realization dawned and she frowned. "I know that I must return to Chepstow, William," she pouted. "I hoped that you had forgotten. I suppose now that you will have me on my way within the week."

"Aye, you must return soon," he said vaguely, his eyes still fixed on her low, swollen stomach. He was a man who had been raised among women, and though he had paid little attention to their ways, something bothered him about the way she carried the child.

Nothing more was said as she finished dressing, choosing a gown of ruby satin embroidered in pink roses on the bodice and hem, the bodice gathered beneath her breasts to allow for the fullness of her stomach. The long sleeves, the tips of the inseam meeting the hem of the garment, were made full from the shoulders, artfully covering the fullness of her figure. A long translucent veil of pink was attached to the fillet of rubies about her forehead, covering her forehead and cascading about her shoulders and back to the hem of the gown.

"You look like a queen." William smiled appreciatively, crossing to her. "It is fortunate that Eleanor is still on the continent, arranging for a bride for Richard."

She smiled at him, reaching up on her tiptoes to kiss him lightly. "You are gallant, sir. You make a very fat woman feel beautiful."

"Fat with love," he said, grinning, bending down to kiss her deeply. She stirred in his arms, responding, her mind blotting out her earlier disquiet.

D'Erley came for them, and as they left the room William, unable to shake his earlier unease, leaned to John, speaking in a low voice so that Isabel did not hear. "Send for Lady Marshal, tell her that we have need of her."

The vast room at Saint Paul's held a vitality of energy that could be felt by all of those present, particularly by Isabel, whose sense of power felt nourished as her shrewd grey eyes moved among the barons present. Count John she passed over lightly, preferring to ignore that dark prince, moving to Hugh, a great blond giant, his quiet intelligence now overshadowed by Geoffrey, bastard prince and now archbishop of York. He held the Plantagenet beauty but a softer version as gifted by his beautiful mother, Henry's favorite, Rosemond. The tragedy his mother had lived showed in her son, a determined acceptance of his position veiling the strength ever-present in his Plantagenet blood. Aye, she thought, Richard and John should worry. This one was a threat, or would be had he not chosen to follow the path of the church. He was loved by the people; that had been confirmed upon his entrance to London. The council had been delayed a full hour, a company of knights sent to aid Geoffrey's own vassals in order to see him to Saint Paul's through the cheering crowds that had gathered.

Her eyes moved to Walter de Coutance, the archbishop of Rouen. He sat at the head table talking with William, and it gave her the opportunity to study this man sent by the king to still England's strife. Greying, the tall man still did not bend under his encroaching years. His eyes held an insight that she sensed could cut to the heart of any problem or the reasonings of man.

But she also sensed that solutions would be seen only by his way of thinking; the hardness behind his expression confirming that he would brook no other suggestion once a decision was made. She hoped that he was one to see reason before it reached that point.

Her gaze, instantly softening then turning to one of fierce pride, moved to her husband. Quiet, assured strength, accepted by his peers and his superiors. Heads turned to William as he spoke, his words taken as the voice of reason, and she again marveled at his gift, brought to a man born landless. A man who had gained his power through the strength of his sword, his steadfast loyalty tempered with wisdom. A man whose word was his bond, whose talent for diplomacy was unsurpassed. And he was hers.

The council began as each in turn presented their grievances to the council consisting of Walter de Coutance and the justiciars. "When my papers were presented to the chancellor he was said to have replied, 'I alone know the mind and reasonings of the king!' The man will not respond to a higher authority! He will see England to his own end!" Geoffrey claimed, his blue eyes darkening with controlled rage.

"He refused to concede to me though I informed him that his lands were forfeit!" Count John interjected. "He claimed that he, as chancellor, had been condemned against law and justice."

"We all are aware that he refused to acknowledge my position." This came from Hugh, who was at Geoffrey's right. "Had I not accompanied his men to Saint Martin's abbey, my life was forfeit—and this because I disagreed with his position though the northern reaches were to be under my control."

"He leaches England," Geoffrey rejoined.

"He works within the law," de Coutance reminded him. "He maintains the king's goodwill in his collection of taxes."

"The king will maintain the goodwill of the people and the barons only by allowing them to exist within a

reasonable means," William interjected. "It is true that
Longchamp works within the law, milord, but he works
against its intent. If he is allowed to move along his
present course, the throne may well be in jeopardy. We
are here to support the throne, and Richard Coeur de
Lion, and it is not served by William de Longchamp.
The four of us," he indicated the others who sat with
them at the council table, "were appointed by the king
to act as associate justiciars to aid the chancellor in gov-
erning England in the king's absence. Not once has he
consulted with us, nor has he given notice to our advice." The other justiciars confirmed, each in turn,
William's words. It was then that William presented the
letter he had received from King Richard, authorizing
him, along with the other associate justiciars and the
archbishop of Rouen, to take whatever steps necessary
to govern England in the event that the chancellor did
not follow their advice. Action was then taken swiftly,
to the grim satisfaction of Count John, Geoffrey, and
Hugh de Puiset. Longchamp was deposed as justiciar of
England, his titles stripped, and Walter de Coutance
made justiciar in his stead.

As the council was disbanding, groups gathering
to discuss the outcome and effects of what had been
done, a breathless, disarrayed messenger burst into the
chamber, his eyes wide with news. "Milords!" he
gasped, while all eyes turned to him in wonder, "the
chancellor has escaped from the Tower!"

In the commotion that followed, only one noticed the
change that had overtaken Isabel where she sat in the
pews on the far side of the room with the other ladies
and knights who were observing the proceedings.
William had motioned to d'Erley, and as the knight
approached his eyes had come to rest on his wife.
"Isabel," he murmured as John reached his side. The
knight's gaze followed William's and he too paled as
they found his lady. Isabel's head was bent, her hands
grasping her stomach, her eyes closed as she appeared to
be fighting some inner agony. William and d'Erley were

at her side in moments. "Isabel, what is it?" William demanded while fearing the answer.

She looked up at him with a weak smile, gritting her teeth through her pain. "It appears, milord," she gasped, "that our child has chosen this untimely moment to make his appearance."

# 13

LIFE moved progressively forward, the people engaged in daily pursuits of profit and need. Menial tasks were completed, conversations between acquaintances who met on the street were engaged in normal course. Laughter was heard, disagreements occurred, and lovers found their private places. Members of the London guilds met, discourse on commerce was dispensed with quickly as their discussions and minds turned to those who thought themselves in power. Rumors ran rampant through the streets to the countryside and beyond, but those of wealth who met about tables in back rooms knew the truth of matters dear to kings.

The castle at Winchester bustled with activity. Messengers came and went with spaced timing carrying news from the north, where Hugh de Puiset again waged siege against Tickhill, and Count John's forces took what remained from the fleeing chancellor. William had rushed forward to capture the ill-fated miscreant before he could depart England's shores, and the archbishops of Rouen and York waited, receiving each bit and taste of news with calm deliberation and relish. Their minds however, while filled with matters of siege and state, took moments to turn to the upper levels of the castle, where another event was taking place. Both sent up prayers for William's lady, neither wishing to be the one to greet their foremost knight with ill tidings upon his return from the king's business.

The pain grasped her again, cutting deeply into her body. It began with an awareness that it was intimate, to an ache deep in her back, only to spread quickly over her middle; a pulling, gripping pain that encompassed her entire body, blotting out all thought, all feeling but her agony. Each time she was certain that it would never end, she would spend an eternity with pain that she could not bear. She fought against it, vaguely aware of voices about her. Their words were undiscernible, a mesh of voices, adding to her misery and she cried for them to stop, to take the pain with them. Miraculously, after what seemed forever, the pain ceased and she was left damp and spent, yet with a dull knowledge accompanied with terror that it would begin again and this time it would not stop.

"Isabel," a soft voice said, "dearheart, you must relax."

Relax? How could she relax when it hurt so much! Oh, Sweet Mother, how could anything hurt so much? Why didn't someone make it stop! Oh, William, please make it stop!

"We have sent for William, Isabel. Please, you must relax."

William? They had . . . her thoughts were silenced as another pain began and she grasped the sheets, wrenching them in tormented fingers as it swept over her, and she did not realize that she cried out.

Below, a commotion was heard as a large company of knights burst through the door into the large entry chamber of Winchester. The largest of them strode to the staircase, taking the steps three at a time as he half ran to the upper chambers of the castle. Reaching the doorway he almost knocked down a serving maid who was leaving the room with soiled linens. He drew back, allowing the startled girl to pass, and her eyes grew wide with shock as she regarded the immense knight whose eyes seemed to burn at her. His eyes were indeed lit with ferocity as they fixed on the linens in the girl's arms, the blood-soaked sheets searing into his brain with a terror he had never known. He burst into the room and his eyes turned to the door of her chamber, the moment striking to his heart as he heard a deep, pain-filled cry coming from beyond the door.

"Isabel!" he cried, lunging for the door.

The door opened at that moment and Elizabeth stepped out, closing it quickly behind her, but William's attention was only on what was behind her, in that room.

"William!"

He felt hands push against him and he looked down at her, his fuzzy mind slowly focusing on the object of the voice. "William! Stop, you cannot go in there as you are!"

"Elizabeth!" he choked, his face and voice filled with the terror he felt. "What has happened? Is she . . . "

"The birth is difficult," she said firmly. "But you can not go in there until you can control yourself. Come over here and sit down." When she saw that he was not listening, his eyes still fixed with agony on the door, she became more determined. "William! Sit down! Annie, fetch some wine for Sir William, quickly," she snapped at a serving girl, whose eyes were wide with amazement over the sudden appearance of the marshal. She managed to guide William to a chair and saw to it that he drank a full measure before she offered him another. "The birth is difficult," she repeated when she saw that he was in control of himself. The thought passed quickly through her mind that this man, undaunted when faced with his own death, should cringe with terror when faced with the pain of a young woman. She had reason to feel amazed; it was the first time she had ever seen her brother-in-law afraid of anything. The thought made her gentler, as she sensed his pain and fear. "She is strong and healthy, William, and the babe is positioned normally."

"But it has been two days!" he groaned. "Why has it not come? What is wrong?"

"She is afraid," Elizabeth answered. "I believe that the first day was false labor, but she so exhausted herself that when it began in earnest she could not relax. Now she is frightened and is fighting against herself."

"How much longer can she last like this?" his tortured blue eyes turned to Elizabeth, and she swallowed involuntarily.

"As long as she needs to," Elizabeth heard herself saying, unwilling to tell him anything else. "Perhaps, now that you are here. . . . But you must be strong for her, William."

He nodded, then tossed off the remainder of his goblet, welcoming its warmth as it coursed through his weary body. He removed his hauberk and his gambeson beneath as Elizabeth called for Anna to fetch him a fresh chanise while she filled a washbowl for him.

When he finally entered the room, he stared down at Isabel, his heart gripped with unreasoning fear as he saw the lines of agony in her pale face remaining, though the last moment of her pain had gone. The linens beneath her were drenched, as were her gown and hair, though her bedding had been changed repeatedly. He reached down and his strong fingers gently loosened hers from where they gripped the sheets. Sitting next to her he raised her hands pressing them against his lips as his eyes closed. "Oh God," he thought, "You have seen me through tournaments, wars, and the whims of kings. See her through this, she is so dear to me, more than my life."

"William?"

He opened his eyes to find her watching him, and though she had spoken to him he wondered if she truly knew he was there, as her eyes were glazed with a foggy veil of exhaustion and pain. "Aye, I am here, love," he said huskily. He reached out and smoothed back her damp hair from her face. Oh God, he thought, what have I done to her? "I love you, Isabel," he said, not realizing that he had never told her before.

Her eyes seemed to clear on his words and incredibly, she smiled. "I know," she whispered.

"You were unprepared for this." he said, trying to keep his voice calm and even. "Your labor has been long. You have been fighting it. You must relax."

"It hurts so."

The simple statement and the small, almost childlike way she said it cut into him. "I know, love. But that I could take it from you." He turned and leaned against the head of the bed and drew her into his arms, nestling her against his chest, wrapping his arms protectively about her. "Let me take the pain, Isabel," he whispered into her ear. "Give it to me."

He stroked her arms and when the next pain overtook her he grasped her to him, murmuring to her, breathing with her. Slowly, her breathing began to match the even rhythm of his, and he felt her relax in his arms and realized that she was listening to his body and matching its even movement against her own.

Elizabeth entered the room with the midwife. Both women stopped short, amazed at what they found, the almost peaceful look that had come over Isabel's face where she lay in William's arms. "She has had three more pains," William said quietly, bringing a surprised blink from both of the women who had been waiting, braced, for the sound of her screams. The midwife rushed forward and checked Isabel's progress, her face lighting happily as she looked up at the others. "The babe is coming, milord." She grinned. "Normally I would send you from the room now," she added with a chuckle, "but I think 'twould be best for you to remain. You appear to be just what the lass needed. Now, lass," she said to Isabel, suddenly full of business. "When I tell you, you push, but not before."

William held her, his eyes fixed on the drama as he continued to murmur soft words of encouragement to Isabel. His eyes widened as he saw the head appear, then the shoulders, wincing as a cry tore from Isabel at the moment, and his attention was again drawn to her comfort. Then it was done, and to his total shock and amazement the midwife was holding his son, her ruddy face contorted with a huge grin as she laid the babe on Isabel's stomach. He was barely aware of the slap the woman applied to the tiny bottom of his son, for his eyes were fixed on the small body, and the loud boisterous cry filled his ears, the tiny fists and arms trembling in protest of the outrage, the eyes shut tightly as he screamed his rage to the cold world he had entered.

William found himself ushered from the room, and suddenly he was facing the closed door, his mind filled with the miracle he had witnessed. He took a deep breath, finally absorbing what had occurred, and he suddenly spun about, grabbing up the nearest object—which proved to be a startled Corliss, who squeaked as her lord spun her about, laughing.

"My lord!" she cried. He set her down abruptly, still laughing, and to her total shock he leaned down and planted a resounding kiss on her lips, leaving her breathless. Stunned, she stepped back but he was gone, slamming the door behind him.

"I have a son!"

William brought the conversation in the room to an abrupt halt as everyone turned. Seeing the blank looks on their faces, he repeated the announcement, and the room broke into uproarious laughter and congratulations. The men rose to gather about him, joining in his happiness with hearty jests and resounding claps to his back.

"We have cause for celebration!" the archbishop of Rouen offered, motioning to a serving lad.

"Oh, Lord," Geoffrey muttered good-naturedly, "I sense a drunk coming on."

"Why not?" William laughed. "We have not had the opportunity to celebrate your homecoming. It will be a double celebration!"

"What of Longchamp?" Walter de Coutance asked, handing a goblet to William. "While I rejoice in your good fortune and am as willing to imbibe as the next man, there is that matter."

"The matter is settled." William grinned. "Long-champ is under guard in a cellar in Dover."

"A dark and dank one, I trust," Geoffrey observed, greatly pleased by the news.

"Presumably." William laughed. "He was . . . "

His words were cut off as the door opened and John d'Erley entered, a shy Allan fitz Ulred following timidly behind. "William! I just heard! God's breath, man, the news is good!"

"Which news?" William laughed.

"Your son, of course!" d'Erley roared. "What else, is there more?"

"Aye, there is, we were . . . "

"The men send you their greetings and congratulations," John interrupted in his elation over the news. "Have you not heard the cheering from the bailey? The heir is being welcomed with great rejoicing!"

"Perhaps, William," de Coutance offered with a wry grin, "we should continue this celebration in the great hall where all may share in it. Then you may tell everyone of your other news." So the party began.

In the late morning William tried to open the door to his wife's room and stopped, holding the doorlatch momentarily to gain support. He closed his eyes until he felt the world come to rest once again. He slowly opened his eyes and gradually focused on Elizabeth, who was crossing the room to him, a smirk clearly set on her lovely face.

"You poor man," she said, unsympathetic laughter in her voice belying her words. "Why will you men do this?" she took his arm. "Come with me, I believe that I have the cure." She whispered to Corliss, who was eyeing her lord with a shy, embarrassed look, and the girl quickly scurried from the room. Elizabeth led William to a chair and fought a chuckle as he lowered himself into it with a painful groan.

"Damn it, woman," he growled, squinting into the early morning light. "Close those shutters!"

"You will recover," she laughed softly. In a few

moments Corliss returned with a tray supporting a goblet of foul brew, which William later accused Elizabeth as using for an attempt upon his life. On her urging he threw down the goblet's contents in a gulp. Swallowing, he leaned back in his chair, his mouth drawn into a grimace as he shuddered slightly. He turned to her, his eyes peaked, and his mouth opened to say something, but he froze, his eyes growing suddenly wide as a look of horror fused his expression.

"Sweet Mother!" he gasped, leaping from the chair. He disappeared behind the garderobe screen as Elizabeth gave into a hearty laugh. "Corliss," she said, grinning, "bring some watered wine, quickly."

William emerged from behind the screen and glared at her, pausing before he returned shakily to his chair. "I won't forget this, Elizabeth," he growled. "Do not think, because you are my sister-in-law, that you are safe. Consider your life in jeopardy."

"I shall take note of your warning," she laughed. She took the goblet from Corliss and handed it to William. "Here, drink this. Now tell me, do you not feel better?"

"A little," he acknowledged begrudgingly, drawing from the weak wine.

"Good. Now, your wife is waiting for you. And a son, William."

William opened the door gingerly, a feeling of reverence holding him back. She was half sitting in bed, her hair spread over the pillow as she slept, her lovely face relaxed, a soft smile touching her lips in sweet, unencumbered dreams. He approached the bed slowly, his eyes drinking in her loveliness as he was filled with his love for her. He leaned over and brushed her forehead with a light kiss, then sat on the edge of the bed as she roused, her mouth drawing into a delightful pout before she awoke.

"William." She gifted him with a soft smile.

He leaned over and kissed her. Leaning with his arms propped on either side of her he smiled down at her. "You look beautiful," he said gently. "Do you know how much I love you?"

"Aye," she smiled, "I know. Have you seen our son?"

"Not since last night. I wanted to see you first."

"He's beautiful."

"Could he be anything else?"

Her eyes moved over his face, and a glint of amusement shone from her eyes. "You have welcomed our son into the world quite properly, it would seem, milord."

"Aye, as have all with me." He grimaced, his head pounding in response.

"I . . . I am sorry to have been so much trouble, William," she said, biting her lip.

"No trouble," he offered gently, bending down to kiss her again. "I am only thankful that everything turned out well."

"But I brought you from . . . " It suddenly occurred to her that he was still here. Why had he not returned to his duties immediately? "What has happened, William? What of Longchamp?"

"You do not want to talk of that now," he chuckled, seeing the determined look return to her eyes.

"Aye, but I do! William, what has happened?"

She struggled to sit up and he laughed, forcing her down to the pillows. "Isabel, be easy! I will tell you only if you behave!" She lay back with a pout. "Longchamp is being put on a ship for the continent even as we speak." He grinned.

"Tell me!" she brightened.

"Would you believe me if I told you that he attempted to leave England disguised as a woman?" he said, grinning.

"Nay!" she gasped, then her face crinkled up with laughter. "As a woman?"

"Aye, as a peddler. Complete with skirt and veil, with a bolt of cloth beneath his arm to aid his disguise. But his lack of English once again served him ill, and a group of fishwives became suspicious, one flipping the veil from his head, whereupon he was discovered. A cry went up and our esteemed chancellor found himself locked in a cellar of Dover. We have granted him exile, and he is even now on his way to Normandy.''

"Exile?'' she snorted. "You should have seen him to the block!''

"You are a bloodthirsty wench.'' He grinned, leaning down to nuzzle her ear. His lips moved across her cheek to her lips, where he kissed her resoundingly.

"William,'' she gasped breathlessly. "Mark me well, you will all rue the day when you allowed that despot exile. How can you be so forgiving?''

"He is the choice of the king,'' he murmured, his lips moving to her other ear. "Richard will deal with him when he returns. For now your 'despot' is safely deposited in Normandy.''

She gave in to his kisses, warmed by his love, while a part of her mind stirred restlessly to the thought that Longchamp was still at large and fully capable, to her reasoning, of causing misery to England and those she loved.

He stood looking down at the small, vulnerable being who lay in the cradle sleeping. He blinked as the baby, who had been making no sound and suddenly began to breathe in panted rhythm, its little chest heaving with exertion.

"What is it?'' William exclaimed in a horrified whisper. "Is he all right?''

Elizabeth, who stood nearby, moved to his side and looked down at the sleeping infant. "He is fine.'' She smiled.

"But he is breathing oddly,'' William insisted, his whisper becoming louder.

"He is breathing like a baby.'' She smiled tolerantly, glancing with amusement at the anxious father.

"Are you sure?'' he asked, doubting Elizabeth's wisdom though she had been through this eight times before with her own.

"Quite sure,'' she assured him. "William, I have things to do and I shall leave you alone with your son. Short of his doing something miraculous, such as speaking to you, you will trust that he is normal and there is no cause to give the alarm?''

"Aye," he answered somewhat sheepishly. "I shall try to contain myself."

When Elizabeth had gone, William knelt by the cradle and occupied himself with the fascinating endeavor of watching his son sleep. So vulnerable, so trusting. His whole world occupied with eating, sleeping and filling his napkin, he thought with delight. Trusting that someone will care for you. And we shall, he thought. Your mother and I. She will nourish you, giving you the means to grow, and I will protect you. On that, my little son, I pledge my life. And someday, when you are grown to a man, all that I have worked for shall be for you. The lands, and the responsibility. Oh, aye, that too, for only in responsibility, well met, comes satisfaction, a feeling of accomplishment. I pray that you understand and do not grow to resent me as I teach you, knowing that I do so in love, even in moments when I appear hard. And misunderstandings will come, for it is inevitable between father and son. He leaned over and kissed the soft forehead gently, smiling as the baby stirred in his sleep.

A feeling of incredible tenderness filled him as he watched his son sleep. Taking a deep breath he left him, allowing Anna, the baby's nurse to enter, and made his way to his wife's chambers. A deep peace filled him, a peace he had never known before.

# 14

As he crossed the hall, Waverly paused to fix his gaze on Master Will. The toddler approached Beaumont from behind, the large blue eyes of the youngster fixed with anticipation on the knife that hung from the knight's belt. Waverly opened his mouth to call a warning, but Beaumont turned just as the child's hands would have closed on the tantalizing object. With a burst of giggles the small boy was swept into the knight's lap, and a smile touched the lips of the solemn steward. He determined that the child was in no peril, and with a glance at Isabel he continued on to his own duties.

Isabel too had observed her son's activity from the corner of her eyes even as her attention appeared to be caught by the others who had gathered about the fire in the great hall. She smiled gently at her son, who had curled up against Beaumont's chest and was now absorbed in tracing a small finger over the brightly colored birds embroidered on the knight's surcoat.

The babe brought joy to a house of sorrow, the mood beneath Chepstow's parapets having been plunged into grief with the news of the death of John Marshal. Isabel grieved for Elizabeth and she wondered how she fared, grateful that Elizabeth had her children to comfort her. Her eyes turned again to her son but she knew, had it been William, that his loss would have been a void that could not be filled, even with the strain that had continued to grow in their marriage. Her gaze shifted to her husband, and she bit her lip with despair at the lines of sorrow etched in his face. John Marshal had been more than a brother to William, he had been a friend. Upon learning of the death, William had quickly dispatched a contingent of his knights to see the body to Cirencester, where his brother would be interred at Bradenstroke Priory. "What will you do?" she asked softly. "Now that the king has returned to England?"

"I will see to the funeral," he answered quietly.

"And then?" she pressed, hiding her surprise that he would take the time, even for John's funeral.

"Then I shall see to my king!" he snapped, his eyes growing cold as they regarded her.

John d'Erley exchanged an uncomfortable glance with Beaumont before his gaze moved to those who had gathered to offer what comfort they could. They were William's closest friends and vassals: Hugh de Sanford, who held his honor for Giffard; Nicolas Avenel, who held honors in Striguil; Ralph Musard, William's constable for Gloucester Castle; and John Marshal, Elizabeth's eldest son, who had brought the news.

John gestured to Tirell fitz Waring, one of William's younger squires, to see to his master's cup, even knowing that the interruption would do little to distract his lord and lady from their approaching quarrel. Allan, though his eyes were filled with tears, stepped forward and saw to the task before the other could respond, though his hand trembled as he refilled the goblet.

"How can you be loyal to a man who cares so little for England that upon his return he reinvested Longchamp as chancellor?" she snapped, her smoky grey eyes flaring with anger.

Though they were accustomed to bluntness between

these two, eyes widened at the vehemence in Isabel's voice and the manner of William's response. "You are in no position to question the decisions of the king, madam," he answered curtly, "or to question mine."

"You can say that to me?" she snapped, her voice rising. "That little despot would have seen my house brought down with his lies to the king!"

"You are forgetting that Richard gave no credence to those lies," William retorted, his anger increasing.

"It is true, Lady Marshal," Musard interjected quickly. "When Longchamp's man sought the king in Syria to accuse William of leading a plot against his throne, the king replied that he would not believe Marshal to be evil or false!"

"Only after the messenger admitted that he had lied," Isabel snorted, still glaring at her husband.

John saw William's growing rage, and he stared at Isabel in dismay. How could she seek to argue with him now, when his grief was tearing at him? And to do so in front of others? Surely, she must realize that his pride would feed his anger. He had kept his grief so tightly in control. Should he explode now. . . . John's eyes softened suddenly, and a smile tugged at the corners of his mouth as he began to realize her meaning.

Will grew restless on Beaumont's lap and the angry voices of the adults caused him to whine unhappily as he pulled at the knight's tunic. "Madam," William said tersely, "I bid you to see our son to his bed. May I also suggest that you may retire." Isabel stared at William for a moment, then she reached over and took Will from Beaumont. Ignoring her husband's anger, she bade them a good night.

Isabel tucked the sleepy child into bed, dismissing the nurse in her need for distraction from her own unhappy thoughts. She kissed her son good night and made her way to her chamber, now regretfully alone with her frustration and anger. She bit back the tears that began to sting at her eyes. Not now, she thought as she swallowed forcefully, I shall not cry. Though her words to

William had been true—indeed, her honesty had given weight to the argument—her purpose had been to drive William to anger. He had been withdrawn and silent since learning of John's death, burying his grief deeply inside of him. But it had been much too easy to anger him, she thought miserably. The years had seemed to draw them further apart; he to his world, she to hers. Her responsibilities were ever demanding, and when she tried to share in his he barely tolerated her opinion, patronizing her until she fled back into her own realm. Oh Lord, she cried silently, was there nothing left between them? Only anger and resentment, lurking like a death-giving growth.

The hour was late when William opened the door to their chamber. He found Isabel asleep in a chair in front of the fire, and for a moment something stirred within him, a remembrance perhaps of an earlier time, a moment of tenderness. But annoyance stirred in him, pushing aside all tender thoughts as he recalled her earlier words, and more, the malignity that had built between them. . . . He shut the door behind him and she awoke, startled with a moment of disorientation. "It is late," he said quietly, "you should be in bed."

She was too sleepy to feel his anger, and she yawned as she struggled to sit up. Wincing at the stiffness in her neck she rubbed it thoughtfully as she watched him move about the room, pulling off his surcoat, then his boots, which he dropped in his path on his way to a small table near the hearth.

"Is it not rather late for that?" she asked as she watched him pour a goblet of wine.

"Are you telling me now how I should conduct myself?" he asked, arching a brow with displeasure.

"I would not dream of it," she answered with sarcasm. "You might as well pour me one too," she added. "I have a feeling that we are about to have a talk."

"Have a talk?" he smirked, handing her a goblet before he took the chair across from her. "That would infer an exchange of ideas, a mutual respect of opinions. As I recall, your manner is bent more to arguments.''

She winced at his words but she regarded him calmly, unwilling to show him how much they had affected her. ''Can you truly expect me to accept a sovereign who will most assuredly bring England to ruin?''

''England?'' he flared. ''When did you become concerned about England—but for that part which is yours?''

''And yours!'' her voice rose in spite of her resolve to remain calm.

''Mine?'' he laughed cruelly. ''Has it ever been? Am I not just the keeper, the steward for what is yours?''

''That is not true!'' she cried.

''Is it not? I wonder . . . '' He paused as he regarded her with an odd look of speculation. ''I wonder how you would have fared with another; one who would have taken it all, making you the chattel you should have been.''

''Should have been . . . '' she gasped. ''Can you mean that?''

He felt a twinge of regret at the pain that crossed her expression, but he dismissed the feeling quickly. The time had come to have it out, and he would see it to its certain end, come what may. ''I do most certainly do mean it, Isabel. I have only myself to blame for what has occurred between us these past four years of our marriage. I had thought . . . '' He was about to say that he had thought, hoped, that in her he had found one with whom he could truly share his life, his thoughts, dreams, his innermost feelings. But he caught himself, unwilling to share that vulnerability with her, not now, especially not now that he knew how wrong he had been. It seemed that no matter how much he gave to her the more she withdrew. . . . . ''But it is never too late,'' he answered instead. ''And the matter will be rectified.''

''What do you mean?'' she asked, dreading his response.

''It should be obvious, even for you,'' he answered,

"In the future, you will keep your opinions to yourself with the exception of those which involve the household and our son."

"You mean in the presence of others?" she countered, her dread deepening.

"I mean at any time," he answered icily.

She closed her eyes and drew in her breath. The pieces of her life seemed to scatter, leaving only a hollow shell of pain she could not have imagined. His meaning was agonizingly clear, he meant to shut her off totally from him. "Why are you doing this to me?" she whispered. "I have tried to be a good wife to you. God knows, the months you were gone from us fighting against Reesap Griffith in South Wales, I was diligent in keeping your forces supplied. I helped you to raise funds to support England when she found herself bankrupt. Through me we prospered when Count John rose up against the throne while Richard was held hostage in Germany. While you were with Eleanor, endeavoring to break John's alliance with Philip of France, it was I who protected our lands so that you had something to come home to!" her voice rose as she cried to him, desperate to win a battle that she did not understand. "I even helped you to raise the funds to ransom your precious king! William, what do you want from me?"

He regarded her silently, allowing her to finish her plea. His eyes remained stony, chilling her with a remembrance of the first time they met. "Aye, you have done all of that, and more," he answered quietly. "I could not have asked more from my closest ally."

"Then what?" she cried. "What more do you want from me?"

"A wife," he answered, regarding her with frighteningly vacant eyes. "I have allies, Isabel. men who will fight for me and by my side. I have no need for more. What I need from you is far different." Seeing her baffled expression, he affected a smile. "Our bed, for a beginning. Wifely duty, if you must consider it thus. At least, before Will was born, I believe you tried. Since then . . ." he waved his hand, dismissing what had gone between them. "You come to my bed with disdain for my touch; there is obviously no feeling for me in you."

"That is not true!" she gasped, a sob escaping her that he seemed not to notice. But even as she protested she wondered how close he had struck to the truth. There were so many moments when she thought about him and she felt desire well up in her until she thought she would go mad with wanting. Until he was there, and touched her, and it seemed to die with the contact, despite her love for him. But she had ignored it as too painful to deal with, a solution beyond her. Now, that moment she knew would come, had come. He was forcing her to face the terrible void in their relationship and worse—the depth to which she had hurt him.

He watched the contortions that passed over her face as she fought with her inner struggle, and he wanted to feel what she felt, to understand and accept, even now. But he could not, too much had passed, too much pain, too much effort, too much need. "Go to bed, Isabel," he said with distaste, turning his attention to his goblet.

His abrupt dismissal stunned her for an instant, then provoked a defiant wall of anger which surged forward. "I do not wish to go to bed!" she rejoined with a snap.

"I do not care what you wish!" he roared, turning on her with an exploding anger. "Go to bed!"

"Why? So that you may exercise your husbandly rights—without regard to my feelings, my needs!" she cried.

It had been over a month since he had made love to her, if it could still be called that, and his needs were suddenly fed by raw anger and frustration. He felt a sudden need to punish her, to force his will, to make her understand how it would be. Combined with his physical needs, his thoughts overcame all reason. "Your feelings, your needs?" he repeated quietly. "Get into bed, Isabel."

His voice was low and struck her with more force than his anger had done. She gasped, stunned by his intent. He is going to force me, she thought wildly. Her mind raced for a means of escape, even as she knew there was none. He could beat her into submission, such was his right. Clear thought eluded her. The fact that he had never so much as raised a hand to her simply did not occur to her at that moment.

With immense effort she willed herself to be calm. Her whole being was repulsed by the thought of what he was going to do, but she forced herself to move to the bed and her fingers reached up to the neckline of her gown. Submit, she reasoned as her fingers trembled, and soon it will be over. Her gown dropped in a pile at her feet, quickly followed by her shift. She closed her eyes and shivered, as much from his intent as the cool air in the room.

He had watched with detachment as she undressed, while vaguely aware that his rage had begun to dull. The light of the fire behind him played across her body, and he felt himself stir as his body responded to the sight of her beautiful form. Gradually he felt something inside of him soften, and he rose to come to her.

She trembled and her eyes flew open as he touched her. Had she been thinking clearly, she would have wondered as to the gentleness of his touch as his hand passed lightly over a breast, his fingers lingering on a nipple. But her mind was blank to such thoughts, and when she looked up at him her eyes were torpid. His hand ceased in its pursuit, and his eyes narrowed imperceptibly as a muscle twitched in his jaw. Interpreting her reaction as abhorrence to his touch, he swore violently under his breath and swept her into his arms, dropping her in the center of the bed before he stepped back to remove his own clothing.

As he turned away something inside of her snapped. She had been numb with hurt, confusion and guilt. She had complied almost as a penance until the shock of the bed snapped her out her stupor. Her eyes darted to him as he stripped off his clothes, tossing them carelessly about in his newfound determination, and she rebelled. Intent on escape, she crawled from the bed, rolling to the side away from him, but from the corner of his eye he saw her intent and was quicker. He lunged toward her and pulled her across the bed toward him as she shrieked at him and tried to twist about, kicking wildly, her arms swinging at him as she tried to fight him off.

"Damnation, Isabel!" he roared, his control breaking. He pulled her toward him across the bed as she clawed desperately at the sheets. Her feet hit the floor, and she would have turned to fight him, but he pushed her face down into the bedding. In spite of his words he had not intended to force her, but his renewed anger, after feeling himself once again soften to her, the raw aching grief he had held so tight, within which seemed to burst, with demanding release, the contact of their struggle, and the sight of her bare, rounded buttock, strained his nerves beyond endurance. He pulled her toward him to the edge of the bed, and grasping her firmly about the waist he entered her from behind. He heard her gasp as he filled her with him, plunging into her in a need he could no longer control.

She cried out, the sound muffled into the bedding, not believing what he was doing to her. But even as she denied what was happening new feelings began to sweep over her. She wanted him, she wanted him to make her feel again. But not like this. She found herself pushing against him, crying out for him even as she fought him.

Later they lay side by side. Neither spoke. Isabel's face was turned away, her eyes filled with tears of humiliation she refused to shed. She fixed on a candle burning on the far side of the room, its light flickering in an uneven dance of rainbow hues through her tears. She focused on it, willing her mind not to act on its pain. He had not hurt her and she knew that he could have beaten her. Most women of her day sported the bruised evidence of their husband's displeasure, while William had always shown patience, tenderness—but somehow that made it worse. She felt degraded, used, her self-respect gone, her pride badly damaged. "Is there so little left between us, William?" she said at last with a sad resignation in her voice.

"There is whatever you would have there be," he

answered grimly, but she could hear the sadness in his own.

"What does that mean?" she asked, turning onto her back to stare sightlessly at the darkened ceiling.

"It means that I have done all that I can to mend this thing that is between us."

"Oh?" she twisted her head to stare at him in the dim light. "Is that what you have just done?"

"I have tried to be patient, Isabel, to understand your unhappiness."

She bit furiously at her lip in order not to cry. She supposed that to his way of thinking he had tried. So had she. "I do love you, William," she said softly, sniffing back her tears.

"Perhaps you do," he said tiredly. "But our love is not enough."

"You . . . you still love me?"

"It does not matter, Isabel. We have done too much to hurt each other. For now I think it is best that we live apart for a time."

"You . . . are leaving me?" She felt herself grow cold.

"I will be leaving at the end of the week," he said, the statement coming out almost as a sigh. "I will leave you John d'Erley and Beaumont with their knights."

"For how long?"

"I do not know, Isabel. Richard is determined to settle the problem with his brother once and for all. Then . . . I will let you know."

"But what of Will? Whatever there is between us, have you no desire to see your son grow?"

"He is yours, Isabel, until he is seven. Then you shall send him to me."

A soft cry escaped but she bit it back. What was happening was rending her, but she knew that somehow she would have to bear it, that he had made his decision and there was no way she could change it. "But what of me, William? What shall I do without you . . . and without Will?"

"Do what you have always done, Isabel, that which you love best. Care for your lands."

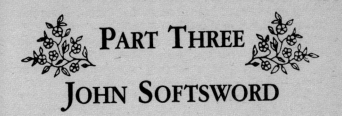

# PART THREE

# JOHN SOFTSWORD

# 15

DEEP in thought, Isabel stared into the glimmering coals of the dying fire, barely aware of the chill that had descended on the room. William had been correct; the lands had sustained her. The days that had passed since his leaving, filling over three years, had moved with remarkable swiftness, her hours filled with tasks, leaving her little time to dwell on the matter of her loneliness. Her lands had thrived under her firm hand, their affairs barely touched by the matters of England and the strife between those in power and those who would seek to be. Count John had been driven from England and now resided at the French court, biding his time until he could return to press his claim against his brother's throne. Isabel was not unaware of these events; she made herself privy to whatever knowledge was necessary for the protection of her lands. Her interest was sharpened due to William's association with the Plantagenets. As was her duty, she kept him, and his vassals, well supplied with food, arms, and equipment. She received each of his occasional letters with longing, secreting them to a private moment, drinking in each word even as she forced herself not to acknowledge the increasing formality in which they were written. Other letters arrived with more frequency to their son. As she read them to Will, the child hung on each word with wide-eyed eagerness for news from his father, and she found herself swallowing back tears for the warmth, the love written in each line that was wrenchingly missing from her own.

He had returned to Normandy with Richard, the king barely settling his suit with his brother before he was pulled back to the continent. And this time he had taken her husband with him. The distance separating them seemed unsurpassable. Aye, the days had been filled, she had made them so. But the nights, when nothing could fill the empty hours but loneliness, guilt, and a good measure of self-pity. Was all of her life to be this? Soon, two short years more, Will too would be gone. She had no doubt that William would send for him. That part she could accept. Will would enter into fostering in two years in any case, and where better than to be near his father? William would keep him close under the guidance of another he could trust, of that she was certain. Ironic, she mused, that their separation would allow William to see more of his son than most fathers.

She thought of her son, her child, made more precious by the absence of another in her life. He was the image of his father, with dark hair and eyes of cerulean blue, which already showed the determination of his sire. William would be proud of him. She swallowed, visualizing the two of them together, while she. . . . Nay, she would not give in to self-pity. She wanted this for her son. He needed William. As for her. . . . She was a survivor. She would go on. The village destroyed by fire in Hertfordshire would have to be rebuilt; funds would be needed, craftsmen. She would purchase additional sheep for the highlands near Tiefe. And there was the matter of the mayor of Saint Brides. The man was disreputable, he would have to be replaced. And Kilkenny. John's men had been threatening mayhem again, in spite of his promises. They would feel her hand—a word to her uncle, Donnell. The market at Chepstow had been going well. She had expanded it with new merchants, allowing the villeins to bring their own crafts in addition to their produce. It allowed them extra coin, and the quality of their goods did not compete with the craftsmen. She must remember to try it elsewhere. As for Normandy . . .

She felt a sudden chill, and she realized that the fire had grown low in the cold hours of the October night. She rose wearily, feeling far beyond her years, as she added wood, then returned to her chair as the fire began to lick and devour the added fuel. She focused on the sputtering and snapping of the yellow and orange flames and slowly became mesmerized by their leaping dance. Remembrance of early stories told to her by her mother invaded her mind, tales of premonition and "sight" experienced by her Celtic side, including Eve herself. By staring into the fire her mother had seen her father in battle; he had been brought to her across time and miles. She wondered if she too could hold such a gift, but as she stared, concentrating on the flames, they remained illusive. Finally giving up, she rose and prepared for bed, determined to face the prospect of another day. There would be no easy way, she thought grimly, no gift of sight or visions, but only what she could bring by her own merit.

The servant moved rapidly up the stairs circling the tower of the keep, pausing to light the oil-soaked rag torches, which lined the narrow stone walls, as he went. He knew that in moments the keep would be a beehive of activity, and in spite of his feeling of urgency it would be his neck if the torches were not lit and someone stumbled and fell on the steep, slippery steps of the tower of Rouen. He attempted to light the last torch near the door to his destination, swearing under his breath when it refused to catch. Finally the rags sputtered into life, and he pushed open the door to the darkened chamber. Crossing to the bed he was careful not to let his torch drip onto the marshal of England as he attempted to shake him awake.

"Sir William!"

Pulling himself from sleep—the urgency of the servant's manner stirred him instantly awake—he twisted about to stare up into the pale distress of the other man's face. William's feet hit the floor, and he was grabbing for his chausses before the man could speak, every part of him sensing the matter.

"Milord, the king is dead," the man stammered, stepping back as William practically pushed him aside. "Bring my gambeson and hauberk!" he snapped, pulling his chanise over his head. Allan and Tirell had leapt from their pallets and were fetching the garments almost before he had finished speaking. William glared at the servant, who was still standing at the center of the room, uncertain of what to do. "Rouse the others but bid them to remain until they have heard from me. Awaken Nicolas Avenel first of all. Have him join me in the hall immediately."

"Damn you, Richard," William thought as they made their way through the rain-soaked streets of Rouen. "You fool! To lose your life and your kingdom, and for what?" The heavy rain pelted the large group of riders, catching in their helmets to run in rivulets beneath their chain mail, soaking the gambesons and wool tunics beneath. They pressed into the deluge, almost thankful in spite of their misery for the driving rain, as it served to clear the crowded streets from their normal fair. Mercenaries had gathered from about Europe and were more often than not besotted by hours spent in the taverns; whores followed the armies to ply their trade; and black marketers hawked their goods by whatever means available. Often as not it was necessary to pass through the city with swords drawn even with the largest of company, and to traverse at night was the worst sort of folly. But William was for once unaware of his surroundings, leaving his safety to his men, his mind on his destination, and to the recent past.

"Your greed was your downfall, Richard," William swore to himself. "That, and your damnable pride." A priceless gilded shield and a trove of ancient coins had been found on the lands of Achard, lord of Chalus. As the man was vassal to Aimar, the viscount of Limoges and a Poitevin baron, word had been sent to Richard, due a portion of the treasure as suzerain. But Richard, always eager for coin, had demanded it all. When Aimar refused, Richard set out with a small party of knights to drive the point home. William was in Vaudreuil with Hubert Walter, the archbishop of Canterbury, and a number of other barons when word reached them that Richard had been struck down while riding before the walls of the castle of Chalus as he took shots at those on the wall with his crossbow yet was armed only with his shield.

William had left within the hour for Rouen, where the state treasury of Normandy was kept, the key to the duchy. He had spent the past eleven days guarding the treasury while waiting, hour by hour, for word of his king. His face was grim as they now rode into the priory of Notre Dame du Pré, knowing what he must face.

"Ah, William," the aging archbishop of Canterbury smiled wanly as he looked up from his papers upon William's entrance. He rose from the table, dismissing the priest who had escorted the marshal, and took it upon himself to pour them each a goblet of wine. "Here, drink this," he offered. "Remove those wet garments—and stand by the fire. It won't do to have a chill."

William removed his hauberk and gambeson gratefully, then took a place before the hearth as he drew from his goblet. They fell to silence, each thinking of their loss and what it would mean to England, and the responsibilities that were now placed on them.

"John or Arthur?" Hubert Walter said at last.

William looked up, a smile touching his lips, as he had been waiting for the question. "You know my mind," he said quietly. "John."

"And you know mine, William. Arthur."

"The son is nearer to the land of his father than the nephew," William answered.

"Arthur, as the son of John's eldest natural brother, Geoffrey, should succeed to the throne," Walter insisted as he refilled William's goblet.

"The law is not clear, Your Eminence. Besides, Arthur is his mother's son," William pressed grimly.

"From his birth she saw him as the reincarnate of Arthur of legend, returning as the salvation of England, and thusly named him! Yet she gave him no love for England, rather taught him it was his divine right to rule! Perhaps, had Geoffrey Plantagenet lived, he could have instilled some feeling for England in his son. But he did not, and when Eleanor would have sought to teach her grandson the hate of the mother for the queen was instilled in Arthur. Nay, his is not the hand to rule England."

"Would John be better?" the archbishop asked rhetorically, his voice laden with doubt.

"Aye, he would," William answered, turning from the fire as his back grew uncomfortably warm. "I have no love for John, Your Eminence, and he will bear watching, but of the two he is the better choice. His mother bore him in England; that alone gives him preference in the minds of the people over a boy of thirteen who has never set foot upon English soil. It often amazes me, but in spite of John's follies he appears to be popular with the people."

Hubert Walter snorted and began pacing slowly across the room. "And when they find that they have erred?"

"That situation, if it should arise, will be faced then. For now, I must repeat, there is no choice. To foist an unwanted king—a child, at that—upon the people when there is this threat from Philip would be disaster."

The archbishop continued to pace, his head bent in thought as the only sounds in the room were the crackling and hissing of the fire and his robes as they swept across the floor rushes. At that moment Isabel came to William's mind, as she did so often, even at moments such as this when such thoughts were totally unexpected. He felt his heart constrict as her face and voice came to him, and his mind formed a comment she would make at such a moment. It had become almost a mental game for him, his loss of her never having left him. He recalled her astonishment upon learning that Richard had made this man archbishop of Canterbury. Her eyes had begun to dance and her mouth drew into an amused smirk as she threw an outrageous comment to him about the fact that her own private keeper in the Tower should now be the keeper of England. Suppressing a smile with great effort, he had hushed her as his eyes had darted about to those present to see if another had heard. His expression softened as he remembered but then hardened once again with the loss.

Finally, the archbishop ceased pacing and stopped before William, drawing the latter's attention from his musings. "You have it then, William," he sighed deeply. "I fear that your arguments are well founded, particularly in reading the mood of the barons. But, Marshal," he added sadly, regarding William with doleful eyes, "nothing of which you have done, will you have such cause to repine as this."

William shifted in his saddle as his eyes moved beneath his helm to the valley below. He could feel the restlessness of his men behind him, so near to home yet held at this impasse. Five hundred knights, seven hundred men-at-arms, men who had served him through battle and the tenuousness of guarding the peace, and the most difficult time, that of waiting. All had served him faithfully, and now it was he who kept them from a hot meal, a warm bed, and the other softer comforts home would allow. Yet he hesitated. Nothing, not the battles, not the disputes with kings nor the uncertainty of kingdoms, had left him with such irresolution as one slender woman had.

Allan drew his palfrey up to William's mount. His face, now filled to a handsome youthfulness, turned to William with question. Drawing a deep breath, William urged his mount forward and down toward the lazily moving river Wye, which stretched through the valley.

They clattered through the outer bailey, bringing the serfs to a halt in their labors as they stared with amazement, their gaping eyes fixing on the banner carried at the head of the entourage. The knights began to disperse their men-at-arms to their quarters, the latter eager to return to families not seen for over three years. It was a small party, with mayhem left behind them, which

entered the inner bailey, their mounts met by groomsmen who rushed forward from the stables as they dismounted. William hesitated as he stared at the large
doors at the top of the steps. Longing pulled him toward
those doors even as a feeling of dread of the unknown
washed heavily over him. Suddenly angry for his indecision, and not a little cowardice, he dismounted, pausing
to backhand Horse across the nose as the ill-tempered
beast attempted to bite the groomsman, and strode up
the steps and pushed open the door. His anger sharpened to find there were no porters at the door. God's
breath, would she allow anyone to enter?

As he stepped about the hall screen, his eyes moved
swiftly about the immense room, taking in each part as
he noted those present. She was there. She rose slowly
from her place at the head of the table, her face paling
as their eyes locked. Lord, he thought, becoming unsettled, the years had been gentle on her. All traces of
childhood had gone, leaving in its place a woman of
breathtaking beauty. Her hips were fuller, her breasts
more rounded to a still-slender waist. Her hair, the long
blond mass of silkiness his fingers could best recall,
hung loose to her hips. A fillet of sapphires was about
her forehead. Her eyes, large, slightly almond-shaped,
were the same captivating smoky grey that had haunted
his dreams.

The room held a deathly silence. William's knights
moved in behind him, their smiles fading at the tension
felt by all as William and Isabel regarded each other.
Even John d'Erley and Beaumont, who had risen with
broad smiles upon William's entrance, were silent, their
eyes now moving between the two.

She stepped from the table, and it was then that
William noticed the child at her side. His small hands
grasped to the folds of his mother's gown as his eyes
fixed on this large knight dressed in fur tunic and leather
leggings who had suddenly appeared among them. The
boy looked up to his mother and frowned suddenly. He
saw a glimpse of tears in her eyes, and he suddenly felt
rage, the first of his life, at this stranger who had caused

his mother to cry. Loosening his hold, he stepped forward, his small fists clenched at his side to control the fear he felt at confronting this large stranger. "Who are you, sir?" he cried, his tender voice strained. "Dare you enter Chepstow without invitation?"

William's brows arched in amazement, even as his mouth twitched with amusement and pride at his son's courage. It was his intention to respond, but Isabel answered her son's question. "Will," she said softly. "Go—and greet your father."

The boy looked up at her with shock and back to William. The child looked puzzled, momentarily at a loss as he studied this man whom his mother said was the source of his letters, the quintessence of his dreams. Seeing his son gather himself up, William stayed were he was, sensing the importance of what Will felt to be his duty. The boy approached, his small chin held up even as William could detect a glimmer of fear in the deep blue eyes so like his own. He swallowed at the likeness he saw in the child, feeling the years he had missed in the boy's life. The child stopped before him, pausing only a moment before he offered his hand. "Sir," he said with a slight tremor in his voice. William ached to grab him up and hold him close. Sensing what such a scene would do to the boy, he merely smiled and bent to grasp the boy's wrist in formal greeting. "My son." He bent, kneeling to eye level as he continued to regard Will seriously, lowering his voice. "I have missed you. Perhaps now we can come to know one another."

The child's chin quivered for an instant. "I would like that, sir."

"As would I," William answered with a smile. Isabel's voice drew his attention, and he looked up to find that she had joined them, though her attention was on those with him. "Nicolas, see to the knights. I have sent to the kitchens for more repast, there is ample for all at the tables."

William glanced about as he stood up, finding that the servants were busily setting up additional trestle tables. Smiling gratefully he turned to Isabel. Their eyes met with what was almost a physical shock, the years passing between them in a kaleidoscope of memory. He fought the impulse to reach out, to touch the soft tendrils that framed her face. Regret filled him as he dismissed the thought, angry with himself for his weakness and his longings. The years that had passed had brought him as much peace as he could reasonably expect, as it must have been for her. It would do neither of them good to stir up old memories and pain. Leave it alone, he told himself, you are only here to assure yourself that they are both well. "Your table is well set, madam," he said abruptly, glancing at the bounty that was being set before his men. "It is obvious that there is no need here; that you have fared well. But then, I never really doubted that you would."

The coldness of his words was hard to bear. She had looked up to find him standing there. A dream from the past, suddenly, miraculously there. Feelings deeply buried came rushing back willy-nilly, filling her with memory, and with them longings she had denied. Dust-covered and obviously exhausted from a long, forced ride, he wore the evidence of what the years had done to him, the responsibilities placed on him. It showed in his face, his so loved face, more handsome than her dreams had allowed her. His eyes carried new lines at the corners but they were still wondrous, piercing into her soul with a startling blue intensity. For a moment she had thought she had seen warmth, a longing in his expression as he regarded her and hope had been reborn, filling her senses, vanquishing the loneliness and the endless pain that had remained with her like a dull ache. All to disappear in a single, coldly given statement. The eyes had turned as cold as his words, and a great sadness enveloped her. Bracing herself, she answered with a stiff smile, gratified when her voice betrayed none of the bitter disappointment that was filling her. "Life has been good, William." Turning to a passing servant, she missed the flicker of pain that passed over William's eyes at her response. "I have ordered your meal to be served in the lesser chamber. I presume that you desire some peace and moments of privacy with John and

Beaumont," she said, turning back to him.

"You will join us?" he answered with a questioning brow.

"If that is your wish."

"It is. There is much to tell you."

Isabel found ample opportunity to study her husband at leisure while he ate, as his attention was held by John d'Erley and Beaumont, who plied him for news. It was obvious that while they had been her mainstay during the years of William's absence, their minds and hearts had been with William. She had tucked a reluctant Will into his bed, assuring him that his father would spend time with him on the morrow, and the moments away from William's presence had given her time to bring her emotions and her thoughts under control. The past three years had afforded Isabel much time to learn about herself. No pain, no loneliness, no amount of hurt could totally destroy her. Only quality of life could be affected. Even from ashes, once there came acceptance, some measure of happiness could be found. She watched him now, her chest constricting painfully as his eyes wrinkled at the corners as he laughed in response to a quip from Beaumont. Those deep blue eyes and the dark curls wrapping about his ears, remembered by the touch of her fingers as well as by her mind. His shoulders broad beneath the fit of his chanise and deep fur of the sleeveless tunic. The strength of his hands as they tore apart the capon he was eating and the remembrance of the gentleness of their touch. She loved him, more deeply than she ever had. He had no way of knowing of her determination, that she fully intended to have him.

She smiled at the thought, sobering quickly as he took the moment to glance at her, only to find her expression as placid as before. Nay, William, she thought as she leaned across the table to refill his tankard. You shall not know how much I want you, not yet. You have kept yourself from me, and our son, for over three years. Aye, you left in pain and frustration, caused by me. But what of my pain? Nay, William, I will not have you think that fleeing from me is ever a solution to our problems. Nor that I am a wench to submit compliantly beneath the hand of her master. You must show me that you want me as much as I do you.

"John was well met in London," William was saying, "the barons concurred and gave their oaths freely, assuring their choice over that of Arthur. The coronation occurred without event, which is more than I can say for when the ducal coronet was placed upon his head in Normandy. The fool dropped the spear."

"During the ceremony?" d'Erley gasped.

"Smack in the middle of it." William smirked.

"From your reactions I assume that the matter is serious," Isabel said, speaking for the first time.

"By Norman custom a spear is used in the place of a scepter, milady," Beaumont explained. "It is believed that to drop the spear is a sign that the king will someday lose the duchy."

"Pah, if John loses Normandy it will be by incompetence, not because he dropped a spear," Isabel scoffed.

"The man is now king of England, Isabel," William said quietly. "Be it your intention to hold fast to old grudges?"

"On the contrary, my lord, I fully intend to give him every opportunity to prove himself as an able and just king. I believe in giving everyone another chance, particularly when it is important."

John and Beaumont quickly stifled their smiles at the comment. William's eyes narrowed and he studied his wife speculatively as he wondered as to the depth of her words, but John smoothly distracted him with another question. "Are you going to share with us news of a more personal nature or leave us waiting?"

"What are you talking about?" William asked, puzzled.

"Oh come now, William. Or should I say, Earl William?"

The others turned surprised stares to William, who flushed. "How did you know?"

"When I checked to see that the men were properly quartered, Allan could not resist showing me your belt," John answered with a grin. When he saw William's frown he added quickly, "Do not be angry with the lad. When I entered the knight's quarters he was cleaning it.''

"Tell us!" Beaumont exclaimed.

"I have been granted the earldom of Pembroke." William shrugged. As the others broke out in hearty congratulations William stole a glance at Isabel, whom he noticed was strangely silent.

"An honor well deserved and long overdue," she said softly. Her eyes, filled with pride, grew moist at the revelation. So long deserved, so long in coming, she thought. Damn Henry Plantagenet, damn Richard Coeur de Lion, she thought. Why did it have to be John? Her feelings ever strong for Ireland, she felt hard put to accept anything from that Plantagenet, even for one loved and so deserving. Ugly contemplations crossed her mind, but she pushed them forcefully aside. Nay, she would think of those things later, not now. This was William's moment and she would do nothing to spoil it. Besides, her mind was on their marriage, and for once the Plantagenets would not interfere. "So, now I may truthfully address you as milord?" she observed, her eyes suddenly dancing.

"If you wish," William answered as his mouth twitched with a smile. "However, I am certain that you will continue to refer to me by whatever name comes to mind at the moment."

"Ah, but now I shall be careful to preface it with 'milord.' '' She smiled wickedly.

The laughter in the small room lifted the mood, and William and Isabel regarded each other with an openness that had not been there since he had walked through the doors to the great hall. Slowly, she allowed her blatant desire to enter her eyes, knowing that no one else was watching at that moment. It was gone quickly and she turned to John with a warm smile to answer a question.

William was shaken. Had he imagined the look she had given to him? He watched her closely as she laughed easily with John, then struggled to dismiss it. He had to be wrong, a moment, perhaps, wishing to see what was not there. How, after all, could a feeling for him de-

velop in his absence? Loneliness for him, if indeed she
had ever felt such, did not compensate for frigidity.
Desire for his company, perhaps, but not for his body.
Nay, she should have welcomed the years without demand upon her person, unless. . . . He looked at her
sharply as an ugly thought entered his mind. Had
another reawakened her? He felt a rage fill him as he
glanced at the others. Who? John? Beaumont? His fists
clenched at his thoughts, and with great effort he
brought his emotions under control as he forced a smile
and gave his attentions back to the others.

They joined the rest of their company in the great hall
soon after. The evening was spent comfortably, in
gaming and conversation, a feeling of peace descending upon the manor not felt for many years. Except for
the principals. Isabel was unsettled, wondering what
had happened. She could sense anger emitting from
William, a new tenseness she could not comprehend.
For a moment they had seemed so at ease, and then suddenly it had all changed once again. Could it have been
the covert look she had thrown to him across the table?
The possibility threw her into a feeling of despair. Had
the years caused such irrevocable estrangement? Could
the suggestion that she might want him, desire him,
cause such . . . repulsion? She felt humiliated and confused. Oh God, she thought, the thought striking her
like a bolt. Could there be another? Someone who had
replaced her in his mind and heart until there was
nothing left for her? With the thought came anger. And
determination. Sweet Mother, if another had entered his
life . . . she would not give him up that easily! Not
again. This time she was determined to fight for him,
with every recourse at her disposal.

But she had no chance that night to pursue her battle.
She retired to her chamber, the drinking and revelry in
the hall lasting into the early hours of morning. She
waited for him to come to her, realizing as she finally
closed her eyes that only exhausted sleep would come to
claim her.

# 16

UPON waking she found the bed as empty as it had been the past three years. She realized with a sinking disappointment that even as she had slept a part of her mind had waited, expecting that welcomed dip to the bed as he finally joined her. Disgruntled, she bathed, plaiting her hair into two thick braids, and dressed, choosing a gown of pale rose silk embroidered with roses of a deeper shade about the hem. She finally descended the stairs to the hall late in the morning to find that William had left at dawn with Will for a morning's ride. The servants bustled about, the evidence of the previous night's events long since removed, but Isabel moved listlessly through her duties, finally emerging from the lower reaches of the manor to find the knights and their ladies gathering for midmeal as the bell rang.

She sensed the moment when they returned, and her suspicions were quickly confirmed by the animated voice of her son as he burst into the hall. He came to a quick halt as he remembered his manners and fought to control his enthusiasm as he came to his mother's side, his voice filled with childish excitement. "Mother, we had the most marvelous time! Father showed me how to track a fox, and he has promised to give me my very own falcon!''

"I am glad that you had a good time with your father,'' she said smiling, dropping a kiss on the top of his head. Seeing such happiness in her son, she realized that he had crossed the gap of the past years with apparent ease. It was well, she thought, for it would make the time when he was sent to William that much easier . . . the thought gripped her painfully but she forced it from her, refusing to dwell on the matter. "See you to the kitchens, love," she said, forcing a smile. "Cook has prepared you a tasty meal."

As she watched him scamper happily away, she heard a sound next to her and turned to find that William had taken his chair at her side. "He is a fine boy, Isabel. You have done well by him."

"Thank you, milord,'' she answered quietly, nodding to the servants to bring in the repast. "But I take little credit. Will's character is due to the manner of the child. He is a joy to me."

"I have not seen Waverly,'' William observed as he trimmed their trencher with the knife that Allan stepped forward to hand him. He heard the slight intake of Isabel's breath and looked up to find her staring at him.

"I wrote to you, William. Did you not receive my letters? Waverly died over a year ago."

He remembered suddenly and inwardly cursed himself for his faulty memory and tactlessness. "I do recall, Isabel. I am sorry. I realize that he was with your family for many years."

"Aye," she said softly, a catch in her voice. "I miss him dearly. Even Julia misses him, though she would never admit it. Gavin has been elevated to that position, though I wonder if he will ever have Waverly's gift for figures."

"Perhaps I could send for Osbert," he offered, referring to his own chamberlain, who resided at Gloucester Castle. "Were he to spend some time with Gavin . . ."

"It is not necessary," she assured him. "I thank you for the offer but I prefer to give Gavin time to prove himself. To countermand his authority now could well cause him to lose what self-confidence he has."

William said nothing but she noted that his jaw tightened for a moment. Oh lud, she thought, there I've done it, I've made him angry again. What would it have cost her to accept his offer? The possible loss of a potentially good steward, she silently answered. Nay, she had been correct in her reasoning. Why could he not see that? Suddenly she lost her appetite and turned to William as she moved to rise. "I have promised to send linens to Tintern Abbey, milord. If you will excuse me, I shall see to the matter now as they should be on their way before nightfall." Relieved that he did not delay her, she left the keep through the kitchen yard. Crossing the inner bailey, she entered the laundry set in the deep walls, passing by the large iron tubs holding the lye solutions for washing, now cooled. From the keys hanging from her belt she unlocked the door to the room that stored the clean linens. She stepped into the room and glanced over the neat shelves lining the walls, which were stacked with fresh sheets and towels kept for the manor. Then her gaze came to rest on a large stack of the soiled linens piled in one corner, and her lips tightened with anger. She would have words with the laundress, she thought, there was no excuse for leaving the wash undone, it was still early in the day. She began to sort through the linens, stacking her choices for the abbey on the folding table set in the middle of the room. It was a chore seen to once a year, the abbey having been built by her great-great uncle, and supported by the deClares since that time.

As she worked, she tried not to think about William but soon lost the battle. Her lips pursed in careful thought as she pulled the chosen sheets and towels from their places. Nothing had gone well since his return. She had felt so full of hope, knowing that someday he would walk through those doors. But it seemed that he had returned as angry as when he had left. If his anger had not dulled after all this time, why had he returned at all? Had he then only returned for Will? The realization that he found her company distasteful filled her with a pain that left her weak. She heard the door open and spun about. Thinking it was the laundress, she was ready with a tart response, only to have the words freeze in her throat as she saw William's large frame filling the doorway. He stepped into the room, shutting the door behind him.

"From the expression on your face I presume that you are less than delighted to see me," he said wryly.

"Nay . . ." she stammered. "I thought you were the laundress. I mean to have words with her," she said lamely, indicating the soiled linen piled carelessly in one corner.

"Then I am not the object of the wrath I observed," he countered, his lips twisting into a smile. "I am gratified."

"Is there something you need?" she asked, confused as to why he would seek her out in this place.

"Only to speak with you," he answered. "But then, do I need a reason to be with my wife, one I have not seen for so long a time?" he added smoothly, giving no evidence of his mood.

"Of course not," she laughed nervously. "It's only that this seems a strange place to visit."

"Oh?" he glanced about the room. "It is private and likely to remain so as your laundress obviously feels herself to be finished for the day. We are not likely to be disturbed."

His odd choice of words added to her unease. "What is it that you wished to speak with me about?"

His brows arched in mock surprise. "My lady, have you no curiosity of what is to be done about us?"

She dropped her gaze, suddenly unable to meet that penetrating stare, and began to chew on her lower lip.

"Isabel, there is no need to be nervous, you are hardly a maid. In spite of your feelings about our, ah, physical relationship, you know that I will not hurt you." Seeing her flush he tensed, her discomfort feeding his deep suspicions. "Or is there something else that causes you to be nervous? Is there something you wish to tell me?"

She looked up at him doubtfully. "What do you mean?"

His eyes hardened for an instant, but it passed quickly as he smiled, and he pulled himself from the wall to step toward her. "Only that I have been parted from you much too long." He stood before her, looking down at her as his eyes moved slowly over her face and body, lingering on the way she filled the rose silk of her gown. Reaching out he drew his fingers through the laces at the neckline, then that of the chemise beneath, drawing the bodice slowly apart. She drew in her breath as the bodice opened, and she saw the desire grow in his eyes. They fixed on the sight of her, now exposed to his hungry gaze. Suddenly, she felt her heart lift as she realized that he did want her! She parted her lips, finding it difficult to breathe; feeling a desire, a wanting she had never known filling her senses, and with it a joy that threatened to burst within her. "Oh, William," she gasped, closing her eyes in an ecstasy of anticipation.

His eyes glittered with anger as he regarded the open passion he saw in her face, but as her eyes opened once more he merely smiled gently, hiding the rage that had begun to fill his own senses. Damnation, but she was beautiful, he thought, angry that he could feel his body respond to her loveliness. But he had to find out, had she truly changed? If so, he would discover who had brought it about. And then, God help them both.

He cupped a breast in his hand, his own breath drawing in painfully as he touched her. He rubbed a nipple with his thumb until it constricted, tightening beneath his caress. Leaning down he drew the nipple gently into his mouth, teasing it with his tongue, until he heard her moan deeply as she pressed against him. His lips moved slowly up her breast to the nape of her neck, planting light, teasing kisses as he traveled to that tender spot beneath her ear. She turned her head, eager to claim his mouth with hers as her arms went up about his neck, pulling him down to her. Her tongue sought his, licking in delicious flutters against his lips, taking his breath away before he crushed her against him, lost against the feel of her. He turned her, pressing her hips between the table and his own growing need, which she felt stir through the thin silk of her gown. The knowledge heightened the desire that was burning within her, that tightened in her middle in a painful, demanding need.

"Shall I take you here?" he asked huskily, pressing her back against the table.

"Aye, William!" she gasped against his lips. "I cannot bear it!"

So there had to be someone else, he thought, someone who had reawakened this need in her where he had not. Would she tell him if he asked? Nay, it would take more than a simple question. "Cover yourself," he snapped, pulling himself from her.

"What?" she gasped, her eyes opening in confusion. He repeated the order and she flushed. Humiliated, she only thought to do as she was bid. Her fingers shook as she rebound her bodice, but somehow she managed, and the moment also gave her the opportunity to think about what had just happened. What was his meaning, how could he do this to her? Had his intent been to humiliate her, could he hate her that much? "Why, William?" she choked as anger began to replace shock.

"I owe you no explanations, Isabel. Surely you should be relieved, judging by your past response to me." He noted that she had finished restoring order to her garments. "Let us return to the hall."

"I have no desire to return there with you!" she snapped.

"You have no choice, Isabel. For others we shall become the loving couple, for I shall have no further scandal upon us, is that clear?" he added, grasping her arm to emphasize his meaning.

"Since when have you concerned yourself with what others say?" she hissed, glaring up at him.

"Since our son has become old enough to be hurt by the words of others," he answered coldly.

"Our son?" she twisted, trying to pull her arm from his grasp. "What has Will to do with what is between us?"

"Take care, Isabel," he growled, his grasp tightening painfully. "In spite of everything, I have tried to be generous with you. But I will not have the mother of my son becoming the object of gossip where it may fall on his ears. You will begin to conduct yourself with propriety until such time I take him from you. If you agree I will continue to be generous—and when he comes to me I will allow you the freedom you wish, with whomever you wish. And I promise that you will not care for the alternatives.'' She gaped at him, stunned by the implications of his words, but he gave her no further chance to speak. ''You will return to the hall and await me in our chamber. I warn you, Isabel,'' he said glaring at the defiance he read in her. ''You will do as I say.''

She complied, while wanting to rail at him for what he was doing to her. How dare he accuse her of . . . her own rage threatened to explode as she made her way to her chambers. She would repay him, she promised to herself, oh, somehow she would repay him!

William was well into his third goblet of wine, a small voice within him cowardly seeking release from the prospect of climbing those stairs to join her. His eyes passed moodily over the small group left to his company, who were drawn into a game of dicing, the others long since having retired. He wondered, yet again, which of them would cuckold him. John? He dismissed the idea out of hand. Damn, he believed in loyalty, it was the epitome of his being. That any of his company should so deceive him rankled him beyond measure. But he was also a realist. She was fair. Oh Lord, she was fair. And unencumbered by the presence of a husband these past three years. It had been a long time to leave her, but the thought that she would be unfaithful to him had never seriously entered his thoughts. After all, had he not left because of her inability to respond? The memory of the deep hurt and frustration of those years came back to him and he stirred uncomfortably.

Another memory, almost forgotten, plucked at him and his mouth drew into a wry smile. Years before while in the Holy Land, he had come across an unusual device. Or, rather, a group of his men had inadvertently discovered it—while divesting garments from the numerous wives left behind by a rapidly departing minor dignitary of the city the Crusaders had taken that morning. William, who had been busy with the matters of garrisoning his men, was drawn to the women's quarters by the sound of laughter intermixed with bellows of frustrated rage. Upon entering the room his men challenged him to solve the dilemma they had encountered, but he found himself no more successful than they. Remembering now, he grinned. Disregarding the physical pain caused the wearer, chastity belts were a handy device, he mused. A warrior knight, secure with the key tucked safely in his belt, could depart with an easy mind. The thought of belting Isabel into such a device, the probable words that would come to her lips as he secured the lock, caused him to chuckle. Too bad that he had not brought one back with him.

Stretching, he leaned back in his chair, the wine and the humor of his thoughts easing the tension he had been feeling the past hours. A cry of anguish from the nearby group brought him about. "Breath of God!" Sir Ralph cried. "These dice are against me? I swear you have bewitched them, d'Erley!"

Guardedly, William observed them for another moment, assuring himself that Ralph's words were given without malice, nor were they taken as such by John, before he returned to his own musings. Taking another draw from his wine, he allowed his gaze to wander about the hall, noting small changes she had made in his absence. A small opening had been carved in the wall on the far wall to hold a small shrine, and behind it a sealed door contained holy relics he had sent her from the continent. A new tapestry graced the wall to his left, depicting a hunt with falcons. His eyes narrowed as he studied the scene, and he wondered if it was the flickering light of the fire behind him that gave the particular expression to the woman in the scene. She was ahorse, the unhooded falcon perched on her wrist, and her mouth appeared to be drawn into a grimace. Memories came rushing back of his last session of hunting with Isabel. His eyes moved to the man in the picture, noting the expression of absorption as he looked to the hunt. His gaze passed back and forth between the two, and he suddenly realized whom she had depicted. He was stunned. It was obvious that she had spent years on that tapestry. And she had chosen to depict them in a particular moment of closeness. Hardly the actions of a woman who was dallying with another man—or men.

William continued to stare at the tapestry, his mind a muddle of thoughts. Over the years, when he had thought of her, it was of the woman he had known. It had never occurred to him that she would change, or that she would be unfaithful to him. Why, now, had he been so hasty in jumping to that particular conclusion? The answer came to him unwillingly, and his mouth turned into a grim smile. In the past three years he had not been celibate. There had been women eager to spend time with him, available to satisfy his needs. None had meant anything to him beyond physical satisfaction, momentary escape. But . . . had that been why he had been so ready to believe the worst of her—that she could draw from those around her to satisfy physical needs as readily as he had? He had returned expecting everything to be as when he had left. Yet there was that look she had given to him in the lesser chamber. She could still fire his blood with such a look—but it was one he had not seen for many years. Was it so hard to believe that it could be for him?

Suddenly, he found that viewing the years ahead without her proved a bleak prospect. Even with the verbal battles, and she was certain to try him to the limits of his patience, he realized with no little amazement that he did not want to live without her. He wanted her. And, by God, he would have her—and this time on his terms. He drained off his goblet in a long pull, and setting it on the table next to him he rose to cross toward the stairs in long, determined strides.

He found her sitting at a small writing desk at the far side of their chamber, writing in a journal by the dim light of a single thick candle, the only other light in the room besides the fire, which burned steadily in the large stone fireplace filling the wall behind her. She had dressed for bed, a sleeveless robe covering her loose-sleeved chemise, her hair tied in a single long braid, which hung to just above her hips. She looked up as he entered, laying down her quill and closing the journal as he stood just inside the closed door, watching her.

"Well," she asked tightly as she stared at her hands, which were clasped on the closed book. "Have you come to ask me if I have been faithful to you?" Before he could answer she rushed on. "Would you believe me if I told you that I have betrayed you to no one? It appears that you have already set your mind to the matter."

"Isabel," he answered wearily, "I came to some wrong conclusions and I apologize. Can we not now speak without accusations? For once can we speak the truth?"

"We?" She turned to look at him with amazement. "I do not recall accusing you of anything, milord! Shall I? Have you been faithful to me?" She rose from the chair and held up her hand as she shook her head. "Nay, do not answer me. That is more than a wife should ask of a husband who has kept himself from her bed these past years. Only one question," she looked at him, her eyes boring into his, bright orbs of grey brilliance seeking the truth. "Is there anyone else?"

"Nay, Isabel. There is no one."

Her shoulders seemed to sag with his answer, but she covered it quickly, turning from him to move toward the fire. He moved behind her to the table, where he passed his fingers over the bleached leather cover of the closed journal. "What is this?"

She half turned to see what he was referring to. " 'Tis merely an amusement." She shrugged. "A journal, a memory of matters told to me by my mother and of our lives. Nothing too personal, milord," she assured him with another shrug to his questioning gaze. "But matters our children and grandchildren might wish to know."

He moved to a chair by the fire. "If you feel the need to write of matters which could be construed as treason I trust that you will not leave it lying about."

"I have only put my own thoughts into it, William," she answered, taking the chair across from him.

"That is what I meant," he countered, with a wry smile.

Her eyes flared but then, in spite of her anger, she too smiled. "I will do my best not to send you to the gallows."

"John is not Richard," he parried. "He has no qualms about hanging a woman. I fear that he would hang us both in such an event."

"Then we shall die together, milord, like star-crossed lovers," she laughed. Her comment caused her to sober as soon as she had spoken, and she turned her gaze to the fire, suddenly self-conscious.

"Are we lovers, Isabel?"

"It would appear that we are no longer, milord," she answered quietly.

"Would it be your wish?" he pressed.

She closed her eyes against the discomfort of his question. "Would you have me answer without knowing your feelings, William? Will you leave me no pride?"

"Then I will answer for you. But first you must understand what has happened, for it must certainly affect our lives. We will soon be at war with France. John has had the temerity to announce that he plans to take Isabella of Angouleme to wife . . ."

"Isabella of Angouleme? But she is affianced to Hugh de Lusignan!" she cried with horror. "William, you cannot have supported such a match!"

"Aye, I have." He grimaced, his resolve fleeing in the face of her condemnation.

"How can you?"

"Damn it, Isabel!" he exploded, leaping from his chair. "Nothing has changed! When will you learn not to question my decisions?"

"But Philip of France is Lusignan's suzerain! He will plead to Philip for support, and it certainly will mean war! Can you not veer John from this folly?"

"He is my king, Isabel! Will you never understand the essence of loyalty?"

"Loyalty?" she cried. "Is it loyalty to your king which brings you to support this match, William?" She leapt from her chair to face him. "Hugh de Lusignan, William? Was it not he who murdered your Uncle Patrick? That foul deed which you have never forgiven? Aye, you are loyal, the man England may look to for strength and wisdom when no other serves her! For that reason, above all, you must not do this! You betray her for your own needs! How will you be able to forgive yourself if she falls because you . . ."

"Enough!" he roared. "God's breath, I have had well enough, I will hear no more!"

"You do not want to hear the truth!" she railed.

"I said enough!" He spun about, striding toward the door, determined to rid himself of her infuriating presence.

"Aye, William. Leave me!" she screamed at him, "flee from me again, is that not preferable to facing the truth?"

He stopped in his tracks, and she could see the muscles of his back ripple beneath the linen of his chanise. Slowly he turned, his eyes glittering dangerously. Involuntarily, she stepped back from him, her eyes widening at the storm in his expression. "Aye, separation is not the answer for us, and I will not make that mistake again," he said icily, taking a step toward her. "I came to inform you that you and Will shall return to Normandy with me, and my decision stands. Be clear to my meaning, you have no choice in this matter. But it will not be as it was." She stared at him in shock, retreating as he walked slowly toward her until she backed up against the writing desk. "You wish the truth, Isabel?" His eyes pierced into hers as he stood over her. "It is this. You will be wife to me, on my terms. Whatever you have shall be given by me. Your freedoms shall be earned. One at a time. To be withdrawn if you displease me." A brow arched as his mouth drew into a grim smile. "Silence for once, Isabel?"

"What would you have me say?" she gasped.

" 'Aye, milord,' would be a good beginning."

"Bastard," she flared, recovering.

He chuckled deeply, his eyes flashing angry amusement as an arm went about her waist and he drew her sharply against him. "Milord Bastard, Isabel, remember, you did promise. And there was another promise given, as I recall. Or did I misread the look you gave me over supper upon my return?"

"I do not know what you mean." She struggled against his hold.

"Ah, but you do. And I most certainly intend to claim that promise." He tightened his hold as his other hand unwound her hair from its plait, his fingers lacing in her hair as he brought her mouth to his. Braced for his anger, her senses shocked at the startling gentleness of the kiss. She desperately tried to block her mind from the feel of his mouth on hers and the length of his hard body pressed against her own. His tongue parted her lips, darting within to claim her mouth as his hand slid down to her hips, pressing her against him tightly. She began to lose her senses. Her nerve endings sharpened with anticipation as a deep ache of desire kindled in her middle, sweeping over her, and she knew she was lost. So long, her thoughts stabbed desperately, so long. Why should her needs be denied? She had allowed that to happen before and what had it solved? Who had suffered more than she? She could fight him now, but she would be the one to lose, for it would merely drive him to another, while she. . . . Her mouth softened beneath his and her arms slowly slid up about his neck. Aye, she thought, I will have this. Perhaps it is the one thing we can truly share. All else must be met, answers found, but this we may have. As she melted against him, her last sensible thought was what a fool she had been.

# 17

SHE had come to see it, to add it to the long list of reasons she so thoroughly despised John Plantagenet, king of England. She waited as the thick morning fog lifted to suspend a heavy grey cloud about the spires and parapets of the Château Gaillard, which perched on the high rocky hill across the river Seine. Isabel's lips tightened as she forced her eyes to the base of the hill, willing herself to see what she had come to see. Tears began to slip silently down her face, and her heart constricted, squeezing out the remaining vestiges of innocence, replaced by a deep burning hatred for the one who, in ineptness and stupidity, had caused it.

There, at the base of the hill, wedged between the French and English forces, huddled those remaining of nearly four hundred women, children, servants, and priests; innocents allowed to starve to death as they found themselves caught between those who vied for power.

Isabel thought of her own children; Will, now a sturdy boy of seven, and Richard, just over two years, born a bare nine months following their arrival at their lands at Longueville, Normandy. Healthy, beautiful children safely ensconced at Rouen in preparation of their departure for England. She could not help but to imagine her own sons scratching out an existence on that bare rock, feeding on weeds, a few berries, and what fish could be caught from the river, until . . .

Had there been a moment of John's reign that had brought them peace? Perhaps there had been a moment of joy, years before, when William had announced that he had become a belted earl by John's hand. Nay, even that portentous moment had been overshadowed by her concern for Ireland. William's loyalty toward Erin, and how John's generosity would effect it, was a matter yet to be tested.

She thought of her husband and her heart warmed. The past two years had proved easier than she had anticipated, though it had been difficult in those first months following their departure from England. He had made good on his threat, and she had stifled under the oppressiveness of his hand. At last she had rebelled. Battles had raged, those in their company quickly growing accustomed to rapid withdrawal when words began to fly between them. She smiled at the thought, now able to laugh at herself as she could never have done before. While neither she nor William would admit it, for something vital would be lost in the telling, an excitement pervaded in their verbal battles. Her life, and she suspected, William's, would suffer dearly should they ever lose the fire that existed between them. And she had not been wrong that last night in England when she had submitted her body to him. There, at least, they had found a common ground, and she never had cause to regret her decision.

As for the rest—somehow she had managed to live with his lack of need to have her truly part of his life. She had learned to suppress the raw hurt that wrenched at her when he excluded her. However, she knew that the constant repression of those feelings as having its effect upon her. She loved him, he was so very dear to her, but at times when it was least expected, she looked at him and she could almost feel hatred. Sheer, frightening hatred, leaving her shaken. It intruded, like an ever-present lurking demon, in moments when she should have trusted him the most. Moments when she felt herself drifting into comfortable dependence on him, she would find herself resenting him, finding fault with the smallest things he would do. She hid her feelings from him, but they were there, lurking. And, somehow, she knew that someday it could destroy them.

Thus they had come to this place in their lives. She thanked God that William had come to his senses in time about the matter that had brought them to Normandy. Loyalty to England was the core of his being. She knew that he would have found it impossible to live with himself if he had aided the cause of bringing her to an unnecessary war. Good judgment had prevailed, and he urgently attempted to stop John from proceeding with his marriage to Isabella of Angouleme. But the king, in the first of a long list of blind judgments, married the girl in spite of better advice.

And it began. John played, captivated by his beautiful young bride, who encouraged his complete attention. Unbelievably, against the frantic advice of William and his other counselors, John found himself at war with France and unprepared for such a war.

William's frustration and anger grew as one inept blunder after another was made by his king. While John languished in a period of inactivity, his dark head turned from the needs of his realm, Maine, Touraine, Anjou, and then Poitou were lost, to Philip's mounting glee, and now Normandy itself lay threatened. William, in a moment of sheer rage, had confronted his king, pressing for him to leave his bride long enough to give attention to his continental empire. John's only response had been the angry cry of "Let be, Marshal, let be!"

Isabel's mount had shifted with her own angry thoughts, and she realized that she must have jerked on the reins, pulling at the mare's tender mouth. She patted the animal's neck and murmured soothingly, but her eyes, fixing once again on the scene before her, hardened to a cold flint.

They had come to this final impasse, and she recalled the desperate, final exchange between William and his king. Philip's forces had moved against Gaillard, the castle that Richard, Coeur de Lion, had built with such loving care, the invincible bastion, the locked door to Normandy. Indeed, it could not be breached. But neither, in the face of a superior army sent by a more astute king, could it be relieved. William had confronted his king at that final war council, urging him to withdraw his troops and sue for peace. He offered to repair to Philip as emissary, to propose a reasonable treaty before Gaillard and Normandy itself were lost to the Angevin empire. John had raged in the face of his barons' agreement with his marshal, "Let those who are in fear flee!" he cried, "I shall stay for at least a year!"

As John cried out, William had grown grim. John d'Erley later recounted to Isabel that he had known in that moment as he watched William that the king was about to hear the plain, unvarnished truth.

" 'Tis your destiny to lead us, Sire," he had said evenly, his eyes cold with controlled anger. "But you have offended too many. You have no friends, none who would rally to you now."

John was stunned at his marshal's audacity. He stared for a prolonged moment in total silence, then turned suddenly and left the room. The following morning it was found that he had left for Rouen and soon after, for England. His departing words to those faithful to him, still desperately holding to towns and castles in Normandy, "Look to yourselves, expect no help from me!"

Thus Gaillard, the last bastion of the Angevin empire, lay besieged by the French, held by its castellan, Roger de Lacy. De Lacy's last chance had come, prior to that fateful war council, from William, who had led a force of three hundred knights, three thousand men-at-arms, and four thousand foot soldiers down the banks of the

Seine. Meanwhile, King John had mustered a fleet of over seventy riverboats, astutely provided for by his soldier-brother years before in case of just such a need. He was to bring the force down the river to join in the attack, but as usual John miscalculated. While William's forces devastated the French army to such an extent that victory was practically assured, John had misjudged the tides. By the time he was prepared to join the attack William had been driven back.

The siege, with no remaining English force to contain it, began in earnest. The French now simply had to starve the garrison. Unable to feed those within, de Lacy had sent out the noncombatants living within the castle walls. But the French had shown no mercy. As the four hundred innocent inhabitants of Gaillard came forth and attempted to cross the river, they were driven back to the castle walls. The gates remained closed upon them, even as they cried for entrance. There was simply not enough food within, and de Lacy stood firm to what he saw as his duty, to hold the walls at all cost.

Stories of the horror reached Isabel, where she awaited William at Rouen. Stories of the cries of the desperate as they groveled for existence week after week; women and children dying of starvation before husbands and fathers who watched helplessly from the parapets of the castle. The men were forbidden, on pain of death, to throw food down from the ramparts, an order confirmed by the periodic hanging from those same parapets of a soldier unable to watch his family starve.

Thus she had come. And her hatred solidified, forming into a calm, cold intent of purpose against the man who had caused it. She watched intently, assuring herself that she would never forget. She did not discount others who were responsible. Philip, his troops who would not allow the innocents to pass through their lines, knowing how the cries and desperate pleas affected those within the walls. De Lacy, who refused to surrender the stone and mortar entrusted to his care, the door to Normandy that had already been cracked open.

Nor the barons of the Angevin empire who had fled to Philip's court in the face of John's treachery, ignoring their own traitorous actions. But most of all, one man; he who had taken the ducal coronet upon his head and with it the responsibility to care. And in that moment her heart turned to Ireland. Never, she vowed. Never would he lay his boot upon her neck. Never would he use her as he did this. Not while she lived.

"Milady, we must go!" D'Erley had drawn his mount abreast of Isabel, and she realized then that he had been speaking to her for some moments. "William will have my head if he knew I brought you here!"

But it was too late. They heard the sound of hoof-beats coming up the rise behind them and pulled their mounts about to face the consequences of Isabel's fool-ishness. William pulled in his war-horse with fury. Horse pulled back against the tight rein in an angry shake of his head as William glared first at Isabel, then at d'Erley, who was looking extremely uncomfortable. "Sweet Mother of God!" he roared, his eyes beneath the dark helm burning with rage. "What is the mean-ing? Have you both lost your senses? The enemy is at the foot of that next rise! Would you enjoy spending the next few years at Philip's court, madam? If you cannot think of yourself, what of your children? Would you have them motherless?"

Isabel fought a smile but kept her face placid and con-trite. She felt in little danger. Philip would not hold the wife of his favorite emissary captive at court; his affec-tion for William was too great. But she wisely kept her opinion to herself, realizing it was hardly the moment to point out William's popularity with the French king. But her own expression turned grim as she turned back to the scene before them. "I had to come, William. I had to see for myself."

He pulled Horse abreast of her smaller mount as his anger faded with concern as he noticed the paleness of her face. "I would have saved you this, Isabel. It is not for you to see."

"Why?" she flared, glancing at him before her

anguished eyes returned to the castle walls, her voice hardening with her rage. "I had to see for myself, so that I do not forget."

They left Normandy, sailing for England with the heavy knowledge that fewer than two hundred survived the siege beyond the castle walls, and many of those died later from what they had suffered. Château Gaillard fell soon after. The door was opened, and Rouen quickly followed. Normandy disappeared from the Angevin empire.

Queen Eleanor died soon after the fall of Rouen, adding an additional burden to William in his love for the great queen. Isabel grieved for her husband, noting the trace of grey that had appeared at his temples. She knew it was evidence of the burdens he carried and the even larger ones he faced.

# 18

ISABEL had never felt such fear. She moved
about the court as an actor engaged in a role, struggling
to keep her emotions in check as she presented a calm,
assured demeanor to those about her. The children had
been sent to Chepstow with a reluctant John d'Erley,
the only one she would entrust them to, though he had
protested leaving her. She kept Beaumont and Ralph
Musard with her; one to send to John in the event the
children were to be taken quickly across the channel to
Ireland, and one to remain with her, to rally the protection of her vassals should the need arise.

She would have chosen to avoid the court altogether;
the moments spent in the king's presence were an ana-
thema, but she would not entertain the constant
pressures by her knights to leave. With great effort she
affected lack of interest over arrivals to Winchester,
forcing herself to cast a most casual glance in the direction of the newcomer as he passed through the hall
doors to the king's chambers. Each time she prayed it
would not be William, even as her heart contracted
painfully when it was not. She knew that John's eyes

were ever upon her, waiting like a preying feline for some evidence of her fear.

William had been denounced as a traitor. His enemies, those jealous of his power and influence, ignored by stronger and wiser monarchs, had caught the ear of John.

Upon arriving in England, William had convinced his king, at least, to sue for peace with Philip. Leaving for France upon his mission he had also been given the authority to assure the lands of those nobles still in control of honors within Normandy, including his own. He had managed to convince John that they would be the foothold to regain what had been lost. But to Isabel's alarm, no sooner had William left her shores than others began to bend John's ear. Shockingly, Hubert Walter, the archbishop of Canterbury, led the feelings against William. His mind fixed upon giving no concessions to the French, he was outraged by William's intent to sue for peace. He laid his plans well, spreading rumors through the baronage that William's true purpose was to regain his lands, even to giving his liege homage to Philip against the good of England. Few believed the rumors but there were those who were all too ready to play upon John's doubts—that one who had ever been quick to doubt those the most loyal to him. John Lackland, John Softsword, living in the deep shadows of his father and brothers. In his insecurities John listened, characteristically failing to remember the loyalty of the one who had placed the ducal crown of Normandy upon his head, remembering only that he had lost it.

Isabel had instantly recognized her own precarious position at court. She had sent the children to safety but knew that for William's protection she must remain. To leave would only add credence to the accusations. Instead, she kept her spine stiffened, her chin held high, ignoring the sharp barbs laced with bitter accusations from the other women, led by Isabella, John's vainglorious and supercilious queen. Isabel noted with interest, and a certain amount of humor, the jealousy that accompanied the women's darts, recognizing them as having nothing to do with her husband's political problems. But she did not dwell on William's poorly disguised popularity with the gentlewomen of John's court, poignantly recognizing that their jealousies could only stem from William's indifference. Moreover, her thoughts were too filled with worry to seriously bother with such triviality. They were fixed with terror that he would suddenly and unexpectedly return to court, not realizing what awaited him. Dreams of dank cells, chains, and the block filled her thoughts, pushing aside all else.

The fact that loyalty to William had survived within the court was proven when word was passed to Beaumont that Hubert Walter had relayed secret messages to France, with John's knowledge and approval, declaring that the marshal had no authority to sue for peace. The intent of those loyal to William was noted by Isabel, but their purpose was ill served. There was no way to warn him. She knew that she and her vassals were being watched every moment; to attempt to send a message would spell disaster, giving fuel to his enemies. She could only continue to play the role of the innocent, hoping that when he returned she could find a way to warn him before it was too late.

She could well imagine William's reaction when word undermining his authority reached the French court. But she had mixed feelings about the outcome, in spite of the fact that it confirmed the opinion she had always held of Hubert Walter, her former keeper in the Tower. On the one hand, knowing William's pride, she grieved for the possible failure of his mission. Yet she rejoiced. Should he return without accomplishing his mission, much of the strength of his enemies would be weakened. Thus, week by week, fate held her heart in a terrifying hold. She played a role of cheerful unconcern—and waited, hiding her dread from everyone.

He returned on a warm spring morning in May without notice, entering the hall just as the court had gathered for the afternoon hours with their king. Isabel tensed, filled with a light-headed feeling of terror. She

sensed his presence before she saw him, her eyes darting
to the door expectantly just as he entered. In spite of her
fear, her eyes feasted on him, the moment before John
became aware of his presence for her alone. He looked
fit, though she saw lines of fatigue about his eyes, his
tall broad-shouldered frame perfectly filling the dark
brown velvet of his surcoat, the wide earl's belt tight
about his narrow waist. The long mantle, richly lined
with fox, fastened to his shoulders with large gold
clasps, flared behind him as his long legs carried him in
purposeful strides down the length of the enormous hall
to where his king was engaged in conversation with a
small group of nobles.

Conversation in the room died as he passed. Bril-
liantly dressed nobles and their ladies turned in hushed
expectancy, their eyes darting between the returned
marshal and the still-unaware king.

As if coming to, Isabel alerted to the danger of the
situation and reached out blindly to Ralph Musard, who
stood at her side, grasping his arm tightly. "Ralph," she
whispered frantically, "could he be aware of the danger
he is in? Oh, why did he not get word to us that he was
returning."

"Be easy, milady," Ralph warned her in a low voice.
"I am certain that he has made himself well aware of the
king's mind. It is not like him to walk into a situation
unprepared."

She glanced at Ralph, desperately wanting to take
comfort from his words, but noticed that his face had
paled as his eyes fixed on William at the same moment
that William had drawn the attention of his king.
Drawn by the sudden stillness of the room, John's face
froze as he turned. "So," he said, his dark eyes glittering dangerously, "you dare to return to us, Marshal?"

"Dare, milord?" William countered placidly. "Sire, I
am but a returned ambassador carrying reports on the
outcome of a mission taken by your gracious leave.
Part, you are aware of. Point in fact—you were aware
before I." He glanced meaningfully at the archbishop,
who stood but a few feet away, his eyes turning cold.

" 'Twould seem that our archbishop of Canterbury had deemed fit to send a covert message to Philip through Ralph d'Ardern. The missive stated clearly to Philip that I presented myself to his court without the power to make peace as given by you. I am certain that it comes to you as no surprise that my mission to effect peace between our country and that of France has been handily rejected by Philip.'' Outraged gasps were heard about the hall, followed by angry murmurs from the barons.

"I know beyond a doubt that you have sworn allegiance to the king of France!'' John cried, his voice rising against the anger he could feel growing about the hall. "You have done homage to him against me!''

Isabel felt her knees weaken at the king's outburst, and she grasped Ralph for support. How could William remain so calm? She panicked. If John could prove the accusation, William's life was forfeit!

"Sire,'' William replied, his voice still betraying no emotion, "whoever told you such has lied to you. Whatever I have given to Philip was by your leave. Not only did you give permission for my homage to Philip for lands on the continent, but you sent letters to him supporting my honors.''

"By the faith, I did not!'' John cried. "What is more, you will go with me to Poitou to reconquer my inheritance from that king to whom you have so feloniously done homage!''

"Nay, Sire,'' William answered firmly, bringing new gasps from those within the hall. "For my lands in Normandy I am his man, and it would be a felony for me to go against him. I have acted within the law and shall be willing to prove it in combat against any whom you will name as champion.'' He turned in the face of John's blazing anger and addressed the barons who were hanging on each word. "Lords, look you to me! This day I am an example for all of you! Attend closely to the king, for what he plans to do to me, he will do to you if he but can!''

John sputtered, his face turning bright red as he

stared at his marshal with hardly controlled fury. He bellowed in response, demanding a decision from the barons. The nobles exchanged uncomfortable glances as they pulled slightly away from the king, and none would answer.

"By God's teeth!" John roared. "I see that none of my barons are on my side! I call for a champion! One among you who will settle this treason in my name!"

The immense room became bathed in an undercurrent of confusion, which was apparent in the rumbling of discontent that spread among the company. Isabel held her breath. Was there one who would come forward to challenge William? Suddenly Baldwin de Bethune, count of Aumale, stepped forward. His eyes passed over the king with a flicker of distaste, then he turned purposefully to the barons. Unseen by those near the king, his lips twitched as he fought a most satisfied smile for an instant before he spoke. "Be silent!" his voice rang out as his dark eyes passed over the room. "It is not for us to judge a knight of the marshal's eminence! It is clear there is no man strong enough to prove that he has failed his lord!"

"I was certain that the king would expire from rage!" Ralph chuckled, ignoring the fact that William was nuzzling Isabel's ear.

"Do not be fooled," William sighed, putting Isabel away from him regretfully while not missing the wicked dance in her eyes as he did so. "He is a Plantagenet. While momentary ravings may cause foaming at the mouth, calmer moments will follow. I have learned over my life to never underestimate them."

"How did you know of what was afoot?" The question came from Beaumont who, with Hugh de Sanford and Nicolas Avenel, had gathered in the small chambers allotted to Isabel for her enforced stay at Winchester. "God knows that we had no way of sending word to you."

"From Philip." William grinned, amused by the amazed eyebrows that rose from his answer. "Are you truly surprised to learn that there are French spies among our court?''

"Oh, William!" Isabel breathed. "You knew he would accuse you, yet you walked into court unarmed? What if someone had challenged you?"

"Then I would have had to best him," William quipped. "My lady, have you so little faith in me? Besides, I had no intention of remaining in France the rest of my life—though Philip did offer me the title of marshal of France." He laughed at the gasps that accompanied his announcement. "He has offered it before, and I assure you that the offer was no more tempting now than it was previously. In spite of the king's accusations, I am no traitor to England."

"And now?" Isabel asked, her voice pleading. "May we go home, milord? Our children are waiting for word of their father, and as for myself, I could use some moments of peace."

"My thoughts exactly, my love." William smiled. "To Chepstow . . . " His sentence was left unfinished as a rap at the door admitted a messenger from the king, who handed William a note, then quickly departed, but not before the lad's eyes took careful note of the marshal, his expression one of awe. Beaumont closed the door on the servant, his mouth working with amusement as he noted the respectful attendance the boy had given to William. His smile froze as he turned back and saw William's expression as he scanned the note. "What is it?" he asked quietly.

William glanced up at Isabel, who had turned away to pour tankards of ale for the men. "The devil has composed himself," he murmured. "Beaumont, take the others and leave us." He handed the message to his knight, who scanned it quickly, his face becoming grim. He nodded sharply, glancing at Isabel as he gestured to the others, and they quickly departed the room, closing the door silently behind them.

Isabel turned back to see the knights retire. She turned to William with questions in her eyes, her gaze dropping to the missive in his hand, then to the sober expression he wore. "What is it?" she asked, her eyes moving again to the closed door and then back to her husband.

"He has given us leave to return to Chepstow immediately," he answered quietly.

"That is exactly what we want!" she laughed nervously. She did not want to ask him what else was contained in the message. No more, she cried inwardly, no more!

He hesitated but knew there was no easy way to tell her. "He demands Will as hostage."

"Nay!" she cried, grasping the edge of a table for support.

He was at her side in an instant, pulling her into his arms. She pushed against him, flinging herself away from him as her mind spun wildly, unwilling to accept what he had said. "You will not give him to him? You cannot! Tell me you will not, William!"

"Aye, Isabel, I will. You know that it must be."

"He is but a baby!"

"That he is not," he said firmly, reaching to her to accept what must be. "He has reached an age of fostering . . ."

"I will not have him here!" she cried. "Not with—him!"

"We cannot refuse, you know that. But I promise Isabel, no harm shall come to him."

The journey home was a painful one. The thought of sending Will to court was incomprehensible to Isabel, to place him into the hands of one she had come to despise more than any living soul. They did not speak of it again. The subject was too painful to face as each mile brought them closer to home, yet she wondered if William's thoughts were the same as hers—recalling a time when he too had been hostage to a king. Would John prove as merciful as Stephen if faced with the sacrifice of a child?

The pain became unbearable when at last they arrived home. As dusk claimed the crenellated walls of Chepstow's massive towers, the brilliant red sunset painted the rough mortar and stone of the battlements in a soft pink hue, softening the gathering shadows that fell about the inner bailey. Even the air had softened to a dreamlike quality, denying the pain of reality that grasped Isabel in a strangling hold.

She drew in her breath as the doors opened and Will came tumbling out, his eyes wide with joy. "How can I bear it?" she murmured. He came rushing into her arms as she bent down to him, his arms flung about her neck as he grasped her in a fierce hug. Her eyes filled with tears, and she looked up over Will's shoulders to find William watching. As their eyes met he gave a slight shake of his head in warning, but his eyes, too, were filled with sadness. Will turned, pulling his arms from her as he stood to face William, his eyes happy but touched with uncertainty of how he should behave in the face of this formidable knight who was his father. The corners of William's mouth twitched as he noted his son's dilemma. He knelt down and offered his arms, which were quickly filled as the youngster leapt forward.

"Papa." Will pulled back after a moment, his face still uncertain as he glanced around at the others, the knights still astride their mighty destriers, and John d'Erley, who had appeared at the top of the stairs. "Are you certain it is all right for us to hug?" he whispered. "I am not a baby anymore, you know."

"Nay, son, that you are not," William assured him with a sober expression. "But when you are a grown man, returning from great battles and conquests, I hope that you will still favor your old father with a hug." He rose, turning to greet John, who had come down the steps, and the two close friends clasped each other in welcome. William saw Will's eyes widen appreciatively, and he threw his son a large wink, bringing a smile from the boy.

They quickly settled in, and the evening was spent in catching John up on the news, all but the matter of Will, which was studiously avoided in front of the child. The gathering clouds had made good on their promise of an impending storm as the wind began to whip about the keep, rattling the shutters violently and whistling mournfully through the high rafters about the large hall. Isabel's heart warmed to the sounds, for once welcoming their promise, as a storm would surely delay the inevitable. She spent the evening half listening to the men as she played games with her son and listened to his recounting of each event that had occurred in her absence; tales of the servants, the antics of little Richard, whom he had visited with his mother and whom he had helped to tuck into bed, and of the hunt for roe on which John had taken him.

William watched them from the corner of his eye, and as the evening progressed his brow began to deepen in worry. It was going to be harder than he had thought. In those years of his absence she had obviously become unusually close to their son. He feared that those years without a father's influence had left Will unable to cope with what lay ahead of him. He could only hope that she had given him strength to face what he must.

At last Anna came for Will, having delayed his bedtime in celebration of his parents' homecoming. Reluctantly, Will slipped from his chair, facing the inevitable, wanting to delay even as his eyes drooped sleepily. He embraced Isabel then crossed to bid his father a good night.

"Beaumont," William turned to the knight as Will reached his side. "Have a pallet prepared in your quarters. He is too old for a nursemaid, and in the future will be your responsibility." As the knight rose, grinning, William turned to the boy, whose sleepiness had vanished at his father's words. "Will, you will no longer sleep in the nursery; that is for Richard. Beginning tomorrow, you shall be Beaumont's page. You'll have much to learn, and I expect you to perform your tasks well. You carry a proud lineage and I trust that you will do honor to the name you carry." He looked up at the rafters bearing the banners of Chepstow. "Someday your coat of arms will hang among these;

what it will tell will be for you to prove, for no one else can give it meaning.''

Will drew up perceptibly, beaming with pride as he followed his father's gaze. "I shall do my best to make you proud of me,'' he said bravely, his blue eyes glowing with excitement and vision.

"Come, Will,'' Beaumont said, waiting, and he led the boy from the hall.

William watched him go, then glanced at Anna, whose hands were tearing at the folds of her apron as her eyes filled with tears. She glanced at William and flushed, turning to flee from the hall, unwilling to cry in front of her master. His eyes shifted to Isabel, who stood aside, stunned as she watched her son disappear from the hall, and she spun on William, her large eyes accusing. Facing her fury, he rose from his chair and strode across the hall to her, grasping her arm. Spinning her about he led her to the stairs, determined to face the unavoidable in privacy.

She half ran to keep up with his long strides, unable to pull from his firm grip as they approached the door to their chamber. Ignoring her protests, he pushed open the door, shutting it upon them before he released her, and she spun on him as her anger exploded.

"Why?'' she cried. "Why now? Could you not leave him to me for the short time that we have?''

"Especially not now,'' he answered calmly, facing her rage. "The boy should have been taken from his nursemaid long before this.''

"But . . .''

"He will go to John's court as Beaumont's page,'' he said firmly. "That, along with the sixty knights of Beaumont's honor, will allow him protection from John. I can delay a few weeks, no more. In that time he must learn his duties as a knight's page, and learn to depend upon Beaumont as his master. It will make the parting easier.''

Her mouth opened in protest but closed sharply as his reasonings began to be absorbed. Blinking, she stared at him for a moment, then her shoulders drooped in submission. He was right, of course. It was the only way to protect him from John. "I will miss him so." She swallowed, fighting back her tears.

"I know," he answered, feeling her sorrow. He drew her into his arms, holding her against him as she sobbed against his shoulder, allowing the grief that she had been holding inside of her to come. As she grew quiet in his arms, he tilted her head up to his, and his mouth closed over hers in a gentle kiss. She responded, needing his warmth, his strength, and she relaxed against him. Gradually the kiss became deeper, changing, and she stiffened as she realized his intent. She couldn't, not now! Her mind raced, denying what he was expecting of her, now when she could only feel grief for the loss of their son! She pushed away from him, her eyes wide with denial, as she stepped back. "Nay, William, not now!" she whispered.

"Not now?"

"I . . . I couldn't!" she breathed, shaking her head as she stepped back from him.

His eyes grew dark, and she could see how angry her response had made him but she flung the knowledge from her, still horrified that he could expect her to submit to him. He took a step toward her. "Aye, now," he said softly, but with a resolve that startled her. "Now. Most definitely now. I will not allow you to pull away from me again. To spend weeks grieving, keeping yourself from me as you wallow in self-pity while you use our son as an excuse."

"Self-pity? Excuse?" she stammered, her own anger flaming at his words.

"Aye, just that," he answered, stepping closer. "Self-pity—as the grief will be for yourself, not Will. Your loss, not his. An excuse to return to the way we were before when you had only your feelings to consider, your needs. Nay, Isabel. We have come too far to return to that; I will not allow you to do that to us."

She gasped as he reached out, pulling her to him. He held her tightly as he stared down at her. His eyes burning with his intent, he pulled apart the laces at her neckline, his hand slipping beneath her bodice to fondle a breast. His eyes held her own, unblinking, as his fingers teased a nipple, his meaning deliberate, until he saw her falter, her lids dipping in half-closed response to what he was doing. He pulled the bodice further apart to expose a breast, now open to him in the flickering light from the candles and the low fire. He cupped it in his hand, caressing it tenderly as he possessively feasted on the sight of it. He knew she was watching him, knew the effect it was having on her as he felt her slump against him. Slowly, he lowered her to the deep furs spread in front of the hearth. Pausing only to release his chausses and lift her skirts, he filled her with him, sliding into the warm, moist sheath that opened to him as she spread her thighs, her need suddenly as desperate as his own. She clasped him to her, her legs wrapping about him as her head tossed wildly, incoherent words called to him to help her, to bring her to that place where she could forget, where her pain could be eased. Swells rippled over her, tension bursting in shattering release, pulling her from her existence to a plane of otherworld where only he could take her.

They lay breathing heavily, sated passion coming to rest as he held her to him, a protective arm about her shoulder. She finally stirred in his arms as she regained her breath. "Oh, William," she whispered, wanting to accept. "Will he be all right?"

"He will be fine," he murmured. "It will be far worse for you."

He rose up on an elbow and bent to kiss her lightly. Slowly, gently caressing her between his efforts, he drew her clothing from her, then shed his own. His eyes moved over her lovingly as it lay open to his appraisal before the light of the fire, his hand moving lightly over her body, following where his eyes rested. "There is another matter dear to your heart that must be seen to, my love," he said as he teased a breast, trapping a nipple lightly between a finger and thumb.

"What?" she gasped, desire returning rapidly under his attentions.

"Ireland," he answered calmly, bending to tease the nipple with his tongue.

The word startled her even as her breath drew in sharply at what he was doing to her. "Ireland? William, stop it! What do you mean?"

His hand cupped her breast, drawing it to his mouth after he murmured softly. "We are leaving for Ireland as soon as Will and Beaumont have departed for London."

She squirmed against him, her hands attempting to stay him from his purpose even as her thoughts spinned dizzily. "William!" she gasped, "what are you talking about? William, stop it!"

He chuckled and rose up to look down into her shocked eyes. "Is it not clear, milady? There are matters to be seen to across the Irish Sea, and I have determined that now is the time. Would you rather remain here? It can be arranged if you prefer, although it does surprise me somewhat. I would have thought . . . "

"William! Damn you!"

His brows arched in mock horror. "Damn me?" He shrugged with a grin. "And I thought to please you . . . "

# 19

THE wind circled in punishing gales to batter those gathered tightly to the beach, their eyes closed to the stinging flurry of the sand that rose to torment them. The surf pounded against the jutting rocks enclosing the small stretch of land, affording small measure of protection.

"We must hurry, milord, the storm is well upon us!" the lieutenant shouted, straining to have his voice heard against the wind.

They prepared to depart the beach as the ships riding in the harbor left to withdraw, their unloading delayed until a more opportune time as their sails unfurled to again set out to sea in face of the impending storm. Reality replaced the essence of the dreams, and Isabel accepted the homecoming, so different than she had imagined, and she allowed the Irish kern to assist her into the saddle of the mount. She twisted about to find William, who had already mounted and was shouting orders to his men. They rode from the beach inland, their destination reached well after the storm had broken, the party arriving soaked and exhausted at Wexford.

They drew before a well-lighted manor, the inviting glow from within drawing like a beacon. William slid from his mount, appearing at Isabel's side to lift her down. Assuring himself that John had seen to Richard, he threw his cloak about Isabel and rushed her to the door and within as it opened before them.

She blinked against the brightness that greeted her, her eyes straining to adjust as she glanced around, absorbing her surroundings. The large room, set with comfortable furniture of massive portions, struck familiar recesses of her memory. Then her eyes came to rest upon a tall man with light hair intermixed with grey, his blue eyes fixed upon her with open pleasure where he stood before the hearth. He grinned, stepping forward to greet her.

"Uncle Donnell!" she cried, rushing forward to be folded in his arms.

"Lord, Isabel. Is it really you?" he chuckled with obvious pleasure. "You were but a wee lass when last I beheld you." He held her from him to look at her closely, his shrewd blue eyes taking in what he saw. He glanced up at William, who stood nearby. "Milord," he said, offering his hand. "Welcome to Erin."

"There are those who will not be pleased that you are here." Donnell motioned to a servant to refill their goblets as he sat before the fire with William. Isabel had disappeared to tuck a weary babe into bed and supervise the unpacking. "Times have changed little, I fear, since Isabel's father arrived on our shores."

"I have heard of a time when *you* sought to see all English from Ireland's shores." William smiled. "Could it be that you are now of a different mind?"

"Not different," Donnell Kavanaugh grinned wryly, "merely tempered with the wisdom of experience—and patience. Experience, which has taught that all English are not necessarily of the same mold. There are those, as in the case of Isabel's father, who become more Irish than English, yet bring us strengths we sorely need, if we but heed them."

"And patience?" William regarded the older man through narrowed eyes.

"Ah, patience. That most difficult of virtues, particularly to the young. To wait, knowing that all things worthwhile come at their appointed time."

"And who shall determine when that time shall be?" William's eyes flickered with humor, thoroughly enjoying the exchange.

"Fate. The gods." Donnell smiled, waving a hand to emphasize his words. "Man passes it by unrecognized, but it occurs, nonetheless. Youth rushes on, seeking answers of its own making. The old ones ignore it, for to grasp opportunity would take far too much effort. But to each age, there is a time by design or accident, then forces work together and progress is achieved."

William's mouth twitched. "Ah, but what one determines as victory another must measure as defeat—unless what is achieved benefits both equally."

"Exactly, my lord earl. It would seem that . . . "

Their conversation was brought to an abrupt halt by the entrance of a middle-aged woman. Of average height, her full figure was little concealed beneath the rich fabric of her loosely fitted kirtle, a style long out of date in England. Her greying hair was pulled back severely in a long braid, her face dominated by stern green eyes, deep lines etched into her forehead, and the corners of her mouth suggesting that her normal manner was one of disapproval. Those self-suffering eyes fixed on William, then dismissed him as they moved to Donnell. "They are settled in, though why the household need be disturbed at such an hour is beyond me."

"My dear," Donnell said tiredly, tossing a look of apology to William. "May I introduce our guest, William, Lord Marshal, earl of Pembroke, Isabel's husband—and lord of Leinster." He emphasized the last words, which were lost on the woman as she glanced at William and nodded tightly in greeting. "My lord, my wife, Katherine," he added with an edge of fatigue to his voice.

Before William could respond, she turned once again on her husband. "Do you know what she has brought with her? A cat! And she expects it to live inside!"

"The animal is a favorite," William explained by way of apology, while concealing his shock over the woman's behavior in deference to her husband, whose embarrassment was apparent. "He is well traveled, even as far as Normandy, and will cause no trouble." He couldn't believe that he was actually defending Shad. It had only been a day since he had hoped the animal would be lost at sea. "Isabel will not be parted from him."

"Katy, 'tis a small thing, hardly worth attention." Donnell sighed. "I apologize for my wife's tongue, Earl William, I fear . . ."

"Ye need not be apologizing for me, Donnell Kavanaugh!" Katy snapped, pulling herself up to glare down at her husband. "I'm perfectly capable of express'n me own feel'ns!"

As Katherine, who was obviously the bane of her husband's existence, launched into a rapid-fire discourse on their ill-timed arrival, William retired quickly. He bade his host a hasty good-night before seeking out the chambers he would be sharing with Isabel during their stay in Wexford. She turned from her unpacking as he closed the door behind him, and upon glancing at his expression, she burst into laughter.

"I see that you have met Katy."

"Whatever did your uncle do to deserve her?" he asked, rolling his eyes.

"He fell in love with her." She shrugged, turning back to her task. "But that was a long time ago. She was different then, or so he thought." She paused for a moment, thinking of her aunt and uncle, and sighed. "But then, it takes two to make a marriage, William. As much as I love Uncle Donnell, he must shoulder part of the blame." She glanced at her husband who had settled into a chair near the hearth. "Katy spent most of her youth quite alone while he sought other company—battles and softer pursuits."

"If what I evidenced below is any indication, I cannot blame him." He grimaced.

In honesty, Isabel could not recall when Katy had not been a shrew, so she let the matter pass. "Katy told me that Mother is at Ferns," she said, changing the subject. "I would like to see her soon. Will we stay here long?"

"Only until I have met with Meiler fitz Henry," he answered, pulling off his boots. "I have summoned the barons and will hold a court three days hence to which he will answer to charges."

Isabel smiled grimly as she grasped the heavy iron arm and swung a large pot over the fire to warm water for their baths. Meiler fitz Henry, she thought to herself, John's justiciar in Ireland. While vassal to William, it was he who fed the unrest, defying all orders while establishing the cause of his own men, and she suspected, John's wishes. "What will you do if he refuses to comply with the decision of the court?"

"He will comply." William ground out the words. "One way or the other. By the way," he added, glancing at the grey-striped fur ball curled up on a nearby chair. "Keep Shad locked up in this room if you value him. In Katy he may have met his match."

The barons began arriving the following morning, and with each the difficulty of their position in Ireland became uncomfortably clearer. Geoffrey fitz Robert, a capable and trustworthy knight of William's household, came first, and it was from he that William began to learn the essence of what had been happening. Isabel had seen fitz Robert arrive from their chamber window and had hastened downstairs. She arrived at the room given to William for his private use while in Wexford only to find that the door had been closed behind them. Disgruntled, she stared at the door for a moment. Then, taking a deep breath she put her hand to the latch and pushed.

The two men looked up with surprise at her entrance, but she managed to affect her own amazement in finding the room occupied. "Oh, William! Forgive me, I did not know you were in here. I seemed to have left my needlework somewhere and . . . Geoffrey! How good to see you! I hope that Glenna is well, it has been so long since I have seen her!'' she rushed on, referring to Sir Geoffrey's wife. She paused and blinked innocently at William. ''Oh, dear, did I disturb you?''

''You may remain, Isabel,'' William said, his brow arching with his effort at calm. ''Unless, of course, your needlepoint is a more pressing matter.'' Seeing the amusement in his eyes, she was relieved, but she also saw his warning to be silent.

Fitz Robert, sent by William in response to Eve's plea years before, began a detailed account of what had happened. As she listened, Isabel complied with William's warning and kept her own counsel, though her rage increased with the recounting, until, finally, she could bear it no longer. ''Then none have been loyal!'' she cried angrily. ''Renault de Kedeville, and even your nephew, John Marshal, have betrayed us, William!''

''I am not unaware of what has been happening, Isabel,'' William said patiently. ''Each will be dealt with. As for John Marshal, 'tis a heady thing to be offered the marshalship of Ireland, with a goodly fief, and he is young.''

She gaped at him, her ire rising. ''How can you excuse him? He was sent by you to inform Meiler fitz Henry that he was not to infringe upon your lands and to remind him that you are his suzerain! Yet he obviously accepted the post of marshal while allowing fitz Henry to continue to work against you.''

''I excuse nothing, Isabel. Fitz Henry has taken possession of Offaly, and he will be taken to account for it, as will those who have supported him.'' He left Isabel to fume, as he turned back to fitz Robert. ''Geoffrey, you are to be commended for your efforts here. New Ross is said to be a thorn in fitz Henry's side,'' he said, referring to the town Geoffrey had built on William's order on the river Barrow.

''Aye, milord,'' the other man said, grinning, his brown eyes glinting with humor. ''We have managed to pull a substantial amount of trade from Waterford. Fitz Henry cannot be too pleased. As for the rest, the barons should be here by sunset. I will say, milord, now that you are here, they are most ready to see the matter to an end, with sword if necessary."

"Let us hope that will not be necessary," William answered grimly. "I hope to unify, not to further divide."

"How can you ever expect to depend upon their loyalty!" she cried. She had waited for him, pacing in agitation in the privacy of their chamber, until he had finally joined her for the night. Waiting until he had relaxed with a goblet of wine, she had tried to broach the subject carefully. It took only moments for the discussion to dissolve into a heated fray. "The king is behind this! He wants you to fail!"

"Of course John is behind it," he responded, resting his head against the back of the chair as he watched her pace across the room. "But it matters not to him who is successful—as long as he does not lose."

"And that is through Meiler fitz Henry!"

"Isabel," he said wearily. "It is unfortunate that your father did not live long enough to teach you the art of diplomacy."

On hearing his words, she spun around, her eyes flaring at him. "He drove the Ostmen from Ireland by sword! Have you forgotten? They would still be holding their walled cities, including the one in which you now sit, had he sought to negotiate!"

"Would he have kept Henry from her shores by the same means?" he asked quietly. "Ireland saw years of peace because he played the game well, Isabel. Yet his daughter would have me throw her into a war."

"His daughter would have John Plantagenet's boot from her neck!"

"As would I," he answered. "A little trust from my wife would make it easier."

"How will you play this game?" she asked, struggling to control her temper.

"That, my dear, depends upon which cards are held by Meiler fitz Henry."

The next few days were strained. The tension was felt by everyone who came and went from the manor. Isabel regretted her angry words to William, and his accusation that she did not trust him bothered her deeply. She trusted him, she told herself, she simply felt that he was wrong. She was certain that war was inevitable, she felt it in the deepest part of her. But she had little time to dwell upon it before another problem came to light. On the third day of arrival in Ireland a suspicion she had harbored for some time was confirmed. The evidence was given as she rushed from her breakfast to the garderobe. She was pregnant again.

Katy Kavanaugh did little to ease the pressure felt by those of the household. Her sharp voice was ever-present over other matters. William watched Donnell with amazement. At first he thought that the middle-aged Irishman was unaware of his wife's shrewishness. Finally, he realized that Donnell had learned to simply shut her out. He found himself thinking of what he would have done if Katy had been his wife. Suddenly, he found that he understood Henry, and why he had locked Eleanor away for sixteen years. His eyes had strayed to Isabel, but he immediately dismissed his groping suspicions, a small smile touching his mouth as he watched her with Richard as she encouraged the child to eat, her eyes rolling comically as Richard giggled at something she had said. Nay, there was a decided difference between a determined woman and a shrew. Isabel could be as gentle, as loving, and as passionate, as she could be angry. And it was always honest temper, however misguided, brought on by matters she felt passionately about. He could forgive that, he even welcomed it when he felt up to a good verbal battle. Aye, she was exciting, but he knew that something deep within her haunted her, keeping her from a complete relationship with him, and he was as helpless now as when they were first wed to understand it. His eyes moved to her banner, where it rested next to his over the vacant table. Something pulled at him about that banner and the meaning of his disquiet, as it had done countless times before. But before he could grasp his feelings, Katy stormed the room, fit to be tied that she had just found Shad curled up in her wardrobe.

The court of barons was held the following morning with William at its head as lord of Leinster. Isabel's eyes fixed stonily on the man summoned before it, Meiler fitz Henry, justiciar of Ireland, and John's man. Short of stature, with thick brown hair, he had large, dark brown eyes, which gave the appearance of innocence, except to those who looked closely to the shrewd light behind them. He stood calmly before his lord, the hint of a smile on his thin lips.

The trial lasted well into the morning, the charges reread and explained to the accused in detail. The greatest offense was that of his seizure of Offaly, lands belonging by law to William Marshal. Fitz Henry had listened calmly, countering with his defense that he had done so in the name of the king of England, that he had acted not as a baron of Leinster but as justiciar of Ireland. As she listened, Isabel heard the drums of war grow louder.

The next day William dispatched Walter and Hugh de Lacy with letters for the king to plead his case. Isabel surmised from bits of conversation she overheard that William was prepared to defend his right by combat. She said no more to him of her own opinion, knowing that the die would be cast. She needed but to wait. The weeks passed, and a semblance of peace descended upon Wexford as they waited for word from England.

At last the de Lacys returned, and with them a message that turned William into a rage. John had received William's envoys—then sent them back to Ireland with the comment that they should worry less about their lord's privileges and more about that of the crown. However, wishing to be the reasonable monarch, and wishing to avoid confrontation between his subjects whenever possible, he summoned William and Meiler to appear before him. The matter was to be settled peacefully.

William ordered their departure immediately, storming about as he supervised the preparations. His rage was unconcealed, fueled by his concern in leaving Ireland to Meiler's men—whom he knew would certainly make mayhem in the wake of his departure. Hours were taken in planning with the knights he would leave behind, preparing for such an event. His mind taken to such matters, he was unprepared for a final point of discord. One that would come from his own wife.

Isabel had no intention of leaving Ireland. She had not seen her mother—and she was determined not to leave Ireland to the greedy clutches of such men as these. They were, after all, her lands, her responsibility. Remembrances of the Château Gaillard filled her thoughts, and with it her oath to never allow John to place such misery upon Ireland. Somehow, she must be allowed to remain.

The answer came unexpectedly the following day as they sat to midmeal and a large haunch of sweet, succulent pork was set before Isabel. William reached over to cut a portion from the meat, then he turned to lay it on their trencher. His eyes touched on Isabel's face, who had turned a ghostly pale, then a slightly tinged green. She flew from the table, followed by the eyes of her husband, who sat completely still, in shock. The portion of meat was suspended from his knife above the trencher. He found her bent over a chamber pot behind the night screen in their chamber. Holding her as she emptied her stomach, he then gently washed her face with a cool cloth before helping her to a chair by a window.

They sat in a long silence as she regained her stomach. Her normal color gradually returned as he stared from the window. "I assume, from your reaction, that you are only a few months along," he observed quietly.

"Aye," she answered, willing her stomach to settle.

"Why did you not tell me?"

"Would it have made a difference?" She shrugged.

"You did not think I would be interested?" He turned his head to look at her.

"I did not think you needed this burden—with everything that has been happening."

"You mean that you knew that I would make you remain at Chepstow," he snapped.

"Can you blame me for wanting to come?" she threw at him. "Besides, I was not certain until a few days ago."

"You were blessedly lucky that you did not lose the babe in the crossing," he said with disgust. "Of course, you are aware that you cannot return now while the seas are high."

The realization made her start, and she fought to control her excitement. Why had she not thought of it herself? "Aye, William," she said contritely, lowering her gaze so that he did not see the gleam in her eyes.

He was not fooled as he regarded her with a shake of his head. "I should take you with me, regardless. The danger here is too great."

"Leave me d'Erley," she said calmly. "He will not allow anything to happen to me. I shall send Richard to Mother, and shall go to her myself if the situation becomes desperate." Seeing his indecision, she played her final card. "William, I am half-Irish. These are my people. They, above all, will not allow anything ill to befall me. If you have any doubt of it, speak with Uncle Donnell."

" 'Tis not the Irish who concern me, Isabel," he answered broodingly. He looked up at her and his face became rigid, but she was elated at the determination gathering in his deep blue eyes. "However, you may leave the barons to me." He did not add that it was her own notions and temperament that worried him far more than anything else.

An assemblage of the Irish and English baronage was

held at Castle Kilkenney, the morning having been spent in councils preparing for whatever might occur in his absence.

Her shrewd eyes catching each nuance, Eve deClare watched with a detached feeling. Had it been so many years since she had stood with Richard, in a hall much like this, when a similar fate for Erin had been faced? She recalled his words years before as they had stood on a hill overlooking Ferns, and he had told her that Ireland's history was fated to be retold again and yet again, perhaps into time itself. Her eyes now shifted to her grown daughter, who was watching and listening with absorption to the decisions that were being made. She could see herself in those eyes as she had been so many years before. She recalled them with pleasure as another part yearned for peace. Soon, she thought, soon Richard. But not quite yet. The clans still looked to her as the catalyst that bound them. She had already spoken with the chieftains. Thus, they had appeared to pledge their support. Henry, Richard, John. Would those who followed after the Plantagenets prove to be different? Probably not. Her green eyes touched each Irish kern with fierce devotion, feeling the essence of Irishness that could never be defeated. Her eyes moved to her son-in-law. Aye, she thought. You are one of the good ones, so like my Richard. And we will use you, without apology, only wishing that there were more like you, that there were enough.

"Lords," William had begun to speak, his eyes moving slowly about the large room, challenging each of the barons, "behold the countess, the daughter of the earl who gave you your fiefs when he came to this land, securing it against the anarchy that threatened it. She remains here among you, with child. Until God leads me back, I entrust you with guarding her faithfully, for she is your liege lady, and I have no right in this land but through her."

The barons raised their hands, holding aloft their lances, the unified roar of assent filling the chamber as they cried their pledge to support their lord's wife in his absence.

Isabel felt a stirring pride at their unity, the two parts of her melded into a oneness, and she experienced, for the first time in her life, her soul and her heart together. Her grey eyes shifted to the woman sitting at the head of the room watching the proceedings, and her eyes misted.

# 20

ISABEL'S eyes fixed on the sea of flickering
lights beyond the city walls. Two thousand men, English
and Irish, lay encamped about Waterford, awaiting the
dawn and the battle that would be faced. They had
driven Meiler's forces to the very border of Okinselagh,
but she knew that the greatest challenge lay before
them. Meiler's forces had drawn back before William's
army much too easily. Rather than giving them a false
sense of security, William's captains had surmised that
Meiler had used the time to gather reinforcements from
the clans in the north. She pulled her fur-lined cloak
more tightly about her against the biting cold as she continued to pace along the wall, as much against the intru-
sion of doubts, as against the weather. In spite of her
resolve not to dwell on personal concerns, it occurred to
her, with a chilling certainty, that she might die. If
Meiler was successful, the outcome was certain. No one
would show mercy. Against such an event, d'Erley had
tried to persuade her to escape to the highlands, to
secrete herself until William's return, but she had refused. She would not flee in the face of that miscreant;
this was her fight, more than anyone's. They were her
people, her lands, and she would defend them. When

William returned she would return Leinster to him intact, or she would not face him at all.

Meiler fitz Henry had left for England soon after William, only to secrete himself back to Ireland while John commanded William to attend the court. William's anger and anguish had been clear in his letters, which arrived with regularity until the onset of winter when no ships could attempt crossing the Irish Sea. Only then did fitz Henry show his colors, as he blatantly took up arms against Leinster, intending to squash resistance before William could return.

She left the wall, making her way to her quarters past the guards, who nodded in silent recognition of her presence, their eyes filled with the realization of what they would be facing in a few hours' time. Their looks haunted her as she readied for bed. Her hand passed over her belly, reassuring herself that her pregnancy showed little. Perhaps she should have heeded John's urging and fled to the hills, giving this babe a chance for life. Nay, she thought angrily as she dismissed the thought as weakness. The battle had yet to be fought.

Her limbs felt heavy. Her mind was weighted with fatigue, but she knew that it would be useless to try to sleep. Wrapping a robe about her, she curled up in a chair before the fire, tucking her legs beneath her. The ponderous weight of responsibility pressed on her as she stared into the leaping flames, and her mind traveled over and over again to the plans that had been made, the advice of her captains in that final war council a few hours past. She trusted them, yet . . . what if they were wrong? Did William feel these doubts the night before a great battle? Could he find the escape of sleep during those final hours before the enemy was met? He had been right about so many things.

William. She sighed, leaning her head back against the chair as she stared sightlessly into the darkened room. She knew that she had been difficult to live with; the problems as much her fault as his. She wished that she could have been all that he had wanted her to be. The realization that she might not survive the day made the answers seem more important than ever.

Would it have been different between them if they could have met of their own accord? She turned back the years and imagined his arrival at Chepstow in a great company of knights. The color, the excitement of a great banquet. Her eyes moved across the room as she laughed at a quip from a knight of her acquaintance, to find him watching her. Slowly, he crossed the room and, as his eyes looked deeply into hers, he drew her into a dance. As the musicians played in the gallery above, the haunting sound of lute and lyre playing to each step as they turned, their eyes locked in heady anticipation. . . . A spark from the fire popped loudly, and she snapped out of her reverie, the dream quickly fading. With its loss she suddenly felt overwhelmed, for what might have been and for what she must face. Self-pity, fear, and grief overtook her, and a slow stream of tears began to course down her cheeks, unheeded. All of these years she had accepted her life, rejecting self-pity for that which could not be changed. Yet never had she felt so alone, so vulnerable, than she did at this moment, now, when she needed strength more than ever before. Never had she ached more to have William's arms about her. Nay! Tears would solve nothing! She wiped them away with the back of her hand, then pulled a kerchief from her pocket and wiped her eyes. Yet somehow, at this moment she could not accept her life. She felt cheated—from what could have been. Resting her head against the chair, she sniffed back the remnants of her tears and stared into the flames, drawing from their steady presence, willing her mind to go blank against the pain of her thoughts. Exhausted, she felt her body lighten. Vaguely she became aware of another presence drawing her down, a dull awareness that the flames seemed to be reaching out to her, claiming her thoughts, as if drawing her into them in an almost physical claiming. No longer able to struggle, she allowed her thoughts to draw deeper and she let go, slipping into the drifting, welcomed release of dreams . . .

"La, and I suppose it's a treat ye be want'n?" The large, robust woman peered down at the small child who peeked up over the edge of the table. Large grey eyes watched the woman hopefully as she rolled out yet another tart to be filled with the plump juicy apples from the garden just beyond the bailey walls. The child wrinkled her nose to the succulent smells drifting about the warm kitchens, and she nodded, her eyes growing impossibly larger as the cook took up a tart, fresh from the ovens and set to cool, and placed it into the small eager hands. "There, be off wi' ye, love, there'll be no more."

The child grinned with delight and turned to escape with her treasure, pausing at the door of the kitchen to tear off a piece, handing it to the lad who was turning the spit with a roasting haunch. The child knew he had been watching enviously, though he never would have asked for himself. He popped it into his mouth, the spicy flavors bursting over his tongue, and he rolled his eyes in appreciation. The little girl laughed at the face of pleasure he made before she slipped through the door to find a secret place to enjoy her own portion.

She ran into the courtyard and came to a halt, puzzled by the commotion as men were scurrying about amid wagons and large horses who pawed the ground nervously, snorting their displeasure from being removed from the comfort of their stables to be hitched to wagons and loaded with sacks and bundles. She watched with curiosity, forgetting for the moment the warm tart clutched in her small hand as she watched the proceedings and wondered what they meant. Spying a loved form and face, she smiled and ran to a large, darkly bearded knight who was ordering the others about in a loud, blustering voice. She tugged on his tunic, bringing him about with a dark frown on his fearsome face, which softened as he spied the small form at his heel.

"What's that you've got?" the knight growled in his tenderest voice. "A tart from cook? Lucky pup! Your papa's looking for you—he's in the great hall. Along with you now." He turned back to his task, shouting to a laggard with a voice that would have woken the dead into living, but the child only giggled, knowing the gentle nature of the knight, yet she scampered away to do his bidding.

She made her way down the hallway of the manor, past the kitchens and the door to the buttery, chewing on the tart as her small legs carried her to her destination. Pausing at the screen passage to the hall, she finished her treat, stuffing it into her mouth as the juice dribbled down her chin onto her dress. She peered around the screen, intent upon sneaking up on her father, to play their game of "boo," which always made Papa laugh and led to tickles and warm kisses.

He sat at the center of the room, bent over a table covered with papers, and she could hear the scratchy sound of the quill as it moved over the parchment. She tiptoed across the floor, wondering why his mouth twitched as she drew near. As she threw up her arms and shouted, "Boo," he spun about, grasping at his chest as his grey eyes rolled heavenward, then he reached out and grabbed her up, against her protesting giggles, drawing her into his lap. Settled, she pushed against his chest with a small finger and frowned. "I do not like this. It is hard," she said, prodding his hauberk and chain mail beneath his tunic.

He squeezed her gently, planting a kiss on her smoky golden head. "I hope you love me anyway."

"I love you, Papa," she sighed, nestling into his arms. He was so strong, and she felt so safe and warm when he held her. It felt, now, like the nights when she awoke from a bad dream and he was there, holding her until she fell asleep again.

He took her small hand and kissed it, drawing back with an odd look on his face as his tongue passed over his lips. "Apple?" he questioned.

"Cook gave me a tart," she said, staring at the grubby hand, then raising it to her lips she licked off the remainder of the tasty treat.

He removed a kerchief from the pocket of his tunic and wiped off her face and then her mouth as his own mouth twitched again.

"Why do you have that on?" she persisted, jabbing

at his chest again. "I don't like it."

"It is part of the reason I wanted to see you. I have to go away for a while, Angel."

"Go away? Why?" She did not want him to go away.

"Because King Henry needs me. He is in a place called Normandy, and he has asked me to come to help him with problems he is having."

"King Henry? You mean the man with the red hair who gave me the doll Kevin broke when he was mad at me?"

"Aye, love, the same."

"But I don't want you to go."

"And I want to stay with you and Mother. But I must go, dearheart, it is my duty."

There was a sound of a skirt rustling against the floor rushes, and the child turned in her father's arms to find that her mother had come into the hall. Why was she crying? She looked back at her father, who was gazing at her mother with a sad look. "Please don't go," she whispered, suddenly afraid.

"Angel, listen to me carefully," he said in that soft voice she loved. "There are times when we must do things we do not want to do. But we must do them because if we don't people will be hurt. Do you understand what duty is?"

She pursed her lips in thought, trying to understand. "You mean like when I have to be nice to Kevin when he visits even though I don't like him?"

"Aye," he answered, smiling. "Like that. You may not like Kevin, but as a lady of this manor, and daughter of the house, you must be gracious to our guests. That is your duty. My duty is to help King Henry when he needs me."

"When will you be back, Papa?"

"As soon as I can, I promise. Every day I will think of you and your mother, and I will not stay away a day longer than I must. While I am gone, I want you to promise me that you will be good and do everything your mother asks of you and help her. Will you do that?"

"Aye, Papa. Is that my duty?"

"Aye, love." He laughed, giving her another squeeze. "Now, go play, kitten, as I would have a few moments with your mother. I will let you sit on Taran before I leave."

Thrilled by the prospect of moments on her father's great war-horse, she threw her small arms about his neck, gave him a sticky kiss, and scrambled from his lap, her mind already on other mischief. After all, he would be back soon, he had promised.

Isabel came fully awake, her body trembling as she stared into the dimly lit room. She realized that her body was cloaked in sweat and that she had been crying in her sleep. She swallowed heavily as the dream floated about her. She knew that it was more than a dream, she had lived it before. She could still taste the tart Julia had given her. She could see the immense knights and the horses as they moved about the chaotic courtyard . . . and her father, she could still hear his voice, feel his arms about her. How could she have forgotten those last precious moments with him? But she had forgotten, or refused to remember. Other times had been recalled, but never those. She closed her eyes, feeling the other-presence that she had felt before she had fallen asleep. It seemed to press against her, yet waft about her gently, as if encouraging, pulling her to accept. Shaken, she threw off her disquiet and rose to cross to her wardrobe. She peeled off her drenched gown and pulled another chemise over her head. Still trembling, she returned to the chair and bent her head to her hands as she rocked slowly back and forth. Why, why now should she be forced to remember? Oh Lord, it had hurt so much! Why was William never with her when she needed him! Nay, even in such torment she knew she was not being fair. Only once had he left her by choice, and she had been as responsible as he had been. She realized then that it had become an all-too-familiar pattern. When he was with her she fought with him, almost as if she wanted to drive him from her. Yet she loathed his leavetaking, needing him, wanting him more than ever when he was gone. Why could she not be complete when he was with her? Was it only the phantom she loved? She stopped rocking. Slowly she lowered her hands and stared vacantly into the low flames of the fire, reason dawning slowly upon her.

"Sweet Mother of God," she whispered.

She dressed quickly, knowing there would be no time to return to her chambers before dawn. She donned the chausses she had set out for morning. Pulling on a re-fitted tunic of William's, she belted the garment about her waist and pulled on her boots. Her thoughts were grim as she threw a fur-lined cloak about her shoulders, but deep inside she felt a renewed hope, a stirring that whispered of a new beginning.

Leaving the manor, she snapped orders to the aston-ished guards to bring her mount, ordering two of them to accompany her, and a third to carry a message to d'Erley of where she could be found. They rode through the city, the sound of the horses' hooves pounding against the hard-packed streets, echoing their journey in the tense, still night air. Arriving at her destination, Isabel slid from her mare, handing the reins to one of the men as she ordered them to wait for her. She hesi-tated for a moment, staring at the steps leading up to the large double doors, filled with a moment of doubt. Tak-ing a deep breath, she walked up the steps and entered the Christ Church of the Holy Trinity.

She paused inside the doors, allowing her eyes to ad-just to the dim light of the flickering flames of the candles. Relieved to find the church empty, her eyes moved slowly over the large room, finally coming to rest on the entrance to an alcove in a far corner of the sanc-tuary. As she entered the alcove, she stood quietly for a moment as her body swayed in a sudden rush of emo-tion. Taking a deep breath she walked forward, her eyes fixed steadily on the sarcophagus centered in the room. Shadows danced across the walls from the candles that surrounded the crypt, illuminating the effigy of her father as he lay in peaceful repose, his hands clasping his sword, his shield with the bold deClare coat of arms over his arm.

She took a deep breath and let it out slowly. *"I was told that you were wonderful, wise, strong, and filled with great wit. Mother said that you kept her in a continual blush the first years you were married. You cherished her, set her apart from other women. You were a man who could love, give of yourself. What would you have given to me?*

*"So many things I would have learned from you that no one else has brought to my life. Things brought from your way of seeing what was ahead of me. The strength you would have given to me, the wisdom, the love. Oh, I am not so foolish to think that it all would have been wonderful. There would have been the arguments—the resistance to what you would have wanted for me! But even from that I would have learned. Secreted your words into my soul—to be taken, bit by bit, resistantly, to grow."*

She closed her eyes, wavering against her emotions before she could open them again, her eyes bright with unshed tears.

*"They tell me that you do not miss what you have never had. Fools! There is a part of you, a resilient part, that knows! There is an emptiness that never allows you to forget that you are less than whole. An empty base that remains cavernous! Oh, God, it effects the whole of your life. You search, you seek for completion, for that which is the most important to understanding, childhood never massing into its proper portion."*

She walked forward, placing her hands on the crypt as she fought back the tears and anger began to well up in her.

*"Damn you! Why did you have to die? Why could you not remain safe for us? Mother has lived such a cold, empty life without you! She did not deserve the empty days, the endless existence with only memories —and they are such a cold substitute! Why, why, why did you leave me? You promised."*

She sank to her knees on the cold stone and allowed the tears to come, giving into the sorrow she had not known was there. Finally, old memories spent, new ones invaded. *"He . . . he has not shut me from his life,"* she whispered at last. *"I shut him from mine—refusing to accept what he would give to me. I have kept myself from giving to him because I have blamed him for being like you. I have hated him for it. You made me aware that everything is fleeting. I've resisted what he would give me, fearing that he, like you, would be taken from me. To love was to be destroyed. . . . But, I understand now—I must take that chance, for it is all that I have. Whatever moments I am given must be taken and held close for without them—without him, there is nothing."*

She rose unsteadily to her feet and brushed back her hair with the back of her hand as she took a long, deep breath. She felt cleansed and truly free, for the first time in her life. A feeling of contentment washed over her—love for the two men dearest to her life.

*"Help me now,"* she whispered. *"Help me to defeat my enemies, even as you have helped me to defeat those from within. Give us your strength and your wisdom."*

She left the chapel, her heart lightened and strengthened to face that which lay before her. The sky was turning to grey as she stepped out onto the steps of the church, and she halted abruptly as she found the narrow street filled with her knights. Her eyes passed over them, gifting them with a tumultuous smile before her gaze came to rest on John d'Erley. He waited expectantly, his handsome brow furrowed with doubt. She smiled at him, realizing that he had been responsible for this show of support. As she began to descend the stairs to her mount, she paused, her eyes fixing on her banner as it began to lift in the predawn breeze. Her brow furrowed into a deep frown as she stared at it for a long moment, as if seeing it for the first time.

"John." She turned to the knight as she settled into the saddle. "Remove that banner. We shall ride behind William's this day." She smiled as his brow arched, and then a slow grin of recognition spread across his face. "Its teeth should prove a sore trial to fitz Henry."

# 21

THE shrouds of fog lifted above the ground in uneven fingers to wrap about the endless rows of tents. Bright, wavering pinpoints of light from scattered cook fires leapt in silent dance against the muted colors of the canvas. The sounds of men's voices and the laughter of women intermittently broke the silence. William stood by the entrance to his tent listening. The man-at-arms stationed nearby took no notice of the marshal's expression, seeing only the elegant cut of the rich blue velvet tunic he wore, envying the warmth of the fox-lined mantle that draped the earl's broad shoulders. He wondered why Earl William remained gazing at the encampment, but he looked quickly away as William's gaze passed over him. Thus he missed the grim set to William's expression, the disgust and anger written there.

The winter past had proved a sore trial for William. Kept to the king's side as the court moved about England, time had been spent in painful idleness as he anguished over what was happening across the Irish sea. And the king had relished his discomfort, even refusing him leave to see to his own lands within England. He recalled a moment with John in mid-January, on a hunting party much like this one. John had called

William to his side while riding from Guilford, and the king's face had been gravely set as he informed William that word had, at last, reached him from Ireland. William's forces had met their gravest battle and it had been lost. The majority of William's knights had fallen, including John d'Erley, who had died from his wounds. The Countess Isabel had conceded the holdings of Leinster and Okinselagh to Meiler, shifting to the will of the throne in order to salvage what she could.

William had effected a pensive and sober regard as he considered the king's words. He knew that his own sources were as trustworthy as the king's, and the unusually harsh winter had disallowed any to cross the turbulent Irish Sea. Sensing the ruse, he merely regarded John with a shrug and answered, "Certainly, Sire, 'tis a pity about the knights. As they were loyal men to England, it makes the affair even more regrettable." The obvious ease with which William saw through his deception caused John to bridle with open anger, itself adding to William's enjoyment, though he was wise enough not to show it. But his pleasure was short-lived as the following weeks passed and still no word was heard from across the sea to the actual outcome of the battle.

Laughter brought William's attention from his musing, and his eyes fixed with displeasure on the largest tent of the encampment from where the sound had come. He was expected there, indeed, he was late in answering the king's summons. William knew full well what it would be about—and he knew that John would delay in the telling, taunting him, twisting the recounting in an effort to cause him to squirm as much as possible in an attempt to twist defeat into victory. A smile touched at William's mouth, and he sighed. He could afford to be generous—but he knew better than to think he could be less than vigilant. The storms had finally passed, and the first reliable word had reached him barely an hour ago. Just as he could be certain they had reached the ear of the king. The victory had been his. D'Erley and Isabel had been successful. With the help of Hugh de Lacy, the earl of Ulster, who had arrived with sixty-five knights, nearly a thousand men-at-arms, and over two hundred mounted sergeants, Meiler had been captured. His lands were forfeit, along with the disloyal barons who were forced to ransom their freedom with hostages confirming their future good behavior. John Plantagenet had lost, and he had never been known to lose gracefully.

William's thoughts turned to his son. The one benefit of the long months spent set at the king's heels had been the time spent with Will. William had been careful not to interfere with Beaumont's authority over the boy, but within his self-imposed rules he had allowed himself many contented and pleasurable hours with his son. He was fiercely proud of Will and knew that he would survive well at court under Beaumont's watchful eye. Before he left England he would be assured that John would not seek revenge in that direction—or he would surely take the boy with him back to Ireland—with or without the king's consent.

Isabel . . . Isabel. Damn, she had beaten them! He was proud of her most of all. He drew in his breath, letting it out slowly. God, how he loved her, even as she frustrated and confounded him.

He had come to a painful decision in the long months when he had had little else to do but to think. He could not live this way. Perhaps if he did not love her it would not matter, but he could no longer live with her contempt. And it was there, though he knew that she struggled to conceal it. Even the verbal battles they had always relished were overshadowed by an edge of tolerance from her. Tolerance, the most destructive emotion she could have chosen. Fight him, hate him, he could have lived with it. But her quiet, patient sufferance of her life was destroying them. He reasoned, in a moment of fairness, that he had helped to bring it on himself by forcing her to live with him. But she had won after all, choosing the one response he could not tolerate. They would have it out—once and for all—or, by God, while he would always give her his protection—he would no longer be able to live with her.

He realized that Allan had quietly appeared at his

side. Seeing Tirell attending him in the shadows, he wondered how long they had waited, unwilling to disturb his thoughts. "I know, Allan," he sighed heavily. "The king awaits."

"Do you think he knows?" Allan exchanged a nervous glance with Tirell, who stepped forward, his young face creased with worry. They had obviously been discussing the portentous outcome of the coming confrontation with the king.

"Of course he knows." William laughed. "And he will do his best to discomfort me. Meiler has lost strength for the throne in Ireland, and John will regain only what he can tonight by his own hand. But we shall do a little bargaining of our own, my friends."

Unaccustomed to the feel of the sand of the beach, Horse sidestepped nervously beneath William, who pulled him back as he faced the two knights who had ridden to meet the landing party. He gave a wry smile as his eyes passed over d'Erley, noting that his friend was attired in full armor. "I was led to believe that peace had been secured, John."

"There are some who are less than convinced, milord," d'Erley responded easily, his brown eyes filled with grim amusement.

"I must say that you look quite well for a dead man." William grinned, then laughed at the puzzled look from the knight.

"Milord?" John queried.

"Nothing John, merely the king's story." William chuckled.

As they rode toward Glasscarrick, John and Jordan de Sackville, the knight who had accompanied him, recounted what had occurred in William's absence, noting the barons who had remained faithful and those who had not. They arrived in Glasscarrick to find that news of William's arrival had spread ahead of him with the usual speed of the traveled word. Particularly, to William's amusement, to those who had been the most disloyal. William ordered large tents to be constructed beyond the city, refusing to enter in order to show his displeasure to those who had betrayed him. He met with the barons in his war tent as the April breeze lifted the canvas in sharp flutters of protest against the tension that could be felt among those present. The ripples shuddered along the roof and the sides of the tent as William stood silently, regarding each of the barons whom he knew to be disloyal with disdain. His intent blue eyes came to rest in particular on Philip de Pendergast and David de la Roche, reminded that the fathers of these men had been Richard deClare's closest allies. He smiled at them. "God save you, milords," he bade them, "if it is right that he should."

De Pendergast and de la Roche fell to their knees, protesting their innocence, which was dismissed with a disgusted wave of William's hand as he regarded the two with ill-concealed contempt. "It is known throughout Ireland, and even to England, that you are traitors. Do not demean yourselves further by senseless protests, milords, further wallowing will only convince me to reconsider my position."

Having settled the matter, William moved swiftly to Kilkennny, where Isabel waited, arriving the next day as the sun settled into a red-gold blanket, illuminating the keep in a deceptive aura of serenity and peace. If only it could be so, he thought ruefully, his mind now fixed to an even greater challenge. For he was determined, once and for all, to settle the matter of his household.

He was informed that Isabel was in the kitchen herb garden, and he made his way there, surprised that she should be thus engaged at such a late hour in the day. He paused at the door leading down to the garden, allowing himself to observe her at leisure as she knelt in the dirt, digging at the weeds that threatened her precious healing herbs, growing to one side of the garden. He suppressed his considerable amusement while he watched her. Could this be the one who had led his forces against Meiler and beaten him resoundingly? His Isabel, who fought him in verbal rages against the injustices of their king, who wielded an iron hand over her considerable dominion? She carried the babe well, he thought, and she glowed with health. Her expression was now drawn up in concentration upon her task, the brown wool of her gown spotted with soil, her hair di-shiveled. Tendrils of gold fell over her face, and sweat glistened on her forehead in the remaining warmth of the turning day.

She reached out a hand to grasp the trowel she had set near her, and she was startled as it was laid in her hand. As her fingers closed on the twisted metal she looked up to find William squatting next to her, grinning broadly. "Would it not be easier to grow the herbs you need at Chepstow, where the soil is kinder, and send them where they are needed?"

"William? Oh, my God, you're here!"

She threw herself at him, almost knocking him off his feet as her arms wrapped about his neck, and she began raining kisses on his cheeks and neck. "Oh, William, I am so glad that you are here! There is so much to tell you!" she gasped between kisses and laughter, and the sound joined with his chuckles as he struggled to hold her off.

"And I have much to tell you," he laughed, finally able to hold her at arm's length. "But it is hard to take any conversation seriously when you are covered with dirt."

"Oh, Merciful Mother, I must look a sight!" she gasped, her hands flying to her face. She stepped back from him in horror, her eyes widening as she spun about and fled from the garden, leaving him to wonder at her sudden flight.

He bathed in the knight's quarters and then at-tempted to follow her but was met on the stairs to the upper chambers by a most determined Corliss, who in-formed him, with surprising authority, that he was to await her mistress in a small room in the east wing. A bemused and disgruntled marshal of England, twice stopping a passing servant for directions, finally found the designated room. Castle Kilkenney, having been built at a much later date than those residences in England with which William was familiar, confounded him. Damnation, he thought, what was the use of these extra rooms? A great hall, kitchens, a buttery, weapons room, pantry, bedchambers, perhaps a solar . . . what possible need was there for more except for the purpose of losing one's way? Ending his search at last, William looked about and noted the comfort of the small room. An intimate table was set at its center. Candles burned low, casting warm light about the tapestries on the walls and floor. A side table set with mets and mazers of venison and mortrews of fish, pasties swimming in thick fragrant sauces, and bowls of blackmanger of chicken blended with rice boiled in almond milk and seasoned with sugar.

But in spite of his immediate hunger, whetted by the fragrant aroma rising from the well-spiced foods, his eyes fixed on the couch that was set against the opposite wall, covered by deep furs and pillows, its purpose all too evident. Perhaps, he mused, the addition of another room was not necessarily unadvised.

The door opened and a serving girl entered, glancing briefly at William before her gaze dropped nervously as she placed the pitcher and bowl she carried on a table behind William. "May I be of help, milord?" she asked, a slight tremor in her voice betraying her nervousness. It took a moment before William could understand her meaning through the thickness of her brogue. Finally understanding, he assured her that he could see to himself, and the door closed quickly behind her, leaving William to chuckle over her rapid departure. He poured himself a goblet of wine from the serving table and eased himself comfortably into a chair at the table to wait. It was obvious that Isabel had taken great pains to present a mood, and he knew that his wife always had a purpose for what she did. Whatever she was about, this promised to be very interesting.

The door opened and he looked up with interest, his eyes widening in appreciation. She wore a pelisse of rich sapphire-blue silk, held at the neckline by a large amethyst. She was girdled beneath her breasts with an exquisitely linked gold belt of delicate lacework. Her hair hung loose, in soft waves encasing her shoulders to her waist. The golden tresses were held only by the narrow fillet of sapphires he had given her in celebration of

Will's birth. But the cut of the pelisse was her own design, clearly cut to hide the gentle swelling of her figure. It emphasized the fullness of her breasts and her hips, swirling about her long legs, giving a subtle hint of their shape and form. He swallowed, taking great effort to hide the effect she had on him. Nay, my lady, he thought, we shall play this game, but it shall not be one-sided. Not until I discover what you are about. However, he did not rise from the table to greet her.

"Welcome, milord," she said huskily, the sound of her voice stirring him uncomfortably. She smiled as she moved to the sideboard. "Are you hungry?" she asked.

"Famished," he said. And soon she served up their suppers, gracefully slipping into the chair across from him. "Have you no questions for me, Isabel?"

"Later, milord, much later," she answered softly, her eyes still downcast as she leaned forward to refill his goblet.

"Ah, aye, well . . . " He shifted, suddenly at a loss for words. Her intent was blatant and it played sorely at him. He struggled with the strong impulse to pull her from the chair and throw her upon the couch and fulfill her obvious expectations, but he held back, determined to know her meaning before he so willingly played into her hands. Blatant, aye, but most definitely effective, regardless of what she was after.

While they ate the conversation was light. They spoke of matters concerning their children. She told him of Richard's latest antics as reported by her mother, to whom he had been sent for safety, and he recounted his time spent with Will while assuring her that their eldest fared well at court.

As she listened, Isabel's eyes warmed to the sight of him. Her chest tightened painfully with love as she drank headily of the luxury of being with him without the encumbrances that had lain between them since the day of their marriage. As he satisfied his palate, she feasted on the crinkles at the corners of his eyes, those glorious eyes, the muscles in his shoulders and arms, the slender strength of his strong fingers, and the knowledge of what those hands could do to her in passion.

Anticipation made her light-headed; thus she kept her eyes downcast when he looked at her, knowing that he would see what was written there. She kept her voice soft so that he would not hear the tremor when she spoke, wanting to delay, to mold the evening with him to the fantasy of dreams she had relived night after night in his absence. She relished the deep timbre of his voice as it sent a pleasurable shock of thrill along her spine, settling in the pit of her in a warm ache that reached into her loins. She struggled with herself not to interrupt him, to blurt out all that she had discovered, to share with him the new life she felt in her soul and mind as surely as a new life grew and moved in her body.

He finished eating and sat back from the table to stretch comfortably as he regarded her through a contented gaze. He had waited throughout the meal for some hint to the game she was playing, but she had thus far played it too well, except for what appeared to be a slight bout of nerves. He considered the alternatives—to allow her to approach the matter in her own way, or bring it to a head himself, now. Feeling the effects of the meal and the wine, he decided on the latter, knowing that his wits would soon be mellowed, not to mention the effect his beautiful wife was having on him—and the promise of the damnable couch in the corner. Well, he mused, there was no more certain way to bring matters to a head than to shatter that self-imposed composure she was trying so hard to affect.

"I have pardoned de Pendergast and de la Roche, along with all but Meiler. He will be brought to answer for his deeds by . . . " He paused as she stiffened and stared at him.

"You what? . . . " she gasped, lowering her goblet to the table.

"As I said, I have pardoned . . ."

"You pardoned them!" Her voice lost its seductiveness, rising to a sudden shriek.

"My dear, you are raising your voice," he answered calmly, hiding his amusement.

"You pardoned them?" she repeated, stunned, her

voice trembling with sudden anger and shock.

"Nothing will be served by attempting to punish all those responsible, Isabel. There are wounds to be mended, and much to be rebuilt. In time . . ." He paused as he noted the sudden slump to her shoulders, her defeat impressing him more than anything she had done since entering the room. Where was her rage, why was she not railing at him? "Isabel, do you understand what I have done?"

"Aye," she whispered as she stared at the goblet that was clenched tightly in her hand. "I am trying to. Do you realize what we went through, how we fought them . . . ?"

"Of course I do. Good God, Isabel," he answered quietly, "of course I do."

She raised her face to his, her eyes filled with tears of anguish. "But . . . you see, I did not," she whispered. "I did not know, William, I never knew. It was terrible, so many died. . . . They suffered so . . ." Oh, God, she thought, what was he doing to her? How could he pardon them? She wanted to scream at him, to throw something! Her fingers clenched tightly on the goblet as she struggled with the impulse. She forced herself to remember the promises, the understanding she had gained about the terrible responsibility of position, her new awareness of Wililam and of thier love. She had to trust him, for once and all she would learn to trust him!

"What of Meiler?" she asked.

"He has forfeited his lands at Dunamase, the remaining to be surrendered to me upon his death. He is done," he answered, still waiting.

"I see." It was all that she said as she rose from her chair and went to the side table for another carafe of wine. He watched with amazement as she came to his side to refill his goblet, her eyes again downcast, though he would have given a goodly sum to see into them at this moment and to know what she was thinking. She began to turn away but he grabbed her wrist. He pulled her back to him and took the carafe from her and set it on the table. "I need no more wine, Isabel." He pulled her into his lap and wrapped his arms about her. "Do you truly understand my decision?'' he asked, watching her.

"Nay, William," she answered, staring at her folded hands. "But I shall try—once you explain it to me." He blinked, feeling totally unsettled by her softly given statement, only to be further shocked as she continued. "But please, William, not now. I do not want to speak of these things now."

"What is it that you do wish to speak of, Isabel?" he asked, relaxing. So, now it would come.

"Nothing, my lord." She looked at him and her eyes softened. "You have not kissed me." She was puzzled by the dark shadow that crossed over his eyes for an instant, but it was gone and he smiled again as a hand reached up to lace his fingers in her hair as he drew her mouth down to his. His lips were warm and demanding, drawing hers open to their gentle assault as his free hand unhooked the clasp at her neck, allowing the soft bodice to fall open. He eased her into the crook of his arm, his mouth drawing demandingly from hers as his hand slipped beneath her bodice. He teased a full breast through the thin silk of her chemise, rubbing the rapidly tightening tip with his palm. Her breath quickened against his mouth, and she moaned softly as she arched her back against his attentions. She felt her pulse quicken and her mind began to spin dizzily as she anticipated what was to come, so familiar, yet now excitingly new.

He drew back to look at her, waiting until she opened her eyes and he saw the puzzled look she gave him as she wondered why he had stopped. "Now," he asked quietly. "Will you tell me what this is about?"

"What do you mean?"

"This," he answered with a sweep of his hand, indicating the room.

"William, I don't understand? I only wanted to please you."

"Isabel, stop it," he said as his voice grew hard. "Since you walked through that door I have been trying to decide upon the game you are playing, though I must admit you have played it with far more skill than before.

As I recall, looking back over the years, first there was anger, then coldness when you refused me. And then, when I demanded you to comply with the least of what I could expect from you, I received a noble tolerance to bear up under my attentions. And now suddenly this . . ." He gestured at the room with distaste. "And I am to slip into your web like a pink-cheeked youth, tripping over myself to meet you in your sudden-found devotion."

"Ohhh," she breathed. As she had listened her eyes had begun to well up with tears until she could only see him through a blur of deep biting hurt and then, suddenly, rage. She was gone from his lap before he realized her intent, half tripping over her skirt as it fell about her ankles, and she stepped out of it, reaching the door as she grabbed frantically for the latch. He lunged, meeting her as the latch caught, and he pushed it shut before his arms went about her. She twisted furiously in his arms and began to flail against him, her cries coming out in choked wails.

"This is my Isabel." He grimaced as his arms locked about her body as she shrieked like a termagant and fought wildly against him. "God's blood, stop it!" he roared, fearing for the babe she carried as she continued to fight him. Her legs struck out as she twisted and struggled frantically against him, her hands seemingly everywhere as she tried to claw and scratch him. Finally he grasped her shoulders, his fingers biting into her flesh, and he shook her sharply. "Isabel, stop it!"

She suddenly ceased to struggle, and her head fell forward against his chest as she slumped in exhaustion. "Damn," she gasped softly.

"God's breath, Isabel," he breathed, pulling her into his arms. "Are you all right?" He felt her nod as she sniffed back her tears. "Now will you tell me what you were trying to do?"

"Seduce you," she answered, her voice muffled against the thick velvet of his tunic.

"That was obvious," he sighed. "But what I would know is why."

"Does there always have to be a reason?"

"With you—aye."

She raised her tear-streaked face to him and blinked —and then hiccuped. He fought a smile as he reached into the pocket of his tunic and brought out his kerchief to wipe her eyes. Sniffling, she turned away from him and sat on the edge of the couch. Pulling at the kerchief, she spoke softly, knowing that he was watching her intently. "You are right." She shrugged. "I planned this for weeks, anticipating your return. I plotted—choosing your favorite dishes to disarm you with a well-satisfied palate. I designed—hoping the cut of this gown would enhance a body five months with child. I schemed— with Corliss, to assure that no others would be about upon your homecoming and we would not be disturbed. I outsmarted myself. Why should my husband believe that I could desire him for himself? Why should he believe that I have ached to have him hold me; that I have missed him beyond belief? How could he know of the things that have happened to me in his absence; things that have brought me to realize how important he is to me and how much I love him. Oh, William," she sighed. "We are a sorry pair. Condemned to suffer that which we cannot bear." She looked up as he lowered himself into a chair near her. "And what of you? How often have you flown to other duties, to obligations beyond our marriage, with eager relief? Relief to escape what you cannot face—that you were brought position and wealth not by merit but by the marriage bed. When will you be able to forgive me for that?"

"Isabel, have I again hurt you so deeply by my silence?" he asked quietly. "It is true, when we were first wed, I did feel that way, but I have not felt so for many years. But you use the lands to keep from me, escaping into them whenever I come too close. It is ironic," he sighed. "I came here to settle this between us, once and for all, and was fully prepared to leave you if we could not—this time for good."

"Why?" she swallowed, staring at him with horror as she realized how close they had actually come to disaster. "Why had you decided this now? You had promised never to leave me again."

He laughed brittlely. "When I left before, sweetheart, I was furious with you, and frustrated. But anger cools, despair does not. Nay, I could no longer bear your sufferance, your quiet tolerance . . ."

"I did do that," she murmured, clenching the kerchief. "I will say it, William. You need not. Whenever I began to feel too secure, too content, it terrified me. I wanted to hurt you, to drive you away from me. I wanted you to go, while it was my choice, before you were taken from me."

"Taken from you?" he repeated, puzzled. "Who was going to take me from you?"

"Not who, William. What," she whispered. She looked up at him and smiled timorously. "William? Do you think you could hold me? I am cold." Tenderly, he wrapped his strong arms around her and she nestled against his broad shoulders. "Is that better?" he murmured against her hair.

"Much better," she sighed. "I am not so naive that I have never considered the possibility of another woman, William. Particularly when we were having problems. But that was not my greatest fear. Actually I never understood what I was afraid of until I—I had a dream . . ."

She told him of the night before the final battle with Meiler, of the dream, of the moments in Christ's Church of the Holy Trinity with her father. He listened carefully without interruption, and when she finished neither spoke for a long, long while.

# 22

"OH my God," he groaned. "I have no feeling in my legs."

Isabel came awake. His words were suddenly clear as she realized where they were and that she was sprawled across him. She suppressed a giggle as she pulled herself off of him and settled against the wall.

"When next you design a love nest, madam, you might consider the size of your husband." He groaned again, stretching out with great effort as his muscles protested.

"It was not my intent that we sleep here, milord." She laughed.

"Nor was it mine." He winced, gingerly trying to move a leg.

"I do not recall when it was that we fell asleep," she mused.

He turned his head to look at her. "It was right after you . . ."

"Never mind!" she chortled.

"You are right," he agreed, grinning wickedly as he turned to her and drew her into his arms. "Some things should not be discussed, but demonstrated. Now, where were we?"

"William!" she laughed happily. "We really should get up. Corliss will think something has happened to us!"

"It has," he muttered, nuzzling her neck.

"Aye, milord," she sighed, "indeed it has." The memories of the past night caused her to close her eyes as her body tingled with blissful contentment. Wordlessly, he had lifted her from the chair and had carried her to the couch, where they had passed the night letting their bodies speak for them, drawing closed the chasm, sealing it firmly with an eloquence no words could have met.

The babe chose to turn at that moment, fluttering against William where his stomach was pressed tightly against hers. "So she wants to play," he murmured against Isabel's neck. "I'm glad someone got some rest last night."

"Are you so sure it is a she?" Isabel smiled.

"I can hope," he answered in a muffled voice. "A little moppet, with golden curls like her mother." He shifted his weight and rose up on his elbow to lean his head in the heel of his hand as he pulled the fur covers back, drawing them down away from her. His gaze moved leisurely over her body, and she watched with fascination as his eyes darkened, his desire confirmed as she felt him stir against her leg. His hand traced the path of his gaze with a light, teasing touch, and she felt herself grow warm and the familiar ache begin deep in her body. She lay still as he continued his patient perusal, relishing the moment as she tingled with anticipation. He rubbed a nipple gently, touching no other part of her, the effect bringing a soft moan from her as all feeling focused to that warm, delicious spot. He took the nipple between a finger and thumb, teasing gently as she pressed her head back into the furs. She bit her lower lip and tried to hold herself still, to focus on the sensations he was giving to her. She felt his tongue begin a taunting trace about the tender tip, circling gently before it flicked across in light, easy flutters, to be replaced by his gently suckling mouth, causing her to gasp and arch against him.

She tried to draw her arms up about his neck, but he stayed her purpose, pulling them back to the furs, where he held them at her side as his mouth traveled lightly down her body. Her skin tingled beneath each butterfly kiss as he reached her swollen stomach, where he lingered gently before traveling farther to her thighs. He spread her legs gently with his hand, his fingers searching that sweet core, spreading her open to him until his tongue found what it was seeking. She moaned, arching against him as the fire began to spread over her body, the deep bittersweet ache grasping at her to begin its outward push, the tension drawing in her until she cried out for him. He pulled himself up over her, sliding into her to fill her with him, and she arched up against him, the tension returning as she began to move with the rhythm of his body, each stroke drawing her higher, until together they tumbled over the top, their release found at the same instant, their one body entering that other world to soar for an endless instant before floating softly back.

They lay wrapped in each other's arms, waiting for their hearts to still, a sated peace wrapping them in companionable silence. "Oh, William," Isabel murmured at last. "I would stay there forever."

"Nay, love," he chuckled. "Sadly, each time is only for a moment. But I promise to take you there as often as I can."

"A promise I intend for you to keep, milord," she parried sleepily.

"One that is easily met." He rolled from her, almost falling off the side of the couch as he caught himself with an oath. He straightened up and turned back to slap her bottom as she settled back into the furs. "Up! When next I bed you it will be in a more comfortable place to romp. For now there are other matters to see to—my son, for one. I instructed John to see Richard home at first light, and I fear the child is probably even now wondering what happened to his parents."

"Oh, William! Why did you not tell me!" she cried. She leapt from the bed and began to gather her clothes.

"Other matters were on my mind," he said, shrugging, as he poured water into a basin to wash.

They emerged from the room to find that John had returned with Richard and was gathered with the knights in the great hall for midmeal. It was not until they spied the laden tables that either realized the lateness of the hour, and Isabel found her face growing warm at the speculative glances that met them. Richard slid from his chair and rushed to her, wrapping his small arms about her neck, his dark grey eyes dancing with excitement as he giggled against the kisses she rained on him. William swept the child into his arms and carried him to their places at the vacant table. She slipped into her chair while wishing that William would stop that confounded grinning at the comical roll of eyes that John was throwing him.

"Merciful Mother, William!" John quipped loudly, "I was beginning to reason that I had imagined riding in with you yesterday!"

Isabel's cheeks burned hotly as she focused on the food that was being set before them, and she silently cursed d'Erley—and her husband, who was laughing heartily at John's quip—and the knights, to a man, who were joining in the merriment at her expense. She promised herself that unless they were to return to England soon she would send for their wives. Ladies in residence would stifle their barbs soon enough, she thought, or at least give them something else to think about than what she and William were doing. Her eyes raised to John and her mouth drew into a smile. Moreover, it was high time that John d'Erley found a lady of his own. She vowed to see to the matter personally.

As they ate their meal William chatted happily with his son, who was contentedly ensconced in his lap, sharing his meal with him in lieu of the empty place next to John. She was gladdened by William's attitude toward his sons, allowing them to take occasional meals out of the nursery even at such a tender age. So much can change so quickly, she thought, thinking of her older son, as she wondered for the thousandth time how he truly fared. Forcing her thoughts from this sorrow she looked up in time to see Richard reach up and touch his father's face. His eyes widened as he drew his small hand back quickly. "It hurts!" he said with surprise.

"Aye, son, your father needs a shave." William smiled. "Your mother would not allow me the time this morning."

Richard glanced at his mother and she could see the question in his large grey eyes. "You answer that," Isabel tossed at William as she returned to her meal, ignoring his chuckle.

"Sir William, what would you like for me to do with this?" The question came from Allan, who had appeared behind William's chair. Isabel turned to find him holding a large basket. "It came with the baggage this morning."

William glanced quickly at Isabel, then turned back to his son. "Richard, would you like to see what Allan has in the basket?"

Richard slipped from William's lap as Allan put the basket on the floor, barely pulling the lid off before a wriggling black and white object popped its head out, to the immediate squeals of delight from Richard. "Papa, it's a puppy! Is it mine?"

"Nay, Richard, it is mine. But there is another surprise for you in the bailey." William looked up at Allan, who nodded in agreement. "I have brought you your very own Welsh pony. Would you like to go and see him?"

Richard looked at his father in shock, his face filled with excitement and pleasure, and he was gone, his small hand clasped tightly in Allan's as he practically pulled the laughing squire across the hall and out the door.

"Yours, William?" Isabel asked with amazement, as she stared at the squirming puppy William had taken from the basket.

"He's a beauty, isn't he?" William asked as he held up the wriggling puppy. "Pure wolfhound. He should be a great hunter."

"Indeed," she smirked. "I suppose you have named him Dog."

"Nay, I've decided to call him Trac. It means . . ."

"I know what it means. Courageous one." She glanced at the other dogs, who had been chained while Richard was about, and her brow furrowed with doubt. "He seems little to be put with the other dogs. Perhaps . . ."

"Oh, this one will be raised apart," he answered quickly. "I shall keep him with me."

"With us?" she countered. "But Shad . . ."

"Shad will get used to him," he tossed back, his smile unseen by Isabel as he turned to place the pup back into the basket. "After all, as you say, he's only a puppy."

They finished their meal, then retired to bathe and change. As they walked down the long hall to their chamber, William's arms were locked possessively about the basket, and Isabel could not help but notice the particular lightness to his step. Her brows furrowed, but then she shrugged her puzzlement aside and swept by him as he opened the door to their chamber. A soft fire burned on the hearth, and William glanced about with approval to the comfort of the room. His roving gaze came to rest upon Shad, who was curled up on a cushion placed on the hearth, and his grey head lifted in greeting as they entered.

"Hello, Shad," William said softly as Isabel crossed to the wardrobe. "I have brought someone for you to meet." He set the basket down and flipped off the lid, whereupon the pup scrambled out, its wriggling body intent upon new vistas. Shad's yellow eyes fixed on the wolfhound as it ran about the room, sniffing in each corner. For a moment the large yellow eyes widened, and then, unnoticed by William who was watching the pup, they narrowed to constricted slits as he sat up and began to clean his front paws. Isabel, now changed to her robe, came to stand by William. She watched the pup as it scampered about the room, running to William with ill-contained eagerness, then on to another discovery.

"William, perhaps you should put him back in his basket for the night," Isabel said doubtfully.

"I will. Let him run a bit."

The pup continued to scamper about happily, and

then he suddenly saw the cat where it sat bathing itself, apparently unconcerned by the new arrival. William fought a grin as the dog froze. It stared at the smaller animal, who was on eye level only a few feet away. The hair on the back of the pup began to raise up along its spine and its body stiffened.

"William, I . . ."

"They have to get to know each other, Isabel," William said sternly. "After all, they are going to live together."

The dog eased slowly forward, freezing every few inches. With apparent feline disdain Shad continued with his grooming, ignoring the approaching wolf-hound. Only inches from the cat the dog froze once again and its body began to tremble.

"William!" Isabel whispered, laying a hand with alarm on William's arm. "I . . ."

It happened suddenly, a wild flurry of fur, grey, black and white, with ear-splitting screeches and yipes. What exactly occurred was uncertain, but a moment later the dog was gone and Shad was calmly sitting at the door waiting to be let out. Isabel quickly crossed to the door and cracked it open to allow the cat to slip through. Her mouth was working furiously as she fought not to break into laughter, but she turned and was lost. Helplessly, she collapsed against the door as she found William on his hands and knees reaching under the bed, calling his dog.

Having bathed and changed, they joined the others in the field beyond the keep, settling beneath a small copse of trees with John, Ralph Musard, and Nicolas Avenel to watch Richard with his new pony. Allan had put the black pony on a long lead and was walking him slowly about as Richard's happy voice carried to them over the still afternoon air.

"Are you certain that the pony is not too large for him?" Isabel asked doubtfully as she watched her son.

"He will be fine," he assured her distractedly as he watched Trac ferociously attack a leaf that had blown across his path. He settled his back against the trunk of a tree and closed his eyes sleepily. "Allan will watch him," he murmured. "However, if you are uncertain you could take Allan's place. I was merely going to discuss the king's disposition of Ireland, but you do whatever you think best."

She had begun to rise but froze on his words. Her eyes darted from her son to her husband. Ignoring the laughter of the men, she resettled on the grass next to William and smoothed out the rust wool of her gown as she looked at him expectantly. "Well?"

He opened his eyes and grinned at her affectionately. "We have been given new charters and I have retained administration of the lands . . . but there were concessions made. The king's court will have jurisdiction over matters such as arson, rape, and treasure. The king will also retain the right of custody in the event of unmarried minor heirs."

"Then the barons in Ireland are no longer independent of the king's will," Isabel said softly.

"The only true independence Ireland has had since William the Bastard is that which France could give her by drawing English armies to the continent. As for the king, it is my guess that he will be kept far too busy with matters in England to bother with what we do here."

"May I assume you are again in favor with the crown?" John asked.

"Aye, but I have determined that at this point in my life I would prefer that my relationship with the court remain somewhat cooled," he explained, glancing at the pup, who had begun to snap and snarl at a cricket he had cornered in the grass. "The king knows of my loyalty, but I will not allow him to use it against England. I informed him that it was my desire to remain in Ireland for a time; to see to these lands my wife has brought to me."

"He accepted?" Nicolas blinked.

"I believe that he was well rid of me!" William laughed. Their attention was drawn back to the field and to Richard, who was calling for them to come and watch. "I will go," William said, jumping up.

Isabel watched as he strode across the field to his son,

and her eyes narrowed pensively. At first her heart had soared with William's news. They would remain in Ireland indefinitely, perhaps for years! Away from the politics of the court, the struggles for power, the treachery, the compromise, always so deeply affecting their lives. It was the chance she had only dared to dream about, never imagining that it would ever happen. To live with him, to raise their children together. Yet there was something that disturbed her . . .

"It looks as though you will have that time of peace you have so longed for, milady," John said quietly.

"So it would seem," she answered distractedly.

"I would have expected you to show more enthusiasm . . . "

"Do you fear that it will be short-lived?" Ralph asked.

"Nay, my good friends, I rather fear it may be too long," she said quietly, watching William as he readjusted the girth on the pony's saddle. "The only thing that could cause William Marshal to leave England is fear."

"My lord earl, afraid?" John snorted, with disbelief.

"Aye, John," she answered. "Of himself. I fear that this voluntary exile is due to no desire on the part of the king but to what William fears he might do should he remain."

"Surely you do not infer that William would ever be traitor to England, milady?" Ralph gasped.

"Nay, Ralph," John answered, his eyes changing to understanding as he smiled with grim sadness at Isabel. "Never to England."

"Then what?" Ralph Musard pressed. "To the crown?"

"Nay, Ralph," Isabel answered, turning her gaze to the knight. "To John Plantagenet."

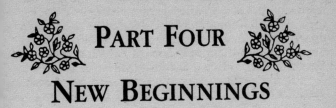

# PART FOUR
# NEW BEGINNINGS

# 23

ISABEL turned as her eyes moved slowly over her reflection in the long mirror, and her hands slid over her waist and hips. "You are certain they are wearing the style in England as well?" she murmured.

"Aye, it is exactly what the queen is wearing."

Isabel glanced at the reflection of the young woman sitting behind her. "It will mean a whole new wardrobe, Cailin, and for you as well."

"I know," the young woman sighed wistfully as she glanced down at her growing belly. "Although it will be many months before I will need it."

"The time will go quickly," Isabel smiled. She looked back at her reflection and decided that she approved of the newest style. The gown was a bliaut, a soft sleeveless gown of pale silk clasped at the shoulders. It fitted the body in soft folds to the hemline and was gently bloused at the waist by a heavy gold-link girdle. A chemise of sheer white linen beneath had long sleeves layered in gathered folds and was fitted with buttons to the wrists. A long, dark blue mantle of soft wool was gathered into the large sapphire clasps at the shoulders, and was folded back to reveal the gown beneath. Her hair was bound up into a crespin, a thinly woven net of gold threads, over which a short veil of sarcenet, or transparent silk, partially covered her forehead and the crespin, and was held in place by a gold fillet studded with sapphires. A barbette of thin blue linen ran under her chin and covered her ears. "You say the men's sur-coats are shorter?" she asked, turning back to the young woman who was busy selecting a sweetmeat from a tray on the table next to her.

"Aye, and the shoes have squarer toes. John refuses to wear the shorter tunic, he says that it makes him feel indecent."

"How short are they?" Isabel blinked.

"Only to the knee, but they are still split on the sides for riding. I think they are attractive and would make him look most handsome."

Isabel smiled at the comment as she moved to the bed, where bolts of rich fabrics had been laid, the result of John d'Erley's recent trip to England. He had gone to attend to their affairs across the Irish Sea—and to give him time alone with his young wife. A fruitful journey, Isabel mused, glancing again with affection at the preg-nant young woman. A good match, she thought, con-firming the decision she had made years before. A brief conference with her mother had brought forth Cailin to Castle Kilkenny, presumably as a companion for her, as she was then nearing her birthing time with Matilda, the daughter William had wished for. Isabel had casually introduced the young couple, knowing instantly that she had been successful. John had been struck dumb. His brown eyes had widened as he gaped at the lovely young maid with large green eyes and exquisite hair of straw-berry blond. Her fresh rosy complexion heightened to a pink hue as she looked up through thick lowered lashes at the tall handsome knight. John was clearly lost, to William's amusement as he stood nearby watching the proceedings. He had not been misled for a moment, knowing full well that a maid would never be selected as waiting-in woman for his wife. Isabel had glared at her husband, who was grinning broadly behind John's back. But to her relief he had withheld comment, and she suspected that he approved of her reasons, if not her methods.

The past seven years in Ireland had been as a dream. Her relationship with William had grown and strengthened, even beyond their love, forming an impregnable bond that withstood whatever discomfort King John threw in their direction. The game William played with his king came to a head when William de Briouse arrived at the marshal's door, fleeing with his wife and children from the wrath of his king. The former exchequer of England was believed by many to have been responsible for the death of Arthur Plantagenet, and thus Isabel was horrified when William unhesitatingly offered the family sanctuary. But William was convinced that if de Briouse had been responsible for the foul deed, and he had his doubts, he had acted on the orders of his king. Her opinion swung to William's when John pursued de Briouse into Erin, his meager excuse that the man owed him money. It became obvious that the king's only motive for turning upon a loyal friend was to silence him. When de Briouse and his family fled to Scotland, the king turned upon William, accusing him of harboring a traitor to the throne. William audaciously responded that he had given de Briouse shelter as an act of mercy, something he would do for any who arrived at his door in a miserable condition. John had returned to England in a rage, once again confounded and frustrated by his marshal, as none would take up his cause against William. But he had also finally come to realize that the earl could be a formidable and dangerous enemy. To soothe matters he restored William to full favor—and then secured his own position by demanding that Richard join his brother at court.

Livid, Isabel was forced to comply, knowing that their lands in England would be forfeit if they refused. When William would have sent Richard into Beaumont's care along with his brother, John d'Erley observed with a wry smile that one of them was enough for any man, and Hugh de Sanford was made guardian of Richard.

Over the years Isabel could often be heard to comment, "This too, shall pass," and it proved true in the matter of her sons' absence. To her joy they had returned with John d'Erley, both well and hardy, and Isabel's contentment was complete. Her first-born were now home, and her family, which had grown steadily over the years, was together for the first time. Matilda, now seven, had been followed in quick order by Gilbert, Isabel, and the babe now nestled in the nursery under Anna's watchful eye, little Sybil, just three months.

Finished with her sorting—of her thoughts as well as the fabrics—Isabel turned to find Cailin watching her, her large green eyes passing over Isabel's still-slender figure. "Do you think that I shall ever see my waist again, milady?" Cailin sighed as her hand smoothed over her growing stomach. "How do you manage to remain so slender after so many babes. The births have not affected you in the least."

"By not eating sweetmeats," Isabel quipped as she fixed on the tidbit Cailin had carefully chosen from the tray.

"Oh." The girl said with chagrin. She hesitated, then dropped the morsel back on the tray, glancing at it again with longing. "Do you think that John would still love me if I was fat?"

"John loves you to distraction," Isabel answered as she refolded a length of amber silk. "But I do not think that you would like yourself very much." Isabel laughed suddenly as a pile of lavender wool began to move and a grey paw shot out from under it to grasp at the air before it disappeared again.

The door opened to admit Corliss, her arms laden with more fabrics and furs, who was followed by a lad who was similarly encumbered. "Well, milady, we're going to be hav'n a busy winter with all of this," she observed, dumping her bundles on the bed.

"It is just as well as the work will be prove easier for you than your normal duties," Isabel observed as she spied Corliss's waistline. "New life appears to be blooming out all over Kilkenney—it should be a full harvest this spring. Your lad did not waste any time."

"Nay, milady," the girl blushed. "Brenton's a one, he is," she added, referring to the stableman she had wed but a few months past. "Now, if ye 'ave other matters ta tend to, milady, I'll see ta this."

"Aye, Corliss. Now, do you think you can manage with these, I need to see William about a rather pressing matter."

"Aye, milady. If I be need'n help there's plenty I can call."

"Fine. We'll work on the blue silk and the amber linen later today. You can place the rest away. And what are you going to do the rest of the morning, Cailin?" she asked, turning to the young woman.

"I thought I would take a walk," Cailin answered.

"That would be good for you," Isabel laughed, seeing to the heart of the matter as a pink flush crept up the young woman's cheeks. "I spied John from the window a bit ago, he was walking toward the tiltyard. But then, I surmise that you know that."

Isabel left the chamber with a smile touching her lips, her thoughts now on her own pleasures. She had not seen much of William since John's return, and she sighed with a rush of contentment as she anticipated some moments alone with him. Aye, the years had been good to them, William's contentment coming as a welcome surprise to them both. He had kept in close contact with his allies in England, but since the matter of de Briouse the king had kept his distance.

She discovered from a sleepy-eyed knight that William had been in the knight's quarters but had left some time before. She followed his trail to the kitchens, to learn that he had grabbed a quick breakfast of bread and cheese before leaving through the kitchen yard toward the stables. Isabel stepped gingerly across the yard, avoiding the puddles and mud left from a brief storm that had passed over the previous night. Finally reaching the stables, she paused just inside the door as her eyes adjusted to the dim expanse of the rows of stalls, her nostrils flaring to the heavy smell of hay and horses. She moved into the dimly lit building and made her way down the long line of stalls, her mouth drawing into a smile as she found him with Horse. His back was to her as he brushed the animal, his attention drawn fully to the task. Trac, who had been curled up sleeping nearby, raised his massive black head as he prepared to growl a warning. Seeing that it was Isabel, he merely sighed and stretched out to go back to sleep. She watched William leisurely for a moment, her loving gaze following the breadth of his back beneath the fur tunic he wore to the strength of his arms under the heavy linen of his chamise as they moved along the side and back of the huge animal in smooth, even strokes. Her gaze moved lovingly to the grey at his temples, the sharp outline of his profile as his heavy brows furrowed in some private thought. The tendons on the back of his hand stood out as he gripped the brush, tensing with each stroke as Horse munched contentedly on hay from the manger to which he was securely tied. She felt desire well up in her, and she realized, with a sudden rush of tingling pleasure, what she had come for, hoping that she would find him alone. A wicked gleam flared in her eyes as she considered her intent, and she bit her lower lip to keep from laughing out loud. She approached him slowly, unaware of the gentle swing of her hips moving with anticipation. Stopping behind him she leaned back against the wall of the wide stall.

"William?" she said softly.

He turned with surprise to find her there, and he stopped brushing the animal as his brows raised speculatively. "Isabel? Is there something wrong?"

"Wrong? Of course not. Should there be?"

His eyes moved over her, noticing her gown. "Good Lord, is that the new style Cailin spoke of?"

"Aye," she answered, glancing down before she looked back at him with concern. "Do you not like it?"

"Aye, it's becoming. I suppose it will mean an entire new wardrobe."

"Of course. Do you mind?"

"Would it matter if I did?" he grinned. A frown crossed over his expression as he noticed the absent sleeves. "It is rather revealing, isn't it?"

"I do not think so," she answered, holding her arms out. She saw him shrug before returning to Horse's grooming. "Wait until you see what we shall make for you," she murmured to his back.

"What?"

"Nothing, my lord earl," she said sweetly. She watched him work for another long moment and realized that he had no intention of stopping. Slowly a gleam came into her eyes. "I had a wonderful dream last night," she said.

"Oh?"

"Aye," she sighed heavily. "It must have been a dream, for when I awoke my bed was empty—as it was until late into the night. John must have had much to tell you."

He turned and his brows arched speculatively as she reached up and unfastened the cloak, allowing it to drop into the hay at her feet. She stifled her laughter as she saw his eyes widen, knowing her message was explicit. He tossed the brush aside and stepped toward her, his eyes darkening with desire. "Shall we return to the keep, milady?" he murmured huskily.

"Must we wait, milord?" she answered with a throaty whisper. "There is no one here. If we are brief . . . "

As he pulled her into his arms his mouth came down upon hers, drawing her breath away in its ferocity. He could feel her laughter deep in her throat as a hand cupped a breast and his body pressed her against the wall. Then he was lifting her skirts, searching beneath as her laughter changed to a moan. She began to move against him, writhing against his searching hand, her eagerness matching his own. Her own hand slipped beneath his tunic to loosen the lacings of his chausses, slipping within to pleasure him as he was doing for her. Her hand closed on his swollen member, which pulsated at her touch, bringing a deep groan from within his throat. He lifted her up against the wall, pulling her legs about his hips and entered her, thrusting deeply as she gasped with pleasure. Her arms wrapped about his neck as she moved against him, matching his movements with her own. She cried out, the sound muffled against the fur of his tunic. She pressed against his shoulder, feeling his own climax as he shuddered, his hands holding her hips tightly against him.

"Jesú," he whispered. His body trembled as she clung to him, her own body shaken and weak. He pulled himself from her gently as her legs slipped down his body and came to rest on the stable floor, and she leaned against him for support. They did not speak for a long while. Then finally William drew back and helped her to adjust her clothing and the veil, which had become slightly lopsided. "I must remember to be more understanding to Will," he murmured as he readjusted his chausses.

"What about Will?" she asked, pulling her eyes from his fascinating task.

"I caught him in the loft last week with one of the laundresses." He grinned. "Next time I shall enter a stable with more discretion."

"Will . . . here . . . " Her eyes moved involuntarily to the loft. They returned to her husband and they widened with shock as she realized his meaning. "With a girl . . . ?" her voice raised.

"Isabel, he is growing up."

"But—"

"I had a talk with him about responsibilities," he added, struggling not to laugh at her stunned expression. "I'll not have him running about deflowering maids and leaving me to face disgruntled fathers. He assures me that the girl was no maid and more than eager to . . . "

"My baby. . . . " she murmured.

"Your baby, indeed!" He roared with laughter, wrapping an arm about her shoulders as they turned to leave the stable. "I suggest, madam, that you take another look at your eldest chick."

And she did. They entered the hall as the bell was rung for midmeal, and she had just finished washing her hands when Will entered the hall with Thomas de Mere and Sebastian Briose, close friends of his who had entered William's service upon Will's return from England. Her gaze moved over Will appraisingly and she sighed, realizing that he was, indeed, a man. He was the image of his father, tall and broad-shouldered, his body filling the fine cut of the brown velvet of his tunic, and, like his father, incredibly handsome. Enough to turn the eye of any fair maid, she sighed, facing for the first time that her baby was child no longer, but a man to himself. She realized then that he would be knighted soon, and then wed. . . . Nay, she thought, rejecting the possibility. He was only sixteen . . . and then she sighed raggedly. He was old enough. She looked up to find William watching her with a gentle smile of understanding.

"Look ye to the nursery, milady," he murmured as he leaned over to trim their trencher. "I have done my best to keep it filled so that you do not grieve over what you cannot change."

"Aye, we are fortunate, and deeply blessed, William," she sighed again as she leaned back in her chair. "We have never suffered the loss of a babe . . . "

"Nay, in that we are unique," he agreed, reaching to the mazer of venison Allan had set before him.

Aye, blessed in their children and the life they had been given there. Her eyes moved to Matilda, who sat near Will and his cohorts, her large blue eyes wide with awe and love for her worshiped older brother. Unruly dark curls had escaped from the long plait that hung down her back, and she brushed them back unconsciously as she hung on Will's every word, a frown crossing her fair brow as Will gave his attention to the maid who sat next to him, sharing his trencher.

Isabel's thoughts turned reluctantly to those who had been lost to her life. So many gone, and with them her childhood passing to memory. Uncle Donnell, Gervase, Lavinia . . . only Katy remained, too irascible to leave this world with the others of her time. Even she had mellowed, discovering a love for her husband, an understanding that had come with his passing that she had not found in living with him . . .

But the greatest loss had been that of her mother, gone these past two years. She still missed her desperately. She savored the memory of the few years she had had with her upon returning to Ireland, but each year since Eve's passing seemed to grow harder to bear instead of easier. When a parent remained one need not face mortality, nor the realization that solutions must be found from within. Resources suddenly seemed frighteningly spare. The great wisdom one had always found and used with courage and enthusiasm, even defiantly, seemed at once inadequate. However, from somewhere was found the courage to go on, to reach forward in facing the terrifying choices that threatened and impelled, the simple necessity of continuing overcoming the doubts . . .

"The good fathers of Saint Salvator are in need of funds, William," she said suddenly, pulling herself from memories that would only serve to plunge her into a depression. Someday, she thought, someday I will be able to remember them without pain. . . . "What shall I tell them?"

"Send them half of what they ask for," he sighed. "I am certain that it will be twice as much as they need and less than they expected."

The abbey, along with Tintern Minor, had been built and was supported by William, in addition to the vast development of commerce and farming he had instigated since their arrival in Ireland. Leinster's economy, along with the establishment of new boroughs and towns and the expansion of the port at New Ross, had swelled under their hands. Isabel had marveled at William's capabilities, talents he had hidden in the early years of their marriage. It had begun slowly, Isabel seeing to the lands while William focused on gaining stability among the barons following the conflict that had brought them to Ireland. Gradually, the latter coming to a rest, he had begun to make suggestions, improvements she accepted readily, particularly in the manner of financing, talents in which he was exceptionally astute from a lifetime of necessitated economy and creative thinking.

The matter settled, Isabel's gaze came to rest on her eldest son once more, his easy laughter capturing her attention as he shared a joke with his companions. No longer able to avoid the unavoidable, she sighed, giving up her claim to his childhood, replacing it with a deep pride in the man he had become. Contentment washed over her as she set to her meal, and she did not notice that Trac, lying as always close to William's chair, raised his massive head. His ears cocked forward to some unheard sound, his lips drawing back in a silent feral snarl in an instinctive acknowledgement of an interruption that would soon irrevocably change their lives.

The trestle tables had been removed, and Will was allowing William to beat him soundly in a rousing game of chess when Isabel reentered the hall after checking on the occupants of her nursery. The laughter of her men drew her to the gaming table, and she stood by William's side, her hand on his shoulder as her shrewd eyes took in the play of the game.

"This pup thinks he can best me," William muttered as he studied the board.

"I?" Will said with mock horror. "Sire, as I do draw breath, you shall always be my superior, in all that I do," he quipped.

"I reason that you think that you are letting me win," William countered, glancing up at his son. "I suggest that you play for your life, as you are in for a rude surprise," he added, finally moving his king.

"You taught me the game, how can you reason that I could best you?" Will laughed. He glanced at the board, frowning for a moment before he moved a rook.

William answered by moving a bishop. "You have

decided that since I have begun to show some grey in my hair that I am well into my dotage and that my brain is addled as well.''

''Father, you do me a disservice,'' Will parried with a chuckle, controlling the gleam that came to his eyes as he spied the move and quickly countered with a rook. ''I ever concede to your greater wisdom.''

William studied the move for a long moment. ''You would do well to do so, my son, but with more care and attention than lightly given words.'' He moved a bishop and leaned back with a hint of a smile. ''Youth makes a habit of giving far too much weight to quick action, when careful study would better serve. But then, that is a value gained with age and time, a condition despised by youth. Checkmate.''

It took a moment for William's last words to register, then Will's gaze darted to the board. Affirming the situation, his eyes grew wide with shock as those gathered about broke into laughter. To his credit, he joined into the humor, fully capable of laughing at himself when the joke was well deserved.

As gibes were tossed about, it was only Isabel who noticed that Trac had come alert. His large brown eyes fixed on the doors to the hall, and he gave a low growl. A moment later the other dogs who lay sprawled about the hall, well out of the large wolfhound's domain, rose from their haunches and gave up the cry announcing an arrival to Castle Kilkenney. William brought them to silence with anticipation as the porters admitted a messenger in Beaumont's colors, his garments mud-splattered as evidence of his forced ride. He crossed the hall to William, extracting a message from the leather pouch he wore as he approached, his face lined with fatigue as he laid the missive in William's hand.

Isabel motioned to the steward to see to the needs of the messenger before drawing her attention back to her husband and the message he had torn open. She started as he rose abruptly from his chair, his handsome face fused with rage.

"Father, what is it . . . " Will began, stopping as John laid a warning hand on his arm.

"Sweet Mother!" William bellowed, his eyes again scanning the contents of the parchment. "Mother Mary and Joseph!" he roared, leaving the table to stride away, his head still bent to the message. He halted as his eyes darted to the rafters. "Now he's done it! The damn fool!" He spun back to the silent group, his eyes filled with anger and disbelief. "Our king has been excommunicated by the pope! The edict has been set against all of England!"

Gasps were heard about the hall, with cries from a number of the ladies, who were silenced by a glare from Isabel. "What has he done?" she asked calmly, turning back to William.

"The fool refused to accept the pope's choice for the new archbishop of Canterbury," he said, gritting his teeth.

"But Father, is it not the king's right to . . . "

"Not when he needs the Holy Father's support against France!" William roared. "Philip has been waiting for this opportunity! What is that fool thinking of?"

"Who has the Holy Father chosen for archbishop?" Isabel inquired.

"Stephen Langton," William answered, his mind spinning back over the years to a night spent in a warm tavern in Paris. "He is a good man. John's pride, as usual, has interfered with his judgment."

"What will happen now?" Will asked.

"England is in chaos. With excommunication, marriages cannot be performed, funerals are without consecration from the church, Masses are. . . . What could he be thinking of? He has little support from the barons as it is, he trusts no one, draws faith from no one, and now he believes that he can rule without the support of the church?"

Isabel had been listening quietly, her mind working as she recalled what William had told her about his visit to

France years before. "Langton is known to you," she observed quietly, the soft deliberation of her voice drawing William's attention.

"Aye, there is no reason for John to reject him. He is English-born and would be a perfect choice."

"And the Holy Father, you knew him in Paris as well?"

"Aye. I knew him as Lothario de Conti de Segni, when he was a priest at the University of Paris. I spent time with both of them."

"So you have told me. You said he was an exceptional man. Could you not write to him? Perhaps, William, in that you understand John Plantagenet so well, you could help him to understand what drives the king to make these decisions."

"Aye." William regarded his wife with a ghost of a smile. "I shall do what I can. Let us pray that one of them will see reason. I deeply fear that this does not bode well for England. Let us hope that I am wrong."

# 24

Isabel leaned out over the railing of the ship carrying them eastward, mesmerized by the wake of white foam that was cut by the path of the moving vessel. Her gaze lifted to the land that was quickly disappearing from view in the thick fog, and she knew that part of her life, a precious part, was slipping away.

William's letters to Innocent III had proved ultimately successful. John had agreed to accept the pope's choice for archbishop of Canterbury, and the pontiff, in return, had reduced the excommunication. While the edict would remain in effect against England until Stephen Langton was confirmed upon English soil, William's involvement had restored him to full favor by an ecstatic and grateful king. To Isabel's way of thinking, this was a doubtful benefit.

Had the matter rested there, England might have entered a long sought-after period of peace. Innocent, however, had been in negotiations with Philip of France, declaring him king of England in a final move to bring John Plantagenet to his knees before the church. Although the pope now rescinded his decision, Philip was of another mind. Draining the French cof-

fers, he had assembled an immense army, and his preparations to see his son, Louis, on the throne of England
had proceeded too far forward to turn back.

Invasion by Louis, the French king's son and heir,
was imminent. The result was a unification of the English people behind their king as nothing John himself
could have done. William had written immediately to
his king, committing his vassals. They had departed
Ireland within the week in the company of over five
hundred barons and knights of Ireland whom William
brought to the cause.

She felt strong hands about her shoulders, and she
turned her head to press her cheek against their familiarity, gaining comfort from his presence.

"Perhaps someday we will return," he said softly.

"Nay, William," she answered wistfully. "Those
years were a gift. While they shall sustain me, I do not
expect to see them again. Now we must face life once
more." She turned in his arms, reaching up to touch his
beloved face. "You have been too long from England,
my love. She is in pain and in need of you. Now I believe
that I am strong enough to share you with her."

"Will would have led the van if Father had not
restrained him!" Richard grinned, lifting his goblet to
his brother to soften the statement. "He had to threaten
him with mayhem if he did not return to the vanguard."

"The important thing is that you are safe, each of
you," Isabel remonstrated. The months of waiting were
ended and her prayers had been answered. The French
had been routed at the port of Dom, and her men had
returned to her safely.

"He acquitted himself well—once he learned how to
take orders." William smiled, his voice touched with
pride. "As did they both. Though I will say that my life
was easier when Will was Beaumont's squire and responsibility."

"He was knighted by the king himself!" Richard enthused, unable to hide the envy in his voice. "Beaumont

would not allow me to leave the rear lines, even to aid his left,'' he added sulkily.

"Be easy, Richard,'' William said as he stretched out his long legs. "When he feels that you are ready you will be given that position by his side. Would you want him to depend upon you while you are still green? Besides, once you have found yourself in the heat of battle you will long to be once again among the baggage train.'' Will's eyes darted to his father. Seeing his look of disbelief, William chuckled. "Well, perhaps not. But, Richard, you dream of war being glory and conquest. The truth is . . . something far different. Mark the bruises and cuts on your brother's body. Your mother spent over an hour on him with her sewing threads and salves.''

They sat before a comfortable fire in the large manor Isabel had established for the household in London. Upon their arrival at Bristol she had journeyed to Chepstow in the company of her personal knights while her men saw to the king's business with the French. But she had departed Striguil after seeing to its welfare, sensing that a London residence would better see them to the events ahead. She had no intention of remaining across the breadth of England while her family immersed itself in the politics of John Plantagenet; and she sensed that the drama was barely beginning to unfold.

"Reality is indeed a far cry from that of our dreams, Richard,'' Will said, gritting his teeth, his mood souring as he regarded his father. "Never would I have imagined that England could become vassal to Rome, or that my father could support it!''

Isabel drew in her breath as Will spoke, and her eyes shifted to William. She saw, with dismay, the storm that gathered in his expression at his son's words. "Will, you have no right to speak to your father in that tone. He . . .''

"You need not answer for me, Isabel,'' William retorted. "Especially in that I am fully aware that you agree with him.'' His angry gaze returned to his eldest son. "Aye, there is no question but that I have supported the king. He cannot contend with the disobedience of the barons, the pressures from Rome, and the threat of the French. By becoming the pope's liege vassal he has gained the church's support. Moreover, by accepting John's fealty, Innocent is forced to withdraw his support of France. Philip cannot now attack England, as to do so he would be attacking Rome as well."

"Had you not aided him with the Holy Father, we would now be well rid of him!" Will replied angrily.

"And have Louis in his place," William countered evenly. "Would you see a prince of France on the throne of England? Do you hate John that much?"

"He is not the man for England," Will replied coldly.

"He is English," William said evenly. "He is our king."

"He is a murderer!"

William sighed raggedly as he shook his head. "There is no proof that he murdered Arthur, Will."

"Who else would have murdered a prince?" Will snorted.

"Anyone who sought to find favor with John," William answered. "With the despots he surrounds himself with it could have been one of many."

"Then he is as responsible as if he had done it by his own hand," Will countered.

"Will," Isabel interrupted, her concern growing at the tone of the conversation. "What you speak is treason. Would you outlaw yourself along with Eustace de Vesy and Robert fitz Walter?"

"Humph," Will snorted. "De Vesy is an outlaw because the king knows he hates him for trying to seduce his wife, and fitz Walter because he is unpopular with the people. If he had not walked away in Normandy without a fight, fleeing to Philip for protection, he would be at the king's side still. John sent him away to distract from his own part in Normandy's loss."

William listened, his eyes narrowing as he studied his son. He sensed, hearing the bitterness in Will's voice, that his son's hatred for his king lay far deeper than he had suspected. "Will," he said quietly, "whatever you suffered during your years in his company must be placed aside for the good of all we hold close. If you cannot revere the man, do not neglect your loyalty to what he represents. It is true that power corrupts John's judgment. He rules with chicanery instead of justice; he weakens strategy with a lack of boldness, and victory makes him imprudent. He surrounds himself with violent men who see only to their own purses while blinding himself to those who would give him loyalty. Aye, I understand him and know his faults. And I do not expect you to ignore your beliefs nor your sense of justice. Fight him, coerce him, ply him with every resource you possess, but judiciously. Above all, keep England for England!"

As Isabel listened, her own feelings of rage over John's capitulation to Rome softened somewhat; her intent was now on soothing this antagonism between her husband and son. "Where is the archbishop to meet with the king?" she asked, changing the subject.

"Magdalen's Hill at Winchester," William answered, pulling from Will's defiant gaze.

"Then I may assume that the archbishop landed without difficulty?"

"A heavily armed escort was provided, but his arrival was met well," William answered.

"Well, I am certain that the Marshal family will deport themselves well upon the meeting," she added, glancing at her older son with warning. Will shrugged moodily. His eyes moved about the large room, coming to rest with lightened interest upon a bewitching, dark-haired maid who had joined the company set apart from the family. The young woman had chosen the moment to look up and her dark eyes caught Will's. She smiled, a slight blush rising on her cheeks before she looked quickly away. Seeing the exchange, Isabel fought her own smile. What else is this world, she mused, could better distract a young man's interest from a discussion of politics? She answered her son's unasked question. "Her name is Levene, daughter of the count of Fountaine. She has been sent to me for fostering so that I might prepare her to serve the queen.''

"Well," Richard tossed out as he rose and attempted to stretch cramped muscles. "I am for bed."

"As am I," Will agreed, pulling his gaze from the maid. "If I am to deport myself well in the king's company as Mother has suggested, I shall need my wits about me." He offered a grin to his father. "I fear it will take great effort, and I shall do my best to meet the situation well."

As William watched his sons depart the hall, his brow furrowed deeply and he rubbed his chin in thought.

"William," Isabel said quietly, "I fear that Will must have suffered much in those years he was taken from us."

"Aye," he sighed deeply, turning his attention to her. "He was never abused physically, of that I am certain. Beaumont saw to his care faithfully. . . . When I was with Will he seemed content, but whenever I questioned him about the court he withdrew, unwilling to talk about his time in the king's company. His loathing for John is all too obvious, and I fear that we may never know what has caused it. I can only pray that it does not lead him to do something foolish."

The morning of July 20 burst forth with summer warmth. The wild grasses melded in blanketing shades of green, background for the sprinkling of flowers, which painted a sweep of rioting colors about the hills, providing a rich canvas for the party that met on Magdalen Hill. The dark-haired king, resplendent in royal robes of purple velvet, his helm replaced by a gold circlet, lent sharp contrast to the Saxon fairness and the scarlet canonicals of the archbishop. Electricity could be felt between the two, the open defiance that sent an almost physical shock among those gathered. William watched guardedly, posed for reaction. Perhaps he alone, of all those present, truly understood the import of what was happening, even more than the principals. Both English-born, the opportunities for understanding and contribution were unprecedented, yet . . .

All watched breathlessly as John dismounted and prostrated himself before Stephen Langton, the archbishop of Canterbury. He rose slowly and regarded the prelate for a long moment. At this moment his genuflection would have been followed by a kiss of peace laid lightly on the bishop's ring, but it was forbidden to him. Until Langton was formally installed in Canterbury the king remained under edict of excommunication. John rose slowly from his knee, regarded Langton for a moment, then suddenly, to everyone's shock, he threw back his head and laughed uproariously, the sound filling the still morning air. Pressing his hand to his lips, he threw the primate a kiss and spun about, swinging easily into his saddle.

Isabel gasped and her eyes darted to her husband. While the large company on the hill broke into easy laughter, thoroughly appreciating John's handling of the awkward moment, she sensed a more dire meaning to his gesture. Her suspicions were confirmed by the expression on William's face as he exchanged a quick glance with her, and she closed her eyes in an instant of dread. John Plantagenet had humor, perhaps his best characteristic, but she knew better than to credit his behavior to his wit, as the others of the court had obviously done. Nay, it lay much deeper, this easy gesture. She shuddered involuntarily, sensing what was to come. Her dread deepened as she glanced at Will to see his reaction. His handsome jaw was set, his eyes flaring with anger as he watched the departing back of his king. She closed her eyes in a silent moment of prayer, even knowing as she did so that God had chosen not to listen.

The door opened slowly, the light from the torches in the outer hall framing a slender, cloaked figure. Hesitating for a moment, the form slipped into the dark room, closing the door quickly behind. The shapeless figure moved down the long row of narrow beds that lined each wall, finally coming to stop beside one. Another moment's hesitation, and slender fingers began to unlace the ties at the throat of the cloak. The heavy mantle slid to the floor as a narrow spear of moonlight shone from a high slit window, illuminating smooth flesh. She raised the corner of the blanket and slid in beside the sleeping figure. She lay still as he turned in his sleep, then she slid her hand lightly across his chest and pressed her body against his harder length.

Will stirred in his sleep, turning to the feel of warm softness against his body. He nuzzled against the warmth, his dreams forming into tantalizing pleasure as he felt arms go about his neck. He came suddenly awake, realizing that a leg had slipped between his to rub against his hardening member. He jerked back, rising up on his elbow to stare down incredulously at the woman in his bed. "Are you mad!" he hissed. His gaze darted about the room to the sleeping knights.

"Oh, Will," she murmured huskily, "do not worry about them, they are all sleeping and not likely to awaken, judging from the amount of wine they consumed tonight. It was quite a celebration your parents gave for the archbishop's investiture. Now hold me. I . . ."

"You are mad," he whispered furiously. He rolled from the bed and pulled on his chausses, then grabbed for her cloak. Yanking the blanket from her grasp, he pulled her from the bed and threw the mantle about her shoulders. Gripping the upper part of her arm, he pushed her out of the room and down the long hallway, not stopping until they had reached the recessed doorway to the pentice leading to the upper floors. He spun her about in the shadows of the archway, and she cringed at the fury in his face reflected by the flickering torch on a nearby wall. "Damn it, Levene, what were you thinking of?" he snapped.

"I just wanted to be with you!" she cried, twisting in an effort to release his grip.

"Be with me? In the knights' quarters? It was a miracle that no one saw you! Have you no concern at all for what would be said?"

"But you never come to me anymore!" she whined. "I have not seen you for days and days . . ."

"You know what has been happening . . ."

"I do not care! If you wanted to see me you would make the time!"

His grip slackened. "Perhaps you should listen to your own words."

"What do you mean?" she stammered, unsettled by the way he was looking at her.

"Exactly what you said, my dear. If I had truly wanted to see you I would have found the time."

It took a moment before his meaning became clear, and her face changed, meeting his anger as she drew up, no longer cringing. "How dare you!" she hissed. "If you think for a moment that once you have found pleasure with me you can merely toss me aside . . ."

"Do not try it, Levene." He gave a short, angry laugh. "You threw yourself at me and we both well know it. And I was certainly not the first. As for the pleasure . . ." He caught her hand by the wrist before it struck him. "None of that, sweetheart, it is not lady-like."

"And you are no gentleman!" she spat, trying to pull her wrist away.

"I have not claimed to be."

"I will tell them that you seduced me!"

"I and how many others?" he laughed cruelly.

"I do not know what you mean." She stiffened.

"Nay? Come now, Levene. You have been like a bitch in heat since you came here. I saw you with both Thomas and Sebastian after you turned your attention on me. Rather frantic work for so short a time, wouldn't you say? It is almost as if . . ." He stopped, his eyes narrowing suddenly as he saw her blanch in the dim light from the hallway. "So that is it," he said quietly, releasing her wrist.

She clenched the cloak instinctively about her, her eyes filling with a rush of tears as she spun about to the door. He grabbed her shoulders and turned her back to him. "How far along are you?"

"What does it matter to you!" she choked as she struggled against his grip.

"I asked you a question," he said, gritting his teeth, his anger returning. "Now answer me!"

"I'm not certain, two or three months, perhaps . . . " she hissed. "Let me go!"

"What were you going to do if you had managed to snare a husband—once he found out the child could not have been his—or mine?" he asked with disgust.

"It would not matter!" she cried. "Nothing would matter as long as I did not have to go back!"

"Where? To your father?" He watched with amazement as she appeared to crumble at his question. "You're afraid of him." When she did not answer he pressed another question. "Where is the babe's father?"

"He doesn't want me," she whispered, unable to look at him.

"Never mind," he said wearily, suddenly feeling the hour and the tension. "Go to bed, Levene. Get some rest. And do not worry."

She stared at him. "What do you mean?" she stammered.

"I will try to help you," he said, shrugging. "We shall talk about it tomorrow. Just . . . go to bed."

Will watched as Levene departed into the dim light of the stairwell, then he returned wearily to his own bed. As exhausted as he was, he lay awake for a long time, an arm propped beneath his head as his thoughts settled into a sullen depression. Why had he promised to help her? He owed her nothing. He had been attracted to her, admittedly more than any other woman he had known—and there had been many. They had used each other for their mutual pleasure, and that was the end of it. But he would help her, he reasoned. She was his mother's ward, and as such he would help her.

He rose early, the matter far from his mind as he sought an early breakfast, entering the great hall even before many of the guests had risen from their pallets along the walls. He was to meet with his master-of-arms to consider the pages of his father's household, to choose two of the hopeful company to enter his service as squires. As he munched on a meat pasty he mentally checked off the merits of each of the older boys, carefully measuring their talents and abilities.

"Sir Will," a servant had approached and had waited to be noticed, finally tugging on the edge of Will's sleeve. "Lady Marshal requested that you attend her as soon as you had risen."

Will closed the door to his mother's chamber behind him as a quick glance toward the bed confirmed that his father was already up and about. "Good morning, Mother. You wished to see me?"

Isabel turned from the window, and a shadow crossed her face as she regarded her eldest son. "Aye. There is some breakfast there if you have not eaten," she added distractedly as she waved a hand toward a small table set with bread and cheese. She turned back to the window as Will, who was still hungry, helped himself to a generous measure. "Sybil was not feeling well at vespers last evening," she said finally.

"Is she all right?" Will asked with concern, coming to stand by her.

"Oh, aye, she is fine, just a slight cold," Isabel assured him. "But she was restless during the night and could not sleep. I went to the kitchens for some warm milk for her . . . " She turned to look at him. "As I was returning to the nursery, I passed by the knights' quarters . . . "

He stopped chewing and returned her gaze. "You saw me with Levene," he said quietly.

"Will, how could you!" she blurted, her voice rising as she moved away from him. As she spun about to confront him she lost her composure. "She is my ward! She is my responsibility! I will not have you rutting about like some wild buck! Well," she glared. "Are you not going to say something?"

"Mother, I wish you would trust me on this. I would really rather not talk about it."

"You'd . . . " her eyes grew wide with amazement. "You cannot be serious! We *will* talk about it! Or would you rather speak of it with your father?''

"I do not wish to speak with either of you about it,'' he pressed, leaning a hip on the windowledge. "There's—it's a private matter.''

"Nay, you are wrong, Will, it most certainly is not a private matter! As my ward she is my concern, most particularly in a matter such as this! How long have you two been carrying on? I am certain that I do not need to ask if you have been intimate with her—it is all too obvious! How could you take advantage of her—and me?'' He began to say something, then paused, and she could hear him swear under his breath. "Oh, you have good reason for dismay, Will, but it saddens me that your concerns are not for the right reasons, but only that you have been caught!''

"I am not the one who has been caught,'' he murmured.

"What?''

"Nothing. Mother, look, you will have to decide whether or not to believe me, but, I did not enter into the, ah, relations, lightly. I would not take advantage of a maid, be she your ward or no. Moreover, I cared very deeply for her.''

Isabel studied her son for a long moment. "This is fortunate, Will. I suggest you encourage that emotion, for you will have little choice now but to marry the girl.''

He looked up at her and leaned back against the window embrasure as his eyes grew stony. "Nay,'' he said quietly. "That is no longer an option, even if I wanted it. Perhaps, if I were Richard, or Gilbert . . . ''

"What are you talking about?'' she snapped.

"Since you are obviously going to force this issue, I have no choice but to tell you. She is with child.''

Isabel's mouth dropped open with shock as she absorbed his words. "She is pregnant?'' Her face began to whiten with rage as she regarded Will with fury. "She is with child and you repudiate her now . . . now that . . . ''

"For God's sake, Mother, of course not!" he stormed, now angry that he had been forced to discuss the matter at all. "The child is not mine!"

"Not yours?" she said, suddenly numb.

"Nay, she was with child when she came here. She was in love with someone who would not marry her. Do not be too angry with her, Mother," he added quickly, seeing the rage return to Isabel's expression. "She is afraid of her father and what he will do. She hoped . . . well, she hoped that she would be married before it was discovered."

"She was going to pass it off as yours?" Her eyes widened.

"Can you blame her . . . "

"Blame her?" she cried. "For passing off her bastard as heir to Striguil?"

"And what if it was Matilda?" he interrupted. "What if she found herself in this position?"

"She would not!" Isabel answered contemptuously.

"Would not what? Fall in love? Find herself with child of a whoreson who would not wed her? It could happen, Mother."

"But she would come to me, not try to pass herself off . . . "

"Exactly. But then, Matilda has a family who loves and cares about her. And a father she is not afraid of."

Isabel stared at Will and then, very slowly, she softened. "Aye. Good Lord, the poor child. I must. . . . " She stopped and regarded Will oddly. "Just what were you going to do?"

"I had been giving it some thought." He shrugged. "I thought to take her to the Convent of Saint Mary's. After the babe was born . . . "

"What were you going to tell me?"

"I hadn't quite decided yet." He grinned.

For a moment she fought a smile, and then she grew serious once more. "Why, Will?" she asked softly. "Why would you do this?"

He shrugged his broad shoulders again. "Perhaps I

feel a little of the responsibility you accuse me of lacking."

"Responsibility? But the babe is not yours."

"True, but it could well have been if things had been different. And," he sighed. "I like her." He did not add that he had also grown to dislike her when he had discovered that she had given favors to his friends. Hurt and betrayal had quickly destroyed what had begun to grow between them.

"Well. In any case, your plan is a good one. Aye, Saint Mary's. After the babe comes . . . I will speak with her. If she is truly afraid of her father. . . . Well, we shall deal with it."

"We can keep this between the three of us?" he asked. "The fewer that know of it . . ."

"Of course. There is no need for anyone else to know —and the fewer that do, the better her chances will be to reestablish some sort of life for herself."

"You have a rather unusual banner, milady."

Their gazes followed the archbishop's to Isabel's banner, which hung suspended above them in the arched rafters of the hall. The reworked device was marshaled, or cut in half from top to bottom, the left quartered with the bottom half those of her father's chevrons, the top the repeated lion of her husband, which dominated the full right side of the lozenge.

"It has special meaning for my parents, Your Eminence," Will laughed. "Though neither of them will attempt to explain it."

"Would you care for more wine?" Isabel asked the prelate, changing the subject. She could feel William watching her, and she glanced up at him with a dazzling smile as she refilled the archbishop's goblet.

"I can well understand why a mere tavern maid would not interest you," Stephen Langton murmured to William, who sat at his side.

William's brow furrowed with puzzlement at the statement, then he smiled, remembering. "Aye. And she has never ceased to hold my interest." He grinned.

"Something you have not told me about, my lord earl?" Isabel asked sweetly, overhearing their comments.

"Nothing worth the telling, my love," William assured her.

"Indeed." She smiled. "Well, perhaps later." She turned to refill John d'Erley's goblet.

"Sorry, my friend," Langton chortled.

"There's nothing to apologize for," William assured him as his eyes followed Isabel. "It should provide for a rousing discussion later—fortunately I have nothing to hide." He turned back to Langton as his thoughts returned to an earlier discussion. "If the Holy Father's purpose in giving England to Philip was to bring England to his way of thinking, I fear that he seriously erred. Nothing could have served more to unify the barons, even to those who are in the greatest dispute with the king."

"I agree." Langton sighed. "That is why I performed the Holy Eucharist at Winchester upon my arrival. A Mass of thanksgiving—and to mend breaches."

"We have heard . . . " John hesitated, unsure of how to phrase his thoughts.

"What have you heard, Sir John?" Langton smiled. "Tell me."

"Only that . . . the Holy Father is furious with you for the Mass. That by doing so the edict was lifted."

"Aye, you are correct, but I do not regret the decision. Ill feelings between the people and the church must be placed aside."

"The pontiff has reason to be unhappy about what you've done," Will interjected, his voice tinged with anger. "He has lost his hold on his vassal, John Plantagenet, and with him, England."

"Will! That is quite enough!" William stormed, affronted by his son's rudeness.

"Nay, William. I do not take exception to the truth, however painful it is to hear. I cannot argue with the fact that the Holy Father is deeply upset that he has lost his control of the king—and he will not give up control easily.''

"Where do you stand on this matter, Your Eminence?'' Will asked, his tone changed by the archbishop's honesty.

"My heart is, and will always be, with the church—and with England.'' He smiled.

"An evasive answer,'' Will countered.

"Will, for the love of God . . . '' William choked.

"Aye, for the love of God.'' Langton smiled. "It is his work I attempt to do. However, you are wrong, young William, the answer was not evasive. I do not believe that the two need be at odds. I am English and Catholic, and in my mind and heart the two are not in conflict.''

Will had opened his mouth to respond, but William silenced him with a glare. "Do you mind if I enter this conversation? Rome's new legate has imposed serious fines upon the crown for what he interprets as damages occurring during the excommunication. They have amounted to hundreds of thousands of marks—every parish priest has placed claims. The barons will not stand for it, a fact of which I am sure you are aware.''

"Aye, and so I have advised the Holy Father. The matter will be settled to everyone's satisfaction.''

"I seriously hope so,'' William said, shaking his head. "The barons are again polarizing on the matter, and if you truly care for England . . . your efforts may effect what Philip of France could not.''

"Philip is quite busy in Flanders.'' Langton shook his head. "The Flemish have drawn his armies, and it should keep him from England for quite a while.''

William's mouth twisted into a wry smile as he thought of Philip, now engaged in a war across the channel. It must have been quite a shock for him to learn of the pope's change of mind, he mused. Knowing Philip he could imagine his reaction upon learning that the vast army he had so painstakingly raised and trained, the expense levied on the French treasury, was for naught. Not to mention his reaction when he realized that he had been used as a pawn by Innocent III to bring John Plantagenet into line. No wonder Philip had looked quickly for another adversary—

His attention was brought about as the archbishop rose to leave. "As ever, I have relished your well-set table, Countess," he said to Isabel, then he turned to William. "Do not be hard on the boy, William," he murmured. "He has the energy and enthusiasm of youth. Age will allow him patience and wisdom, along with its disadvantages, soon enough."

"Hummm," William muttered. "If he lives that long."

As the archbishop departed with his company, John d'Erley rose and offered his hand to Cailin. "Enough of the king, Philip, Flanders or any other problems," he said, stifling a yawn. "I am to bed."

The knights and their ladies soon followed his lead, but William spoke up when Will would have gone. "A moment, Will."

Isabel stiffened at the tone to William's voice, and she motioned to Richard to leave, but William stopped her. "Nay, Isabel, Richard will remain as well so that he might know how I feel about certain matters."

"Father, if this is about what I said to . . . "

"Nay, Will, this has nothing to do with tonight. That matter can be taken up at another time." William rose from his chair and stood before the fire, taking a moment to compose his thoughts. He stared into his goblet for a long moment, rolling the liquid slowly about the sides, then finally looked up at Will. "I had a visit today from someone who brought news of a rather disquieting nature. It was disturbing for a number of reasons," he glanced up at Isabel, and she started at the anger she saw in his eyes. "It seems that my family has sought to keep rather important information from me." He looked back at Will, and his eyes had grown icy. When he saw that Will was about to speak, he silenced him with a glare that made Isabel shift uncomfortably. "It seems," he continued sternly, "that a certain young maid—recently under our care—one whom my wife had informed me had returned to the home of her father—is now ensconced at the Convent of Saint Mary's. And, it appears, that this young woman, who was delivered into the hands of the good sisters by my own son, is with child."

"William . . . " Isabel started to rise from her chair.

"Nay, Mother." Will put out a hand to stay her. "I would hear what he has to say."

"But . . ."

"Be still, Isabel," William said angrily. "At least he is willing to face up to what he has done—now that I know! It is obvious that *you* were not going to tell me! Imagine my pride to hear of it from a virtual stranger!"

"Who are you talking about?" Richard looked from one to the other then realization dawned. "Levene?" His shock, touched with awe, turned to his brother. "Levene? Good God, Will, really?"

"Shut up, Richard," Will snapped, his eyes still fixed on his father. "So . . . you know. And you naturally assume the worst of me. I took her to the convent, so the babe must be mine."

"Are you implying that it is not?" William said, gritting his teeth.

"I am implying nothing," Will answered, rising from his chair. "I do not intend to answer. Indeed, there has been no question asked. It appears that you have already decided upon my guilt." He turned and left the hall without looking back, leaving them in silence.

"Richard, go to bed," Isabel said shortly as she rose from her chair. "Now!" she added when he hesitated. As Richard left the hall she turned to William, and her face was set with determination.

She found him in the stable as he was cinching the saddle to his destrier. She glanced at the packed saddlebags that lay nearby, and her heart contracted painfully even as she forced herself to remain calm. "Will?"

He half turned but did not stop what he was doing.

"Mother, it is cold out here, go back. I was going to come to you before I left."

She watched him for a few moments as she struggled to find the right words. "You—you don't have to leave." She tried to keep the pain from her voice. "I told him everything. Please do not be angry with him, Will. We should have told him from the beginning. I believe that is what he is really angry about—that we kept it from him. Think of how he must have felt, to find out this way. It was natural that he would assume . . ."

"Mother, that is not why I am leaving." He smiled sadly as he turned to her and leaned on his saddle. "I have to go."

"But why? If not this, then . . . why?"

Will stared at the floor for a long moment, then raised his eyes to hers, pleading for understanding. "He was so quick to believe the worst of me. It wouldn't have happened if things were not so strained between us. Perhaps then, when we both can view each other from a distance, we might come to understand each other better. I need time. Time to myself to decide— what I believe in, who I am. After all, how can I expect him to understand me when I do not understand myself?" His eyes suddenly misted as he stared past her at some unreachable point. "God, can you imagine what a life he has had?" he said wistfully. "The tournaments, the battles, the politics—all those years when he was responsible only to himself. The things he must have seen, learned, experienced . . ."

"But what of your responsibilities here?" She reached for what she knew and could feel was slipping from her. "What of Striguil, the lands, they are yours!"

He looked down at her and laughed softly. "Mother, I am not running away. I need time. As for the lands, they don't need me. They have him—and you."

She stared at him for a long moment. "I suspected as much," she sighed raggedly. Then she reached into the pocket of her bliaut and handed him a small weighted sack. "I brought this for you. If you need more you may claim it from any of our castellans." Swallowing, she fought back her tears as she reached up and touched his face. "Please," she whispered, "take care of yourself."

He pulled her into his arms in a fierce hug, then quickly let her go. Picking up the saddlebags, he tossed them behind the saddle and led the mount from the stable. Drawing her into his arms once again, he released her and swung into the saddle. She stood a long time, watching the gate from which he had ridden. As the cold began to bite through the thin mantle about her shoulders, she forced back her tears once again and returned to the hall, where she knew William would be waiting.

# 25

"IF you begin to think that you are a victim,
you become one," William answered, drawing from his
goblet as he regarded the other man carefully over its
rim.

Langton shook his head. "The king has made them
so, but he was not the first. His father and brother, as
those before them, effected the result. But William, it
must stop! Somewhere, at some time, freedoms must be
given to those who have not the power to take them for
themselves. That is the responsibility of the barony."

"And the church?" William eyed the archbishop
shrewdly. "I believe it said that true freedom is gained
only through the kingdom of God. Is it the intent of
Rome to now assure paradise on this pitiful kingdom of
earth?"

"Point taken." Langton laughed, but then sobered as
he leaned forward to regard William seriously. "You
know perfectly well that what I mean to accomplish is
not condoned by the church. But let us parry no longer,
William. We are both English. What I mean to do is for
England, and it is right!"

William rose and stretched, stepping to the fire where

he turned to have his back against its warmth. "So you have it, Stephen, let us not mince words. I have enjoyed the many hours we have spent together before this fire over the past months. Now tell me, why are you really here?"

"To learn from you." Langton grinned, leaning back in his chair. "There is no one in England who knows more of common law and the government's administration than you—nor one I could trust more to tell me the truth."

William snorted. "Truth? Just what truths are you seeking?"

"Truths which will lead to freedom," Langton answered quickly, his eyes gleaming with some secret purpose.

"Freedom?" William chortled disbelievingly. "Freedom for whom? My God, man, look around you! Philip is posed at our door; the pontiff is demanding that England be placed at his feet and is draining it dry to bring it down; the barons are engaged in continual bickering, each vying for position and power as they look for any excuse to wage war against the crown! Or perhaps you expect something miraculous from a king who is barely clinging to his crown and has no idea of what is happening! And you are raving about freedom?"

"Aye, William, freedom. Can you not see? There is a catalyst which can bring it all together, a dawn of reason never seen before, a new beginning! The people, William! You did it—you were nothing but what you effected by will, by drive to accomplish something in your life. I did the same—the son of a simple laborer of Yorkshire—and now the archbishop of Canterbury, for the love of God!"

William regarded the prelate for a long moment, then shook his head. "You are mad."

"Perhaps so." Langton grinned as he leaned back again. "But you know that I am right. What is more, you will help me."

"I am not even certain of what you are asking me to

do," William grunted as he refilled Langton's tankard, then his own. "And I am not certain that I want to."

"You have already helped me more than you can know."

"Humph," William snorted as he returned to the fire. "Why do I know that there is more—much more?"

"There is." Langton laughed. "In a few days I will be holding a Mass at Saint Paul's. I would like you to be there."

"A Mass?" William repeated, his eyes narrowing. "And what else?"

"Nothing else—if you wish it so. You will decide at that time."

Silence hung over the room as William turned to his own thoughts; the only sound for a long while was the fire as it snapped and cracked behind him. "I have heard that Will has been spending a great deal of time with you," he said at last.

"Aye, he has. I have enjoyed his company, William. You should be proud of him."

"I am. And I hope to remain so." He paused as Trac, who had been sleeping by the fire, rose up, and the tip of his tail began to wag tentatively as he turned his massive head toward the doors to the kitchens. "I believe my lady is about to join us." William smiled. "I, for one, am starved. May I offer you a late supper?" he added, effectively bringing the conversation to a close.


William opened the door to their chamber, his body aching with fatigue as he pulled his cloak from his shoulders and tossed it on a chair near the door. The fire burned low on the hearth, beckoning him to its warmth as did the pitcher of wine she had left on the small table nearby.

"You're back."

His head jerked about as she rose from the bed and reached for her robe. "You need not get up," he said softly. "It is late."

"I haven't been sleeping," she said, crossing to the table to pour him some wine. "Unless you are tired.

Would you prefer to wait until morning to tell me what happened?''

"Nay," he smiled, dropping into a chair. "I am tired but sleep would be impossible." He reached for the goblet she handed him and waited for her to settle in the chair next to him. "I don't know where he found it," he mused out loud as he stared into the fire. "Unbelievable. Good God, Henry had destroyed all copies."

"William, what are you talking about?"

He glanced at her with a grim smile. "He planned well," he mused, turning his gaze back to the fire. "The most powerful barons of the realm were there, but the Mass was only an excuse. The gathering which followed was his purpose, although it was attended by only those of his choice, and must be kept in confidence . . . Sweet Mother, if word spread . . . ''

"William, what did Henry destroy?"

He looked up at her with almost an expression of surprise to find her there. "Oh, aye. Well. Old King Henry, the First, love. His coronation charter. All copies had been destroyed by him—or so we thought—the only reason I knew of its contents was because of my relationship with his grandson. Henry told me of it once . . . '' He glanced at her with a sheepish grin. "While well within our cups—but I had forgotten . . . until tonight."

"A charter? What did it say?"

William laughed softly at the question. "What did it say? A better question would be what will it effect? Civil war, most likely." He ignored her gasp as he took a long draught of his wine. "Old Henry had great visions for England. His coronation charter spelled out those dreams but, for reasons of his own, he destroyed it later. Somehow, Langton has obtained a copy. I know it is authentic—I saw the signature and the items are as Henry recounted them to me. Simply," he laughed softly at his choice of word, "they remove many powers from the throne, giving them to the barons—and the common man. It declares that those outside of the class of nobility have rights, and that those rights should be incorporated into the law."

Isabel blinked, wondering if she had heard him correctly. "What?" she whispered. She felt a trembling excitement begin to stir within her as she leaned forward, her eyes wide as she almost feared to believe what she had heard. "Oh, William! Could it be true?"

He smiled at her enthusiasm. "Oh, it is true enough. I know what you are thinking. Freedom for Ireland, as well as England. No more of what you consider to be the rule of an inept, despotic king, one who would allow women and children to starve at the gate of a besieged castle. Isabel, if only it were that simple," he sighed deeply. "If only it were that simple. My God, what Langton's done."

"What has he done, William?" she asked softly.

"He has loosened the devil." He shook his head, staring into the fire. "There will be war, Isabel. The worst kind. Not from without, but from within. English against English. And there's not a damned thing I can do to stop it."

She rose from her chair, clasping her hands before her as she regarded him. "Then, perhaps my lord earl, you are not meant to."

He glanced up at her as his brow furrowed with doubt. "Are you wishing for bloodshed?" he asked. "Isabel, can you realize what you are saying?"

"Aye. I can and I do," she said, returning his look evenly. "You told me once that if laws were unfair, they should be changed. I recall words of my father's—that the only right we are born with is that which enables us to fight for what we believe in—to die for it if necessary."

He regarded her steadily. "Will was there," he said quietly. "Are you prepared to see him die for it?"

She stiffened at his words, wavering slightly as she closed her eyes, then opened them once again as she took a deep breath. "If it is what he believes in," she answered.

He rose and looked down at her as his eyes held hers intently. "So be it," he said softly.

"Do you mean it?" she whispered, returning his

steady gaze. "William, it will not happen without you."

"I mean it. But I must be allowed to handle John in my own way. Langton has agreed, can you?"

"Langton . . ." she gasped, her eyes growing wide with understanding. "You . . . you already agreed!"

He chuckled deeply. "Aye, I have agreed. But I will tell you what I told him. I will do everything that I can to avoid war. If concessions must be made, then compromise must be met. I will handle John, but I fear, in spite of his enthusiasm—or because of it—Langton will not be able to control the barons. He simply will not understand that there are those who want the king's head and will use the charter as an excuse to have it. I meant it when I said that the devil is loosened. I fear that we are facing a hell that we have yet to imagine."

William shifted in the saddle, his hands tight on the reigns of Horse as the animal moved restlessly, sensing the tension of his rider. The marshal's eyes moved slowly beneath the visor of his helm as he felt the hot June sun take its toil. The rivulets of sweat trailed down his neck into the collar of his gambeson, already damp beneath the sweltering heat of his chain mail and tabbard. Months of labor, the hours spent laboriously writing reason into the Great Charter, pressed with the knowledge of what would occur if they failed . . . The arguments with Langton, struggling for each phrase, the endless hours spent sparring with the king, finally convincing John that no choice was left to him but to sign. Now it was upon them, the moment when it would come to pass—or fail, thus throwing England into a ferocious civil war. His eyes fixed on each of the barons who waited across the river Thames, knowing well those who waited, and those who hoped that the effort would fail and they would have the excuse . . . He could feel Philip of France breathing down the neck of his gambeson along with the sweat of his labors, waiting . . .

He glanced at his king who sat at his side, ready, though with understandable reluctance, to cross the river to sign the charter . . . and again recalled the time spent arguing for reason, finally convincing John Plantagenet that the alternative was the loss of his throne . . .

His eyes moved to a singular figure among those waiting across the Thames, and he winced involuntarily, a sharp spear of pain stabbing him before he could throw it off. His son, among those who would see England's throne in ashes. The law cast aside, chaos. . . . He wondered how far Will would go if the charter were not signed . . .

The sound of cheering reached them as they approached the northern shore of the island where the negotiations were to take place. John pulled his mount to a halt, his dark eyes burning with fury as he regarded the company who awaited him on the opposite shore. The island was filled with armed knights, the warm morning sun illuminating helms, and the bright colors of the rich brocaded surcoats and banners bearing the coat of arms depicting many of the proudest families of England. William's eyes narrowed with anger as he saw two of the assembly separate and ride down to the shore, Robert fitz Walter and Eustace de Vesy.

"Let us have done with this travesty!" John spat petulantly, his fury turning on the archbishop, who rode at his right. Urging his mount forward the small party crossed to the island and to the sumptuous pavilion that had been erected for the event.

Isabel waited in the tent that had been set up on the north shore near that of the king's. Through the day she had watched from a distance with the other ladies of the court. Her concern grew as the sun moved slowly across the sky to lengthen shadows as the barons and knights moved about restlessly, impatiently for a conclusion to the proceedings within the pavilion. As the sun receded, casting the meadow in dusk, it was obvious to all that the matter would not be concluded quickly. It was late when he came to her. Silently, she helped him to divest his armor and served him a light supper, waiting for him to tell her in his own way.

"He has capitulated," William said at last, his voice showing fatigue and strain. "But, as ever, he is in a high dudgeon, and his acerbity compels him to argue each point. Langton and Saire de Quincey, who acts for the confederates, have rewritten the draft, again and yet again, changing words if not the intent, to satisfy him.''

''It will be signed?''

''Aye, it will be signed. But he continues to play the game as a tyrant. At this rate it will take days, and that alone may cause it to fail.''

''What do you mean?'' She leaned forward to refill his tankard.

''A few of the barons have already departed, with great disgust and flurry.''

''But why? If they know the charter will be signed . . .''

''You saw them when we arrived. Mounted, in full regalia. They expected the matter to be concluded quickly—only to find themselves trapped in armor beneath a broiling sun. And, there are those, such as fitz Walter and de Vesy, who use the charter as an excuse, hoping that he will not sign it. Damn!'' He hit the table with his fist in a flash of frustrated rage, causing the tankard to spill. ''If it is not held together now, all is lost! They have finally found the spine to gather together for a worthwhile, unified purpose, but it is one based upon personal greed and avarice! They profess their cause to be for the good of England while hoping they can use it for revenge upon the king for personal grievances! And through it all we may yet live to see Louis of France on the throne of England!''

''But John will sign,'' she repeated as she cleaned up the spilled ale and refilled his tankard.

''Aye, I have said so—if he is quick!''

''Aye—if he is quick,'' she paused thoughtfully. ''Or if you can convince the barons to remain, no matter how long it takes,'' she finished with a poignant smile.

''Obviously,'' he snorted.

''There is something which will draw and hold men in spite of discomforts,'' she tossed out, leaning against his side as she slid an arm about his neck.

He laid his arm about her waist and looked up at her, grinning. "Are you suggesting that I provide women for them all?"

"Not that kind of amusement, milord," she answered with a smile. "Nay, there is another, even more effective, way to hold their interest."

"I am waiting."

"A tournament, milord, a small war to release their energies."

He stared at her for a long moment, then threw back his head and roared with pleased, relieved laughter. Isabel's suggestion was taken as a stroke of brilliance, and William immediately organized a tournament to follow the signing of the charter. With the tantalizing promise of a tournament, the barons continued to grumble and swelter beneath the burning July sun, keeping cool by the eventual shedding of their armor beneath their heavy surcoats and the continual dousing of cool water by their squires, but they remained.

> no freeman shall be taken, nor imprisoned . . . but by the lawful judgment of his peers, or by the laws of the land . . . holding chattels, franchises, or any right . . . all the forests that have been afforested in our time shall be disafforested . . . shall put any man to his law upon his bare word . . . all merchants may, with safety and security, go out of England and come into England . . . this charter given at the meadow called Running-Mead, betwixt Windsor and Stanes, the fifteenth day of June, in the seventeenth year of our reign. John.

"It is done," she sighed as she buckled William into his hauberk.

"Aye," his voice was muffled as he pulled his tabbard over the hauberk. "Now let us hope that it will have some lasting effect."

"You think it will not?" she frowned as she handed him his helm.

"I believe that John will seek revenge for the humiliation he has suffered the past four days—and the barons will retaliate."

"If you believe that, then why did you support it?" she looked up at him with amazement.

"Because, my love," he murmured, taking her face between his large hands. "As you have so often reminded me, change must begin somewhere. The document which was signed today is ultimately worthwhile —now we must defend it. Surely you did not think that it would be easy?"

"Are you firm that I may not remain to watch?" she asked, changing the subject to strike on a matter more immediately dear to her.

"Watch a melee?" he chortled as he turned to pick up his mantle. "There will not be a safe place within miles of here. Where would you view it, from a tree?"

"An interesting thought," she mused.

His head jerked about, and he saw that she was seriously considering it. "That would be interesting, indeed," he smirked, glancing down at her. "Those fair legs dangling from a branch. Perhaps I could use them as a diversion for the opposition. Enough. Your escort is waiting, without. See you gone so that I may attend to business."

Begrudgingly, she allowed her household knights to escort her back to their London manor. She released them upon their arrival, as they fairly twitched with eagerness to be returned to the melee, and passed the remainder of the day with Cailin and the children. The two women listened for the sound of horses as the day progressed. Their emotions were mixed, knowing that the early arrival of one of their men meant that he had been bested, only to be released upon promise of ransom. Yet the fact of their absence was a double-edged sword. It could mean the possibility of injury or worse—or that they had been thus far victorious.

Their nerves were sorely strained. As the room dimmed into darkness, the candles were finally lit. Suddenly the sound of a mounted party was heard from without. They laid their needlework in their laps as their eyes fixed with anticipation upon the door. It was flung back and John, Beaumont, and Richard entered, their clothes and faces covered with dirt, their expressions alive with enthusiasm.

Cailin flew from her chair to John's arms, and the room was filled with happy laughter, except for Isabel, who looked past them for some sign of William. Seeing her concern, Richard stepped forward and gifted her with a great hug. "You should have seen him, Mother! He was magnificent!"

"Where is he?" she asked, reaching up to push aside a stray lock of hair that had fallen over his forehead.

"He attends the king at Windsor." He shrugged, then glanced about. "I'm starving! Is there something to eat?"

"Of course." Isabel turned, motioning to a serving maid who had appeared at the sound of their arrival. As the girl disappeared into the kitchens, Isabel turned back to her son who had dropped wearily into a chair.

"Do not worry, Mother. He said he would be here soon. Lud, what a day!"

"Richard acquitted himself well, milady," Beaumont assured her, a touch of pride in his voice. "He held to my left and did it nobly. Henceforth he shall be my shield-bearer."

Richard gasped as his gaze darted to the knight, and he beamed with pleasure, visibly drawing up at the announcement. "I am proud of you," Isabel said softly, touching his dear face. "As your father will be. Now, wash up," she added as a serving lad entered with a pitcher and washbowl. "Your food will be here soon."

The meal was a happy one, hearty eating interspersed with a boisterous accounting of what had occurred, each vying to best the other with feats of prowess. But Isabel listened with one ear, the other waiting expectantly for the sound of William's arrival. At last it came, and she rose up from the chair to meet him at the door as her eyes searched his face for some signs of what had happened. He smiled at her and leaned down to brush her lips with a light kiss before he greeted the others. Grinning at their enthusiastic welcome, he settled into his chair at the head of the table and grabbed for the food that was left. As Isabel took the chair at his side, he looked up at her and gave her a wink.

"What are you going to do with the fortune you earned today?" John threw at him with a chortle.

Isabel blinked, now listening as she had not before. "What fortune?" she asked.

"The one he gathered in ransoms!" John roared good-naturedly.

"Indeed?" she looked at her husband with puzzlement.

"I took a few." He shrugged as he helped himself to a capon.

"A few?" John blurted. "What he left for the rest of us was pitifully spare!"

"Aye," agreed Beaumont. "I find it passing strange, milady," he added, smiling. "He seemed to concentrate upon those who led the revolt. A mere coincidence, I am certain."

William smiled slightly, then turned his attention to his meal.

"What is this?" Cailin laughed. "We were led to believe that you three felled all that were there."

"You must have misunderstood." John grinned.

"Aye, now that father is here," Richard laughed. "Indeed, we spent the better part of the day cleaning up after him. Even Will . . . "

"What about Will?" Isabel jerked her head about to stare at Richard.

"Father knocked him on his ass," Richard chortled. "He was there one minute, and the next . . . "

Isabel spun about to William. "You did not hurt him!" she gasped.

"Nay, he wasn't hurt," Richard assured her. "Except perhaps his pride. He went limping off toward the lists, rubbing his backside . . . "

"Richard, that is enough," William warned.

"Lord," John sighed, leaning back in his chair, "I haven't had such a good time since . . . William, do you remember that tournament near Saint-Pierre-sur-Dives?" He chortled at the memory, Beaumont joining in as he recalled the moment. "It had lasted for several days, and we were poor as friars. We settled in a small inn at the center of the melee and were drinking ourselves into oblivion while wondering how we would pay the bill. William happened to look out of the window, and suddenly he jumped from his chair and rushed out the door without so much as a by-your-leave."

"There was no time." William laughed.

"We watched from the window," John continued, warming to his story. "To this day I cannot believe what I saw. A knight, we never did discover what side he was on," he observed with a chuckle, "had fallen and was about to be trampled beneath the destriers of the knights in combat about him. His leg was apparently broken and William, seeing the fall from the window, rushed out and pulled him from beneath those flailing hooves. Then, supporting the weight of his armor and that of the knight's, he threw him over his shoulder and carried him into the inn. He plopped him down onto the table between us and said, 'Here we are, lads, the ransom to pay our debts!' "

"What do you expect from a man who climbed a rope in full armor . . . " Beaumont chortled.

"I beg you," William held up a hand sheepishly. "Do not recount that one. As I recall, I caught hell from Henry . . . "

"What happened?" Cailin said, her eyes bright with interest, as she looked from one to the other.

"We were besieging a castle in Normandy," John pressed forward, oblivious to William's discomfort. "William could not wait for the ladders. He rushed forward as the ropes caught and pulled himself up the length of the wall. We arrived at the battlement to find that he had felled those along the wall, and he was sitting on an opponent . . . "

"I was tired." William shrugged with a slight smile. "But, enough of this," he added, seeking to change the subject. "It has been a long day."

Isabel frowned as she noted the weariness in William's voice. "What of the king?" she asked quietly.

"In spite of his understandable reluctance to sign the charter, I must admit that in the end he purported himself well," William said quietly. "However, upon our return to Windsor he went into a rage. He rolled about the floor, foaming at the mouth, shouting curses to everyone—a typical Plantagenet reaction. It took over an hour to calm him."

"What will he do now?" Isabel asked, watching William carefully, knowing that he would hide his deepest concerns.

"Time will tell," he said quietly. "John has a remarkable capacity for being a great administrator—but his lack of control reduces him to a petty tyrant, emotions ever ruling his judgment. And, I fear, he has surrounded himself with those who will but encourage the worst from him, blinding him to whatever reason he might possess."

"Can you not make him see reason?" Isabel asked, even knowing the answer.

William sighed deeply. "He will never trust anyone who is not totally dependent upon him. That is why he has surrounded himself with mercenaries. He knows that I will never be under his control. Nay, he will not trust me until the day comes when he has no one else."

# 26

WILL'S fingers played lightly over her shoulders as he stared into the darkened room, his thoughts already fixed on matters other than the woman in his bed. She turned and stretched against his hard length. Her hand slid over his chest as she sighed with contentment. "I should be going." she whispered. "It would not do for me to be found missing from my pallet. Cook would have a fair fit." When he did not answer, she rose up on an elbow and peered down at him in the dim light of the few candles still burning in his chamber. "Do you wish for me to leave?" she pouted.

He turned his head and looked at her for a long moment as if he was just realizing that she was still there. "Whatever you wish," he said casually, returning to his own thoughts.

"Do you wish for me to stay the night, milord?" she murmured, her hand seeking lower beneath the covers.

He jerked as she found her target, and he turned to grin at her. "I thought you were worried about cook."

"Let her find her own pleasure," she laughed softly, plying him with her expert fingers until she felt him respond. He shifted his weight and reached for her, drawing her under him as his mouth came down on hers in a brutal kiss. She moaned as her arms went about his neck, and she pulled him to her.

Much later, well sated, he rolled from her and threw himself from the bed. He pulled on a robe as he crossed to a table that held the pitcher of wine and goblets brought by his bedmate hours earlier. He poured himself a goblet and sank into a chair near the fire. Losing himself to his earlier thoughts, he was unaware when she left the bed and came to stand behind him. After a moment, she came about to stand before him, her hands on her hips and quite unconcerned with her nakedness as she regarded him coldly.

"May I gather that milord is through with me?" she asked, sulkily.

He looked up. His eyes passed over her slowly before his mouth drew into a wry smile. "Do you expect more?" he asked quietly. "There are coins on the table by the wardrobe. Take what you will."

Her eyes gleamed for a moment, and she crossed quickly to the table, where she took a fair measure. Slipping on her clothes, she returned to him. She picked up the pitcher of wine and refilled his goblet as she gifted him with a smile, feeling satisfied with herself and her evening's work. "Is there anything more I can do for you?"

He looked up and shrugged with a slight smile. "Nay, I assume we are both satisfied."

"Well . . . " She hesitated. "I am, milord. But I fear that you are not. What bothers you I fear I cannot help you with."

He glanced up at her again, and his mouth drew into a smile at her words. Suddenly, he grasped her wrist and pulled her onto his lap. "You are a wise wench." He laughed. "How is it that you are not married?"

"You said that I was wise, milord." She smiled, tossing the coins in her hand. "Would a stablehand or a serf bring me this?"

He threw back his head and laughed. "Point taken, lass!" His arms went about her waist and his voice lowered. "Keep me occupied while I am here and there shall be more."

She glanced at him from the corner of her eye, telling herself inwardly to hold her tongue, cursing herself for what she knew she would say even as she said it. What was there about him that made her care? "Why do you bother with the likes of me, when there is another who holds your heart, milord?"

He stiffened as his brow furrowed into a furious frown. "What are you talking about?"

"The reason that you are here," she tossed out, with a shrug of her shoulders. "The Convent of Saint Mary's, 'tis only a stone's toss away and . . ."

"That is none of your affair!" he snapped, withdrawing his arms as he reached again for his goblet.

"Of course it isn't," she said, watching him. "But everyone knows . . ."

"Enough!" he snapped, pushing her from his lap as he stood up. "You best leave."

"Aye, milord." She complied, grabbing up the remains of his supper dishes. She faced him as she turned to leave and watched him for a moment as he stood staring broodingly into the fire. "Happiness can be found when we think with our hearts," she said softly.

He turned to glare at her, but the door was closing behind her, leaving him to stare at its silent span for a long moment. He sank back into his chair, feeling suddenly bereft and lonely. Damn, he thought, pushing aside the unwanted feelings. What was the matter with him? Everything was happening as he wished it. His father was in Wales, commander in chief of the army driving itself against the southern Welsh, who were doing their part to divide the forces loyal to the crown. They had attacked Pembroke, assuring that William would be drawn into the fray. In so doing they had eliminated the one most feared as the confederation drove to complete their plans . . . soon John Plantagenet would no longer be king of England. Everything he had wished for. Then why was he so miserable?

His thoughts turned to the one sequestered but a few

miles from where he sat, and his mind filled with the memory of her large blue eyes, the raven hair that curled gently about her face. . . . Her laughter, the large pools of her eyes when they filled with tears. . . . He could feel her loneliness, her fear. . . . Restlessness filled him, and he rose from the chair and crossed to the window. The sky had begun to turn from black to grey, announcing the arrival of dawn. Soon she would be rising, he thought. Her day, he knew, would be much as the one before, and as tomorrow, and the next. Until . . .

Why had he come here? At first he had told himself that he was merely assuring himself of her well-being—for his mother's sake. Was it not natural for him to feel protectiveness for her, even extending to the babe?

Gradually, in the hours he spent with her, she began to trust him. Bit by bit, she told him of her past and, with growing horror, he began to understand the atrocities she had suffered under the hand of a heinous and demoniacal father.

Following each visit he found her filling his thoughts with increasing, and disturbing, regularity. It was compassion, nothing more, he reasoned. Yet, now he began to wonder, to question the emotions he was feeling.

His jaw tensed as he thought of the hours past. Twice while embracing the wench it was Levene's face who had forced itself into his thoughts. Nay! he thought irascibly, it was impossible! The relationship would never be allowed! His mouth suddenly twisted into a rapacious smile. On the other hand, he thought, nothing is impossible. He crossed to the wardrobe and pulled fresh garments from the closet, his mind set to its purpose.

He rode into the convent as the sun broke over the walls, melting the courtyard in a soft glow of morning. Sliding from his mount, he announced his arrival to a startled nun, who fled quickly to the Reverend Mother, leaving him to pace the small room where she had left him to wait. He paced anxiously as his mind, now set, raced with desperate thoughts. What if she would not come? What if she refused him? Finally he heard the sound of a door opening, and he spun about to find her standing there, her large blue eyes wide with surprise and question. He strode across the room and stopped before her, taking her hands in his as his gaze moved over her face, memorizing each feature before he drew her gently into his arms, and he murmured to her softly. "Levene, love."

Isabel paused and looked up from her ledgers. Leaning back in her chair, she rubbed her eyes with the tips of her fingers, feeling the strain of tension and worry. She sighed as she picked up her quill again and attempted to complete the work, but soon found herself staring, unseeing, at the unfocused columns of figures. He should be here soon, she reasoned, he had sent the message a fortnight ago.

It had been her duty to greet William upon his return from Wales with the knowledge that England was in chaos. That John was systematically laying waste to England in an effort to punish the barons who were disloyal to him. Encouraged by the pontiff's refusal to accept the Great Charter and the order from Rome for the barons to lay down their arms, John had thrown himself into action. The king surrounded himself with mercenaries, miscreants bearing the dubious names of Dennis the Damned and Mauger the Murderer. They claimed themselves to be Satan's Guards and had followed him about the breadth and length of England, seeking to dispel the barons who would revolt and who now found themselves without leadership. Stephen Langton had been recalled to Rome to answer to the pope's displeasure and it was unlikely that he would return soon.

John left behind him a blackened England as he cut his swath of revenge, setting to torch each residence where he had previously spent the night. Moving from Rochester to Scotland, his maddened mind was set upon revenge against those who had dared to confront him at Running-Mead. William, learning that the panicked barons had appealed to Philip of France for aid, had set sail immediately. Even as he prepared for departure, he had realized the futility of the gesture, but determined that the effort had to be made. He hoped to play upon Philip's fear of displeasing Rome, and thus Philip would forbid his son, Louis, from making claim to the English throne.

Isabel forced herself back to the long column of figures before her, finally able to draw comfort from her work as she had done for so many years, when she heard the sound of horses from without. Rising from her chair she crossed the Great Hall, greeting him as he entered from behind the passage screen. He pulled her into his arms and held her tightly. Turning his head he claimed her mouth in a deep, drawing kiss, comforting and warm. "I came as soon as I could. Ah, love, you do feel good," he whispered, kissing her again as she clung to him.

She drew him to the chairs near the fire, seeing to his comfort before she would allow him to tell her of his news. She was shocked by his appearance. There were heavy lines of fatigue about his face and a bitterness in his expression she had never seen before. She served him a meal herself, dismissing the servants as she saw to his needs. Settling into the chair next to him, she waited as he ate, holding her endless questions until he finally sat back in his chair with a heavy sigh. He glanced up at her with a hint of a smile. "The future does not appear so bleak when I am with you," he murmured, reaching out to trail a finger along the line of her cheek.

"Was it so bad?" she whispered, turning her head to lay a kiss on his palm.

"I have begun to think that humanity is basically mad," he answered as he reached for his goblet. "Philip and Louis put on quite a show. Their act was superior to any of the players you have brought to this hall, my love. Philip played the part of the great supporter of Rome, decrying the intent of his son, assuring all that by his life he would uphold the pope's command to let be! Louis played his part equally, claiming the throne of England for his wife, Blanche of Castile. He cried out that she was the true claimant to the throne, that John had forfeited his right when he murdered Arthur. Philip was so certain of his playacting before those attending the conference that at one point he turned to me and winked! He knew that there was nothing anyone could do, not even the pope's legate . . . I fear that we shall soon see Louis here . . . '' He turned to Isabel. ''What of the king? I traveled here so quickly that I have not had time to inquire.''

''The same,'' she sighed. ''He is somewhere in the north. No one knows exactly where he is, until the blackened evidence of his passing marks where he has been. But . . . there is other news . . . ''

He caught the hesitance in her voice, and his eyes narrowed as he then reached out to lay a hand over hers, where it rested on the arm of his chair. ''Do not fear to tell me, love. I would rather hear dire news from your lips than from any other's, as it is easier in the hearing.''

''I received word that the king has arranged for a conference between you and Will.''

''Indeed,'' William grunted, reaching to refill his goblet. ''He imagines that I will persuade my son to join us. When is it to be?''

''At your convenience. Aimery de Saint Maur, master of the Templars, will conduct him safely here. We need only send word of the time. Please, William, you must do this. For us, to mend this breach . . . ''

''Mend the breach?'' He glanced at her, his eyes a mixture of anger and sadness. ''You need not worry for your son, my love. For once I used my influence with Philip for personal reasons. I spoke in private with him before I left France, and he has assured me that Will shall be found in high favor should he be successful. And,'' he sighed, ''if John should succeed, I can promise you that Will shall come to no harm. In any case our son shall be safe—at least from all but me.''

She closed her eyes, thanking God that he had seen fit to answer her prayers. Opening them she once again regarded her husband. ''And what of you?'' she whispered. ''Will you be able to forgive him?''

''Do not ask me that question now, Isabel,'' he grumbled, looking into his goblet which he was slowly turning in his hands. "I cannot answer. Let us see what he can possibly say for himself." He placed the goblet on the table and stared at it for a long moment, then turned his head to look at her as a strange light crossed his eyes before he grinned. "Enough of this. There are other comforts I seek, milady, and I have ridden hard to find them."

She blinked, recognizing the look he was giving her. "Now?" she said dumbly.

"Now?" he repeated. "What is wrong with now? Is it too late, too early?" His eyes narrowed. "Are you having your flux?" he asked bluntly.

"Nay," she smiled, finding she could still blush after all these years. "But, you seem so exhausted, and worried . . ."

"Sweetheart," he grinned, rising from his chair as he offered her his hand. "Have you not learned yet that making love to you is the greatest comfort of all?"

"Aye," she returned with an arch to her brow. "For men it appears to be the cure-all."

"And what would you know of other men?" he asked, his own brow arching.

"Milord," she smiled sweetly, "we women do talk."

"Really?" he asked, suddenly interested as he looked down at her. "And what would Cailin be saying about John?"

"Oh, nay, milord!" she laughed softly. "Are you not the one who staunchly protests the gossip of women? Are you now seeking to lower yourself to that level? Really, William, you have always assured me that men never gossip!"

"We don't," he grunted. Then his mouth twisted into a grin. "We merely seek to mend notes of discord."

He swept her up into his arms and moved toward the stairs, pausing at the foot of the long span. Looking down at her, he sighed softly before he began his ascent. "As soon as our lives are settled once more, madam, you might look into the possibility of a room such as the one we have at Kilkenny. I recall that it saved much time—and effort on the part of your husband."

She nestled into his arms as he carried her to their chamber, drawing on the comfort and security he gave her. She nibbled at his ear as he carried her down the long hallway, drawing a grunt from him, then a reprimand as she continued her pursuit, followed by a threat of what was certain to happen to her somewhere in the shadowed recesses of Chepstow's corridors if she persisted.

"Is that a promise?" she murmured to his ear, bringing a soft chuckle from him as he finally pushed open the door to their chamber.

"Now then," he countered as he settled her onto the bed. "Is this not better than the stairwell or the pentice? Here we will not startle the servants nor the horses in the bailey."

"The horses in the bailey?" she chortled.

"I have known you to be somewhat—ah, boisterous in your pleasure, madam." He rolled his eyes as he began to rapidly discard his clothing.

"Do I detect a note of criticism, milord?"

"Hardly," he grinned, joining her on the bed as he began the removal of her garments. "Would I be the one to protest when my wife enjoys her pleasures—as long as I am the one to give them?"

"Give me pleasure now, William," she said, suddenly anxious. Their easy humor was pushed aside as she reached for him, everything forgotten in her need of him. "Oh, please."

"Isabel," he said softly, drawing back to look at her. "What is it?"

"I—I want another child, William," she murmured as her hand slipped about his neck.

"Is that not up to the fates?" He smiled gently at her as he pushed back her hair from her face.

"If you wish," she murmured, pulling him down to her.

He pulled back and stared at her oddly. "Isabel?" His thoughts moved quickly, calculating the births of their children. But for Will and Richard—and he had been gone from her those years—each were almost exactly two years apart. "Isabel, how did you manage it?" he asked, intrigued.

"We have our ways, milord. A sponge, dipped in herbs of. . . . Never mind, William." She looked up at him with concern. "You are not angry?"

"Of course not. It is your body that bears them. You have given me six beautiful children. And I have worried about you; I will not see you as I have seen others, worn out from childbearing. In fact, I have kept myself from you when I thought you most likely to quicken, fearing that you would come to child each year. I would not have that for you."

"We do seem to be fruitful." She smiled up at him.

"But you are telling me now that I have been over-cautious? You could have told me," he chided her. "It could have saved me much misery—in more ways than one."

"Nay, love, you did not sacrifice for naught. The sponges do not always work by themselves. I have been aware of your concern, and it has meant much to me. But now, William, I wish—I want another. It is time."

"But why now?" he asked gently.

"Sybil is three . . . " she shrugged her shoulders.

"Isabel." He stopped her and turned her face to him. "Why now?"

She looked up at him in the dim light of the fire and her eyes filled with tears. "Oh, William," she said softly. "So much is happening, perhaps the end of much of what we know. I need—I need the feeling of new life within me. Life only you can give me. Something to hold, should . . . "

He laid a finger on her lips, keeping her from completing her thought. "Shush. Nothing is going to happen," he whispered. He bent down, his lips replacing his fingers as he claimed her mouth, drawing her deeply into a kiss which drew breath from her.

She gasped, moaning against his mouth as she pressed her body against his. Her arms slipped about the broad span of his chest as she pulled him to her. "Oh, please, William, help me to forget."

\*   \*   \*

In spite of the king's urgency, almost three months passed before the fated meeting between William and his son. William had delayed the event as long as possible, using the time to his advantage in the hope that Will would come to his senses. They met at Tintern Abbey, the presence of the good brothers lending a stable influence to the hostility felt between father and son. William arrived late in the morning, his shrewd eyes instantly measuring the forces Will had brought with him. Knights and men-at-arms in Will's colors and those of the Knight's Templars lounged restlessly about the grounds of the abbey, coming to attention at the arrival of the marshal of England and his company of two hundred knights and Irish kerns. He was met by Aimery de Saint Maur, the stark white of his surcoat emblazoned with a red cross, in startling contrast to his darkly tanned face and his deceptively gentle countenance. The enormously built master of Templars greeted William with a grin and a hearty clasp of their wrists.

"It is good to see you, William," he offered sincerely. "We missed you sorely in Acre."

"That was long ago." William returned the greeting, truly gladdened to see the knight once again, they having spent many pleasurable hours together in earlier years. "I am grieved that it is you who must perform this duty."

"Do not feel so, my lord earl. I deem it an honor to do whatever I can to help to mend this breach."

"I am not overly optimistic, Aimery, and you should not be. Where is he?"

"Inside." The knight jerked his head toward the abbey. "He is having a bad case of nerves, though he does well to hide it."

"He should have them," William said grimly.

"He has impressed me greatly, William," the knight added as his eyes narrowed speculatively. William's expression had turned stony as he stared at the abbey. "You should be proud of him."

"So I have been told." William gritted his teeth as he

began up the sloping hill to the large stone structure looming over him, the deep shadows it cast matching his mood.

William met with his son in a large room in the north wing. The brothers had provided a light meal and beverage before they silently retired in tactful deference to the two men who stood regarding each other in studied appraisal. Glancing down at the meal set on the table between them, William pulled out a chair and settled himself. "I am famished. You can watch me eat or join me," he said, reaching to fill their tankards.

Will sank into the chair across from him and reached for his tankard, but he only toyed with it, turning it in his hands as he regarded his father, who had helped himself to a generous portion of venison. "I believe that the purpose of this visit is to provide us with the opportunity for a magnificent reconciliation; the outcome to be that I shall see the errors of my ways and return to the fold, as it were, dedicating my sword and spurs to the name of Marshal and to my sovereign."

"I was not aware that you had forsaken the name of Marshal," William said, his mouth full of bread.

Will picked up a slice of the venison, taking a bite as he regarded his father carefully. "I would think that you would be the first to accuse me."

"Because you follow your own course?" William washed down the bread with his wine. "Then I am guilty of same and should similarly be condemned. My father supported Mathilda while I was for the son. And *neither* were on the throne," he added. William's eyes glinted with amusement as he swished his fingers in a bowl of rosewater before helping himself to a tart of blackberries.

"Then why are we here?" Will asked.

"You said it yourself. John would see you by my side."

"Then you support my actions?" Will regarded his father with disbelief, as his expression became filled with guarded hope.

William leaned back in his chair, and when he again

spoke his voice had hardened. "I support your right to follow a path that differs from my own. I support your right to fight for what you believe in. But to the matter of placing Louis of France on the throne of England, you will find me on the opposite side of the field. When my father supported Mathilda, and I, Henry, neither of us had given our oath to King Stephen. When a knight pledges his oath, he pledges his honor. Without honor your coat of arms are *vale proditor* and your honor lost. When you took your knight's vows, you pledged that oath to John Plantagenet. Do you recall the words you said? 'I become thy man of such tenement to be holden of thee, to bear to thee the faith of like and member and earthly worship against all men who live and can die . . . ' He alone, Will, is your suzerain."

"You have taken both Philip and John as yours!" Will snapped, rising from the chair.

"Philip is my suzerain for my holdings in Normandy," William said with control. "But in all matters English, I am John's man."

"All matters?" Will spun back on him, his eyes blazing with anger. "What of the Great Charter. You helped to write it! What of your dealings in Ireland—all against the king's interest! What of Normandy—you are one of the few English barons who still retains lands there—and by your friendship to Philip, not John!"

"In each of the cases to which you refer the law has been strictly adhered to, as you well know. I helped Langton with the charter to save John's throne and avoid a civil war; my disputes in Ireland were with Meiler, never in open conflict with the king; and as for Normandy, my oath was given to Philip with John's consent. But then, you know all of this." His eyes narrowed as he regarded his son with a deep sadness. "Will, why do you hate John so?" He held up a hand. "Nay, do not tell me the obvious. I am all too aware of John's faults. It goes much deeper than that. What happened to you during those years at court?"

Will's eyes turned hard and his mouth twisted with disgust. "Happened?" He gave a quick laugh, a hard, brutal sound that made William wince inwardly. "Ah, I see. You would like for me to tell you of some devastating experience, a happenstance that changed my life, causing me to forever seek revenge upon John Plantagenet. Well, you will be disappointed. I simply lived there, observed, experienced the court of our king. He never laid a hand on me, oh, except one time when I had spilled a bowl of fruit and received a cuffing . . . nay, the king was quite solicitous. In fact, he so enjoyed my company that he kept me with him continuously. Through his rages, his pleasures—whatever had struck his momentary fancy—or whoever had struck his interest. Aye, I came to know John Plantagenet very well. Well enough to know that he is the wrong man for England."

William envisioned what his son must have seen, kept at John's side, a pet for the whims of the king—or as revenge against the boy's sire. He felt rage well up in him, but he fought it down, knowing that the moment must be met with calm. "Will, I cannot change the events of your boyhood any more than I can change mine. What we have lived, experienced, must be drawn upon to make us stronger if we are to survive with principles intact. You are a man now, and you will be called upon to answer as a man. If you flaunt the laws that have been made for us to live by, what shall your code be? Those you make for yourself? How will you answer the next man who has chosen to do the same, though he be in conflict with you. We have worked to change the laws, Will, both of us—"

"You mean the charter?" Will said with contempt. "And where is it now? The pope has annulled it! So much for the law!"

"Patience, Will. I do not believe that the charter is lost. But it will not be regained by a civil war, or under the hands of Louis! Now, more than ever, the barons must unite under an English banner."

"I will never raise my banner for John Plantagenet!" Will reaffirmed, waving his hands against his father's words.

"We have not much more time," William sighed, rising from his chair. "Will you at least think about what I have said?"

"If you will give me the same courtesy," Will answered sullenly.

"I imagine I will think of little else," William rejoined. He took his cloak from a chair where he had tossed it upon entering the room and pulled it about his shoulders.

Will had turned away from him to stare from the window at some distant vista, but he turned as his father would have left the room. "I have been in the north for some time and have heard little of news of home. I assume that everyone is well?"

"Aye, and everyone misses you," William returned. "Your mother sends you her love, and Matilda has been pining for her eldest brother. She has been driving Richard to distraction."

"Give her a hug for me." Will grinned. "And tell Richard to be patient. Soon our little sister's thoughts will turn to lads other than big brothers." He paused for a moment, hesitating uncomfortably. "What of Levene?" he asked offhandedly. "How does she fare?"

William sighed deeply as he tied the lacings of the cloak at his throat. "Have you had no letters from your mother, then?"

"Nay, I have been moving about, and they have not caught up to me."

"I fear that the lass is gone, Will," he said softly. "It is such a pity . . . "

"Gone?" Will paled. "What do you mean? Where did she go?"

"She's . . . " William frowned at the way Will was looking at him, and he stirred uncomfortably, something odd about the way Will had asked the question. "She is dead, Will," he said gently. "She did not survive the birth of the child."

"Dead?" Will repeated. He stared at William with horror, and his jaw worked as he opened his mouth to speak, then closed it again. He turned away to the window, gripping the casing with his fingers, which turned white from the intenseness of his grip.

"Will." Worried, William took a step toward his son. "Are you all right? I had no idea you felt this way about the girl."

"I am fine." Will grimaced. "Please. Let me be."

William hesitated, his heart heavy for what he realized his son was suffering while knowing there was no way to help him. He crossed to the door, but as he placed his hand on the latch, Will stopped him.

"What of the child?"

William shook his head. Will nodded slightly and turned back to the window as William left, closing the door quietly behind him.

Isabel listened quietly as William recounted the few hours spent with their son. She was curled up on a cushion on the hearth, a greying Shad purring softly in her lap while Trac slept peacefully at William's feet, age having brought the two opponents to an understanding of tolerance. "I can pray that he will come to understand the dangerous path he takes," William sighed wearily. "And that he will not be forced to pay for mistakes of youth for the remainder of his life. But I fear that his hatred of the king will fuel the decisions he now makes."

Isabel's eyes filled with anger as she thought of her little son the victim of John Plantagenet's whims, the things he must have been forced to do, to see. . . . Her own hatred of the king flamed her imaginings, and she had to swallow before she could speak. "What will he do now?"

"I imagine he will bide his time in the north until an answer has come from Philip." William glanced uncomfortably at his wife. "He asked about Leven," he added quickly. "Isabel, I fear that the lad was in love with her."

Isabel started and her face paled. "Are you certain?"

"As certain as you would have been had you seen his reaction."

"Oh, Sweet Mother," she whispered. "How much is he expected to carry?"

"Isabel, most of what he has done has been by his own making."

"Aye, that is true. As with us all."

"It will either break him—or make a man of him," he said. "But we are going to survive, Isabel. Even Will."

"Survive?" she repeated, sniffing back the tears as she smiled up at him. "Aye, milord," she agreed. "We will do that."

# 27

On May 22 the fleet of Louis of France appeared off the Kentish coast near Sandwich. John Plantagenet had rallied his pitiful force on the shore, fully convinced that he could repel the mightier army. William rode into the English camp as dawn rose over the Channel behind the ships of the invading army. He was intent upon making his sovereign see reason, knowing that the future of England rested upon his power of persuasion with a king who had gone mad. He dismissed those attending the king with a look that brooked no argument, sending them scurrying from the royal tent, and faced John's raving alone. Surprisingly, the king's temper was quickly modified, evidence of his defeat in the slump of his ample shoulders and the pouting scowl that he presented to his marshal.

"You must retire, Sire, and quickly," William began reasonably. "Your army . . . " he used the word cautiously, "is uncertain. Their pay is seriously delinquent. Moreover they are, almost to a man, of French descent. I must question their loyalty should they be put to the test against Louis's forces."

John brooded. He stared at some distant spot in his

tent. "What is to happen, Marshal? Is there no one loyal to his sovereign?"

William fought back his contempt for this man, who had been given so much, whose talents could have brought him to greatness, but whose innate suspicions and mistrust of those most loyal to him had destroyed it all. "I am here, Sire," he answered, "and there are others upon whom you may depend. But you must not delay, Your Grace, Louis will be here within the hour."

John Plantagenet fled the Kentish coast, and Louis entered England against meager resistance. He entered London on June 2, then advanced to Winchester, easily taking the castle as the king of England retired into the west. William returned to Chepstow to bide his time as he reinforced his armies in the western regions and watched for Louis's next move. When word reached him that Louis had made Will marshal of the court, concerned eyes turned to William for his reaction. Upon receiving the news, William merely grinned as he tossed the parchment on the vacant table and returned to his meal. "Let the pup enjoy his illusions," he laughed. However, a short time later word arrived that William did not dismiss. An event that spelled the beginning of the end to Will's venture as a supporter of Louis of France.

The first few days of July proved hot and muggy, leaving those at Chepstow lethargic and prone to laziness. A cold supper had been taken in the solar and William was entertaining Matilda and a wiggling Gilbert with a game of merels so as to allow Isabel some moment to herself. She sat nearby fanning herself with a letter from Elizabeth Marshal in an attempt to repel the oppressive heat of the late afternoon. "Elizabeth has offered an interesting notion," she mused. "Do you think that now that Innocent is dead that Stephen Langton will find favor with the new pope?"

"From his last letter I conclude that he no longer is considering joining the order of Carthusians," he answered with a grin. "Though I never gave that threat much credence. It is the most fanatically rigid of the monastic orders, and I cannot see Stephen as part of it. However, I fear that he will not regain favor with the new pope. I doubt that he will ever be forgiven for what he did here. He will probably spend the rest of his life in Rome. Matilda, you are not paying attention, that was a poor move.''

"Then he will never see England again," she mused. "How very sad, for his heart is here."

"Father, is it true that the king has lost England's treasury?" Matilda said suddenly, her thoughts giving evidence to William's suspicions about the game. "It is said that he lost it while crossing The Wash. Is it true?"

William started at the question. "Where did you hear this, Matilda?" he queried. "I had just learned of it myself."

"I overheard John talking to Ralph." She shrugged. "Is it true?"

"Aye, it is true." William shook his head, still unable to believe it himself. "The sword of Tristan, the crown, orb, and scepter of England, along with the treasury, all lost into the muds washing into the North Sea. The king removed it from Winchester when threatened by Louis's arrival and dispersed it among the monasteries throughout England for safekeeping. Until recently —when he ordered that it all be brought to him."

"But why?" she asked, puzzled as to why the king would do such a thing. Even in her young mind it seemed irrational.

"The king has not been well," William offered, moving his piece on the board.

"William," Isabel admonished. "The girl has a mind as quick as your sons. She deserves a fair answer. Gilbert, put your father's playing piece back on the board. Answer her truly. The king has lost whatever reason he had."

Matilda's brow furrowed as she considered her mother's statement. "I know that he has not been the best of sovereigns, but at least he remained within England. King Richard spent only six months here the entire time he was king. He could not have cared much for us—but people say he was wonderful.''

William's eyes widened at the depth of his daughter's statement, and he smiled, adding a new respect to the intense love he felt for her. ''Your mother has her prejudices, love.'' He grinned, glancing at Isabel, who threw him a nasty look. ''But you are most astute and have touched upon the heart of the matter. John's heart is with England, where Richard's never was. John has, on occasion, shown brilliance as an administrator. But while both had great faults, Richard was able to effect that which John never could; he gave the people an image of greatness. While John showed the mettle of a petty tyrant, Richard was the glorious warrior. He gave the people something to be proud of, and for that they forgave him his shortcomings.''

''While the king gives them nothing to focus upon except his faults.'' She looked at him steadily as she considered his words, turning them over to reason.

''Exactly.'' He smiled.

''Then it is more important for a king to appear great than to be so.''

''Well—not exactly.'' His brows furrowed at her logic as he tried to ignore Isabel's chuckle. ''He should be both.''

''Actually, it seems to me that, in this event, the people are correct in their estimation of the king,'' Matilda continued, with a brow furrowed deeply in serious thought. ''Aside from his ineptness as a military leader he is a lecher, forever demanding unreasonable considerations from the ladies at court. I heard that he required the payment of two hundred chickens from the wife of Hugh Neville so that she might leave him to lie with her husband for one night.''

There was a collective gasp from Isabel and William at their daughter's casual comment, but before either could respond Isabel's attention was drawn to the doors.

''William,'' Isabel said as she rose from her chair. ''Someone is coming.''

On her words a greatly agitated John d'Erley burst

into the hall. "John, I thought you had left to . . . " William paused before John's barely controlled alarm. "What is it?"

"William, I rode as quickly as I could," he breathed heavily as he attempted to catch his breath. "I intercepted a rider at the border to Striguil, and thought I should bring word myself. William . . . Will has attacked Worcester."

John d'Erley shifted his eyes to William. He wished he could have seen William's expression beneath the shadows of his helm and could know what he was thinking. He had followed William's gaze to the portcullis of the town as they crossed beneath the gate, and he had silently blessed the saints that no bodies hung from the parapets and no heads were spiked at the walls. They would have been insults against William's possessions that he would have been unable to forgive—even to his son. William had left his forces beyond the city walls, where they ringed Worcester in an unmistakable force under the direction of Musard and Avenel. He brought with him into the city only his personal guard and Beaumont, who had insisted upon facing his former squire. The small party moved slowly along the narrow cobbled street of the town, approaching the square. The only sound heard was the sharp click of the hooves of the destriers as they struck stone, and the sound echoed against the buildings lining the passage. Hands rested upon hilts of swords, as yet undrawn upon William's orders, while the eyes of the knights moved about the closely set buildings for signs of ambush.

The street suddenly widened into a large square set before a large church, which dominated the smaller dwellings to the east and west. Grimly, William noted that the square was filled with armed knights and men-at-arms interspersed with Will's colors and that of Louis of France. Will stood at the top of the stairs leading into the church, his manner apparently relaxed as he watched William's approach.

William pulled Horse to a halt before his son and was

aware of John and Beaumont, who had stopped to pull their mounts to face away from him, as did Allan, who protected his back. William regarded his son silently for a moment, then pulled Horse's head about so that he was abreast of the welcoming committee on the stairs. He leaned his arms on the pommel of the saddle and gestured for Will to come forward. Will hesitated for a moment, then descended the steps slowly as William reached up to scratch under his visor as he stared at the ground.

When Will came into his view, William leaned down so that no one beyond their small group could hear him. "Will," he said quietly. "Leave the city and take those damn French with you."

"I am in possession, milord," Will said through gritted teeth. "I claim this city in the name of Louis of France."

"Will," William continued, again scratching the itch that was plaguing him. "Worcester is mine. I suggest you leave."

"Nay, milord," Will said obstinately.

"Hmmm." William paused. "I see. Well now. You have, by my estimate, two, perhaps three hundred at your back. I, on the other hand, have over seven hundred beyond the walls and can summon more with little effort. I ask you to consider carefully what your decision should be." He stretched, rubbing his back for a moment, and did not miss the grin Beaumont wore though the knight had not taken his eyes from those lining the west wall. Leaning down once again, he turned his head to look at his son. "Will, there is no disgrace in retreat when it is the only reasonable recourse. I shall withdraw now, and on the morrow I shall reenter the city—one way or the other. I suggest that you be gone."

"It would have been quite a coup had he pulled it off," John said, grinning. He was pacing slowly about the war tent with a tankard in his hand.

Ralph Musard, who was slumped in a chair at the trestle table centered in the tent, shook his head. "Pah.

There is no way he could have done it with that meager excuse for an army. He did well to flee.''

Beaumont looked across at Musard and frowned thoughtfully. He glanced at William, who was stretched out on his pallet with an arm propped behind his head as he stared at the roof of the tent. "I agree that Will knew he could not hold out against our forces; moreover he knew that we would come.''

"Then he was a fool,'' Musard countered, as he lifted his tankard.

"Will is no fool,'' Beaumont responded as he struggled to hold his temper. "No one knows that lad better than I . . .''

"Nor has more face to lose should he display ineptness in such matters . . .'' Musard drawled.

"You are braying like an ass, Musard!'' Beaumont shouted, his face reddening as he half rose from his chair. Musard countered by rising to meet the angered knight.

"Enough!'' William roared.

Reluctantly, the two knights lowered themselves back into their chairs as William rose from the pallet. He ran his fingers through his hair in a gesture of frustration as he regarded the two, who were still glaring at each other. "I'll tolerate no bickering between you,'' he snapped. "Particularly on the matter of my son. Whatever you think of him, Ralph, he is my heir and the day will come, should you outlive me, when he will be your liege lord and will demand your fealty.'' His brow arched as he regarded Musard keenly. "Will you be able to give it to him?'' he asked softly.

Musard shifted uncomfortably. "Has it come to a pass when we may not voice our thoughts, milord? Would you question my loyalty?''

"To me—never, Ralph. But to my son? That answer can come only from you.''

"I cannot condone his loyalty to Louis!'' Musard answered, his voice rising. "I have tried, William, but I cannot! Can you?''

"Aye.'' William smiled. "Today I have.'' He laughed

at the stunned looks of the other three men. "Beaumont was correct—Will knew we would come. As I watched him ride from the city this morning with that pitiful group of French men-at-arms, it occurred to me, as it has to Beaumont, that he was not a fool. So then, why? Then I considered what I would do, were I ordered by Louis to attack my father's holdings . . ."

"That's it!" John exclaimed, suddenly seeing William's reasoning. "Louis ordered him to attack you—as a test of his loyalty, or in the hope that you will not throw your forces against your own son. Will, who cannot refuse, takes only a small force with him, knowing full well that he will be forced to retreat upon the appearance of a larger force—thus he keeps his honor and his oath to Louis!"

"He never had any intention of fighting you!" Beaumont beamed, relief showing in his well-lined face.

"That is my guess," William answered, glancing at Musard, who looked less than convinced. "Only time will prove it out, but for the moment I choose to give Will the benefit of the doubt."

"Well," John grinned, reaching for the flagon on the table. "That settles the matter as far as I am concerned. Shall we . . ."

His words were never finished, as the tent flap flew back and Nicolas Avenel entered with John Marshal, William's nephew. "John!" William exclaimed, with obvious pleasure. "I thought you were in Newark with the king . . . !" His words froze in his throat as he realized that John was in a state of near exhaustion. "Sit down," he ordered. "Beaumont, pour some ale . . ."

"Milord," John Marshal gasped, startling William by falling to one knee before him and clasping the edge of his surcoat. "Milord," he repeated. "The king . . . the king is dead."

William stared at him. His ears roared, as if filled with a great force of rushing water, and for a moment all other senses seemed to stop. He was the first to recover as he turned to find the others in a similar condition, and he snapped at Nicolas to raise John to a chair.

He poured a tankard, handing it to his nephew as his eyes darted again to the others. While their expressions were filled with a mixture of horror and shock, he knew they had regained their reason, and he turned back to John Marshal. "How?" he asked quietly.

"I—I do not know for certain," the young man choked. He drew from his ale to ease his dry throat, then looked up at William miserably. "Some say he was poisoned—that the blood of a toad was put into his wine. Others say it was a fever . . ."

"What do you say?" William asked firmly.

"I do not know," he groaned. "But I believe that when the treasury sank into The Wash he gave up his heart. He knew then that all was lost. I—" he turned his eyes to William. "I think he wanted to die."

William sighed. "John never would realize that his wealth was in men, not coin. The loss of England's treasury would signal the end of hope for him . . ." William turned slowly. Suddenly he struck the table with his fist. "Damnation!" he roared. "Damn him! To leave England now when she can spare him the least! He fled from everything, all of his life! And now, when Louis is here, to leave England in the hands of . . ." His tirade ceased and his face drained of color as he spun back on his nephew. "The prince," he gasped. "Where is the prince?"

"Wiltshire, milord." The young knight hesitated. "The king's body is being brought to Saint Wulstan for interment. Thomas de Sanford has ridden to bring young Henry forth. It was felt that he should be removed from his mother's influence as quickly as possible. We are all aware that the queen would stop at nothing to grasp power through the child." He hesitated again as he glanced at the others before looking back to William. "Milord, I have been sent to repeat the king's dying words to you. . . ." He cleared his throat and slipped from the chair to kneel before William, his eyes bright with his purpose. "His words were these . . . 'Lords, I must die. I cannot resist this disease. For the love of God, beg the marshal to forgive me the wrongs I have done him, for I repent them fully. He has always served me loyally, and he has never acted against me no matter what I did or said to him. For God's sake, lords, pray him to pardon me. As I am more sure of his loyalty than that of any other man, I ask you to entrust to him the care of my son, who will never succeed in holding his lands unless by his aid.' "

William stared at him for a long moment, then slowly raised his eyes to the others, who were watching expectantly, their expressions filled with amazement. William turned from his nephew, who had risen to his feet, and he gripped the edge of the table as he bowed his head in anguished thought.

"William," John d'Erley said quietly. "Will you accept the guardianship of Prince Henry?"

Slowly, painfully, the words came out. "Accept? How can I not? If all should forsake him . . ." He raised his head to look at the others. "I would carry him on my shoulders, isle to isle, from land to land, and would never fail him. Nay, even though I had to beg my bread."

He rallied then and straightened as his thoughts filled with the matters at hand and what needed to be done. "John," he directed to d'Erley. "Choose two messengers and ten knights to ride with each of them. They must be ready to leave within the hour." To Beaumont and Musard, "Order that camp shall be broken before first light. We ride first to Saint Wulstan and to the king. And for you, John," he turned to his nephew, "go with Beaumont, he will make a place for you in his tent. You look as if you could use some rest."

When the others had left he set to his writing materials, not trusting the messages he intended to another, even the faithful Father Delano. If they fell into the wrong hands, he wanted no one accountable but him. When John returned with the chosen messengers he was sealing the last message with his ring, pressing it into the softened wax. He rose, handing one to the first of the men. "This goes to my son. John will tell you where he is likely to have gone. Give it to no other. If you are waylaid, you are to destroy it—even to your life." From the look of determination in the man's face William knew John had chosen well, and he turned to the other. "You will carry this to the countess, telling her that a contingent of knights will follow. She is to go with them, leaving all others at Chepstow."

When the knights had left, John d'Erley turned to William. "Why do you send knights for her? She has sufficient . . ."

"Chepstow's vassals will need to remain where they are," William said, gritting his teeth. "I have told her to prepare the keep for siege upon her departure as well as sending riders to our other holdings with the same message." He turned to John and smiled grimly. "We must reach Henry before Louis learns of John's death."

"Then perhaps we should not delay for the funeral," John offered.

"I must have a moment to speak with the barons, who will assemble. Sanford can be trusted to do his best. If we are quick, we should have just enough time."

"May I ask . . ." John hesitated.

"Anything," William said. "You know that, ask."

"Why the message to Will?"

"The king is dead." William shrugged. "It is time to discover where Will's loyalties truly lie. If, upon the news, he remains with Louis, then we shall know."

"And if he tells Louis of John's death?"

The two men exchanged a long look. "Then he is no longer my son," William answered quietly.

John Plantagenet's body was interred in the church of Saint Wulstan in great pageant and ceremony. His large body lay in repose, clad in the white robes with the red cross of a crusader. The irony of his choice of robes, chosen before his death, was not lost on those present. Immediately after, a meeting of the barons was held which proved ultimately successful, as William's power of persuasion confirmed their loyalties to the young prince. Messages were sent from the meeting to assemble a council at Gloucester. The next morning, as dawn broke, William set out with a large company toward

Wiltshire to meet with the future king of England.

The dawn had broken with leaden skies as the heavens released an icy mist that clung about the group of riders. Their breaths added to the heavy fog along with that of their mounts as the destriers continuously shook their massive heads to rid them of the moisture that gathered about their ears and eyes. By midday the sun reluctantly made its appearance as they reached the large meadow near Malmesbury. William raised his hand, bringing the long column to a halt as he spied a group of riders approaching. As they neared the center of the meadow he could make out the slight form of a boy riding with a knight. He urged his mount forward while snapping an order to John to accompany him while instructing the others to remain where they were.

The shrill cicadas kept uneven measure with the rustling rhythm of the destriers as they moved slowly through the tall grasses toward the prince's party. They met at the center of the meadow. The prince, looking small and vulnerable, sat mounted in the arms of his old retainer, Rulf of Saint-Samson, boldly prepared to meet the marshal of England. The large blue eyes of the nine-year-old betrayed the brave set to his body and flickered with a moment of fear. He regarded the large man who sat looking down at him with eyes that appeared to the child as fierce and angry beneath the shadows of his helm. The boy's chin quivered slightly as he began to speak, though his young voice carried to those with him. "Sir, you are welcome. I give myself to God and to you. May God give you his grace so that you may guard me well."

William was unable to respond as he regarded the young prince, so obviously frightened yet facing, with courage, whatever was to come. The thought passed swiftly through his mind that this child had not known what would greet him. The hatred and strain of betrayal that ran throughout the baronage for his father would most certainly give cause for him to doubt his future. A quick sword thrust and it would be over. Even at such a tender age, like thoughts must be passing through his mind, William thought. And he did not doubt for a moment that Queen Isabella's viper's tongue had taken its effect upon the child. He noted the pathetic circlet of gold set upon the child's head, and he almost smiled. Strange, the things one thinks of at such a moment, he mused. It looked oddly like a woman's torc, or necklet. He shook his mind free of the thought and he dismounted. Ignoring the surprise on the child's face, he knelt in the grass of the meadow, and removing his helm he looked up at the prince. His voice was solemn as he spoke. "Sire, by my soul I shall do what I can to serve you in good faith and with all of my powers."

The prince's mouth dropped open slightly and his eyes grew wide, as if unable to believe that the marshal was actually paying homage to him. He glanced up at Saint-Samson, and he saw that his old retainer was overcome as he unashamedly wiped away tears with the corner of his sleeve. He turned back to the marshal, who had remounted and was now waiting. "Where are we to now, my lord of Pembroke?" he asked, gaining his courage.

"To Gloucester, Sire," William answered. "Your barons await."

The boy nodded with a seriousness far beyond his tender years, and they rode to join the others. From the corner of his eye William again noticed the circlet about the boy's forehead. "Your—ah, coronet, Sire," William observed. "It is unusual."

"It is my mother's." The boy shrugged. He glanced up at William and a tentative smile crossed his attractive features. "When word reached us that you would be coming, we . . . she could find nothing suitable for a crown and took this in its stead. It is one of her favorite torcs."

The two men burst out in laughter, to be joined by the prince, at first with a giggle then a chortle, easing the tenseness of the small group as they rode toward the company of bemused knights who awaited them.

# 28

IT was dark before they rode into the bailey at Gloucester keep. The large doors were opened wide by the porters, and the light from within spilled over the party as they dismounted. William lifted the prince from his saddle. As he set him onto the ground, he pulled the boy's gown straight and checked his appearance. The child's blond Plantagenet beauty was marred by the tight set to his jaw and the paleness of his face as his large blue eyes turned up to the top of the stairs and the men who were waiting for him. Seeing the boy's dismay, William laid a hand on the small shoulder and bent to his ear. "Be of good heart. Within the keep there are only those who wish you well, and I am at your side."

As they entered the hall a deafening cheer of "Fiat!" rose from the gathering. The enthusiasm and warmth of the oath was missed by the boy as he jumped at the sudden outburst. William felt Henry start beneath his hand, and he squeezed the boy's shoulder gently. Henry looked up at him and smiled tentatively, then broke into a broad grin as William winked at him. William slipped his hand to the boy's back and ushered him to a chair set by the hearth. Standing by his side, he watched with a shrewd eye as each of the barons came forward. Kneeling before him, each took the hands of the prince into theirs, and they gave their oath, in turn to receive the kiss of peace from their young prince. William watched carefully; his ears were tuned for a voice carrying something less than expected, his eyes observing those who bent before Henry for a flickering note of betrayal.

The prince stifled a yawn as the last of the barons came forward, and his small shoulders slumped with fatigue. He glanced up at William, who smiled gently at him and then his fair brow furrowed with puzzlement as William nodded to someone beyond him. He turned to find a beauteous lady rising from a deep curtsy before him. Her eyes were gentle and full of understanding as she smiled at him. "Sire," she said softly. "It has been a long day for you. I have come to see you to your bed."

"My Lady Isabel, Countess of Pembroke," William offered, leaning down to the prince. "You may go safely with her. Sleep well, Your Grace, I shall be here if you should need me."

"My love, you look exhausted." Isabel rubbed William's shoulders as she stood behind his chair in the privacy of their chambers. Her fingers sought the tense muscles of his neck and shoulders, pushing with a firm gentleness until she could feel them relax.

"Was he well settled?" William asked, his head rolling back to the pleasure of her touch.

"He was frightened," she sighed. "Such courage for one so young. Perhaps now, for the first time, I can realize what happens to those who become king. So much responsibility is placed upon them, so much they are expected to understand, to give to us, when they are but children. Small wonder that they become—distorted. I tucked him into bed even as he protested the attention, declaring that it was quite unnecessary. Yet his voice quivered, his chin trembled even with his protests. I sat on the bed and drew him into my arms and—he cried. He cried, William. It was some time before he slept.''

"That is the reason I sent for you, love," he murmured as he closed his eyes and relaxed under her attentions. "A woman's touch," he sighed.

"Whatever will happen to him?" she asked, her gaze fixed sightlessly as her fingers moved against his shoulders. "Even his own mother does not truly love him. She has never had time for him—until now."

"He will become king," he said shortly. He drew away from her hands and rose from the chair abruptly, rolling his shoulders wearily as he turned to her.

"Isabella will attempt to rule in his stead," she observed. "And someone must, he is only a child."

He looked at her oddly for a moment, then turned to a nearby table to pour himself a goblet of wine.

"That is not watered," she warned him.

"Perhaps it will help me to sleep," he countered, drawing from the goblet.

She watched him for a moment, her eyes narrowing as she sensed there was something he was not telling her. She had not lived with him for all of these years for nothing. "William?" Her whole being tensed as she posed the question. "Who shall rule in his stead?"

His eyes shifted to her, and a crooked smile pulled at his mouth, almost sheepishly. "Those below have suggested that I should do so."

Even as she had sensed the answer he would give, she was stunned by his reply. She took a deep breath and let it out slowly, then her own mouth drew into a smirk. "How far below?" she asked with an arch to her brow.

"Not as far as you are suggesting," he chuckled. "Only to the hall. I know. I too was stunned by the suggestion."

Seeing his turmoil she realized suddenly that he was actually considering the offer. She was frightened. The offer was dazzling, overwhelming. But she felt intense pride too. There was no doubt in her mind that there was no other more suited for the responsibility. But she was fully aware of what it would mean to their lives, and to him, physically and emotionally, should he accept the regency.

"D'Erley, John Marshal, Beaumont, and Musard met with me privately," he shrugged. "Only Beaumont was silent, drawing immediately into his cups. I fear that he is totally unable to accept the prospect. My dear nephew extolled upon the honors to the family, as could be expected. Ralph centered upon the gains to those close to me; the coin seems most dear to him," William laughed shortly. "Where he deems they will come from I have no idea."

"And John?" she asked.

"John advised against it," he said soberly, sighing deeply. "I suspect that he is correct. He alone pointed out what I fear most—the difficulties it would place on our lives, the drain to our resources."

"What did you say to them?"

He turned to her and smiled. "I told them that the only thing to do at this point was to go to bed."

She laughed as she crossed to him to undo the lacings on his surcoat. "Most wise, milord. It is certainly a matter to sleep on."

He pulled her into his arms, bending to kiss her ready mouth. "Not only to sleep on," he murmured. "I reason that pleasant distractions are called for."

"Milord," she parried huskily as she lifted the surcoat from his shoulders. "Do you rush to escape to the warmth of my bed when you are offered the administration of England? What can a mere woman offer to compare to that?"

"Everything," he murmured as he pressed his face into the bend of her neck, bringing a moan from her as his lips began to probe. "Your bed brings me comfort and ease, release, gentleness, passion—this . . ."

Her laughter was silenced by a gasp as he drew her gown up, and his hands found their target upon his last words. She jumped slightly as his fingers slid between her thighs, then she pressed against him, her mind spinning with the need he had invoked with his touch. His

other hand had been busy unlacing her gown, slipping it
from one shoulder to reveal a breast ready for his attentions. "Milord," she gasped. "I have had a knight
make love to me and then a belted earl. Now I am about
to be seduced by a regent of England. Ever you give to
me a new experience."

"And if it proves to be but an earl who shall have
you?" he queried, pausing as he raised his head to look
at her.

She looked up into his eyes, seeing the doubt and
anguish in those dear blue depths. "Then I am content," she whispered, drawing his mouth down to hers.
"For in you I have all that I shall ever want, or need."

She opened her eyes, realizing before she was fully
awake that it was dawn. She turned her head to watch
her husband in sleep. Reaching out a hand she traced
the line of his jaw with tender fingers, careful not to
wake him, wishing that she could prolong his sleep. The
day ahead would be trying for him, regardless of the
decision he would make. Should he decide to accept
the new responsibility thrust upon him, their lives would
irreversibly change, hers as well as his. She considered
the alternative—some measure of peace, time with him,
years of growing old with him. Firmly, irrevocably, she
placed the thought aside. She would never think upon
those dreams again, what could have been. Her eyes
filled with tears as they drank in each feature, softened
in his sleep. She had been given a rich, full life. Everything she had ever wished for, he had brought to her,
even the strength to accept what she needed to give.
Dear William. So fierce those many years ago when she
had faced him in the Tower of London. How different
her life could have been had she been given to another.
Her thoughts turned to her parents, thoughts she had
not had in years. If their love had been half so sweet,
they had indeed been blessed. How much more she had
been given, so many more years.

Even as she felt his doubt, she had none. She slipped
quietly from the bed and crossed to his wardrobe. Open-

ing the doors, she pursed her lips for a moment, then reached for the garments she had chosen. She wanted no serving women, nor even Allan this morning. She would shave him, dress him, prepare him. A last time, hers alone.

The morning had drawn well past midmeal, and still the council pressed on. The arguments, the reasonings, the pleas had been presented. All knew that the time for decision was well at hand. She watched the conflict cross his face as he turned to the barons, the anguish clear as he faced the council. "Chester is as good a choice!" he cried out. "And a full ten years younger!"

Ranulf of Chester rose from his chair and regarded William with a smile as he shook his head. "Nay, Marshal. That cannot be. You have been the best of our knights, a man feared and loved, so wise that you are considered the first of us, even beyond England. I say to you in all loyalty that you must be chosen. I will serve you, and I will carry out to the best of my power all the tasks you assign to me."

"There is nothing more to add." The papal legate turned to address Peter des Roches who was presiding. "Let us recess so that each may consider what he has heard."

A few members of the barons and clergy retired to a wall chamber, and William sought out Isabel as she entered to find her husband. "Is Henry well?" he murmured.

"Aye, milord," she answered, her eyes searching his face for some signs of the stress he was under. "I left him with Will, who was teaching him a game of draughts."

"I thanked God when Will appeared at the portcullis," William grimaced and turned his back to the others as he whispered, "I had begun to give up on him."

"Nay, William, you did not." She smiled. "But I am relieved for your sake that he did not delay further. You have enough pressure on you without worrying about our son.''

Their attention was drawn to a heated discussion by others in the room. It was the legate who ended the argument, evidently given to reasons of why William should accept. He turned to the earl and smiled, his humor given lightly though his eyes regarded William with deadly seriousness. ''It will give the earl a most precious opportunity. One who accepts the responsibility is certain to receive penance for those sins he has committed here on earth.''

William and Isabel were soon left alone and William's eyes fixed on the legate who was the last to leave. ''As he says, it does give me that opportunity,'' he said quietly.

''Pah.'' Isabel tossed her head, glancing at the closing door. ''Do not think upon your sins as a means to choose, William. You are far likely to gather considerably more in the years to come should you accept. Then what shall be gained?''

He chuckled at her comment as the door opened and John d'Erley entered, followed on his heels by Beaumont, Musard, and John Marshal. ''Well?'' John shot at him. ''God's blood, William. Have you decided?''

William threw up his hands in desperation as he regarded his friends. ''Counsel me!'' he exclaimed. ''By the faith that I owe you, I see myself entering a sea without bottom or bank! May God come to my aid! They are entrusting to me an almost hopeless task. The child has no money; the church is pressing; Louis is within London, his father seeking to see him on the throne; and if that is not enough, there is no precedent to govern my actions as regent! They are turning over to me a helpless government!''

''We will find the funds,'' Isabel answered, the quiet force of her voice bringing the men's attention to her. ''The church is yet seeking to find its strength with a new pope. As for Louis, you are not John Plantagenet. Louis will not resist you once you set your mind to throwing him from England's shores. As for the matter of precedent—make your own, milord.''

''William,'' John d'Erley blurted out enthusiastically, encouraged by Isabel's words. ''She is right. After all, what if you should fail? If each baron should turn to Louis, if every domain in England should be passed to him, if you should be driven to Ireland for refuge, what of it? The honor for attempting to the task shall be yours, as only you have the courage and strength to try!''

The sounds of the men's voices mingled, forming in her mind as one, as Isabel moved to a window. She leaned against the embrasure, and her eyes passed over the landscape beyond the castle walls. England. Her eyes drank it in, her mind seeing what was beyond her vision. This, then, was what it all had led to. Even in her imaginings, she would not have reasoned it so. Striguil would be hers, her lands, as they always had been. And for him—England. A smile touched her lips, drawing upward in spite of the inner doubts, the pulling fears. No time for doubts, she reasoned. That child, that tender prince safely sequestered in a chamber a few doors from where they stood, engaged in a game of draughts with Will. His future was to be dreaded, a lifetime of doubts, of conflicts, of uncertainty. Nay, their future was determined. The French would be driven from England, as Louis was no match for William; the funds would be found to stabilize the country—she began to tabulate the funds found within her own resources, knowing what could be drawn from others. As for them—her hand went to her belly, softly stroking that of which she had not yet told him. New beginnings. Life remained forever growing, for each turn. We are survivors, William, she thought, turning her eyes to him. For us, when we have nothing else, there will be love.